CW01647033

THE DIARY OF A WOMAN SCORNED

Published by Chalcedon Books

ISBN 978-1-84396-607-4

Also available as a Kindle ebook
ISBN 978-1-84396-608-1

A catalogue record for this
book is available from the British Library and
the American Library of Congress.

The author gratefully acknowledges
Cornell University for allowing her to quote lines
from 'The Tiger' by Laura Riding Jackson.

Pre-press production
eBook Versions
27 Old Gloucester Street
London WC1N 3AX
www.ebookversions.com

For my Tuesday morning art group and in memory of Karen, the most patient of art teachers.

THE DIARY OF A WOMAN SCORNED

Geraldine Pinch

CHALCEDON BOOKS

Regina versus Margaret Jennifer Claridge

Items placed in evidence

Document A
Diary in defendant's hand-writing
dated October 19th to December 12th 2018

Two pages were removed prior to the
diary being examined

Psychologist's report attached.

October 19th

I read once that even sweet old ladies swear when coming round from an anaesthetic. Today, I found myself rolling ugly words around my mouth and spitting them at the paper-jammed printer. It feels as if I have been anaesthetized for most of my life. I am only just coming round, angry and confused.

Nina says that I should write down my feelings. She has given me a large notebook to do it in. The sort bound in pieces of old sari fabric – discarded fragments of other women's lives. Putting something on paper makes it so final. I would rather open a new file for my diary entries, so that they float in the limbo of a blue screen. Then events can be deleted at a touch and everything will go back to the way it was. But I am hopeless with computers. Like animals, they seem instinctively to know when someone is afraid of them. I might press the wrong key and lose the one sentence which turns out to explain what is happening to me.

So, I am writing in the first page of my new diary with the gilded pen which David gave me for our anniversary. I used to be a great diary keeper, writing an account of each day last thing at night. That stopped soon after I got married. I felt too self-conscious scribbling in front of David, knowing that he was waiting for me to turn the light out. Now, the black ink sinks into the creamy paper as I try to listen to myself. People constantly say to me, 'You're such a good listener, Meg'. Am I the only person since Hamlet's father to be poisoned through my ears? Family, friends, colleagues, even people on the bus, tell me their troubles at leisurely length. Deirdre is the worst.

David refers to her as Deirdre of the Sorrows. She always has trouble to report – with her finances, her job, her new man, her old man, her kids, his kids... I murmur sympathetically and offer rational advice which is never taken. Then she goes over it all again, while my wrist begins to ache from holding the phone to my ear and a mean little inner voice starts squeaking, 'It's your own fault, Deirdre. What did you expect from a man who's already left two wives?' I suppress the squeak and ladle out more sympathy. Eventually, there may be an, "Anyway, how are things with you?" Before I can answer, Deirdre usually says, "You're so lucky not to have kids, Meg, or money worries. I'm dreading the phone bills." Then she's off again about her problems. She did it last night, so I never had to say, "Well, actually..."

With Nina, I am also the listener, but now she talks about what I should do next. Nina is like one of those scrubs which claim to make you radiant by removing the top layer of your skin. She abrades me with gritty advice. "Don't imagine that he's going to come back. His pride won't let him. The younger woman always wins, until it's her turn to be dumped." This makes me understand that I have been dumped. Taking the rubbish out always was David's job. Nina says that I must move on as quickly as possible – as if I were a bystander rubber-necking a car crash, not the passenger lying in the wreckage.

October 20th

I have never been a morning person. David is always up first. He slips out of bed and puts in an hour's work before waking me with a cup of tea. I shall have to replace him with one of those mumsy machines that combines alarm-clock, radio and tea-kettle. If it can be programmed to kiss me on the cheek and ask me how I slept, I shall hardly notice the difference.

Today I am woken by the cats wailing to be fed. They hate any alteration to their routine so they miss 'food-provider one'. Vincent and Theo are failing to realize that divorce is 'an exciting opportunity for major life-style changes.' It says so in the self-help manual bought for me by Nina. The book is full of stern warnings against self-pity but if I don't pity me, who will? Who would care that one more middle-aged, middle-class woman has been left by her husband for the usual reasons? Being a victim has somehow become blameworthy. As a woman scorned, I am not allowed to scream and shout about my wrongs to anyone but my best friends for a strictly limited period – probably about six months. After that dignified silence is my only option.

Not stunned silence. It is two weeks since David left and Nina is the only person I've told.

I carry on with my life. I ring my mother every day. I paint. I teach. I shop. I cook. I scrape all the uneaten food into the recycling bin.

My heart lifts when I hear his key turn in the lock and the front door opens but David has only come to collect more of his clothes. When he rang to arrange this, I just said, "Of course," and he thanked me for 'being so understanding'. Understanding is the last thing I feel. In the bedroom, I watch him pack white shirts and dark suits and it doesn't seem any different from all the times he's gone away on business. I nearly ask him whether he's sure he's put in enough socks.

Years ago I vowed that I would never be the kind of wife who whinges when her husband puts his work first. By any objective standard, David's work as a Crown Prosecutor is more important than mine. What does it matter if a painting, which may at best end up on a greeting card, is going well compared to whether thugs and rapists walk free to stalk more victims? Some jobs take over your whole being, like a parasite. I thought that was something we would always have in common. I reach for my sketchbook whenever an idea comes or lose track of time painting the furled petals of a summer rose. David carries his work home with him; sometimes in the form of briefs to be studied, sometimes like a penumbra, barely visible but always there.

Often when he came home I would be itching to spill out the petty troubles and triumphs of my day to the one person to whom they ought to matter but I learned to read his face. I could tell when he was too caught up in the present case even to pretend to listen. I used to wonder how he could let go at the end of a trial. For weeks, even months, he would be utterly absorbed in the lives of a set of people in crisis – the accused, the victims, the bereaved. After the verdict, whether he wins or loses, these lives rarely seem to haunt him. "You can't get too involved," he would say, "It's unprofessional." I don't think he ever saw the people in his cases as real, even when they were standing in front of him in the witness box. Once he closed the brief, he forgot about the people in it as if they were characters in some trashy thriller he'd read on a plane. Is that what happened to me? Did I become unreal to him too?

As he closes the suitcase, David says, "Have you seen a solicitor yet about filing the petition?"

"Petition?"

"The divorce petition."

Divorce. It is the first time that the word has actually been spoken.

"You'll want a reliable firm who won't rip you off. Not Hadley and Stokes, because I'll be using them, but there's..." He reels off some names and then says, "There's no hurry about selling the house. It would probably be better to put it on the market in Spring anyway, when the garden's looking at its best."

The garden I have spent nearly fifteen years making. I realize then how completely David has uprooted himself. He has already moved on to his new life. "I understand," I say and for a moment, I do. I go down to the front door with him. As he leaves, I stand on the top step and give him a little wave in case the neighbours are watching.

That afternoon I go online to look for a solicitor. It's extraordinary how many there seem to be in Bristol. Like locksmiths or dentists, you never notice them until you need one in a hurry. I ignore the firms that David suggested and look for websites which mention the D word. A short walk away is a firm claiming to be 'Family Breakdown Specialists.' I like the sound of this. Perhaps a no-nonsense solicitor will whip out a spanner and fix my marriage breakdown so that I can proceed on my journey to a contented old age. I ring them straight away and request an appointment. The receptionist asks what I need legal advice on. I say, 'marriage' and then 'marriage breakdown'. She asks if there are children involved. I say, 'no' and then 'yes'. After she takes my details I am offered an appointment with a Mrs Patel in two days time. I can always cancel if David comes back before then.

October 21st

Will writing down everything that happens help me to see what I should have done? Hear what I should have said? Today I nearly forget that it is a Wednesday – the day I teach two painting classes. I grab the handouts I've managed to print off. Then I race around the house because I can't remember where I've put things. What old memories shall I discard to make room for new ones?

The morning I noticed my first grey hairs.

The disastrous holiday in Naples when I was sick the whole time.

The 'How quickly can I get rid of her?' look on the faces of gallery owners as I bring out my portfolio.

All the cold afternoons watching David play rugby and the loads of muddy washing afterwards.

Almost every conversation with my mother-in-law.

The night David told me about Rosa.

Surely that should create enough space to remember where I put my reading glasses?

I get to the church-hall with barely enough time to heave out the trestle tables before the ladies start arriving for the Introduction to Drawing and Painting class. The room fills with chatter about what everyone and their family has done since the previous week. As I put out the jars of water, willowy Janet is describing her latest diet, Joanne and Candy are trading information about how to get their sons into the right school, and Pam and Jean are talking about some television programme which involves torturing demi-celebrities.

Eventually they all sit down and I remind them about last week's session on Cool and Warm colours. Janet's phone starts playing the Blue Danube and she rushes out into the corridor to answer it. Today, I only seem to have cool colours left in the palette of my emotions. I don't wait for Janet to come back. I pass round a handout on pigment types and talk about the importance of tonal values. Candy and the one whose name I can never remember have their heads together, whispering about some piece of gossip. Pam has her phone out too and appears to be texting somebody. I wish I was the kind of old-fashioned teacher who could confiscate their phones and make them all keep quiet and concentrate. I can't because they are only here to relax and have fun. To them, painting is just an alternative to Pilates or coffee at Waitrose. If I push them too hard, they'll flock to some other leisure pursuit instead.

I raise my voice and say that we are going to mix all the shades we need for a painting from just three colours, Lemon Yellow, Windsor Blue and Permanent Rose. Several people haven't bought the colours on my Essential Materials list, so it takes another five minutes to make sure that everyone has the right squeezes of paint on their palettes. I explain how to add one colour to another a little at a time. Most of the class mix their paints too quickly and carelessly and end up with liquid mud. Splash together all the bright colours the eye can see and that's what you get – a depressing sludge-brown which must be the true colour of the universe. Joanne seems on the edge of tears as she vainly tries to lighten the mud with more Lemon Yellow. I tell her that she's mixed the perfect colour for painting shadows.

I make coffee at eleven and the chatter spikes again. For the past two weeks I've found it comforting to listen in on cheerful conversations. It made me feel that a world of happy families still existed and I could be living there again soon. Today, I feel like screaming at them, 'It's all a lie. You think you're loved but you aren't.' I go and hide in the cloakroom till it's time to start work again. I get them painting muddy landscapes and I make myself say something nice about every picture, however dismal. At twelve-thirty the class seems reluctant to leave. They linger in the doorway reminding each other about programmes to watch and making plans to meet for lunch.

When the last of them has gone there is barely enough time to chew my way through an energy bar before I must set things up for the afternoon flower-painting class. I didn't have time to buy any flowers today. I snatched whatever I could find in the garden – a cobwebby branch of cotoneaster, bleached grasses, blotched leaves, mildewed Michaelmas Daisies and earwig-eaten dahlias. I take them out of their wrappings of wet newspaper and stuff them in jam-jars. Only four people turn up – Evangeline, the two Sarahs and Rodney. I tell them that I've deliberately chosen damaged or dying specimens so that we can create paintings about change and decay. There is a line from a poem by Robert Graves that has always stuck in my head – 'It is all too easy to admire a flower'. People don't look beyond the surface prettiness for meanings. Van Gogh was probably the most serious painter who ever lived and he used the colours of putrefaction to paint dying sunflowers. Yet his sunflower paintings are still regarded as pretty and used to decorate shopping bags and pencil cases. Gauguin wasn't fooled. When he saw the sunflower sequence hanging on his bedroom wall, he knew that living with Vincent in the Yellow

House wasn't going to work out.

I try to explain some of this. Retired nurse Evangeline nods and smiles, Rodney keeps adjusting his bifocals, Sarah seems thoughtful and the one I think of as 'Other Sarah' looks cross. She aspires to Botanical painting and doesn't approve of imperfect specimens. I paint a demonstration leaf, starting with strident oranges and reds. I dab out most of the colour and drop in splashes of Burnt Sienna darkened with Ultramarine to mimic the spread of rot. Evangeline hums, Rodney asks questions and takes notes, Sarah watches closely and Other Sarah picks out the least-damaged dahlia and starts drawing it.

When they've all chosen what they are going to paint I go back to my leaf and put in more shadows. I surround it with leaden greys till the fiery streaks on the dying leaf seem the last glimpse of colour in a monochrome world. I sit there for a long while until Sarah asks for help with the texture of a seed-head. Then I look around again.

Rodney is painstakingly drawing every fiddly twig on the cotoneaster, Other Sarah's dahlia is annoyingly good. Evangeline should be the ideal pupil. I love her lilting Jamaican accent and she always pays attention. She always has the right materials. She always tries to do exactly what she's been shown. Yet somehow her paintings always end in a shapeless mess. Her daisies have lost the light from their centres and the petals have dripped down into the stems. Evangeline laughs, shaking her whole body, and says, "I'm hopeless." Usually I laugh with her and reply, "Of course you're not." Today I nod solemnly like a doctor confirming a fatal prognosis. Then I give them the speech about failure being part of the process of learning. It sounds quite convincing. Failure is something I ought to know a lot about by now.

When I get home, I check my phone for messages. There is one from Nina, insisting that I meet her for coffee on Friday. I wish I hadn't told her about David and Rosa. It wouldn't have happened if Nina hadn't turned up at my door two days after David left. I had forgotten to cancel our planned trip to an exhibition in Bath. Now she rings every day to check on me. I've tried not answering when her number shows on the phone but then she comes round to see if I'm 'all right'. What she sees is that I'm 'all wrong'. I am stuck in denial and I haven't cried in front of her, which apparently is a bad thing. "Don't be so stoical, Meg," she says. I ask if there is a set number of tears I'm supposed to cry and suggest that I use a bucket so that I can keep count. She says that this doesn't sound like me.

People usually tell me that I am a nice person. Niceness and goodness are easily confused but niceness is merely a negative quality. Niceness is just refraining from being nasty. It costs comparatively little to be nice and niceness is valued accordingly. I fear I am the moral equivalent of one of those sickly Victorian paintings of curly-haired children playing with fluffy kittens. Except not as saleable. I must paint over the canvas and trowel a new image on top. Something spikier. Something less vulnerable. No more Mrs Nice Guy.

Nina is always telling me that I should be more assertive; except towards her of course. Self-assertion won't work if I'm trying to push some weak and wobbly self into the light. I need to remake myself. How do I do that? With lots of little changes? Or by doing something big? Something totally out of character, something there is no way back from? I'll have to think about that.

October 22nd

I am late for my appointment with the solicitor because I stop to listen to a chugger. I shouldn't have felt sorry for the young man because everybody else was hurrying past with averted eyes, as if he had some awful facial disfigurement. He starts his pitch by asking, "How are you today?" This requires the ritual response, 'I'm fine, thank you,' but I can't get past the, "I'm..." I stand there with my mouth hanging open, trying to decide how I am. The chugger just fills in the pause with, "Great!" and launches into his set speech about how polar bears and whales and cuddly orang-utans will all be saved if I sign a direct debit form right here and now. He hands me a leaflet with a panda logo.

The giant panda, what an idiotic symbol for a charity bent on conservation. A beast too stupid to eat anything but bamboo. Bad at sex and bad at mothering. If ever an animal was past its use-by date, it's the giant panda. And me – the obsolete woman. It is tempting to sign up for a wildly generous standing order on the joint account, which David will have the odium of cancelling. I smile and say I'll think about it.

I arrive at the Solicitors and stare at the brass name plates. As a child, it used to puzzle me when my mother began sentences with, 'After I lost my husband...' Once, when she said this at a tea party, I piped up, "But daddy isn't lost. He's at the cemetery, in the third grave in the row by the yew tree." There was an electric silence. Then someone murmured, "Children are so literal." My mother passed the cake and the tea-cups started rattling again. Now that I too have 'lost' my husband, I understand the fog of bewilderment she must have lived in during those first few years.

I make myself go in. I speak to the receptionist. I sit in the waiting area, trying not to make eye contact with anyone. All the other women waiting seem younger, smarter and happier than me. Perhaps they are all dumpers, rather than dumpees, here to negotiate killer divorce-settlements. I sit up straight and attempt to look like someone ready to discard my old husband and move on to a better one. I don't respond the first time my name is called because I am trying to be someone else.

"Mrs Claridge?"

"Yes, here, yes."

Mrs Patel shakes my hand and asks me to follow her. She is much younger than I was expecting. When did I start thinking of young as a term of abuse? I'd vaguely imagined that Mrs Patel would be a matronly figure, with a cushiony bosom to cry on. This Mrs Patel has a plump face but the rest of her is whippet-thin, as if head and body belong to two different people. Her office is small and dark, suggesting that she doesn't come high in the firm's pecking order.

Mrs Patel starts by saying that this twenty-minute consultation is free, and then explains what her fees will be if I decide to 'proceed'. I nod as if I am listening. I am wondering about Mr Patel and what he thinks about his wife specializing in marriage breakdowns. Does it make him nervous?

"And your full name is Margaret Jennifer Claridge?"

"Yes but please call me Peg."

No-one has ever called me that but it suddenly seems right. So much harder and sharper than Meg.

"And how long have you been married, Peg?" she asks.

"Thirty years," I answer, "minus one day."

David told me he was leaving the day before our 30th anniversary. I was sitting there with the Eating Out section of the local paper in my lap, trying to decide which restaurant to book a table at for our anniversary dinner. I keep going over what happened next. David doesn't seem as interested as usual in where we should go. I suggest the Hotel du Vin but he says, "Meg, there's something I have to tell you." I gulp in air. I think he is about to say that he has some awful illness. He's been looking haggard recently and I've been pretending not to notice because David hates fuss. Then he confesses that he's been 'seeing' Rosa Winston . Idiotically, my first reaction is, "But she's fat!" I think I even say it aloud. His expression warns me that any belittlement of Rosa will be taken as an insult to him. Rosa has to be worth leaving a marriage for, or he might look stupid. David hates looking stupid more than anything. Me, I hate being stupid. Stupid enough not to notice that my husband was doing much more than look at Rosa Winston.

Mrs Patel is explaining the grounds on which you can petition for a divorce. There are only five, which hardly seems adequate for all the things that can go wrong in a relationship. She ticks them off on her fingers – adultery, unreasonable behaviour, desertion and two kinds of separation. I pick one.

"Adultery."

"By which party?"

It takes me a moment to understand. "Him! My husband. David."

"So, you wish to petition for divorce on the grounds of your husband's adultery?"

No, I wish for this not to have happened. I wish for Rosa never to have been born. But I must have nodded because Mrs

Patel moves on. "Are you currently separated?"

I almost shake my head because I still feel conjoined. 'I will cleave to you only...' Cleavers are nasty weeds. When you try to pull them up they stick to your fingers, your sleeve, your hair...

"Has your husband moved out of the marital home?"

When your husband announces that he is leaving, you expect him actually to leave. David seemed curiously reluctant to do this. He continued to sit in his usual armchair.

"I hope we can be civilised about this, Meg."

"Yes," I said.

So when the oven-timer buzzed, I took out the casserole and laid the table. David poured two glasses of wine, as if it was any normal evening. I served the lamb and apricot stew and watched David eat it. Then I asked when he would be joining Rosa. He explained that Rosa had gone to London to visit her parents and would be away for another week.

"Perhaps you could go to a hotel?" I suggested.

He looked surprised, as if a hiatus between women was something he had never considered, but then he nodded. I stayed downstairs while he packed a suitcase. As he went, David said, "Take care of yourself, Meg."

"I'll have to now, won't I?"

When I finally went up to our bedroom, I found that he had left my anniversary present on my pillow. It had obviously been wrapped by an assistant at the expensive shop where David bought it. I took off the ribbons and wrapping paper slowly and carefully to expose the old-fashioned fountain-pen. I'd been hoping that David was going to surprise me with an eternity ring.

I half-woke in the night; my cold feet searching for David's warmth. Panic hit when I realised that, for the first time in thirty years, I didn't know where David was. Then I corrected myself. I obviously haven't known where he was for a long time.

"Yes, he's moved out."

"And do you have any dependent children – children under eighteen?"

"We...I have no children."

"Before going any further, you should consider Mediation."

"I don't think...Rosa – the other woman – she's pregnant." I start to gabble. "David expects to be made a judge soon. In the past, leaving his wife after getting one of his Juniors pregnant would have scuppered his chances but considering what judges get up to nowadays, it's probably a recommendation."

Mrs Patel's eyes flicker with alarm. "Your husband's a barrister?"

I nod and I can see her making the assumption that my husband will have the very best legal advice that money and cronies can provide.

"And do you work?"

"I'm an artist."

This answer seems to complete my demotion to 'undesirable client'. Mrs Patel frowns and then explains that Mediation is not just for couples who think their marriage could be saved. Apparently it provides a valuable opportunity to discuss issues such as the division of property with a neutral mediator. I am beginning to hate the word opportunity.

Mrs Patel says something about the importance of keeping channels of communication open and begins to type on her laptop. I am fascinated by the maroon of her nail varnish against the milky coffee of her skin. I start thinking about how I would mix the colours to paint her hands. Raw Sienna perhaps, with a dash of Naples Yellow.

"Peg? Mrs Claridge?"

I realize that I must have failed to answer a question I haven't even heard.

"I'm sorry. This has all been rather a shock."

"Of course." She gets up as her well-behaved printer starts spewing documents. "This will explain the different stages in legal separation and divorce. This is a list of the information you will need to provide."

She hands me a sheaf of paper, warm from the printer.

"What happens if I just...do nothing?" I ask.

"I wouldn't advise that," says Mrs Patel.

October 23rd

Every morning now I wake with that sick feeling I used to get as a child on exam days. In the kitchen I notice 'C's B' written on the calendar. It is my mother-in-law's birthday next week. Will David remember? I always buy the present and choose the card. David just signs it. For a moment I consider sending an email to remind him. Then I recall that I've heard nothing from Celia. Will the prospect of a grandchild reconcile her to the thought of a black daughter-in-law?

At least there will be no more Christmas or Boxing Days with Celia in Chipping Camden. The mothers mix badly. David's father was the only one who could make them get along. After he died, we would rocket from one mother to the other during holiday seasons. "And never," David would say, "the twain shall meet."

As I walk into Clifton village to meet Nina, I encounter more Chuggers. They wave leaflets about guide-dogs for the blind full of pictures of chocolate-eyed puppies. Presumably actual blind people are not deemed cute enough to attract the dosh. A pink-haired girl urges me to sponsor a labradoodle. Who would trust their life to something with a name that silly?

"Do you have to be blind to get a guide-dog?" I ask.

The girl has done her homework. She spouts statistics about how many partially-sighted people qualify for guide-dogs. That isn't what I mean. If I had a faithful creature to lead me where I need to go, perhaps I wouldn't feel so lost. This time I do sign up on the spot for a £20 a month sponsorship. David hates dogs. He was badly bitten by an Alsatian as a child. When we're out walking, I always get between him and any large dog.

Will Rosa know to do this?

At the café my instinct is to slink to the shadowy regions near the toilets but Nina has bagged a window table. I sit there feeling as if I have a scarlet D on my front, hoping not to see anyone else I know. Nina has ordered for us. Her prescription for me is a Viennese coffee and a sticky slab of chocolate and cherry cake. I tell her about my interview with Mrs Patel. Nina pronounces it a good thing that my solicitor is a young woman.

"She'll be keen to make her mark and impress the Senior Partners."

I suspect that Mrs Patel is just going through the motions with cases nobody else would want until it's her turn for something more profitable.

"She'll fight harder for you," claims Nina.

"When did this become a battle?"

"Meg, there's no such thing as a civilised divorce. David may still be fond of you – I'm sure he is – but he isn't on your side any more. Your interests are opposed and he'll want to come out a winner. Men do."

I sip my over-sweet coffee. I'd always assumed that in any divorce both parties were losers, just like in a real war. "Surely, women want to win too?"

"No, we just want the man to feel sorry for what he's done."

This sounds horribly true though I don't see how never-married Nina knows. She seems to have the knack of staying on good terms with all her ex-boyfriends. Perhaps because she never moves in with them or lets them stay in her flat for more than one night at a time. I stare down at my plate and realize that if I start eating, in future my favourite cake will always remind me of the way I feel now. "Damn David."

Nina tells me that it is normal for someone in my position to feel anger and healthy to express it.

"What, even if I feel like murdering Rosa?"

"Murder away, as long as the mayhem stays inside your head. People sometimes ask me how I stay so calm during infuriating meetings. I tell them it's due to my Yoga classes but actually it's because I sit there imagining horrible fates overtaking the incompetent treasurer or the woman bleating about health and safety."

We giggle over this and invent some horrible fates for Rosa. She shall be smothered with her barrister's wig. She shall prick her finger on one of my roses and die of tetanus. She shall be poisoned with the Cadmium Yellow from my paintbox.

"Still, you better confine yourself to wishing her triplets and cellulite," suggests Nina, "Rosa isn't worth spending the rest of your life in jail for."

"Oh but it wouldn't be for life; more like ten years."

Thanks to David, I know a lot about sentencing and how little a human life seems to count for nowadays. There wasn't an exact moment when I realized that people rarely get the punishment they deserve, it just seeped into my consciousness. Rosa is still safe. I don't think I could ever harm a pregnant woman. How could you pass judgement on someone who hasn't even been born yet? David's child.

I take the cake away with me, saying that I'll eat it later. On the way home I risk a fine by throwing it to the pigeons, who pick suspiciously at the cherry-halves. Pied beauty. I love these dappled street-bandits, no two of them feathered alike, but I can't stay to watch them feast. I have to pick up some materials and get to the Day Centre for my Friday afternoon art-therapy session.

Since I've been volunteering, the group I work with has been re-labelled several times. I think they are currently known as 'Mentally Impaired Adults with Behavioural Difficulties'. There are six of them today. Pete and Etta are the two I'm most familiar with. Scrawny Pete who in three years has never said a word. He draws everything vanishingly small, as if he's trying to shrink what he sees so that he is the biggest thing in his world. Etta never takes off the knitted hat that looks more like a tea-cosy. After my first session with Etta, I was impressed by the bright picture she'd painted of a house with a girl looking out through an upstairs window. She has produced the same picture every week since, whatever I've been trying to get them to paint. She is sometimes forced to use different colours but it is always the same house and the same face at the window. These two follow their obsessions quietly. The others often moan, rant or scream. Carl eats the paint if you don't watch him. At least my Wednesday morning class never does that.

Jake, the psychiatric nurse, is endlessly patient in a detached sort of way. When he's not needed to calm or assist someone, he sits in a corner reading the 'Sporting Post'. He looks up from his paper when I say, "Today, let's paint how we feel when we're sad." Elderly Morag starts swearing, but she does this most of the time so I'm learning to tune it out. I hand round big sheets of sugar paper and get out boxes of wax crayons and poster paints.

"Some people think blue and grey are sad colours. What colours do you think of when you're sad?"

"Red!" cries Tom, whom I think of as the rocker, because his body is never still. Given a choice of colours, Tom always picks red. Jake frowns when he does, but then Jake knows much more about the patients than I do. Nobody else answers my question, I try again.

"Perhaps you could paint something that makes you feel a bit sad – like a rainy day." Or waking up to find no-one lying on the other side of the bed. "What makes you sad?"

"Jam!" shrieks Carl.

Jake and I exchange looks. "All right, Carl, if jam makes you feel sad, you paint that."

Brain-damaged Joe is trying to say something. Jake has to interpret for me, "Sad when no-one comes."

Joe was an electrician before he came off his bike. Jake says that Joe's wife no longer visits. I know that this should put my own troubles in perspective but somehow it just adds to them.

Morag grabs a crayon and slashes it across and across the paper. Tom rocks to and fro as he tells me a confused story about a dead puppy. Jake holds Joe's wrist to help him draw, so I'm not sure which of them is creating a picture made up of empty circles. Carl gets paint all over himself. Pete is drawing a tiny leafless tree. Etta quietly paints her house and today nothing could seem sadder than the lone face at the window.

October 24th

Weekends are bleak but this morning I wake up thinking, 'This is the day that David will come back. He will walk through the door, sit down in his favourite chair and tell me that it was all a mistake.' I decide to stay in all day, because if go out I might miss him. I could work in my studio but what if he rings the doorbell instead of using his key? I don't always hear the bell from the end of the garden, even if I leave the back door open.

So, I pick up the obese Booker Prize-winning novel I've been meaning to read for weeks and sit in an armchair by the front window. The cats are pleased by my inactivity. Theo perches on the back of the chair. Vincent sits on my lap, kneading and purring. It's soothing at first but then it strikes me that this is the same noise he makes at the Vet's, when he's hunkering down as the needle goes in. His relationship with me must also be based on fear. Fear that I'll stop feeding him. Fear that that I'll shut him in when he wants to be out or out when he wants to be in. Fear that I'll punish him for some offence that he can't understand. Are human relationships grounded in fears too? Fear of having less sex than other people. Fear of growing old alone.

When the phone rings I rush to answer but it is only Deirdre. She launches straight into a tirade about Callum coming home later and later after evenings at the pub with his mates. When she pauses for breath, I say mildly, "At least he's still coming home."

"If he carries on like this, he might as well not bother."

"You don't mean that," I say, but she probably does. When things get tough, cut and run has always been Deirdre's policy.

It worked better when she didn't have three kids, a sheep-dog and a fluctuating number of rabbits.

"But when I want to go out for an evening," she continues, "it's a different story. The fuss he makes about getting supper for the kids. All he has to do is open a tin of beans..."

Eventually, I tell her that I have to go because I'm expecting David home any minute. "You spoil that man," she grumbles before ringing off. She makes me sound like a spaniel waiting by the door with the master's slippers. Is it 'spoiling' to welcome my husband home with a a kiss, however ratty I may be feeling? I've tried to make this house a sanctuary from the grim world of David's work, a tranquil place where he would always want to be. Can I have failed so badly? I refuse to think so.

I make myself a sandwich and go on sitting by the window. All afternoon I watch cars squeezing in and out of the Residents Parking places but none of them is David's black Saab. My Saab too officially, though I rarely drive it. The cats get more and more restive. At dusk I go into the kitchen to feed them. Afterwards, Theo shoots out through the cat-flap into the garden. Vincent, perpetually baffled by the cat-flap, stares up at me mewing sadly. I only open the back door for him a little way. I dare not look out into the garden at night in case I see Rosa haunting the glass-house.

When we first looked at this house it was the glass-house built against the end wall of the garden which attracted me. Much of the wooden frame was rotted and most of the glass was either cracked or missing but I could see that it would make a wonderful studio. The garden itself was no more than a yard with a few miserable shrubs surviving on the edges of the crazy-paving. David muttered about how gloomy it was but

I was already imagining the perfect town-garden with raised beds of herbs, a lion's head fountain and roses trained up the walls. I ignored all the work that needed doing to turn three shabby flats back into one house, the narrow knee-cracking stairs and the near impossibility of finding a parking space in the street and persuaded him to buy it. Now, when we meet new people, David likes to drop into the conversation, "We live in a Regency house in Clifton." William IV and not quite Clifton actually but I never correct him.

David holds drinks parties in the garden on summer nights. I remember feeling sorry for Rosa the first time she came. She seemed very much the new girl, not chatting easily with her colleagues. She wandered into the glass-house, which I had decorated with candles inside water-jars. I saw her shimmering through the glass; her toffee-apple skin, her marmite-black hair, her lemon yellow dress, all under-lit like a Caravaggio. David saw her too. When he went in to talk to her, I thought he was being kind to a shy Junior. Now I wonder if Rosa, like Miss Elizabeth Bennett, only fell in love after doing a quick house-valuation. I bolt the back door, as if that will keep Rosa out of my home.

October 25th

When I woke up this morning the sick feeling was back. I read over yesterday's entry and cannot understand why I sat by the front window until almost midnight waiting for David to come home. Now it is Sunday and I have promised to take mother out to lunch. I put on a Sunday-best dress that goes with my favourite necklace but without David to help me I just can't fasten the fiddly clasp. After several minutes of trying I fling the necklace across the room, like a toddler having a tantrum. Then I leave early to catch a bus because I don't have the car. I don't even know where the car is.

The Sunday bus-service is unreliable. When I get to Orion House, mother is standing in the doorway of her flat with her hat and coat on.

"I was getting worried," she says.

I kiss her powdery cheek. "I'm only a few minutes late."

"If we don't get to The Scriveners Arms before twelve, we might not get a table."

"I've booked a table, Mum."

"Isn't David coming?"

I tell her that he is working on a case, which is bound to be true. We make several attempts to leave the flat. After I've found her stick and her gloves, I'm sent back to look for her reading-glasses. This must be what it's like trying to get a toddler off to nursery school. A joy to come for David and Rosa.

What used to be a short walk to the nearest gastro-pub now seems a very long way. Mother clutches my arm with her left hand and taps the ground ahead with her stick as if she expects the paving stones to turn into quicksand at any moment. When she nearly slips on some wet leaves as we cross a road, I realize that she's right to treat everywhere beyond her sheltered-housing complex as a landscape of hazards; a danger map marked with muggings and broken-hips rather than pirates and dragons. As we chat about how negligent the council road-sweepers are and ask what we pay our taxes for, I see real fear in her eyes. What can it be like to dread the snap of a bone every time you leave your front-door? I suppose that in twenty to thirty years, I shall find out. I've read that most accidents to old people happen inside the home but it would be cruel to point this out. Most hearts break inside the home too.

We reach The Scriveners Arms safely and slowly cross the wood-effect laminate that has replaced the garish carpets the place used to have. Their yellow and orange patterns seemed designed so that people could throw up on them without anyone noticing but at least they weren't slippery. Mother objects to the table we're offered because there isn't enough light, so we shuffle off again to table nearer a window. I order two dry sherries and try to be patient while mother struggles to read the menu. I suspect that her reading-glasses are no longer enough to help her decipher wavy typescript on a grey background. After a few minutes, I solve the problem by reading items aloud as if pondering whether to try them – "The warm goat's cheese salad sounds nice but it does have beetroot in it" – until mother says, "Well, I'm having that. Do make up your mind, dear, or we'll be here all day."

As we wait for our food, the conversation runs along its usual track. This would madden David but I find it soothing. I have to acknowledge that my mother has become small-minded. I don't mean that she's petty or mean. Simply that, like Pete in my Friday group, she has shrunk her world down to a size that she's comfortable with. Her main interest in life is the doings of her neighbours at Orion House. My role is to remember the cast and plot of this very dull soap opera and ask appropriate questions. I'm glad to be able to do something for my mother that no-one else would.

"So," I begin, "did Mr Parsons' son finally visit, or did he come up with another excuse?" The non-appearance of Mr Parsons' son lasts until the main courses arrive. Then mother switches to her other favourite topic, the news from Rob and family in Abu Dhabi. My brother rings her about twice a month which apparently qualifies him to be described as a wonderful son. The job of keeping in touch with me has been delegated to my sister-in-law. Harriet calls when she wants a fresh audience for her complaints about the other wives at 'the Club' or the misdeeds of the latest maid. She often sounds as if she's living in a Somerset Maugham story rather than the 21st century but I just make sympathetic noises.

Mother prods her turbot with her fork as if she's making sure it's dead. "Poor Rob has to work so hard, and in that heat..." We cover the current state of the oil industry and move on to her worries about what sort of education James and Chloe are getting. She is very fond of her grandchildren, except when they're actually here.

Over dessert, it's back to life at Orion House. I believe that she tells the other residents how proud she is of her 'daughter the artist' but she rarely asks what I'm painting. As mother doesn't care to dwell on unpleasant things like rape and murder, she has always found David's work distasteful. She does remember to ask after Celia. I tell her that I haven't seen my mother-in-law for quite some time. She goes, 'Tsk, tsk,' but I can tell that she's pleased.

When the bill is brought, I let her win the argument about whose turn it is to pay. Every time I use the debit card, I'm afraid that it might be refused because David has decided to close our joint account. Can he do that? I must ask Mrs Patel.

The return walk to Orion House seems even slower. Back at the flat I open a stubborn jar and then try to adjust the central heating – jobs that David usually does for mother. As I'm about to leave, she surprises me by saying, "You're very quiet today. Are you all right, dear?" I almost tell mother about David but the sight of a bicycle in the communal hall distracts her into a long anecdote about Mrs Tranter's Polish cleaner and the offending bicycle. The moment passes.

When I get home, I see the pile of paper from Mrs Patel which I've been ignoring. I ought to start reading all that information about how to get a divorce. I promise myself that I'll do it tomorrow.

October 26th

The book on how to survive your divorce tells me to choose a word each day that sums up how I feel or how I want to feel. Among the suggested words are angry, sad, hopeful and strong. I shall start with – discarded. Discarded like a toy no longer played with, like small change that isn't worth retrieving from under the sofa, like once-favourite jeans that no longer fit... Now that 's a more comforting simile. The jeans will still fit someone and in a few years time they'll be prized as vintage. They should run Vintage Women Fairs to go with the Vintage Clothing Fairs. For sale – one bride c.1988. Any reasonable offer considered.

In the kitchen I find myself with a mug of coffee in each hand. Why is it so hard to remember that there is only one person at the breakfast table now? I pour the coffee in David's mug down the sink and sit down to read the notes about the stages in getting a divorce. I learn that, 'if both parties are in agreement' I could be divorced within six months. Only six months to undo thirty years. Nearer thirty-three years if I count from when I met David at the private-view for my first professional exhibition.

At the time I was walking on air, entranced by the idea that all these people had come to see my paintings. Now of course I realize that the gallery owner must have rung everyone in her address-book in a desperate attempt to rustle up a crowd. So there they stood, sipping cheap sparkling-wine when they'd hoped for champagne, exchanging gossip and occasionally looking at my pictures. "At least you can tell what they're meant to be," I heard someone say. He couldn't. They were meant to be the sunlit landscapes of my hopeful mind.

David had been dragged along by his mother. I was the only young woman in the room, so I suppose it was natural that he came over to talk to me. After a while he asked if I would be at the gallery tomorrow because he'd appreciate my help to choose one of the pictures as a surprise present for his mother. Naively, I didn't suspect his motives. I genuinely thought that my paintings were more interesting than me. The next day, when David asked me out to dinner, I think my inner light dimmed for moment. I still said yes to handsome charming David but our first date did cost him a picture. The gallery owner made sure of that. A painting of a narrow path winding through an impossibly flowery meadow towards golden hills. Celia hung it in a particularly dark stretch of corridor. I wonder if she'll take it down now.

I read on and discover that as 'the petitioner' I am expected to provide details of my husband's adultery. Dear God, what kind of details? I drop the piece of paper as if it was a stained sheet. I pace around the room several times before making myself pick up the paper and continue reading. I will be asked to specify persons, times and places. Persons – only Rosa Winston as far as I know but I start to wonder. There have been other attractive trainees over the years.

When we talk about his life in Chambers, David likes to refer to his Pupils and Juniors by nicknames – Haughty Hanna, Pointless Peter, Um-Er, Bling-Boy, High-heels – now what was her real name? Belinda something. A pretty red-head with a penchant for ridiculously high-heeled shoes. When Belinda came to dinner, she tripped in the living room and spilled her glassful of Burgundy all over the sofa. While I tried to clean up the mess, David was fussing about whether she'd sprained her ankle. Was he just being a considerate host or... No, don't think about it. Concentrate on what you do know.

Times – days or nights when I thought David was working. Places – at David's Chambers? No, surely too risky. At Rosa's home? How would I know the address? At some cheap hotel? Not here, please not here, on the days when David knows that I'm out.

The phone shrills. I see that it's Nina calling and pick up straight away. She starts to ask about my weekend but I spill out my disgust at having to prove the 'facts' of my case against David.

"Really? I didn't think the courts were interested in the sordid details now that no-one's supposed to be to blame for anything."

"Apparently they are."

"Well, what did David say during his confession? He must have told you when the affair started."

"I'm not sure. Some months ago, I think."

"Didn't you ask him how often he'd been meeting Rosa?"

"No."

Why did I sit there so dumbly? Why didn't I demand to know the where and the when and the how often? I can't even remember everything that he did say. When David started to tell me about Rosa, I thought he was asking me to forgive him. I was preparing myself to be magnanimous.

Nina goes into practical mode, using the tone of voice she must employ when she's trying to get one of her committees to agree on a sensible policy.

"I expect all the law requires is a few sample dates. Since

David wants everything settled as quickly as possible, I'm sure he'll provide the information your solicitor needs. You have made another appointment with Mrs Patel?" She interprets my silence correctly. "Meg, you must get moving on this. The situation isn't going to go away if you crouch in your hole quiet as a mouse. There is going to be a divorce whether you like it or not, so take the initiative and get the best deal you can."

The best deal. I am losing a husband not buying a car, but I promise to ring the solicitors the moment Nina is off the phone. I actually do. When I'm offered an appointment on Thursday, I hear myself saying that it's too soon. I arrange to see Mrs Patel a week from today. A lot can happen in a week.

October 27th

Word of the day – pointless. That's how so many things feel now. I get up and open the wardrobe but it seems pointless to worry about which clothes go together. I just dress in the first things that come to hand. In the kitchen, it suddenly seems pointless to make real coffee or bother with toast and scrambled eggs. I eat a slice of bread smeared with jam and go out to the glass-house. Even though it seems pointless to teach people who don't really want to learn anything, I put together some material for my Wednesday morning class. Then I fill a water jar, lay out my paints and prepare to get on with the current painting.

This year I am trying to capture the mood of each month in my garden by painting studies of flowers and foliage to cut out and collage. I have already picked a coral-stemmed leaf from the tree peony. I must work quickly to record the extraordinary moment, between waxy summer green and brown winter mush, when the plant sends up a distress flare of crimson. I choose and thin my colours and start painting. The shape flows from my brush as it should but when I sit back to look at my work it too seems pointless. Just lines on paper. I drop in more colour. While the paint dries, I watch Theo chasing leaves and stalking birds in the garden. He switches from play-hunter to potential killer and back again all in a minute.

The peony leaf on the page is still as lifeless as if I'd been copying some plastic table-decoration. I focus on the real leaf. The crimson is already deadening to unpolished bronze at the tips but I try again. And again. Then I tear the thick sheet of paper into strips and drop them in the box of scraps I use when I want to test the strength of my washes. I get out last month's collage, to reassure myself that I can do this. I study the elusive colours of the fleshy sedums, the fluorescent tutus of the fuchsias, the sugar-pink nerines and cobwebby asters of September. Then I start to wonder why I bothered to spend so many working hours on something that is unlikely to fetch more than £400, even after I've paid for the framing.

I should have lived in 17th century Holland, when painting flowers was a lucrative profession. For years I've suffered from my own form of Tulipmania – an obsession with producing the perfect image of a tulip. The Netherlanders who gave fortunes for the bulbs of flamed or feathered tulips never understood that the broken colours were symptoms of disease; beauty caused by a virus. Did Rosa's charms infect David simply because of her proximity? After a spell of fever and grumpiness, will he suddenly wake up feeling better? Feeling married to me again.

When the phone rings later, I see David's mobile number flash up. I reach out to answer. Then I let it ring. Even if he's ready to say that he's sorry, I'll let him suffer for a bit. It's his turn to wait.

October 28th

My word for the day is – reflective. This morning, when I stared at myself in the mirror, I could not trust what I saw. I looked the same as usual, which cannot be right. When my Wednesday morning ladies arrive, I abandon the lesson I'd prepared and tell them that they are going to draw me. I want to see myself through their eyes.

I thought they'd all say life-drawing was too hard but most of them are excited by the idea. I sit down on a chair in the centre of the room. When Pam wails, "Where do I start?", I just say, "Head or feet and then keep the line going."

I pose for ten minutes and then walk round to look at what they've done. I see that I am mainly made up of smudges and of lines which don't quite meet. That seems about right but I let them try again. I only hold the pose for five minutes; the quietest five minutes we've ever had in this class. Everybody concentrates hard for once. Candy and Janet even ignore the chirruping of their phones telling them that they have new Text messages.

When I stand up, it is like taking the cork out of a bottle of sparkling conversation. Words and laughter froth out as I go around the circle. "Mine looks like a scarecrow..." "I can't do hands..." "The head's too big..." "That was fun..." "We'll have to try a nude next..." "Ooh, let's have a lovely nude man..." Janet's drawing is surprisingly good for a beginner. I'd thought that my pose was a relaxed one but she has drawn the slump of defeat.

I hand out sticks of charcoal and large sheets of paper and sit down again, keeping my back straight and my chin up. I make them draw several three minute poses. They all improve except Candy, who sulks if she can't do something right the first time. Then the drawings are spread out. I try to make constructive comments but I notice that when they had to reduce my figure to essentials, they mainly drew my clothes – boldly-patterned and textured clothes with a stick-woman inside.

After coffee, I let them take turns being the model. While I help everyone with their drawings, I keep thinking of the image of me which they've created. Peg the stick-woman, with a face to scare off crows – or husbands. At what point does slim become scrawny?

I can't concentrate in my afternoon class either. I'm afraid to do a demonstration, in case the marks I make still seem pointless. I set them to painting white flowers on black paper and talk about letting the shadows create the shapes.

I still feel shadowy when I get home. As I enter the kitchen, Theo crashes in through the cat-flap. There is no sign of Vincent, even when I open a can of cat-food and start forking it into their dishes. I go into the living room to look for him. Books are leaning drunkenly on the shelves. There are gaps in the CD tower. My heart thuds. 'Burglars', I think. Then, 'What if they're still in the house?' I whirl round, poised to run out into the street and seek help from the neighbours, but my eyes have been registering the losses. What kind of burglar ignores a flat-screen television and a Bose music system but takes the Folio Society edition of Trollope's novels? David has been here while I was out.

I've always liked the way our different literary tastes cosy up on the shelves, my volumes of poetry against his Victorian novels, my art books against his biographies. Now they've been separated. So have our musical tastes. David's opera sets are no longer slumming it with my folk-rock albums.

I rush from room to room to see what else he's removed. Most of the post piling up on the hall table has gone and his winter-coat is no longer hanging in the cloakroom. From the dining room he's taken his rugby trophies and a photograph of himself with his father. In his study, the chess set is missing and the draw in the filing cabinet where we keep all the financial documents is open and gutted. There is a lighter patch on our bedroom wall where a picture of his old college used to hang. I was right first time. I have been robbed; robbed of parts of my shared life with David.

I'm so furious that I ring his mobile but I'm switched straight through to his message service. It's too late in the day for him still to be in court. Perhaps he's doing something with Rosa that he doesn't want disturbed. I leave a message – '*How dare you sneak into the house and take stuff when you knew that I'd be out? You don't live here any more. I want your keys back. If I don't get them, I'll have the locks changed.*'

I can hear faint wailing from the garden. Vincent is sitting in my trough of herbs. David must have let him out. I wonder how many hours Vincent has been stuck out there, waiting for someone to open the back door for him. It's only later, when I'm sitting with Vincent in my lap unravelling tangles in his fur, that I think of checking my own phone for messages. There are two – one from Nina inviting me to go shopping with her on Saturday and one from David asking if he could come by and get some of his things today.

October 29th

At eight in the morning the doorbell rings. I'm still in my nightie and an old dressing-gown of David's that is warmer than mine. I stumble into the hall and open the door. David is standing on the doorstep, holding out a bunch of keys.

"You should remember to use the chain when you're opening the door," he says. "I might have been anyone."

I gape at him. He hands me the keys.

"I'm sorry you were upset, Meg. When you didn't reply to my message, I thought it was all right to come."

I realize that I am being put in the wrong. "You know I'm out all day most Wednesdays."

"I thought you'd prefer not to see me."

No! I almost say it aloud. My instincts are still telling me that he is the one I always want to see. I start to reach out for him but the jangle of keys in my hand stops me. The keys are all David is giving back to me.

"I'm meeting with my solicitor again on Monday," I say.

"Good. Which firm did you choose?" He frowns when I tell him. "They're just a budget outfit..."

"So I'll be saving you money. You were intending to pay my legal costs?"

He seems startled but replies, "Yes, of course."

"Apparently we could save even more money if we went to an official Mediator but I didn't think you'd fancy that."

"God, no."

For a moment, we are in complete accord. Neither of us can bear the idea of picking over our feelings in front of a stranger.

"I have to provide evidence that you...of your affair," I begin.

"Do we have to talk on the doorstep?"

"Yes. When did it start?"

"When? Last summer. I did tell you that."

"Did you? I can't have been listening. And where did these... trysts take place? Did you ever meet her here?"

"No!" David looks genuinely shocked at the idea. Perhaps he is the sort of man who likes to keep his wife and his mistress in completely separate compartments. Or his wife and his ex-wife.

"I'll send your solicitor a statement," David is saying, "that's all you'll need. What's his name?"

"Her name is Mrs Patel. By the way, did you remember that yesterday was your mother's birthday?"

"Shit! And she's been so..."

"Has she?"

I close the door on him. Then I rattle the safety chain so that he'll hear me using it.

Later I ring Nina and agree to go shopping with her on Saturday.

"Great. We'll hit Cabot Circus. Some new clothes will make you feel like a new woman." "That implies there was something wrong with the old woman," I say.

Which is a mistake because I then get the whole 'looking on change as a positive thing' lecture. I read the latest issue of *Artists and Illustrators* while she's talking. Thank God videophones haven't caught on yet. I'm deep into an article on a new type of gesso when I realize that she's asked me a question. "What? Oh yes, I'm seeing her on Monday. Must go. I've got stuff to do."

Word of the day has to be – transformation. If I'm going to transform myself, I can't be half-hearted about it. One new outfit won't be enough of a catalyst. I take a roll of bin-bags to the bedroom and fling open the wardrobe and all the drawers. I tug clothes off hangers and start to bag the summer florals and the bold Scandinavian prints, the Liberty lawn shirts and the lace-collared blouses. Skirts and dresses in the sunset colours that I love are fed into gaping mouths of black plastic. I work fast so that I don't have time to think, 'This is the dress I wore when...'

The shoes are easier. With my troublesome feet I've never been sentimental about shoes. Most of the pairs I bag were too uncomfortable to wear much anyway. Next I start emptying drawers. Out go all the museum tee-shirts, the Fair Isle cardigans, the sweaters hand-knitted by Peruvian peasants; the paisley shawls and the long silk scarves. I pluck back a favourite scarf, printed with flowers taken from a Charles Rennie Mackintosh watercolour. As I hold the chiffon, my fingers seem to read off memories – David handing me the small parcel as I lay in bed recovering from flu – my depression lifting as I folded back the paper and saw the crimsons, pinks and oranges of the wallflower pattern – wearing the scarf knotted around my throat when we... I stuff the scarf deep into one of the bin-bags and then sort through my underwear and nightwear.

It is easy to find and discard the slips and teddies and nightdresses that David has given me over the years. They are all black silk, like the traditional QC's gown. I used to tease him about that. The clothes that David has left behind – odd socks, his least-favourite shirts, ties that were presents from aunts – go into the bags too. I lug the bags downstairs and pile them up in the dining room. I fill two more bags with an armful of coats from the cloakroom and three pairs of winter boots that never quite fitted. Then I ring the local Oxfam shop. I tell them I want to donate ten sacks of clothes but I don't have a car. The manageress says she will try to send the van round sometime next week. That gives me plenty of time to unpack the bags if I change my mind.

I wonder if David is colonising Rosa's flat with the things he took yesterday. Is the print of his Cambridge college now hanging in the bedroom they must be sharing? Is he offering her his past as well as his future? The past that is, or was, mine.

October 30th

When the doorbell rings as I'm breakfasting on bread and marmalade, I think it must be David again. I keep the door on the chain and peer out through the crack. Two strange men are standing on the steps and an Oxfam van is double-parked in the street.

"You've got some bags for us," states the older of the two men.

"I wasn't expecting you until next week..."

"We managed to fit you in today but we'll have to be quick."

He gestures at the street where a small car is barely squeezing past the van. I find myself undoing the chain and backing to let them into the hall. They spot the bulging bin-bags through the open door of the dining room.

"There they are, Mike," says the older man, "start loading."

"I'm not sure if I want...I don't think I can..."

"Parting with someone's things is always hard but it's best to make a clean sweep ."

He obviously thinks that somebody has died. In the street an impatient driver is parping their horn. The men work fast to load the van. I stand there, getting in their way but unable to move.

"All dealt with, luv," says the man from Oxfam. "No more reminders and you know the money's going to a good cause."

I manage to nod as he hands me a leaflet and exits with the last two bags of reminders.

Word of the day – severed. For David there may have been a long slow letting go of our marriage. For me, it was as quick as a knife slash. Aren't quick cuts supposed to be less painful?

I am dressed in yesterday's clothes. I put the oddments left in the laundry basket into the washing machine so at least I'll have a clean shirt to wear tomorrow. Then I sit down with my survival guide. It suggests making a list of positive role models. I have always been a list-maker, so -

Georgia O'Keefe? The obvious choice. A successful female artist who kept on developing into old age. Except that I've come to hate her because when I explain that I paint large scale pictures of flowers, most people say, 'Oh, you mean like Georgia O'Keefe.' No, I mean like Margaret Claridge.

Frida Kahlo? A dazzling painter but I'd have to join up my eyebrows and pencil on a moustache to get her bandit look. Didn't Frida write that she mainly painted herself because she was so often alone?

Emily Dickinson? One of my favourite poets but a notorious recluse. I probably shouldn't copy her habits of despising punctuation and hiding upstairs from visitors.

Laura Riding? Another favourite poet but she's famous for failing to kill herself over a love affair by leaping out of a window. There is nothing as embarrassing as a botched suicide attempt.

Lizzie Borden? – Lizzie Borden took an axe and gave her hubby forty whacks. When she saw what she had done, she gave his lover forty-one.

I don't think I've got the hang of this role model thing.

On my way to the Day Centre, I gather leaves from the street-trees and from overhanging shrubs and creepers, looking for the boldest shapes and the brightest colours. Some of the best come from the cherry-trees that have dollops of candy-floss pink blossom in Spring. I remember reading that the golden-amber colour is there in the leaves all along but you can only see it when they're dying.

At the Centre, I spread out the leaves on newspaper while Jake shepherds the group into the room. Joe is missing today. There is a young woman whom I take to be a helper because she's holding Etta's arm, until Jake introduces her.

"This is Annie, who's going to be with us for a while. Annie, this is Margaret. She shows everyone how to draw and paint. Say hi to Margaret."

"Hi, Marg-ret," says Annie with a radiant smile. No-one who has a clue how the world works could look that happy.

I put out boxes of pencils and wax crayons and hand round sheets of paper. Then I show the group how to draw around the edges of the leaf to make the shape. "Then you can colour in the shape with the crayons – yellow or orange or..." I look at Tom and he shouts, "Red, red, red."

I smile at him. "Or red. So, everybody pick a leaf."

Carl grabs a handful and has to be persuaded to part with some of them. Tom predictably takes a scarlet vine-leaf. I have brought some tiny yellow birch leaves specially for Pete and he picks one. Annie seems unable to choose so I hand her a horse-chestnut leaf. She twirls it between her fingers, staring as if it's the most fascinating thing she has ever seen. Morag is sitting with her arms crossed. I put a plane leaf in front of her and she mutters under her breath. Etta has taken some crayons and is already drawing her house. I put a leaf down beside it.

"Etta, shall we draw some trees next to your house?" She shakes her head and hunches over her paper. "Etta, leave that for a moment and try drawing around this leaf." I take her wrist but she won't let me lift her hand. She screws up her face and pulls her hand away. "Etta..."

Jake is suddenly at my shoulder. "Best leave her be," he says.

I switch to helping Carl who keeps puncturing his leaf with his pencil and Tom who is crayoning on top of his leaf. Annie is still twirling her leaf. When I coax her into picking up a pencil she makes only the lightest of marks on the paper. I turn to Morag, who is scowling at her plane leaf as if it was a creepy-crawly.

"Here," I say, "let me help you..."

"Fucking bitch!" Morag stabs my hand with her pencil. Then she grabs my hair and thrusts the pencil at my throat. "Bitch, cunt..." I've never seen such anger in anyone's eyes.

"Stupid bitch..."

Jake is there, trying to pull her off me but she's still gripping my hair. Carl dives under the table. Pete punches Morag in the back over and over. Somebody is screaming. I think it's Tom. "Please, please...." I hear myself saying.

The muscular woman who runs the 'Fitness for the Elderly' class next door bursts in. "What's all this racket? Oh." She marches over and tickles Morag under the arms.

Morag lets go of me. I stumble backwards. Etta has covered her eyes, Tom is still screaming and Annie is beaming at everyone as if this is delightful entertainment.

Jake manages to get Morag to sit down and then asks if I'm okay.

"Yes," I say, automatically, but Brenda, the fitness instructor, takes me off to the cloakroom. In the mirror I see that I'm bleeding at the temple where a chunk of hair has been ripped out. There is a puncture in my right hand where the pencil went in. The administrator of the Day Centre arrives with the first-aid box and the 'incident book'. She explains that for Health and Safety reasons she is not allowed to tend my wounds or even stick on a plaster. Brenda snorts as she reaches for some cotton-wool. "Then go and make Margaret a cup of tea, if you can do that without a risk assessment."

The admirable Brenda patches me up and goes back to martial her class, who have spilled out into the corridor to enjoy the uproar.

I'm drinking disgustingly sweet tea in the administrator's office when Jake puts his head round the door. "No more sharp pencils, eh!"

The administrator starts to say that the Centre is not legally responsible for the pencils. I speak over her. "Are they all right? Is Morag....?"

"I've given her a double dose," says Jake enigmatically. "It'll take the others a while to settle, so we better call it a day."

"She was so angry."

"Don't take it personally. Morag's angry at everything. You were just in the way. Must go, I've gotta get 'em back in the mini-van."

I'm still shaking, so I take a taxi home. As I unlock the door I find myself thinking, 'I'll feel better when David gets home.' I can't stop a picture of him hugging me flashing into my mind. I get myself the comforting mug of hot chocolate that David would have made for me and switch on the gas fire.

When I go through the post, the first item is addressed to 'The Occupier', which is now me. It is a notification that from November 7th all post for Mr David. F. Claridge will be redirected to the address of his Chambers. There it is, in black and white – David doesn't live here any more.

October 31st

Word of the day – bruised. I wake up in need of paracetamol. The back of my hand is damson-coloured. Can you get lead poisoning from being stabbed with a pencil? I think how much worse it might have been if I'd let them use craft-knives. Lying in bed, I wonder if I daydreamed giving my clothes away. When I get up and wrench open the wardrobe doors, all I see is bare hangers trembling as if they're cold. I dress in yesterday's jeans and sweater and the clean shirt I retrieve from the airing-cupboard.

I'm staring into the fridge, trying to work up the energy to cook something for breakfast, when the phone goes. I think it will be Nina, making some change in our arrangements for today, but it is Mrs Parker, the Warden of Orion House. She tells me that mother has had a fall and that she's been taken to hospital.

"When? What happened? Is she badly hurt?" She has to repeat everything before I take it in. Mother fell in her bedroom. She was probably lying there for some time before she managed to pull the alarm cord. She said her leg was hurting so the Warden called an ambulance. The paramedics wouldn't or couldn't say if anything is broken. My mother has been taken to the Royal Infirmary. I say that I'll get there as soon as I can. Then I realize that I don't have a car and that I used up all my cash on yesterday's taxi.

I'm suddenly so angry that David isn't here when he's needed. I nearly ring him. After all, my mother is still his mother-in-law. Thirty years of socks or handkerchiefs every birthday must be worth something. My fingers start to press out his mobile number. Then I jab the off button. I tell myself not to be so pathetic. I can cope with a crisis without running to David. I will walk to the nearest cash machine and then ring for a taxi from there. I go to the cloakroom to throw on a coat and find that I don't have any.

I rush out of the house and half-run to the cash machine four streets away. I arrive breathless and shaking but I manage to type in my pin number and draw out £40. It is only when I have the phone in my hand that I realize that I haven't got the number of a taxi firm with me. I should have made a note of one before I left the house. I try to think of a number for Directory Enquiries and my mind goes blank. It used to be simple when there was just one service. Now I have choices, I can't remember any of them. I will have to get to the nearest taxi rank. I break into a run because I'm picturing mother lying in a cubicle in agony from a broken hip, asking for me, and not understanding why her daughter isn't there for her.

At the rank, there are no taxies waiting. Should I wait for one or take a bus into the centre and walk from there? I'm still dithering when a taxi arrives. I jump in and gasp, "Royal Infirmary". I fumble with the safety-belt and lean back against the seat, my heart thumping. "You all right, luv?" asks the driver.

I glimpse myself in his mirror. A breathless wild-haired woman in a paint-spattered sweater, with a plaster on my forehead. I look more like Mad Margaret from 'Ruddigore' than a respectable passenger.

I try for dignity. "I'm just a bit flustered, because of hearing that my mother has been taken to hospital."

"Ah, fall did she?" says the driver pulling out into the traffic.

"My mum fell off a stool last year; broke her leg in three places. She was trying to get the curtains down for washing. Can you believe it?"

He regales me with the misadventures of various elderly relatives while he drives very fast down side streets to avoid the traffic jams already building up.

We're half-way to the hospital before I remember Nina. I manage to get her on her mobile She's already on a bus to Cabot Circus. When I explain, she tells me I should have rung her earlier. She reminds me that she does belong to a car-sharing scheme. I turn down her offer to come straight to the hospital but agree to call her if mother needs transport home. Nina makes me feel that I am not coping but I tell myself that she wouldn't be so calm and sensible if it was her mother who'd had the accident. Even forming the word 'accident' in my head makes me hear the crunch of breaking bones.

The driver drops me off close to the entrance to the Accident and Emergency Department. I tip him over-generously and rush to get inside. The glass doors won't open. I tap on the doors but no-one inside responds. A passing man in baggy green clothes, who might be anything from a surgeon to an orderly, says, "You have to push the button." I look where he is pointing and see a big button and a small notice. I jab at the button and the doors rumble open.

Inside is a tatty waiting area smelling of disinfectant and vomit. A man with a bloodstained cloth wrapped around his thumb is talking to someone on his mobile phone. A girl, still skimpily dressed for a night-out, is flicking through a dog-eared magazine. A harassed looking mother is rocking a toddler in her arms while an older child plays with some garish plastic toys on the none-too-clean floor. A young man is striding up and down, muttering to himself. There are no doctors or nurses in evidence and I can't even see a reception desk. Then I spot a notice telling everyone to report to a hole in the wall covered by a metal grille.

As I come closer, the shadowy shape behind the grille resolves into a plump woman in a blue uniform. I blurt out my story. The receptionist asks for my mother's full name, consults her notes and then tells me that mother isn't here.

"At least," she adds, "not officially."

"She's been taken to another hospital? How do I find out where she is?"

"She may still be in the ambulance."

"You mean the ambulance is stuck in traffic?"

"It's probably parked outside. We're having a busy morning."

She tells me to take a seat while she sees what she can find out.

I sit down under a notice which threatens that anyone who abuses the hospital staff will be refused treatment. What counts as abuse? Complaining about the length of time an anxious mother has to wait to see a doctor or an old lady has to lie in an ambulance?

After a few minutes the receptionist calls out mother's surname. When I go up to the grille she tells me that they expect to have a cubicle free for my mother in a quarter of an hour. I return to my seat. There is nothing to distract me but ancient copies of *Hello*, leaflets about Sexual Health clinics, or listening to the man with the injured thumb as he tries to rearrange his work schedule.

After ten minutes, there is the sound of a door being

unlocked. A nurse briefly emerges to summon the mother and children. The mother has to drag the older boy away from the toys. They disappear down a corridor and the door is locked again behind them. If the doctors and nurses have to hide behind locked doors, what about my safety? The young man seems to be getting more and more agitated. He is mouthing, 'Must have it, must have it," over and over. He kicks at one of the abandoned toys. The yellow plastic duck squeaks as it skitters across the floor. We all look up but try not to catch the young man's eye.

The girl drops her magazine with a sigh and turns to me. "What happened to you, luv? Someone do you over?"

She's looking at my hand.

"No," I say, "well, sort of. " I give her the gist of what happened.

"Bloody loonies, they should all be locked up."

She shoots a venomous look at the agitated man, who has shuffled up to the grille and leant against it. He starts demanding to see a doctor right now. Whatever the receptionist replies it causes him to start swearing at her. The man with the wounded thumb stops talking into his phone, obviously wondering if he should intervene. After a moment, he decides against. The girl starts telling me how she's waiting for her girlfriend, Debbie, who got 'glassed' at a Hen Night. When I express alarm and sympathy, the girl shrugs, "They were both pissed." I begin to realize how lucky I am to be waiting here on a Saturday morning rather than a Friday night.

Hospital minutes are like country miles: much longer than they have any right to be. The young man is thumping on the grille by the time Security arrives. The two burly men announce that they are going to escort him off the hospital premises and that if he tries to return the police will be called. I expect the young man to struggle but he just covers his face with his hands. Security takes him by the elbows and marches him out.

Two more patients arrive – a woman with something in her eye and a man whose colour is so ghastly that I feel like rattling the grille and demanding a doctor for him straight away. I'm wondering about the mother and the sick child who haven't come back, when I'm finally called. The receptionist tells me that my mother is now in Cubicle 8 and gives me directions. It seems strange to leave the waiting area without knowing how any of the patients' stories will end.

Inside A&E, I have to flatten myself against a wall as an accident victim strapped to a trolley is pushed down the corridor. There is none of the shouting and hustle you would get in an American hospital drama. Just a silent trudge towards the operating theatre. An old man in Cubicle 3 does call out to me as I go past, "Nurse? Nurse!" but I keep walking. The curtains are drawn around Cubicle 8. This is the moment when everything may change. I take a deep breath and open the curtains.

I find my mother arguing with the nurse who is trying to take her blood-pressure. She is saying that she feels fine now and wants to go home. I introduce myself to the nurse and bend over to kiss my mother. "Have you come straight from painting?" she asks. If she's noticing the state of my sweater, she can't be that bad.

"I came the moment I heard," I say. "You've had a nasty fall. The doctors need to check you over."

"I couldn't get up off the floor, that was all. I just wanted the

Warden to help me up, but she wouldn't listen."

"The Doctor will be along soon," says the nurse, fastening a plastic identity bracelet to mother's wrist. "What would you like us to call you, dear? Claire or Mrs Rice?"

"Mrs Rice," says mother firmly. "I don't want the doctor to see me like this." I wince as she squeezes my bruised hand. She tugs me down to whisper in my ear. "I wet my nightie."

I ask the nurse if she can get my mother into a hospital gown.

"Not till Doctor's examined her. Doctor will be along in a minute."

I sit beside the bed holding mother's hand as more hospital minutes tick past. Mother asks what I've done to myself, gesturing at the plasters.

"Just a bit of an accident during my Friday morning class."

"We can't have both of us falling over," she grumbles.

I agree meekly. When I ask, she says that her leg isn't hurting any longer but her face looks very drawn. Or is that just the unforgiving overhead lights?

Mother is complaining about the Warden again when the curtains are wrenched back and a young woman says, "Hello, Claire, I'm Dr Reynolds. Can you tell me what happened to you?" I try not to think that she's too young to be a fully trained doctor, but the spotty face and the flaxen hair escaping from a pink scrunchy aren't helping. Mother starts to tell her story. She tripped in the bedroom on her way to the bathroom and twisted her right leg. She isn't sure how long she was on the floor before she managed to crawl until she could reach the alarm cord.

Dr Reynolds suddenly asks what the date is. My mind goes

blank but mother says, “It’s the 31st of October – Halloween.”

Dr Reynolds asks her how old she is. Mother hesitates.

“Mother hates giving away her age,” I begin.

The doctor ignores me as if I’m both invisible and inaudible and repeats her question. Mother admits to being 82. She is nearly 85. Dr Reynolds begins the physical examination. She prods and pulls and twists mother’s leg. “Does this hurt? Or this?” Mostly it doesn’t. After a while, Dr Reynolds says, “I don’t think anything’s broken but we better get some X-rays.”

After all the rush and panic, tedium sets in. We wait for a nurse to find mother a hospital gown to change into; we wait for a porter to take mother to X-ray; we wait in the queue of patients at X-ray; we wait for the X-rays to be checked, we wait for a porter to take us back to A&E, we wait for a doctor to check the X-rays. I try to produce a flow of cheerful conversation to keep mother distracted. She is not allowed anything to eat or drink in case she needs an operation. I lunch on a Mars bar from a vending machines in one of the endless corridors we pass through.

I begin to feel as if we’re in Purgatory, with a long time still to serve, but around three o’clock, a different doctor breezes in and tells mother that nothing is broken. The leg is merely bruised. He tells her she may now take some pain-killers and go home. Except that mother has nothing to wear but a hospital gown or the soiled nightdress I’ve been carrying around in a plastic-bag. I have to go outside to ring Nina. She cheerily agrees to go to Orion House to fetch a set of clothes for mother and bring them to the hospital.

Just before she rings off, I remember to say, “Don’t mention anything about David leaving. I haven’t told mother yet.”

"Meg! Why...never mind. Let the Warden know I'm coming. I'll be as quick as I can."

Mother is now a 'bed-blocker' but I try not to think about who may be waiting for a cubicle. I chivvy the nurse who brings two paracetamol tablets into fetching mother a cup of tea. There is even a broken biscuit with it. When Nina arrives, she hands over the clothes and stands outside the drawn curtains. I try not to look at my mother's body as I help her to dress.

We wait for a porter with a wheel-chair to take mother out to the car-park. Mother keeps asking if we can go and Nina searches her purse and mine for enough coins to pay for another hour's parking. Eventually, we support mother between us and walk her to Nina's car. I sit in the back with mother but we seem to have run out of things to say to each other. The traffic is bad so it takes forty-five minutes to get back to Orion House. I nearly fall asleep.

"Why is sitting around all day so tiring?" I ask.

"You've both had a shock," Nina says.

I feel more as if I'm jet-lagged after a long flight.

When we get to mother's flat, Nina offers to stay until I'm ready to be driven home but I tell her not to. "I'm going to make mother some supper and see her to bed. Thank you so much for your help."

"No problem." She gives me a meaningful look. "You stay and have a nice talk with your mum."

As soon as she's out of the door, mother asks why Nina isn't married.

"Just hasn't met the right person I expect."

"She is a bit bossy. Men don't like that."

Her eighteen years of marriage and long widowhood

apparently entitle her to be an expert on what men do and don't like. I have been married for longer than mother ever was, but I haven't a clue what men like. Apart from curvy girls in low-cut dresses.

"You must be starving," I say. "Let me get you some supper."

I warm up two of the ready-meals from mother's freezer. After we've eaten she tells me that I ought to get home because David has been on his own all day. I help her to bed and promise to come back in the morning.

On the way out I'm button-holed by Mrs Parker. She starts using the ominous phrase 'in your mother's situation'. She makes it clear that the time has come for mother to have daily help. "Otherwise, it might be a case of looking for somewhere more suitable for her needs."

I say I'll discuss it with my mother tomorrow and escape to the bus stop.

By the time I get home, the front-door is splattered with eggs. The local kids must have thought I was only pretending to be out on Halloween. There would have been no treats for them anyway. David is the one who buys a big tin of sweets and urges any child who comes to the door to take a fistful.

November 1st

Word of the day – panic. I wake up thinking, 'I can't do this on my own'. I think it again as I struggle to scrape dried egg off the front-door. It was a mistake not to do it last night. Now it is as hard to shift as congealed spite.

I jump as a voice close-by says,"Morning, Margaret."

It is our left-hand neighbour, the male half of Derek-and-Susan, picking up sections of the Sunday Telegraph which the paper-boy has dumped on his door-step.

"Haven't seen David around recently," he goes on.

"No," I say, scrubbing harder with a pan-scourer.

"Careful with that. You don't want to take the paint off."

"No," I repeat and keep scrubbing.

"Well, if you need anything. You know where we are."

Did he emphasize the we? Or am I just being over-sensitive?

I suppose the first thing many women in my situation do is to look around for a lover, but the world of water-colourists is not full of alpha-males. I start composing a list of possible men.

Derek from next door, the epitome of cardigan man? Too married.

Widower Rodney from my flower-painting class? Too old.

David's nice unmarried colleague, Mark? Probably gay.

Crispin at the Society of Western Artists? Flirts with anything that has breasts. Probably also gay.

Brunon, our handsome Polish plumber? Marital status unknown.

The nice bearded man who sells me goat's cheese at the Farmers' Market? Too many goats.

Would the world seem well lost for any of these? Hardly.

I could expand the list of possibles considerably if I was willing to declare myself a lesbian. It used to be only death that cancelled all debts but now 'discovering your sexuality' can be used like a Get out of Jail Free card and everyone will applaud. Nina? Deirdre? Brenda from the keep-fit class? No. I just can't see it. There is a rambling message from Deirdre on my phone. She sounds really cross that I was out last night when she wanted to itemize Callum's faults. I must follow one of the suggestions in my divorce-guide and make a list of David's faults to remind myself what I'm not missing.

I give up on the door and set out to visit mother. I shiver at the bus-stop because I don't have a coat. I'm wearing one of David's old sweaters that happened to be in the laundry basket. It has shrunk a bit in the wash but is still baggy enough to let in cold drafts. Two young women ahead of me in the queue sport cotton tops that barely cover their midriffs and yet there's no sign of goosebumps. How do they stay warm? Fat in the right places? Better circulation? Or is it all the vodka women seem to drink nowadays? That's another traditional thing I could do – take to drink, but alcohol never makes me merry. If I drink a little too much I'm prone to burst into tears at the slightest provocation. If I drank a lot too much, I'd probably feel suicidal.

At Orion House, I'm relieved to find that mother is up and dressed, though her cardigan is mis-buttoned. She scolds me for coming out without a coat and notices the sweater.

"You want to keep yourself looking nice for David," she says as we sit down. "Men expect that."

"David doesn't care what I look like." I assume that this is now true.

"Men always care," mother insists, "especially when you're out with them. Your father always used to look me up and down in the hall before we went out and say, "Very nice." If he didn't, I knew something was wrong with my outfit or my hair. George liked my hair to look natural. Not scruffy of course, not like girls wear it nowadays..."

Once mother gets started on the topic of my father, there is no stopping her. Mother still wallows in widowhood. No moving on for her. I'm sure the pain was hideously real after my father dropped dead from a heart-attack while mowing the lawn, but all these years later her grief has become an over-rehearsed act. She knows all the lines – 'I still miss George so much,' 'I could never replace your father,' but she no longer speaks them with much conviction. Suddenly, this is comforting. It may mean that one day I'll be able to say, 'My husband left me for a younger woman,' or even, 'David doesn't love me any more,' and not feel as if I'd just bent a fingernail back. How long will it take? Months? Years? Decades?

I let mother ramble on for ten minutes before getting up to make us some coffee. Then I firmly change the subject. "I noticed you were limping a bit. Is your leg still hurting?" She tells me that she's fine but I don't believe it.

"Did you take the paracetamol before you got up?"

I had left two tablets and a glass of water beside her bed.

"Just half a one. You know I don't like taking tablets."

I do know. This is a why a cupboard in the kitchen is stuffed with packets of blood-pressure tablets that mother won't admit to her doctor that she never takes.

I gulp down my coffee and begin, "Mrs Parker thinks..."

"That woman! She's always interfering, trying to tell people what's good for them."

"It's her job, mother. She thinks you need more help to..."

"I'm staying here. I won't go into one of those awful homes, where they're all gaga..."

I hear the panic in her voice and see that she's gripping the arms of her chair as if I'm about to tear her away from the only place where she feels safe.

"There's no question of that. All I'm suggesting is that you have someone come in for an hour or so every day to help with things like making the bed or getting your shopping in, or to be there when you take a shower – just to be on the safe-side."

"I can't afford it," mother says and that's probably true. She's scraped by on a widow's pension for almost half her life but she owns her flat and has just enough savings to disqualify her from most state help. She has always insisted on paying for the cleaner who comes in twice a week but now she needs financial help. I open my mouth to say, "We'll pay for the extra hours," and then remember that there is no we.

"Perhaps Rob could help out."

Mother looks shocked at this idea. "He's got a family to support, all those school and college fees...I've still got some savings I can use."

"We'll sort something out. Shall I ring up some of the care agencies and get quotes?"

It takes her another ten minutes to agree to this.

"But mind, I want someone English."

"Mother, I don't think you can say that."

"Irish would do," she concedes, "as long as I can understand what they're saying."

"I'll try to find someone suitable," I promise.

I leave without saying anything about David because it really doesn't seem the time.

November 2nd

I can't face the solicitor's waiting room in the shabby clothes I've been wearing all weekend, so I stop off at a charity shop. Not Oxfam, of course. I wouldn't want to meet my old self hanging on the bargain rails. In the Sue Ryder shop, I order myself to choose clothes which until last month I would never have considered wearing. I hold a polyester blouse in a virulent shade of emerald against myself. Just the thing for a St Patrick's Day parade. I pick out an electric blue skirt and a spotted cardigan that looks like a nasty case of measles but I can't bring myself to try them on. I decide to make it simpler and restrict myself to black and white. I shall go into mourning for my marriage for a year and a day. Perhaps that will get me some sympathy.

I choose battered black pumps, a black skirt with a hemline just above my rarely exposed knees, a fuzzy black and white check jacket, and a black t-shirt that I would normally call too skimpy. There are no black coats so I have to settle for a black poncho with a bobbled fringe. I surprise the volunteers by donating most of the clothes I took off in the changing-room and leave the shop with David's sweater in a plastic bag.

In the waiting room I expect everyone to stare at me because I'm looking so unlike myself but of course they don't. Nobody here knows the old me. By the time Mrs Patel calls me in, I'm sweating under the poncho. I almost correct her when she greets me as Peg but I pull off the poncho and sit down.

Today, Mrs Patel's nail varnish is the colour of rose-hips. She confirms that I wish her to handle the divorce proceedings, explains the stages at which fees will be due and gives me a financial document to sign. I make a show of putting on my glasses to read the small print but it might as well be in Armenian for all I take in. I sign at the bottom anyway. Then she gives me my word of the day – realistic.

"It is important to be realistic about the outcome of your divorce. Many woman read about high profile divorce cases among the super-rich and imagine that they are going to be supported in luxury for life, but this is rarely the case."

I keep tugging down my skirt but it won't cover my knees. "David promised that I wouldn't suffer financially."

Mrs Patel sighs. "In my experience, men in your husband's situation promise a great deal initially but once the legal process is under way they tend to become less generous. They have a new family's interests to consider and your husband's legal team will be keen to negotiate the best deal for their client."

"But the divorce is David's fault! I didn't ask for it. He's the one who's left me for another woman!"

Mrs Patel frowns at me as if I'm being obtuse. "Except in extreme cases, courts don't now take the circumstances of the separation into account when it comes to the financial arrangements."

"But I'm divorcing him on the grounds of adultery. He walked out on me after thirty years..."

Mrs Patel flinches slightly as I raise my voice. "If you and your husband can't agree on a financial arrangement, the court will try to divide the marital assets in a fair way. They will not attempt to compensate you for any pain you are feeling. Suing for divorce is not like suing for damages."

But there is damage. I suspect that I may have suffered what the emergency services now coyly call 'life-changing injuries'.

Mrs Patel is moving on. "There are circumstances in which a court might award you a larger than average financial settlement. Did you bring any assets to the marriage?" As I mentally start listing my good qualities, she adds, "Financial assets – money, property and so forth." Mother gave us a tea set as a wedding present. David hated the dainty cups.

"No," I admit.

Mrs Patel types something and then asks, "Are you economically active?"

"I'm sorry?"

"How much are your current earnings?"

I name the pathetic sum I put down on my last tax form. Mrs Patel purses her mouth as if she is sucking on something sour. "Have you ever supported your husband financially? When he was training as a barrister perhaps?"

"Not financially exactly. His parents helped us out then, but we managed on next to nothing..." I'm remembering making curtains for our tiny rented flat, searching junk-shops for furnishings, thinking up seven different ways to serve lentils, but Mrs Patel is focusing on figures. "Were you earning at this time?"

"A bit, whenever I sold a painting, and I did some teaching one or two days a week." "And when you bought your first property, how much did you contribute to the mortgage and other household expenses?"

"Well, I've always paid for my clothes and my art supplies out of my income – mainly. David took care of everything else."

"So the mortgage has been paid exclusively out of your husband's salary?"

"We didn't think of it like that..." I falter.

My solicitor is making me sound like some kind of parasite living off David's work. What about all the hours I've spent listening to him talk about that work, helping him to learn briefs, comforting him whenever he lost a case? What about all the cold afternoons cheering him on during Rugby games? What about the thousands of meals I must have cooked for him over the years and all the sex, whether I felt like it or not. Does none of this count? Aren't comfort and sympathy 'marital assets'?

Mrs Patel starts asking me financial questions, most of which I can't answer to her satisfaction. I can remember the amount of the mortgage we took out and how much is left to pay but I'm hazy about the interest rates. I know roughly how much our savings are but I'm hopeless on pension arrangements. Mrs Patel hands me a twenty page 'Financial Disclosure' form and instructs me to come back when I've filled it all in. She tells me that she will be sending the same form to David's solicitors. She rises from her desk to make it clear that my time is up but I have to ask, "Can David really make me sell the house?"

"If the house is held in Joint Names, he will be entitled to his half-share of the value. He might agree to you buying out his interest in the property, if you can afford to do that."

I nod my head and say, "I see," as if this will be no problem.

On the way home I'm waylaid by another chugger. This one wants me to become a Friend of the Zoo. If I sign up, will the lemurs take me out to coffee when I'm feeling down? Will the gibbons tell me if the new black skirt makes me look fat? Will the meerkats lend me forty quid for a decent haircut? Will the toucans peck Rosa's eyes out? I tell the chugger that I fear the relationship would be too one-sided. He can't think of a reply so – silently – I answer for him. At least the inhabitants of the zoo won't insist on giving me good advice, or if they do, the gist will be, 'All men are beasts.'

November 3rd

Word of the day – rejected, like a misshapen apple in a supermarket. I am not bright and shiny and perfect enough. I am however meticulous about recording my days. I write my diary in bed, last thing at night, just as I did as a teenager. I used to think that having an exceptionally retentive memory was a blessing. Now I'm not so sure.

There was a message on my phone to say that my Friday classes have been cancelled because of 'safety issues'. Is the Day Centre afraid that I'll sue them? Perhaps I should. I wonder what the going rate is for a nasty bruise to my hand and my confidence? It seems appropriate to go out and look at other people's rejected clothes. I give myself a budget of a £100 and try to find a useful black outfit in each of the local charity shops.

The rails are full of little black dresses. Do women give them away because the party they were worn at failed to live up to expectations? I think of my blank social calendar and tell myself I would never wear any of these dresses. I buy one anyway – a clingy wrap-over dress with a peacock-feather design embroidered in silver on one shoulder. I'll allow myself that much decoration. For obvious reasons, nobody has donated a pair of really comfortable black trousers. The only trousers on offer have waistlines or crotches in anatomically impossible places. I eventually come home with the impractical dress, a black cashmere sweater with a moth-hole in one sleeve, two white shirts (only slightly sweat-stained) a black crepe maxi-skirt and some cord trousers, rubbed at the knees, which I'll have to hold in place with a belt.

I spend the rest of the morning on the computer and the phone checking out care agencies and asking for quotes. In the afternoon I ring mother and give her a summary of what I've found out. She starts wavering about having someone come in every day. I start lying about how much it will cost. I promise to visit on Thursday and try to end the call but mother goes on for another ten minutes about a neighbour's mysterious visitor. This is a sign that she's feeling more like herself.

I'm preparing material for my Wednesday morning class when David rings. He tells me that his solicitors have already received the Financial Disclosure form. I'm so taken aback by Mrs Patel's efficiency that I don't listen to what he says next. I didn't ask her to move so swiftly. I thought I could rely on the legal profession to slow everything down to a glacial pace.

"So," David is saying, "rather than put you through all the stress of selling the house in a difficult market, I thought I could buy out your share. Then you can afford somewhere new right away."

"Buy me out..."

"Yes, mother will advance me the money."

That answers the question of whether Celia will tolerate Rosa for the sake of a grandchild. "Surely," I begin, "you wouldn't want to live in this house with a baby? What about the stairs?"

"Rosa thinks..." David pauses, realizing that he has fallen into my trap. Rosa doesn't just want David. She wants the whole life-style, house and all.

"I'll think about it," I say, and I do. I think about Rosa in our bedroom, Rosa in my studio, Rosa in my kitchen, Rosa's baby in the small room I'd secretly picked out as a nursery, even though buying this house was supposed to mark the official end of our hopes for a family. David always said he didn't mind that I couldn't carry a baby to term. It is – was – one of the things I loved about him.

November 4th

I started to read another chapter of Nina's self-help book last night but I couldn't stand the constant exhortations to 'take control' and 'move on'. I feel like a tin woman, too rusted up to move. Is this what marriage has done to me? Any movements I do make will be slow and jerky. Perhaps if I can identify one clear goal, I could progress towards it. The trouble is that the goal I'm now picturing is not one that even the 'all change is positive' brigade would approve of.

I want to phone my brother at his office rather than at home, so I do it before breakfast to allow for the time difference. Rob immediately assumes the worst. "Is it mother? What's happened?" I tell him about her fall and her trip to the hospital. I exaggerate a bit, wanting him to feel, as I did, how bad it might have been.

"Why didn't you tell me before?"

"She asked me not to. She didn't want to worry you."

Rob accepts this. He knows that not worrying the menfolk is a vital part of mother's creed.

I press on to the difficult bit. "The Warden at Orion House says mother needs someone coming in every day to check on her and help her to get up and so forth. Otherwise, she may need to move into a nursing home. We want to avoid that if possible..."

"God, yes. A week in one of those places costs more than a luxury cruise."

"So, I've been researching care at home providers..." I start feeding him figures.

After a bit, Rob breaks in, "That all sounds fine. You just go ahead and make the arrangements, Meg."

I pause. "Well that's the thing. The issue is money. Mother doesn't have much."

I name her exact income. Rob says, "Yes but..." and then stops. He obviously doesn't want to spell out the next bit, "...but you've got plenty of money."

"David and I have helped mother out in the past but things have changed."

"What? You don't mean David's lost his job? But he's a QC...."

"No, I mean that David's left me."

"Left you? David? I would never have thought..."

"For a younger woman."

Rob makes an 'ah that explains everything' noise. "When did this happen?"

"About a month ago. I haven't told mother yet."

"Are you sure it's not just a blip? All marriages have them."

"The blip is pregnant."

"God, Meggy, I'm sorry." Rob hasn't called me that since we were children.

"So," I persist, "until things are settled, my finances are very uncertain. I can't commit myself to paying mother's care bills. I was hoping you could help out."

"Oh, well, yes of course. Chin up, Meggy, we'll sort something out."

'Chin up, Meggy.' What a a stupid thing to say. So why does it make me cry?

At my Wednesday morning class nobody comments on my black clothes but somebody asks if I've lost weight. I know this is deemed to be the nicest thing that any woman can say to another woman but I am not grateful. When I've got them settled, I read out lines from a poem by Laura Riding.

'Ah me, ah me, says every lady in the end,
Putting the tiger in its cage
Inside her lofty head.
And weeps reading her own story.'

Now, after thirty years in its cage, I could free the tiger.

My art ladies are looking blank or baffled. I say that I want them to try painting their inner tigress. Literal-minded Janet complains that she doesn't know how to draw a tiger. I have anticipated this and brought some pictures of tigers, but I explain that their fierce inner spirits can take any forms they choose. I urge them to forget about trying to produce a precise drawing and just let their brushes flow into shapes. Everyone starts getting out brushes and filling their water-jars, except Jean who reaches for a pencil. Candy and Joanne fret about what size brush to use, so I choose for them. I turn on the radio I always bring with me hoping for some tigerish music but everything on Classic FM or Radio 3 seems tinkly and bland.

Putting music on is meant to be the signal to start work but today Pam and Janet are still listening to the new one whose name I can never remember. Could it be Amelia? I mix up a dreamy blue-grey to start my own painting. I catch odd bits of conversation from the far end of the table and flinch when I hear the word 'divorce'. Janet leans across and says, "Yes, it's the grandparents who are the innocent victims, like the children." I find it difficult to envisage Celia in the role of innocent victim, but I suppose she is. I clear my throat and announce that I'm going to demonstrate brush-strokes. I show them how to make strokes of different thickness using the point or edges of the same brush. Then I take my own advice and let the paint flow, hardly looking at the page as I think of my own story.

After twenty minutes, I make my round of the class. Candy and Joanne have produced almost identical paintings of a feline that is more kittenish than tigerish. I ought to treat them like naughty school-girls and split them up. I look over Pam's shoulder and can't help laughing. She is painting an upright tigress in an apron and rubber-gloves doing the cleaning. I help her to sketch in the distinctive shape of a Dyson. This is a very well equipped inner tigress. Janet is producing an accurate copy of the tiger photograph in front of her, which tells me nothing about her inner life. Or does it? I move on to Jean who confesses that she's more of a dog person. It's difficult to tell if she's drawn a canine or feline beast because she's tried to erase so many of its lines with a dirty rubber.

"I know," she says, "just let it flow...but I like to plan things before I actually do them. It's the way I am."

"That's fine. Artists have always done pencil sketches before they start painting. Try doing lots of little sketches instead of focusing on getting one drawing exactly right. Tell me about the image in your head."

Jean looks startled as if I've asked a very personal question. I suppose I have.

"A dog, a big fierce dog, something like a wolfhound."

So, immaculate Jean has an inner hell-hound. Who would have thought it?

As I do a quick demonstration sketch of a long-limbed dog, Janet is looking at her neighbour's work. "Ooh, that's good, Alice."

Of course, her name is Alice. I glance at Alice's painting and see a hunched beast made up of snarly black lines.

"That looks very...angry."

"I am angry," Alice responds, "having to get a court order to see my own grandchildren."

She starts to talk about the humiliation of being interrogated by social workers and the lies her ex-daughter-in-law has allegedly told them. Some of the others chime in with further stories of collateral damage after divorces. I listen open-mouthed, making no attempt to get them back to work. Why did I think that the lives of my Wednesday morning class were all sugar and sunshine? I'm beginning to see divorce as a kind of plague spreading so fast that hardly anyone is immune. "I think we all need some coffee," I say.

After I've handed round the mugs, I look at my own painting. I seem to have an inner porcupine.

I drink more coffee before my afternoon class. The prices at the florist where I normally buy flowers now seem too scary, so I have bought a cheap bouquet from a garage – a few scentless roses lost among cheap ferns and garish carnations all wrapped in shiny pink cellophane. When the group arrives I ask them to imagine the story behind the giving of these flowers as they paint them.

"Are they gesture of affection, a half-hearted apology, or a plea for forgiveness?" "They'd cut no ice with me," snaps other Sarah.

"Good," I say, "put that response into your painting".

Evangeline arrives late, carrying a sheaf of yellow flowers. When I ask her if she wants to paint them, she laughs and says, "No dear, these are for Matthew." She sees my puzzlement and adds, "I'm popping in to the cemetery on my way home. It would have been our Golden Wedding Anniversary today."

Everyone looks touched and sympathetic. Before I can stop myself, I think, 'It would have been better if David had died.'

November 5th

Remember, remember, the 5th of November – the day a formal proposal to strip me of my home arrived in the post. To be fair, David may really believe that I want to leave this house and make a new home for myself as quickly as possible. Nina keeps telling me that this is the sensible thing to do, that moving out of the home I made with David will help me to accept what has happened and stop me living in the past. But I need the solidity of a past. No-one seems to realise how much this house is a part of me. What are those spectres called that look like a woman from the front and a hollow tree from the back? That is what I would be like if I was ripped away from my house without time to gather and store all its memories. So, word of the day – hollow.

Mid-morning, I get the sympathy call from my sister-in-law. "I couldn't believe it when Rob first told me. Who is she? Some secretary?"

"I think secretaries are extinct. Rosa is one of David's Juniors."

"A trainee shark? Then she obviously did it to trap him. Smart girls don't fall pregnant by accident nowadays."

I agree that it seems unlikely. Harriet starts going on about predatory young women. Tactfully, I don't point out that she too is a younger second wife. Rob was married to Silvia for nearly ten years before he met Harriet at a seminar on 'Making Successful Business Presentations'. Harriet's presentation was so successful with Rob that he moved in with her three months later. Shocked as mother was, she took the view that the wife is always to blame if she can't keep her man happy. Since I'd always thought Silvia was a bitch, I never gave her much sympathy. If I knew where she was now, I'd apologise to her for that.

Rob may have thought he was marrying a high-flying, high-earning career woman but Harriet rapidly took to the role of stay-at home mum, or at least, stay-at-home employer of nanny. She is talking about the children now. Chloe is still at the American School in Abu Dhabi. James has chosen to go to college in the states.

"You wouldn't believe the fees at Cornell..."

I see where this is going but I just say, "It's the curse of being the 'Squeezed Middle' generation." I know that Rob's company makes a substantial contribution to Chloe's school-fees.

Harriet changes tack. "And Rob's pension isn't going to be as generous as we thought. It's really worrying."

"Everyone has financial worries at the moment. Mother's annuity pays out less and less. I expect that once Chloe goes off to college, you'll be keen to go back to work."

There is a sharp pause before Harriet says, "It isn't so easy to get a decent job when you've been out of things for a while."

I've a nasty feeling that this is true. Especially if 'a while' is nineteen years. I don't let myself start to feel sorry for Harriet.

"I'm so *very* grateful to you both for agreeing to help mother," I gush, "but I have to go and see her now."

I press the off button before my sister-in-law can reply.

I don't actually have to leave yet. I force myself to pick up Nina's book on surviving divorce again. It opens at a page which tells me to think about what I really want from life. What I really want is for gallery-owners to compete to put on an exhibition of my work because I am the next big thing, not the last small thing but ten. I really want to be given the Turner Prize for painting the perfect tulip. I really want someone to support me, financially and emotionally, for the next ten years while I try to do it. None of these things is likely to happen simply because I stamp my foot and tell the universe that I'm ready for them now. Realistically, the only chance of an upturn in my career is if I become famous for something else. I close the book and head off to Orion House to play the good daughter.

November 6th

The fireworks kept me awake last night. I could hear them but only see the odd flash of colour. All the pain and hardly any of the pleasure, just like my current relationship with David.

No. The fireworks were the same as any other year. I must stop letting this divorce contaminate everything, as if I'd failed to rinse Payne's Grey out of my brush and darkened my whole palette of colours. So, word of the day – rinse. 'I'm gonna wash that man right out of my hair' and out of my life. I look in the mirror and know it won't be that quick or easy. David is more like the permanent dye I use on my greying hair. You just have to wait for it to grow out.

With no Friday class to go to, I have time on my hands today. I should use it to fill in the Financial Disclosure form. Instead, I put on the hideous poncho and go for our favourite walk to the edge of Clifton Gorge. In the sunlight I see that the bruise on my hand now has the colouring of an over-ripe pear. Part of me is relieved that I don't have to go back to the Day Centre. In the past, I've sometimes found the class upsetting but it never impinged on the rest of my life. Morag's attack somehow changed that, brought me into their damaged world and that is a scary place to be.

I push the thought away by going over the dull minutiae of the arrangements I'm making for mother. Someone from the care agency we've picked came to assess mother's needs yesterday afternoon. The supervisor seemed a nice enough woman though mother thought she was 'a bit anoraky'. Mother also objected to some of the 'how helpless are you on a scale of

1-10?' type questions but they have to be asked. The supervisor has promised to find a suitable regular carer for mother, starting from next Friday. That should give them enough time to see if my cheque for the first month's visits bounces. I have sent off an email to Rob telling him the amount he needs to pay into mother's account each month. Acting as if he has already agreed to this should make it harder for him to refuse, though I know that Harriet will try to argue him out of it. I'm surprised by how ruthless I can be when money is short. So much for poverty being ennobling. Comparative poverty. This is Clifton after all.

I've reached the point where the prim Regency streets of Clifton terminate in a wooded gorge straight out of a Romantic landscape painting – 'Pride and Prejudice' suddenly morphs into 'Wuthering Heights'. Even the locals never quite get used to it. I walk past the paved viewing area and climb the grassy swell of Sion Hill. My destination is a bench on a narrow platform at the base of one of the neo-Egyptian towers of the suspension bridge.

Brunel's famous bridge never led to anywhere important. Its purpose was to flaunt Victorian man's ability to tame nature. David loves the bridge, in spite of its reputation as a magnet for would-be suicides. He knows all about its design and construction. In the past, whenever David sat here reciting facts about the bridge, I would rejoice in how gloriously untamed the gorge still looks. Today, this view makes me feel that I'm living close to the edge of civilisation and that it only takes a few steps to fall into wildness. Why did I never notice that before?

I go home and struggle to fill in the Financial Disclosure Form. What I mainly disclose is my ignorance of our finances.

After supper, I change to making that list of things which annoyed me about my ex-partner. According to my divorce survival guide, reading over the list will help me to embrace my new freedoms. Here goes –

Five Things I Hate About David

He argues for a living, so I can never win an argument with him.

He thinks that his mother is wonderful.

He expects his shirts to be perfectly ironed and if they are not, he re-irons them himself with a martyred expression.

He drives too fast on motorways and overtakes in what I consider to be a risky manner.

He has no sense of colour. When he chooses clothes or cars or objects for himself, they are always black, white or grey. He even grumbled when I picked out a pair of ginger cats at the Animal Sanctuary instead of black ones.

Not a dramatic list. If I'm going to recast myself as an oppressed wife I shall have to go darker.

November 7th

Word of the day – work. Nina tried to reschedule our shopping trip to Cabot Circus for today but I told her I had to work on my pictures for the Society of Western Artists' Winter Exhibition. She knows this is true. I go to the glass-house and start looking through a folder of recent paintings. Submission Day is next Friday and I haven't made my choice yet.

As a full member, I'm entitled to submit up to five pictures without fear of rejection. I'd been planning to include at least three of the flower collages but none of them has been framed yet and the best is unfinished. The framer I normally go to is used to rush orders but his charges are high. I wince when I think of the dent three of his frames would make in my own small bank account. Normally, this is the point at which David would say, 'Oh just charge it to the joint account...' Which, come to think of it, is why I've never become competent at dealing with my own artwork. I must go on a framing course. In the meantime, I shall mount the pictures myself and maybe I can find ready-made frames to fit.

I stare at the unfinished August collage, trying to decide what it needs to balance the composition. I cut out various paintings of leaves and flowers – speckled eucomis foliage, star-burst dahlias, orange and red heleniums that prefigure the death-flare colours of autumn – and hold them in place, but nothing looks right. Fellow members of the society often greet me with remarks such as, 'Still painting flowers, Meg?' They would never have said, 'Still painting people, Lucien?' in that patronising tone. Sometimes I answer, 'No, I'm painting time. It just looks like flowers.' When I look back at my own work I can date a painting exactly by changes in technique and emphasis, by what I was trying to achieve and by how far I fell short. Like tree-rings, my paintings record the years I was growing fast and the dry years when I stood still. I'm beginning to fear that this is a dry year.

I stare out through the glass. Instead of thinking about the possibilities of the garden, my gaze is drawn to the house. If I'm to lose this house it suddenly seems important to record what made it my home – layer upon layer of choices and memories and routines. I take my sketchbook and go to the drawing-room. The name was one of our jokes. Our house was never grand enough to have a formal drawing-room but it is a room I often draw in.

I sit down in my usual chair and start to draw; not a naturalistic view of the whole room, just fragments that catch my eye. The floral pattern on the sofa that David called 'too Aunty Dora'. A turquoise glass vase bought during our honeymoon in Malta. The creases and rubs on David's leather chair. The slightly chipped face of a china cat on the mantelpiece. A cobwebby stretch of cornice. Knots in the wood of a half-shutter. Bars of shadow where David's books used to stand. I fill eight pages with drawings before I make myself stop for lunch.

In the afternoon I sit in the room that David insisted on keeping as a formal dining-room, even though carrying food up here from the basement kitchen is a nightmare. If we could divide up the house room by room, I'd give him this one without a struggle. Some of my paintings hang here but they look insipid against the bull's-blood colour of the walls. I draw the claw and ball feet of the mahogany table, the black and white stripes of the satin curtains, the Doric column that forms the stem of a Sheffield-plate candelabra which was a present from Celia. On top of these images I scribble another list.

Five More Things I Hate About David

He has been fucking another woman for over a year

He has never taken my work seriously. I suspect he thinks of my painting as a suitably genteel hobby for a barrister's wife.

He refused to consider adoption, saying he wasn't sure he could love a baby that wasn't his own.

He has nurtured my incompetence in so many areas of daily life. I used to be grateful but now I find myself feeling

Next half-page missing

November 8th

Word of the day – impulsive. Today I followed an impulse and got questioned by the police. On the bus-journey back from mother's flat, I felt restless. I had spent most of the morning calming mother down. She is panicking about the new arrangements, sure that she won't like the person who is due to come for the first time on Monday. I managed to persuade her not to cancel before even giving it a try. She was so set on worrying about a stranger helping her to dress that she only asked once why she hadn't seen David lately.

I had booked lunch for us at The Scriveners Arms but mother didn't feel up to going out. Her world has shrunk again. A walk that was difficult but do-able only two weeks ago now seems as impossible as a polar trek. That thought makes me want to go everywhere while I still can, so after the bus trundles around a huge roundabout, I jab at the bell. I jump down and watch the bus drive away in the direction I should be going. Then I wait for a gap in the traffic.

It isn't easy to dodge across a four-lane road, even in Sunday traffic. Lorries hoot and a car swerves out of my path but I reach the island at the centre of the roundabout. I push through the rough grass, startling small birds into flight. Here I am in another patch of wilderness in the heart of a city, a place where humans hardly ever set foot.

I climb to the crown of the island, spread my poncho on the damp grass and sit down. I'm at the junction of four busy roads and the start of a flyover section of motorway, but from this perspective it looks like a giant sculpture of sweeping grey curves with the vehicles as moving points of light and colour.

I soon find it surprisingly easy to ignore the traffic-noise, just as the cats have learned to ignore as irrelevant any noise that comes from the radio or the television. If Vincent and Theo were with me, their ears and whiskers would be twitching as they registered the buzz and scurry of insects amongst the rustling grasses. I put on my reading glasses to look closer. I see an ant clambering up the lower slopes of my shoe, a lone bee searching a patch of clover for unfrosted flowers, tiny black beetles like full stops against the gaudy yellow of dandelions, scarlet ladybirds sheltering in grass seed-heads, a wedding-veil white paper-wing preying on the last aphids of the year. I feel out of scale; a clumsy giant in this Lilliputian world.

Suddenly I wonder why I've isolated myself in a place where people don't belong. 'No man is an island' but what about a childless, husbandless, fifty-five year-old woman ? Am I an island? I wave at the traffic just to see if anyone notices me. Some children in the rear seat of a bus wave back. Several cars hoot. One driver gives me a thumbs up. Perhaps he thinks this is some kind of protest. Perhaps it is.

I tell myself that I'm the queen of the castle. I shuffle around to flatten the grass beneath me and get into a more comfortable position. Then I bring out the small sketchbook I always carry and scrabble in the bottom of my bag for a drawing pen. A peat-brown butterfly has landed close to my foot. Or is it a moth? It spreads its ragged wings as if it is trying to absorb some warmth from the rare November sun. From a distance it would look dowdy but close up you can see orange speckles on the velvety wings.

I sketch fast and add notes on the colours as it flutters

off. Next my eye is drawn to one of those flies which imitate the warning stripes of a wasp. I do a sequence of five-second drawings to try to capture its flight pattern. Then I try larger scale studies of a wonderfully intricate beetle and an undulating red centipede.

I'm so absorbed that I don't notice the police-car at first. It is only the irritation of flashing lights on the edge of my vision that makes me look up from my sketchbook. A bulky figure is squeezing out of the gaudily chequered door on the passenger-side. Stupidly, I believe that he can't set foot on my island but this isn't a dream, so of course he can. In a few strides a massive policeman is looming over me, his feet crushing the subjects of my drawings.

"What do you think you're doing?" he demands.

Mutely, I hold up my sketchbook for him to see. He frowns in the way that slightly short-sighted people do when they are trying to focus. This small sign of vulnerability makes him seem less threatening.

"I'm drawing all the insects I can find in this patch of grass."

"Insects?" He makes it sound as if I've confessed to some kind of perversion.

"It's for a project," I improvise. "We want to show people how nature is all around us, even in a big city. How rich in life even patches of wasteland are." This is starting to sound like a good idea. What's the buzz-word I need? Ah yes. "It's about diversity."

The policeman twitches like a bullock bitten by a horsefly. "Diversity," he repeats, taking the notebook.

"I think it's going to be called the Wild Bristol Project."

I must suggest the idea to Nina. It is the sort of thing she excels at organising.

The policeman has been flicking through the pages as if he was looking at photo-fits of dangerous criminals.

"Well," he says, snapping the book shut, "you can't do your project here."

"Oh, but isn't this roundabout public land?"

"You're distracting the traffic, causing a hazard. There have been complaints."

"Goodness," I say getting up and shaking out my poncho, "I've never been a hazard before. I'm so sorry. I'll leave at once."

"Get in the car, Madam." After a pause he adds, "Please."

Inside the car, a younger policeman in the driver's seat looks through the sketchbook and seems impressed. He starts to tell me how he really wanted to go to art school but his parents persuaded him that law-enforcement was a steadier career. I murmur something about it never being too late to develop your artistic talent. His partner tells him to get off the roundabout.

As we pull out into the traffic, I ask if I'm being arrested. The porcine first policeman states that he could charge me with behaviour likely to cause a breach of the peace but that he's just warning me not to do it again. I smother the desire to tell him not to be so bloody pompous. Instead, I play the scatty artist, wittering on about how sorry I am to have caused any trouble. Then I suggest that they drop me off at the bus-stop. The driver asks me for my address. When I tell him, he says they might as well take me home. Do they think I'll go straight back to the roundabout, like a drunk to a bottle? Or is just a very slow crime day? The first policeman sits in grumpy silence while his partner asks me whether I do art classes.

By the end of the journey, we're on first name terms and I know that Jack's favourite artist is Grayson Perry. Luckily the name seems to mean nothing to the first policeman. While I'm imagining his reaction to a six-foot potter dressed as Little Bo Peep, Jack confides that he'd really like to try Still Life painting. Perhaps policemen prefer subjects that can't run away. I scribble down the details of an evening class which might suit him, warmly invite him to the Western Artists exhibition and give both policemen a cheery wave from the steps. They wait until I've used my key to open the front-door, presumably so they're sure that this really is my house. I think it still is.

Deirdre rings later to tell me about her latest row with Callum. We go over all the hurtful things he said, and the clever things she should have said back. Then she groans and says, "I don't want to think about it any more, Meg. Tell me something you've been doing, something funny or cheerful."

"I...well, I nearly got arrested today for drawing insects."

I relate the story of my trip to the roundabout.

She laughs and asks, "What did David say about you being brought home by the police?"

I reply truthfully that I haven't told him. If I hadn't got this diary to tell things to at the end of the day, would any of it seem real?

November 9th

When the bell rings around 8.30, I'm huddled under the duvet with Vincent. It's a grey day when there seems no point in getting out of bed and putting on clothes. Perhaps I'm the one who should be paying a carer to get me up and dressed. I assume it must be David at the door and decide to ignore him. When the bell shrills again I suddenly think, 'What if it's the Police, come to tell me that something has happened to David?'. I disentangle Vincent's claws from my nightie, grab the dressing-gown from its hook, rush downstairs and open the door.

Mrs Kingsley, the office manager at David's Chambers, is standing on the doorstep looking embarrassed.

"Oh, Mrs Claridge, I'm so sorry to disturb you. Mr Claridge asked me if I could pick up any post that's come for him in the last few days on my way to work."

We both know that this street, this whole area, is not on her way to work.

"Come in," I say.

There is a small stack of post for David on the hall table. Now that the re-direction order has started it should stop coming, but what about letters addressed to both us? Surely he doesn't have the right to divert those? They are mainly bills anyway. Perhaps he's asked for duplicates.

I realize that Mrs Kingsley is staring at me and I know the impression I must be making – bare feet, unbrushed hair, no make-up, tatty old dressing-gown. I can imagine her telling everyone at the office how I've let myself go. Suddenly I'm angry with David for exposing me to this.

I snatch up the letters. "Here's David's post but if he wants anything else, tell him to ring me and make an appointment."

"I will." She hesitates. "We were all so sorry to hear about...." I just stand there, not giving her any help to finish the sentence. "About you splitting up."

Splitting implies two people going off in opposite directions by choice, not one person leaving another behind. I wonder whether to point this out but Mrs Kingsley is retreating.

"Goodbye then, Mrs Claridge."

As I close the door, I wonder if I will ever see her again. It isn't just David, but everyone associated with him who is vanishing from my life. I go into the kitchen, make myself a mug of tea, grab an oatmeal and apricot bar, and go back to bed. What does it matter now if I get a few crumbs on the sheets? There is plenty of space in the bed.

At mid morning I get the call I was expecting from mother. The agency has sent a foreigner from 'one of those countries that used to be Russia'.

"It won't do," mother insists, "She has some name that sounds like a sneeze and I can't understand most of what she says. It's all smile, smile, jabber, jabber."

I focus on the smiling. "So, she's a friendly type? Not like Mr Johnson's cleaner?"

I hope that this will steer her into the topic of her neighbour's haughty cleaner and it does.

"He says she dusts his ornaments as if they're bugs she'd rather squash. She broke a vase the other day and when he complained she just shrugged and said, 'Gone now.'" After a minute or two she concedes, "This girl seems willing enough but..."

I don't let her finish. "Just try her for a week. Then you can make up your mind. "

I ring off as soon as I have her promise to tolerate the smiley girl for a week. Then I get dressed, go to the glass-house and spread out my sketches of the drawing room. I cover a large sheet of paper with a pastel-coloured wash. While it's drying, I shuffle and reshuffle the sketches until I have the composition I want. So later, when Nina rings, I'm able to say that I'm working on a painting. "Something new, something I haven't tried before."

"That's great, Meg. It just shows that change isn't all bad."

To fend off another lecture on the virtues of change, I mention my 'Wild Bristol' idea. She becomes quite excited. Well, as excited as she ever gets. Nina only seems to do middle of the range emotions, which is an advantage when it's your job to organize wildly emoting artists and performers. I tell her about my drawing session on the roundabout and suggest neglected development sites and railway sidings as promising places for artists to work. Or get arrested.

"We could get some inner city schools involved." Nina starts to talk about possible sources of funding. By the time she rings off, Nina obviously thinks I'm on the road to recovery. She might change her mind if she saw my drawing-room painting with the black void where David ought to be and the prickled creature cowering in one corner.

November 10th

Word of the day – money. I've completed the Financial Disclosure Form. Like the annual humiliation of my Tax Return, it makes me realize how little I earn as a supposedly professional artist. Total sales of pictures last year amounted to less than £3,000 plus a trickle of royalties from images used on cards. My best-seller is a blurry painting of a Madonna lily which features on a Sympathy card – the kind that people buy because they don't know what to say to the bereaved. There is the income from teaching but if I'm really honest about my expenses, the Wednesday morning class is barely in profit and the afternoon class runs at a loss.

What I long to be able to say to David is that I'm keeping the house but otherwise I can manage without him. I don't want to be anyone's official dependant. The very word makes me sound like some kind of addict. How can you make a clean break if you need to keep claiming alimony? It's like slamming the Doll's House door and then having to go back for your handbag.

To stay in my home I'll have to generate a lot more income, especially as the mortgage isn't quite paid off yet. So, possible sources of income –

1) Rent out the spare room. Come to think of it, David's study in the attic could be turned into a bedroom too. Do I really want to share my bathroom with a couple of students? Perhaps if they were male, they wouldn't be keen on long soaks in the claw-footed tub? If I can put up with David's stubble in the washbasin and the dirty towels he drops on the floor as

if we lived in a hotel with maid service, I can probably cope with student mess and grime. I might even enjoy some young company. But would I turn into the kind of eccentric landlady who has cats or lap-dogs instead of children and lives vicariously through her lodgers? Like Mrs Polson in my student days. 'Call me Flo' she used to say but I don't think we every did. God, it's years since I thought about her.

2) Sell more paintings. Which probably means only painting popular subjects. Combinations of cats and flowers always sell. Look at Elizabeth Blackadder. Bluebells and roses are sure bets, perhaps because they symbolize the kind of Springs and Summers we never quite have but always hope for. I could hold my own Open Day in the glass-house, instead of waiting for Bristol Open Studios week. It does mean visitors traipsing through the house, which I don't like. Especially now, when I feel under siege.

3) Raise the price of my classes. I shouldn't feel guilty about this. David gets paid at least £200 an hour for his professional knowledge and years of experience. I've trained and practised as an artist for just as long. Aren't my skills worth at least £10 an hour per head? But can someone like Evangeline afford to pay more? Besides, no-one actually needs my classes. They are one of life's extras, easy to cut out when times are hard. I'm as dispensable as a Grande Latte with chocolate sprinkles.

4) Do more teaching. A lot of my teaching is unpaid, like those Friday classes. I could try to do more day schools or weekend courses at places which pay decently, like the manor house in the Cotswolds where people mainly come for the food and the chance of some mild flirtation. Not so mild in the case of the elderly gentleman I had to fend off behind the bushes on

my 'Painting Nature' day. I could see if any of the studios that run painting holidays want an extra tutor, but some of them don't pay much more than full-board and travel expenses and if I had to put Vincent and Theo in a cattery... That kind of work is for people who need job-satisfaction more than money. When I first graduated it was easy to get part-time jobs in private schools. The main criterion was being less weird than the previous art teacher. Nowadays, even private schools won't touch you without a teaching qualification and a character reference from an archbishop. Besides, I'm clueless about the National Curriculum. Does it even include art? I could find out.

5) Get a part or full time job. Why not? I'm an able-bodied, relatively intelligent woman of 55. This may not be the best time for a career change but there must be opportunities out there. Oh God, I've just used the O word. Still, I could go to the Labour Exchange. Or are they called Job Centres now? There must be such things around here somewhere but, like places that sell video-games or shoe-shops that only stock trainers, I've always blanked them out as something I'll never need. Yes, I'll check where the nearest Job Centre is and go there on Thursday.

November 11th

It is suitably gloomy for Armistice Day. Word of my day – dark. Last night, one of the bulbs went in the overhead light in the drawing-room. David has always been the one who changes light-bulbs. The ceilings are so high in the main rooms of our house that I can only reach the light-fittings by standing on the very top rung of the step-ladder. So, are the lights going to go out one by one until I'm forced to sit in the dark? Is this why so many divorcees rush into a second marriage? They really want a handyman, not a husband. Or a computer expert. Today, I can't even cope with printing out digital photos. I'm not anti-technology. I just feel like an accidental time-traveller, stranded in a future where everyone but me knows how to do things. And now I've lost my native guide... I'm being pathetic. I must add signing up for a computer course to the list of things I should be doing.

I'm nearly late for my Wednesday morning class. As I couldn't get my photographs to print out, I have to stop at a newsagents to buy some bird-watching and poultry-keeping magazines. I can't even remember who it was who wanted to do birds. Candy and Joanne arrive while I'm still unlocking the hall. I ask them to set out the tables while I rip pages from the magazines. There are plenty of characterful shots of chickens but the wild birds all seem to have been photographed by Gortex-clad men obsessed with distinguishing one small brown bird from another in cloudy weather.

As the others arrive, only Janet looks through the pictures with much interest. Then she complains that there aren't any owls. Of course, it was owls she wanted to paint.

"We'll get to owls later," I say as if this was always the plan."Does anyone know if Jean is coming today?"

Pam answers, "I think this a bad week for her. You know..."

I nod but I don't. What is wrong with Jean? Depression? Cancer? Widowhood? As everyone else clearly knows, it seems too late to ask.

I tell each person to pick a photograph to work from and announce that we'll deal with bird shapes first.

"But they don't have any shapes," moans Candy, staring at her photograph of two seated bantams. "They're all feathers."

Perhaps I should have made them draw a plucked chicken.

"The shapes are very simple. Let's do some quick sketches, with brushes, not pencils."

They always hate doing preparatory sketches. Everyone seems to expect to get it right first time but how often does that happen in life? I watch the class peering at their chosen photographs and then making tentative brush-strokes.

"Try doing the shape in one stroke." I exhort them "Don't take your brush off the paper till you've finished the outline."

I walk round looking at their efforts. Pam is making it harder for herself by working on a very small scale. That reminds me of Pete and suddenly I miss my Friday group. Whatever they did, even if it was only red scribbles or stabbing at the paper, was a true expression of their personalities. My Wednesday morning ladies have all learned to conform to a bland socially-acceptable norm, even in the way they draw.

When they've each done several outlines, I demonstrate how to paint feathers. I've brought a magpie feather with me, a relic of one of Theo's more notable kills. I get quite carried away showing them how to lift out paint to indicate the individual pinions. Then shuffling, tapping of pencils and an irritating cough make me aware that the class is restless. I look at the clock and realize that we...I have failed to observe the 11 o'clock silence. I am so obsessed with my own petty concerns that the millions who died in horrible wars can slip my mind. I apologize and suggest that we have two minutes of silence before I make the coffee.

We do it but the silence now seems artificial and awkward. I try to think about all the young men who didn't come back from the last century's wars but I feel nothing. Everyone is subdued during the coffee-break and they go back to their chickens without being harried. At the end of the morning, nobody seems satisfied with what they've painted, which I suppose is progress of a kind since nobody has done good work today. There are groans when I announce that we'll continue with birds next week.

I ask the afternoon class to paint their Remembrance Day poppies alongside some real flowers in various shades of red. Other Sarah objects until I explain that I want to demonstrate the variety of hues within a natural petal in contrast to the uniform red of the artificial petals. She sees the point of that. My own poppy is crumpled and slightly faded. Will the others realize that I dug it out of the bottom of a drawer rather than buying a new one? I begin an outline, complete with the pin through the stem. As I draw, I imagine pricking my finger and a drop of blood falling to spread and spread until it fills the page. Painting can be a form of meditation. If you think about something deeply enough you hope that the thought, and the emotions which cling to it like barnacles, will saturate the painting. Today – nothing.

I wonder if my heart is broken. Usually when we say that someone is heart-broken we mean that they are in the throes of anguish. But that's not it. The real danger is when your heart is too broken to feel anything. Perhaps David's betrayal was just the final blow that broke open an existing crack. I can even draw up a list of people who broke my heart -

The chief social worker who wouldn't accept any responsibility for the terrible death of a tortured child because 'we don't do blame'.

The teaching-assistant who was sacked for telling parents that their child was being bullied because bullies, and the people who tolerate them, are entitled to their privacy.

The foreign driver who can't be deported in spite of killing two children, because he is entitled to the family life he's taken away from others.

The nurse reprimanded for offering to pray for a patient. Belief slipped away from me in my teens but I wouldn't mind being loaned a little of someone else's faith.

The well-off woman who had one of her twins aborted because she didn't want the bother of looking after two babies. Aborted – not just someone coming to an end but someone prevented from being all the things they might have become.

At the time it seemed such an obvious decision for a pregnant art student with no income but a student grant, an unreliable boyfriend, and a mother who was more likely to be hysterical than supportive. Did I mull over all the moral issues before going ahead with the abortion? No. I mainly thought about what my then sister-in-law would say. An accidental pregnancy would have confirmed Sylvia's view of me as a hopelessly impractical person. It is frightening how the most important decisions in your life can be made for such trivial reasons. Was it some little thing I did or didn't do that made David look elsewhere?

"There, there, deary"

Evangeline has taken my hand and is patting it. The others are staring at me with varying degrees of discomfort. I realize that tears are streaming down my cheeks.

"I'm sorry..." I gulp.

Only Evangeline is unembarrassed by my outburst. "It's the day for tears, isn't it? So many of them to cry for."

I nod and thankfully nobody asks me who my tears are for.

November 12th

Today I take a bus to my nearest Job Centre Plus. Plus what? Plus idle people looking for jobs they don't want? Or plus desperate people looking for jobs they won't get? Even on this street I find myself dodging chuggers. The ones from Amnesty International are particularly self-righteous, even though they're paid to accost people. I spot a jaunty Job Centre Plus sign in a nasty artificial green of the kind I tell my pupils never to use when painting leaves. I have vague memories of reading rows of cards when I was looking for summer work as a student but all I can see through the front window is an expanse of scuffed laminate dotted with phone booths and tall machines which look like the automated check-in terminals I avoid in airports. There are no chairs.

I approach the doors but the way in is half-blocked by two brawny badge-wearing men. Bouncers? I veer away, as if I hadn't noticed where I was heading until now. I stop and stare at some garish purple and peach tee-shirts in the shop-window next door. As I pretend to be interested in the display I realize that the tee-shirts are meant to be dresses for women with a lot fewer years and a lot better legs than me. I turn around and stand in the middle of the crowded street, uncertain what to do next. I see the chuggers sizing me up as the weak one to cut out of from the herd. As they move to surround me, I march towards the Job Centre again. I tell myself that the men in the doorway can't be bouncers. The whole place is here to encourage people into work.

One of the men is still standing just inside the door. I get close enough to read his label . It gives his name followed by 'Customer Care Officer'. I smile at him and begin, "Hello, I'm looking for information about possible jobs."

"Are you registered here as a claimant?"

"No, this is my first visit. I..."

"Do you have an appointment?"

"No, I just thought..."

He is jerking his thumb towards a notice on the wall behind him, which doesn't seem very caring, especially as the notice says, IF YOU DO NOT HAVE AN APPOINTMENT WAIT OUTSIDE OR RING A CONTACT CENTRE.

"Can't I make an an appointment while I'm here?"

I crane my neck so that I can see further into the Job Centre. Right at the back I spot some more friendly-looking people and actual chairs to sit on.

The Customer Care Officer moves to block my view. "No, you have to email or ring to make a New Claim Appointment." When I continue standing there he squeezes out a little more information. "You'll have to see the Financial Assessor first. When there's an appointment free, they'll send you a text."

"I don't do texts," I say.

I'm not sure if my phone does either. At my request, David got me the simplest possible model. The bouncer gives me a pitying look. "You can do it all on-line. Ask them to help you in the Central Library."

"I don't think I want to claim anything I just want some information. Don't you have any leaflets?"

"Leaflets?" His brow furrows as if this was a bizarre and archaic request, like asking for a horse and cart in a car showroom. "Wait here."

I stay exactly where I am, watching a young man hunch over one of the terminals, occasionally tapping the screen in a desultory way. An older man is using one of the phones. He keeps saying, "Yes, but..." or "No, but..." He is never allowed to finish his sentences. The bouncer comes back and hands me two leaflets. The one on top is titled 'Tap into our services'.

"Thank you," I say. He's clearly waiting for me to leave, so I do.

I downgrade my word of the day from determined to frustrated and make for the nearest café to regroup. I order a Viennese coffee with a topping of whipped cream and chocolate sprinkles, just to emphasize that I'm back in the frivolous world of women who don't need to work. While the coffee is cooling, I look at a leaflet with the motto – 'When we train you gain.' What I am to gain it does not say. The leaflet urges me to sign up for a free certificate in 'Employability and Personal Development'. I have a sinking feeling that my Employability level isn't high. What kind of personal development do they have in mind? Am I to develop into the kind of person who can endure the crushing monotony of a 9 to 5 job waiting on tables or stacking shelves? I give myself a mental slap on the wrist. I probably should develop into the sort of person who has more respect for useful work and the people who do it.

I look at the other side of the leaflet. I don't think that my Maths and English skills need much improvement, which must surely put me ahead of many job candidates. Perhaps I should take a vocational course, but the choice isn't wide. I could go for a 'must-have qualification in getting work on construction sites'. I thought that a hard hat and plenty of muscle were the only 'must-haves' for building work, though being Polish obviously helps. I don't see myself as a Fork-Lift truck-driver either but I could probably manage a Level 2 Award in 'Door Supervision' . If opening and closing doors is Level 1, what is Level 2? Is Door Supervisor a euphemism for bouncer? If so, there's obviously quite a demand for them to keep the public away from government services. I could do that, especially in my current mood.

I turn to the other leaflet and learn that the machines in the centre are called Jobpoints and the phones are for calling Jobseeker Direct. The whole job-seeking process seems to be designed to avoid human contact. Are job-seekers contagious? Do the gainfully employed fear catching failure from them? Apparently extra help is available for people who are deaf or Welsh but not for bewildered middle-aged, soon to be divorced, women. Since I do still have an internet connection at home, my best bet is to search for suitable jobs on the official recruitment website. I pledge some weekend time to the task.

Meanwhile...I use that word a lot now. I am stuck in the dreary state of meanwhile in which nothing good seems to happen. Meanwhile, I must get back to what I've always thought of as my life's work and finish preparing my entries for the Western Artists Exhibition. The synthetic sweetness of the coffee was disgusting but I leave an extra large tip for the staff. I could end up working in a place like this myself.

November 13th

It is Friday the 13th but bad luck doesn't seem so threatening when you've less to lose. Normally David drives me to the SWA Gallery on Submission Day. This time I have to indulge in a taxi. The driver says he'll be charging extra for my wrapped-up paintings as if they were suitcases. I make a feeble joke about packing a lot into my paintings. He just grunts as he slides the brown packages into the boot of his cab. Actually, the paintings are lighter than normal because of the cheap frames and low quality glass I've used.

After we reach the Gallery, the driver dumps the paintings on the pavement outside the grandiose portico. He doesn't offer to help me inside with them. I give him the smallest possible tip and struggle to fit five paintings under two arms. I'm rescued by a miniaturist who carries the largest of the paintings for me so that I can join the queue in the foyer. Greetings and gossip are bouncing off the stone walls and tiled floor. I try to smile at people I know but don't join in the chatter.

When I reach the head of the queue, the Steward checks to see that each of the five packages is correctly labelled with title and price and my name and full-member status. Then he hefts them onto a trolley as if they really were baggage at the start of a journey. I almost ask him to give back the painting called 'Home – Drawing Room' but I don't want to delay the kindly miniaturist or the painter behind him whose vast canvas is getting in everyone's way. The Steward hands me a receipt for my paintings. I squeeze past the canvas labelled 'Explosion 17' and make for the doors.

Outside, it has started to rain. I walk to the nearest bus-stop. I am on my way to meet 'smiley girl'. By the time I arrive at mother's flat, I am quite wet. I really must get myself a black raincoat. The door is opened by a young woman in high-heels, a short red skirt and a low-cut satin blouse. She would look like a hooker if she wasn't also wearing bright yellow washing-up gloves and her hair scrunched back by rubber-bands. Come to think of it, she still looks like a hooker but of a rather specialized kind. Did I approach the wrong sort of agency? This apparition says, "You are the daughter Maar- gret? I am Aija. Please to come in."

It annoys me to be invited into my own mother's flat by a stranger but I just say, "Yes, I'm Margaret."

She gives me a sunny smile. "I thought you are younger."

I stop even trying to like her.

Mother doesn't get up when I come into her living room. She seems very comfortably settled in her armchair. As I lean over to kiss her, Aija says, "Here is the daughter. I make the coffee for two?"

"Yes please," mother replies, "with hot milk like I showed you."

Aija nods, setting her pigtails bouncing. "Milky, milky."

She retreats into the kitchenette and I sit down in my usual chair, which I notice has been moved nearer to mother's armchair than usual.

"Melody is from Latvia."

I blink. "Melody?"

"It's what her name means in Latvian, or something like, so that's what I'm calling her." This sounds rather like re-naming a pet adopted from an animal shelter.

"Well, if she doesn't mind..." I begin.

"Oh it was Melody's idea. All her ladies call her that, except for the one who thinks Melody is her daughter. The real daughter hasn't showed up in years, apparently. So sad."

As the kettle boils and there is a clash of cups from the kitchenette, I whisper, "Melody seems rather unsuitably dressed for a carer."

"Girls nowadays," says mother vaguely.

"So, you're happy for the moment?" I ask. " You don't want me to ask the agency to send someone else?"

"No, dear, it's nice to have somebody so cheerful about. Of course I have to tell her how to do the simplest things. Girls her age have no idea how to polish anything."

"Well if you're satisfied." I'd expected to have to spend half my morning persuading mother not to reject the help I'd arranged for her. Now I'm rather at a loss.

"You're looking peaky, dear. Aren't you sleeping well?"

I admit that I am not and receive the usual lecture about the importance of not doing anything too stimulating before bedtime. I used to pass the time during this lecture by recalling some of the very stimulating things David and I do...did in bed. Now I find myself thinking 'Perhaps I should try some Ovaltine'. I am only saved by Aija bustling in with a tray, as if she is serving in a restaurant rather than stepping out of the kitchenette.

"The English coffee. Much milk, little coffee. Like you show me."

Aija spoons mounds of sugar into mother's cup and tries to do the same to mine. I put my hand over the cup. "No, sugar for me."

"The sugar is good," Aija insists, "make you sweet."

"No! Thank you."

She smiles as if she's proved a point and turns on her heel.

"We all need a bit of sweetness in our lives," says mother tritely.

I take a sip of the tasteless coffee to avoid answering.

"The brown biscuits," announces Aija, slapping down a plateful of Hobnobs. "Now I finish the dusting."

She moves over to the mantelpiece that frames the gas-fire and dabs at the clock in the centre with an orange duster.

"Why don't you start in the bathroom?" I suggest.

"The bathroom is all finish. Shiny bright."

Aija moves on to a china figurine of spotty dog. It used to be one of a pair but I broke the other one as a child. I steel myself to ignore her.

Then I nearly choke on my coffee when mother says, "I understand now why I haven't seen much of David lately."

'Oh God,' I think, 'I can't have this conversation now. Not with Aija in the room.'

"Who told you? Was it Rob?"

"Rob? No, it's all in The Express today."

She taps the paper lying on the table between us. I pick it up, bracing myself for a 'Top Barrister leaves wife for Junior' headline. It takes me a moment to realize that the story I'm looking at is actually about a murder trial. David is prosecuting and one of his speeches is quoted – "The Crown will show that in a jealous rage, Martin Jenkins hacked his wife Jenna to death and then attempted to burn her body." How stupid, how self-absorbed of me to think that a national newspaper would be interested in my marital difficulties when they have juicy murders to write about.

Beside the story is the photograph of Jenna Jenkins that the papers all printed when she was first reported missing. It must have been taken on a windy beach somewhere. Jenna is wearing a strapless sun dress and her pale hair is floating around her head like an aureole. I remember David once joking that if you want to avoid publicity, murder a plain brunette. If the victim is blonde and passably good looking, the tabloids will splash the case all over their front pages. This was going to be a high profile trial.

Mother is asking me questions about the case, which I evade by telling her that David doesn't talk about his work until a trial is over.

"Such a terrible thing," says my mother, "with his little girl sleeping upstairs and then telling her that her mother had run off. Mind you, she sounds like the sort who might. I expect there will be things coming out about the wife."

Until I married David, I thought of defence lawyers as the romantic heroes and prosecutors as cold-hearted establishment figures. "Why can't you act for the defence?" I once asked and David said, "I do. I'm defending the victim." I wonder if he still believes that.

Mother has been diverted into telling me about the alleged infidelities of the grand-daughter-in-law of the Jacobsons in Flat 6. When Aija declares that she is 'all finish', I walk her to the front door.

"Your mother is the nice lady," says Aija. "Is sad she has no family living with her."

"She has family. She prefers her independence." Even as I'm saying it, I wonder if mother would refuse if I asked her to move in with me.

"Sad," repeats Aija, "but now I care for her every day, not Sundays."

If Aija/Melody is mother's official carer, what am I? Her not caring as much as I should next of kin?

November 14th

Today I finally go on that shopping trip with Nina. I am not in the mood for buying. I'm finding it restful to have so little choice when I get up in the mornings. I toy with telling Nina that I've given nearly all my clothes away but I'm not sure what her reaction will be. Would she see this as a praiseworthy new start or a sign of craziness? I admit to needing a raincoat but insist that I'm on a strict budget. We avoid the smarter shops in Cabot Circus and make for one of the discount stores.

To me, the tightly-packed rails of 'end of line' and 'sample' garments look like a retirement home for failed fashions but Nina goes into Hunter-Gatherer mode. She enjoys tracking down the one wearable thing hidden in a rail of dross. When we find some raincoats, Nina tries to steer me towards the kind of bright colours which she favours herself. I tell her that black is more forgiving. She points out that my figure doesn't need forgiving.

"You're too thin already." What a difference there is between the complimentary slim and the pejorative thin. "Are you eating enough, Meg?"

"Of course," I say.

At Waitrose, I find myself still putting things in my basket because David likes them. Jars of green olives, packets of oatmeal biscuits and tins of anchovies stand unopened in the larder.

I buy the first black raincoat that fits me, even though it has a spotted lining which reminds me of a poisonous toadstool. I amuse myself by talking Nina into buying a flouncy skirt with a delicate floral print on the grounds that if change is good, she ought to try a new look. Then I let her buy me coffee.

While my Flat White is cooling, I tell Nina about my mission to become a Job Seeker. I describe my abortive visit to Job Centre Plus and how I sat up with my lap-top late into the night searching for jobs in the Bristol area. The intangible world of the Internet seemed more evasive than ever. The websites I was trying to get to always seemed to have changed their names. After going from link to link, I was presented with lists of choices none of which were exactly what I wanted.

"It's like trying to find your way around an invisible maze. By the time I gave up, the only vacancies I could possibly apply for were for office cleaners or eye-brow threaders – whatever they are."

Nina laughs but she seems surprised that I'm considering full-time work. "You're an artist, Meg. You can't stop painting."

"I wouldn't have to stop entirely," I say but I know that painting is like music or ballet, you have to practise continually to keep up the standard.

Nina knows this too. "I don't see you as a week-end dabbler. Surely you won't need to work once you get your divorce settlement?"

"Barristers like David, who work as Crown prosecutors, don't make as much money as you think they do. Besides, if I keep the house instead of..."

I don't get any further before Nina attacks this plan. I pacify her by presenting a picture of myself as a den-mother to a household of students.

"Perhaps then I could get by with a part-time job. Something in an art gallery or museum would be ideal. Do you know of anything coming up?"

Nina is not as encouraging as I expected. "There might be something temporary but most paid posts require administrative experience, or a relevant degree."

"Isn't an art degree relevant?"

"I meant degrees in Arts Administration or Museum Studies."

"Perhaps I could get a job as a gallery attendant, or do you need a degree in staring at paintings for that?"

"The guards are supposed to watch the people, Meg, not the paintings."

"Oh." I sip my coffee wondering how much successful arts administrator Nina would have in common with a trainee eye-brow threader.

Later, when I'm back home, Madeline Danvers rings to invite us to dinner. I've never particularly liked Madeline but she always has an interesting mix of people at her dinner parties. I tell her that the date she's suggesting 'won't be possible'. When she offers two others, I have to explain that there is no 'us'.

"We've recently separated. David doesn't live here now."

Madeline murmurs that she's very sorry to hear this and starts extracting information. "Not another mid-life crisis! Men are so predictable. I assume there's a younger woman involved, or is it a younger man?"

This provokes me into giving the bare details. As I talk, Madeline is making sympathetic noises but I can almost see her crossing out my name in her address-book and substituting Rosa's. It's only after she rings off that I think 'She could have asked me to that dinner party anyway.' I would probably have said no, but it would have been nice to be given the choice.

Newly single women are obviously much less popular with hostesses than newly single men.

Newly single. Not yet, especially if I go on ignoring the letter from my solicitor, but should I still be wearing my wedding and engagement rings? What is it that Anne Elliot says in 'Persuasion' about the different ways that men and women love? Something about women loving the longest when all hope is gone. I'm not ready to take off my wedding band when I still feel bound to David in so many different ways. I'm not even sure that it will come off.

My diamond engagement ring though is a family piece. It was made for David's grandmother. I can remember him producing it from his pocket, still in its original velvet-lined box. David had insisted on going for a walk on an unpromising day because he was determined to propose in a romantic setting. By the time we reached the rose garden that was his chosen spot, it was pelting down. We had to take shelter under a spreading conifer, so when he knelt down his damp cord trousers got covered in pine-needles. Ever since, the smell of pine, even in a disinfectant, brings back the giddy mixture of joy and panic that I felt when I heard David say, 'Meg, will you marry me?'.

I know I laughed and kissed him and tried to brush off the needles but I don't actually remember saying 'yes'. I must have done. Or did David just assume that the answer was bound to be yes? Should I give the ring back to him? If I do, will he go somewhere romantic to offer it to Rosa? I imagine him trying to force the dainty ring onto Rosa's thick stubby finger. She has ugly hands. I remember thinking that the first time we met.

November 15th

Sundays are hard. On rainy Sundays like this one we often go – often went out for a late breakfast or an early lunch. Now I dare not go to any of the familiar places in case David has taken Rosa there. Perhaps David and I should draw up a list of favourite haunts and divide them between us. 'You can have the slightly pretentious fish restaurant, if I can have the café that does such good pain au chocolat...' I put on my new hooded raincoat and walk to the Downs. I'm probably safe enough there among the dog-walkers and the weekend-only fathers. I don't see Rosa as the strolling in the rain type.

On Clifton Downs I soon feel out of place as a lone walker with no obvious purpose. The joggers and runners are torturing themselves to reach some ideal of fitness. The dog-owners and single parents are there to allow their pet or offspring to work off energy by rushing around on wet grass. Most of the families are headed for the zoo. A pair of lovers are running hand in hand for the shelter of the trees. I seem to be the only on-looker. If I was a middle-aged man, I'd probably get reported to the police for loitering and staring at children. A small dark-haired girl has tilted back her head and is trying to drink the rain as it falls.

When I walked with David, it was easier to stop myself thinking, 'That little girl might have been mine if I hadn't...' I swat away this persistent thought. I remind myself that if I'd foolishly had that unwanted baby all those years ago, she or he would no longer be a cute child. I never gaze at thirty-somethings chattering into their iphones about school-fees or mortgage rates and think 'they could have been mine'. Now I'm the unwanted one. An inconvenience to other people's lives.

I can still remember how nervous I was that Leo would be angry with me for forgetting to take the pill every day. When I'd missed my first period I hadn't been too worried because I was never that regular but days and then weeks went past and my body began to feel different. One night, after we'd made love, I told Leo that I was pregnant. He seemed to take it well. He stroked the slight curve of my stomach and said, "It must have been meant to happen, babe." Beautiful Leo with his sculptor's hands and long tawny hair and beard to match his name.

The next day, when I came back from my print-making class, Leo's things were gone from my room. I found out later that, like a wandering tom-cat, Leo had several homes. I wasn't the only girl giving him food and shelter and sex. My landlady heard me sobbing and got the whole story out of me. Mrs Polson was very kind. She went with me to the clinic and cosseted me afterwards with cups of tea and hot-water bottles. Mrs Polson did everything for me that a mother would or should have done but as soon as I felt better, I couldn't get out of there fast enough. I never even sent her a Christmas card.

After Leo, I became much more cautious about relationships. I suppose I was looking for someone who was honest and reliable, someone who would never walk out on me as Leo had. I thought I'd found him in David. Even then, I didn't rush into marriage. I was the one who insisted on a long engagement but each day the fit seemed better. Once we were married, I thought there was no rush to start a family. Later, after the problems became apparent, my gynaecologist assured me that the 'termination' I'd had as a nineteen-year old had nothing to do with my miscarriages. Most days I believe it.

November 16th

In the early years of our marriage, David and I talked about his work much more. When he first appeared as a Junior, I used to watch from the front row of the Visitors' Gallery. I was keen to be supportive but I gradually realised that David didn't want me there because he had to be a very different person at work. Playing that role in front of me was harder. Of course I still met him at court for snatched lunches or to travel home with him at the end of the day. Sometimes, I asked the ushers to sneak me into the back row just for the pleasure of hearing his voice. David never even knew I was there. So this morning when I asked one of the ushers if he could get me into the court, he smiled and said, "Court One is packed today, Mrs Claridge, but the bloke from The Sun has sloped off to the pub early. We'll slot you into his place."

During a brief pause in the proceedings, I am ushered into the court and find myself sitting on the end of a row of journalists, very close to the front. Thankfully, I'm on the opposite side from the Prosecution Team but out of the corner of my eye I see David notice me. I don't allow myself to look towards him. I nod and smile at the court artist, whom I've half-known for years, and then study the judge, jury and defendant.

The elderly judge looks like a Tenniel drawing of a tortoise in a wig but I recognize him as His Honour Justice Strang, one of the few judges whom David regards as scrupulously fair. The jury appear to be a carefully chosen cross-section of modern Britain, from perms to piercings. There is an equal number of women and men, and skins of all shades from blue-black to mottled pink. Some have dressed formally, as if for a job interview. Others are wearing the kind of clothes I would reserve for messy painting days. The older members of the jury are poised with pencil and paper to take notes. Twitchy-handed younger jurors seem lost without the phones or notebook-computers that the court doesn't allow and are forced to do nothing but listen. Probably a novel experience for them.

It is only when I turn my attention to the Defendant that the casting seems wrong. Martin Jenkins doesn't look capable of a crime of passion. He isn't the hulking, wife-beating Bill Sykes type or even the creepy little worm-who-eventually-turns Crippen type. He looks disappointingly ordinary. Average height, average build; medium brown hair, a pleasant face, neither handsome nor ugly. There is nothing remarkable about him. Except that, if my husband is to be believed, Martin Jenkins didn't just sit there in stupid silence when his wife told him that she wanted a divorce. He picked up a carving knife and slashed and stabbed and hacked until there was no possibility of her ever leaving him.

The next witness is being sworn in. He can't be very important because it is not David but Rosa who gets up to question him on behalf of the Prosecution. I've always hated seeing David look prematurely aged by the ridiculous grey wig that barristers are forced to wear but the pale curls framing her dark face make Rosa look like one of those girl-playing-boy characters from opera. I am forced to admit that the effect is charming. I lean forward to study her for signs of pregnancy. Her figure was always voluptuous but is her black suit too tight now? It's hard to tell when she's wearing a shapeless Junior's gown over it. Rosa casts a nervous sideways glance at my side of the court. Does she think I'm going to stand up and make a scene? That probably would get my marital problems into the papers.

"When you're quite ready, Miss Winston."

Rosa winces at the Judge's tone and her first question comes out as a gabble. After a few moments she slows down and manages to establish the witness's qualifications. He's a pompous and voluble little man. Rosa has to keep cutting through the flow of jargon to highlight the rather sparse forensic evidence that Jenna Jenkins died in her kitchen. Martin seems to have done an excellent job of cleaning all traces of blood from the kitchen floor, but then according to Saturday's paper, he was a house-husband who had given up his IT job to look after the little girl while his wife earned big money in a Swindon PR firm.

I look at Martin again. He is dressed very neatly and his skin has a scrubbed look. It is easy to imagine him mopping and hoovering and polishing; keeping the house immaculate. Did he do all the cooking too? Jenna seems to have waited until their daughter was in bed and they were sitting down to a late dinner, before telling him that the marriage was over. I assume she was planning to take the little girl with her. What drove Martin to pick up the knife? Was he just trying to stop Jenna talking before the decision became irrevocable? Or was he overpoweringly angry because, after twelve years of marriage, she had no idea of the strength of his feelings, no idea that her discarded husband could be dangerous?

The forensic witness is talking about the blood that had seeped into the chipboard bases of the fitted-kitchen units. They should have gone for solid wood. I picture myself in my own kitchen scrubbing splashes of blood off the oak-topped work-surface. David likes his meat rare and he never seems to notice the mess he makes when he carves a leg of lamb or a sirloin of beef.

Martin doesn't seem to be listening to the evidence against him. He is gazing at the gilded coat of arms over the judge's bench, as if he had a mild interest in heraldry – which for all I know, he does. I wonder if anything about the court seems real to him. Martin has the look of someone who has withdrawn far inside himself and has no intention of coming out until everything is safe. Which it probably never will be. I want Martin to turn his head and notice me; to read my face and know that I am someone who might understand what happened to him that day.

I also want Rosa to stop talking but she is nipping at the witness's heels, moving him on to describe the evidence that Jenna's body was transported on the back seat of Martin's car. Why didn't he put the body in the boot? Perhaps he still thought of the body as her rather than it. The witness is talking about small bloodstains in the car-upholstery 'consistent with seepage from a wrapped body'. Seepage. Horrible word. The witness goes on to innumerate the long fair hairs and woollen fibres tweezered off the back seat. I instantly recall the flaxen-haired, elfin beauty in the newspaper photograph, but the journalist beside me just writes hairs and then starts to doodle in the margins of his notebook. He favours spirals. Martin is now studying the backs of his own hands. I note that he is still wearing his wedding ring.

The fibres are from a tartan picnic-rug. "Of the type," as Rosa carefully states, "in which Jenna Jenkins' half-burned body was wrapped." The very fact that the Jenkins had a picnic-rug suggests happy family outings. I picture the three of them sitting on the rug on some windswept beach, eating boiled eggs and neatly-cut sandwiches prepared by Martin. Of course I have to imagine the little girl, as her name and image have been kept out of the papers. The journalists have confined themselves to the stock phrase about her 'being comforted by family members'. What words of comfort you could possibly offer to a child whose father has murdered her mother they never say.

Rosa has finished with the witness. As she turns away from the witness box, she looks across to where I'm sitting, more defiant than nervous now. It is tempting to give her a round of applause. In any film or TV series, Rosa would be the heroine. Clever working-class black girl who succeeds in the snobbish legal world and wins the heart of her upper-class boss. Of course if the boss was married, his wife would have to be written as a heartless bitch. I clamp my hands together.

The Defence Counsel is coming forward to question the witness. He only makes a token effort to belittle the forensic evidence, extracting an admission that the hairs, fibres and even the bloodstains could have got onto the back-seat some time prior to Jenna's death. They are probably going for a defence of Provocation. Will that work for a defendant who is showing no emotion? I scan the faces of the jury. David is an expert at reading the body language of juries. To me, they are a collective enigma. One woman is frowning. Another is chewing one of her long fingernails. A man has taken off his glasses to polish them on his sleeve. Have they already made up their minds, for or against Martin? All I can tell is that there has been an increase in the small fidgety movements of people who've been forced to sit still for too long.

When the witness steps down, Justice Strang peers at the clock and at his list of witnesses. Then he announces that the court will hear the rest of the forensic evidence after lunch. The testimony about the body and its injuries will probably put everyone off their next meal and judges like a good lunch. We all stand for His Honour to leave the court. As soon as he does, journalists are elbowing past me in the rush to get to the lobby where they can use their phones. I stand there, as the court empties. The Defendant has already been taken back to the cells. I didn't notice him go. Martin is that sort of man.

"Meg, what the hell...what are you doing here?" David is striding towards me, still in wig and robes. He sounds so angry. For a moment I can't speak, can't say, 'Don't I even have the right to look at you after all these years?' Then I delve into my raincoat pocket and bring out the box.

"I came to bring you this."

"What?"

"Your grandmother's ring. I thought you might want to give it to Rosa."

Now he is the speechless one.

"Here," I say, "take it."

"Meg. You don't have to do this. I would never have asked for it back."

But he takes the box. As he does so, I notice that David, unlike Martin, is no longer wearing his wedding ring.

November 17th

Word of the day – independence. I remember reading in one of those magazines I only look at while I'm having my hair done, that older women are fleeing long marriages in droves. Apparently, they are jumping ship to savour the joys of independence before it's too late. Why can't I feel like that? Is it the difference between jumping and being pushed?

Nina rang last night with some suggestions for possible part time work in arts projects, all of it temporary and very badly paid. If I am to be truly independent of David, I will need more than this. Big changes, not little ones. I notify the universe that I require a job that is creatively satisfying and decently paid. I ring Job Center Plus and attempt to make an appointment with an advisor.

The first question I'm asked, by a woman who tells me to call her Sharon, is whether I am 'currently in work'. I find this difficult to answer. As an artist, I am constantly working, at least I was when I could concentrate properly. Sharon makes it clear that she is only interested in 'paid work'. I babble about my art classes and my sporadic royalties and picture sales until she cuts me off by asking if these are my only sources of income. When I admit that I am currently supported by my husband, Sharon informs me that she can't assign me to an advisor because I am not officially unemployed and my level of income renders me ineligible for Job Seeking allowances or free retraining schemes. The Job Centre will not help me to avert financial catastrophe; it will only help me to pick up the pieces after Humpty-Dumpty falls off the wall. I argue and complain but Sharon has clearly heard it all before. She doesn't expect the rules to make sense. She is just there to enforce them. The message is that, for now at least, I am on my own. Before she rings off, Sharon suggests that I look for jobs online.

So I fetch my unreliable laptop and go to the Guardianjobs website and click on the Arts section. Most of the jobs in the south-west region are in 'Heritage' which seems to cover what used to be culture, history and nostalgia. They all claim to be looking for a 'dynamic individual'. No-one has ever called me, or my work, dynamic. Perhaps the adverts don't really mean it. Dynamic people are rarely comfortable to work with. Nor are they likely to be 'team players' which seems to be another essential requirement. I spot a job which sounds perfect for me – Development Manager at a well-known art gallery in Bath – and print out fifteen pages of details.

I make myself some coffee before working through the job description, the message to candidates, the Equal Opportunities Monitoring Questionnaire and the Guidelines on filling in the Application Form. When did everything become so verbose and bureaucratic? I look at the Guidelines first. *Give the names of two referees.* Nina, obviously but I'll have to think about the other. Perhaps I should ask the manager of the Day Centre. She's probably feeling guilty about me and working with the mentally disabled should win me brownie points. *If there are gaps in your employment record please give dates and details-* what if your employment record is mainly gap? Will they think I've been in prison for a long stretch? Some would see my marriage that way. *Give your reasons for changing jobs* – dumped for a younger woman – *'and for applying for this* post' – middle-class lifestyle and period home to support.

I turn to the list of *Knowledge, Skills and Experience Required.* I think I can tick *Good writing and presentation skills* and possibly *Strong time-management skills.* After all I've been a successful freelance and – what do the Americans call it? – homemaker for years. *Able to talk about contemporary art with enthusiasm and conviction.* I certainly have convictions about modern art. I'm not so sure about the enthusiasm, but I could probably fake it. Nina says that murmuring 'Such interesting work' is enough to satisfy the egos of most artists.

Mysteriously, there is another, more scary list of *Required Core Competencies.* In this, *Interest in the Arts* comes bottom. Am I *Confident, authoritative and socially at ease?* Not currently. Could I *Advocate the aims, ethics and mission of the organisation effectively?* It depends what they are. Can I *Improve donor strategy and database capabilities?* Almost certainly not since I lack the required *Sound admin and IT skills, particularly word processing, databases and spreadsheets.* To be truthful I don't really know what a spreadsheet is.

So, what are my Core Competencies?

I can mix colours

I can paint flowers

I can talk about art

I can teach people to paint (except Evangeline)

I have memorized a great deal of poetry

I can sew back a button

My pastry isn't soggy and my soufflés always rise

I can spell all the words that I use

I know where to put an apostrophe

I can recite the names of all the kings of England in order. Forwards or backwards.

There doesn't seem an appropriate space for most of this on the Application Form. I tell myself that I shall fill it in tomorrow, after my classes.

I go out and buy several newspapers and spread them over the kitchen table to read the coverage of Martin's trial. It cheers me a little that Rosa is not mentioned by name in any of the papers. The journalists have all concentrated on the afternoon's evidence about Jenna Jenkins' body. *Blonde mum, Jenna,* as The Sun puts it, was found near a well known beauty-spot a few miles from her house. They claim it was somewhere she liked to go with Martin *in happier times.* More probably it was Martin who thought it was romantic to walk through the woods at sunset, while Jenna would have preferred a night on the town.

According to the forensic evidence, the body was laid on a bed of bracken and covered by branches before being set alight. Martin looked like the Boy Scout type. I can picture him as an earnest boy, winning badges for wood-craft and fire-lighting. As he built his wife a pyre, did he strew flowers on her body? Giving flowers to the dead is such an ancient and enduring custom; the natural poetry of grief. I'm assuming that there was grief by this stage, not just anger.

Rain seems to have put out the pyre when the body was only half-burned. Then, as usual, somebody's dog nosed it out. David used to ask why people kept corpse-hunters as pets. I read that the trial was adjourned for a while when 'one of the jury became distressed by photographs of the body'. Only one? After an upsetting incident early in our marriage, David was careful never to bring those kind of photographs home with him. Yet he and Rosa have to look at them together. How can either of them forget the images of brutality, death and decay without the help of a partner who lives in a kinder, more beautiful world?

November 18th

Lying awake in the early hours, it occurs to me that I don't have to keep still or quiet. David who needs his sleep before a court day, is no longer beside me. Only Vincent blinks and stretches when I sit up and turn on the light. When he was appearing in some big trial, David would quite often slip out of bed and go to his study, or in winter the kitchen, to work. He was very good at doing it without waking me. I remember once wandering sleepily downstairs in search of my morning tea and finding David in the kitchen reading his notes with Theo settled on his knees. Theo who will never perch on my lap for more than a few seconds. They both looked embarrassed when I saw them, as if I had intruded on their private time together. Perhaps I should have taken this incident as a sign that David was keeping some of his relationships secret. At the time, I just thought it was sweet.

I decide to get up and wash my hair. In the bathroom mirror I notice how much grey there is in it. I'd always hoped that when I was ready to relax into old age I'd go silvery-white, the colour of wisdom. Instead, my roots are the dirty-looking grey you get if you wash elasticated underwear at too high a temperature. Is it worth spending £75 at the organic hairdressers to get my hair re-coloured, when David isn't here to run his fingers through it or bend to kiss the top of my head? Perhaps it is if I'm putting myself on the jobs market. Nobody will be fooled by the dye but it shows that you are making an effort to look presentable, or even dynamic.

In spite of my early start, I'm almost late for my morning

class but it hardly matters because I only have more photographs of chickens to hand out. Jean is back. I sense that the others are toning down the usual cheery exchanges and being careful around her. No-one asks her where she was last week so I don't either. I perch on the edge of a table and give them my chicken speech.

"Today, we're all going to do at least ten quick paintings of chickens." I ignore the groans. "I'll do a demonstration before you each take five minutes on a picture based on one of these photographs. When the five minutes are up, swap photographs with your neighbour and start again. You'll probably be quite pleased with your first effort. The next few tries you'll think you aren't making any progress, or even that you're going backwards, but carry on till you've drawn chickens all the possible wrong ways. If you keep looking, you'll start to see chickens as they really are."

"Nasty bad-tempered birds," murmurs someone.

"Get the lines right and the character will be there," I promise, "get the shadows right and the substance will be there. You just have to put in the time until you can do it all automatically. Then you can start to think about what to do with your chickens."

"Count them?" suggests Candy.

"Roast them," counters Pam.

Everyone giggles because my intensity has made them nervous. I don't let them relax. I dip my my brush in some Raw Umber and say, "Watch carefully." I draw the basic chicken shape in one movement, fill in the centre, dab on some Burnt Umber shadows, add the legs, beak and eye with strokes or dots of Payne's Grey and finish with a dash of Vermilion for the comb and wattles. Then I do it again and again and again. "Now it's your turn," I say.

They begin and I walk around, urging people not to lift their brush from the paper until they've finished the outline. I tell Pam not to make the head too big and Joanne not to fret when her Vermilion bleeds into her Umber.

"Just remember what you did wrong and go on to the next one."

After a few tries, Candy is unjustifiably satisfied with her work and everyone else is getting discouraged. I peck and scratch at them. "Think where the wings are attached to the body, Janet." "Don't go for fussy details, Alice. Keep it basic."

There turn out to be a surprising number of wrong ways to draw a chicken but by coffee-time nearly everyone is making progress. Scowls and slumps, and an even greater than usual willingness to stop for coffee, tell me that they don't see it. I try to lift their mood by opening a new packet of chocolate biscuits. I smile as I hand them round and say, "What's everyone been doing?"

There is almost a collective gasp when it is Jean who answers. "We went to the Memorial Arboretum last week to see Michael's name on the wall. It's a beautiful place but it doesn't seem right somehow that everything is so new."

So this is what we don't mention; a soldier son dead in some recent war. Iraq? Afghanistan? I stand there unable to speak, stupidly holding out the plate of biscuits. Others step into the silence with sensitive questions. I back away and put down the plate. How, I think, does anyone survive the death of their child? Then, like a kick in the stomach, I remember that I have. Of course the cases are completely different. My miscarriages were always so early in the pregnancy that the potential babies never became individuals to me. Somehow they, and the one before that I always tried not to think about, merged into a single lost child, more imaginary than real. I never held that child in my arms, or loved and nurtured it and sent it out into the world with hope. How can Jean walk and talk like a normal person? How does she even get up in the mornings?

After fifteen minutes, they all go back to their places without being chivvied. I busy myself at the sink but there is only so long you can take over washing and drying nine coffee-mugs. Then, since it is the only thing I can do for her, I go over and help Jean with her brushwork. She copies my quick strokes for dabbing in feathers and says, "Now I get it." By the end of the morning I feel that I can add teaching people to paint chickens to my list of core competencies.

There are five at my afternoon class. Gina so rarely turns up I'd almost forgotten that she'd paid for this term but here she is, so tanned and wrinkled she might have been dug out of a peat-bog. I used to describe her to David as 'the Constant Cruiser'. True to form, Gina immediately starts talking about her latest cruise to Madeira. Only Evangeline encourages her, with a murmured, "Cruise ships must be nice for people on their own." Like Evangeline, Gina is a widow. Gina's husband died of something asbestos-related and now she's busy spending the long-delayed compensation.

Rodney approaches me in a gingerly way, as if any loud noise might start me crying again.

"How are you this week?" he asks.

"I'm fine," I say defensively.

On the table I have placed a saucer containing three 'Lilac

Wonder' colchicums. I've had them on a high windowsill all week, hoping that they'd open in time for the class and, almost miraculously, they have. Sarah bends over for a closer look. "Ooh, Naked Ladies. Isn't it amazing how they'll flower from the bare bulbs without any soil or water."

"That's the contrast I'd like you all to try for, " I raise my voice to over-ride Gina recounting how she talked the Purser into upgrading her cabin. "The way these extravagant flowers spring out of these hard dry corms."

Rodney is stooping too, in order to examine the orange-tipped stamens.

"Is this the plant saffron comes from?" he asks.

"No! They may look like saffron crocuses but I believe every part of the colchicum is poisonous. Now, this light bright rosy-purple is quite hard to mix. The proportions need to be exactly right."

"Pale Cobalt Violet is a close match," puts in Other Sarah, waving a plump tube of this expensive colour. Other Sarah doesn't approve of mixing colours. She argues that it compromises purity of tone, which sounds a bit racist but is the creed of many Botanical painters.

"Use a ready-made colour if you like, Sarah," I say cattily, "the rest of you might like to watch."

After the colour-mixing demonstration, I give them the usual warning to think about where the whole plant will go on the page before they start painting. I don't dictate which end of the colchicum they should start with because I know that this choice will influence the whole mood of the picture. Gina, Sarah and Evangeline begin with the flower; Rodney, Other Sarah and myself with the corm.

While these two make meticulous drawings, I blend colours, even allowing myself some Chinese White, to capture the matt bone-like quality of the corm in front of me. Sarah is producing beautifully controlled petals with just the right degree of transparency. Gina is splashing down her flower with vim; Evangeline is just splashing. Her paint is far too watery and more grey than mauve. When they think I'm not looking, Other Sarah slips Evangeline a blob of her Cobalt Violet.

As I paint, I know I should be seeing the colchicums as a comforting metaphor. Beauty springing from bleakness, new hope, fresh start, all that kind of thing. I should be linking these implausible blooms to the re-flowering of lives after grief and loss. Jean's stoicism, Evangeline's serenity, Gina's cheerfulness. I try but all I get is a sick feeling that nothing lasts. The flowers are already lolling on their lax stems and losing their chalice shape. Tomorrow they'll wither and by the day after there will be nothing left but bony corms and a few smears of poisonous pollen.

Gina is chattering away in a voice like chalk scraping across a blackboard. "They had all sorts of classes on the *Ocean Queen*. There was 'Drawing for Beginners', 'Cup-cake Decoration' and 'Make a Scrap-book of your Voyage', though that one was full. The session on scarf-tying was good. Do you know how many ways there are to wear a head-square?"

"No," I snap, "Take care that you don't add your orange before the purple is dry. This kind of painting needs concentration."

"Don't worry, dear, I can paint and talk at the same time. Leonard used to say that I could talk through anything, even being kissed."

Evangeline chuckles but I say, "I'm afraid some of us are

finding your talk too distracting."

Other Sarah backs me up with a curt nod.

"Sorry, I'm sure," says Gina in an offended way.

She slams some orange into the approximate centre of her flower and an uncomfortable silence muffles the room. Other Sarah draws on unperturbed. I sense everyone else's enthusiasm is wilting like the colchicums. It doesn't auger well for my 'People Skills'.

On my way home I buy several newspapers but only the local paper has a piece about the Jenkins murder trial today. Other stories are taking centre stage. When I've fed the cats, I get out the application form for the gallery job. The 'personal details' on page one are easy enough to fill in, as are the 'Education, Training and Qualifications' columns. I cross out the 'Present Employer' page and grapple with 'Previous Employment and Work Experience'. *'Note what you have achieved'* the form states. Just at this moment it is hard to believe that I've achieved anything. After doing several rough drafts, I decide that this page and the 'Specific Information in Support of my Application' will have to wait until I'm feeling less tired and more creative.

November 19th

I am writing in my diary more often now. Word of the day is still – tired. I've slept badly the past two nights. It was a mistake to go to the Court. Seeing David and Rosa together, even just sitting side by side in their working clothes, has made the fact of their being a couple more real to me. A couple whose lives are going on without me. Lying in bed, I couldn't stop wondering what they say to each other about me and what they do together when the clothes are off. Intimacies. Things never meant to be shared outside of this room. Do they make love in the same ways that we did, or is everything new with Rosa? I cupped my breasts, remembering the feel of David's fingers on my nipples. He always claimed to like my small breasts. Was that a kindly lie? Are Rosa's spectacular curves what he secretly longed for?

I tried to think about something else and the blank face of Martin Jenkins floated into view. I pictured him tossing and turning in some Dickensian prison cell. Then I realized that, being a middle-class murderer, he was probably out on bail. Surely he wouldn't still be living in the house where it happened, preparing meals for one in the same kitchen? Wherever he is, I'm sure that he keeps thinking back over a marriage that failed without him knowing it until the last few minutes. Could he really have been so blind to his wife's discontent? Most people won't believe that, but I can. Over and over again he must be saying, 'I did everything I could to please you. How could this happen? How could you do this to me...' I groped for the bedside radio and turned on the World Service. I listened to a programme on the economic progress of the Baltic States until the flow of statistics finally put me to sleep.

The phone wakes me in mid-morning. It is my brother, sounding flustered. "I rang Mum and got this flaky woman who told me I should visit more often. Doesn't she realize that I live nine hours flight away? If this is the helper I'm paying for..."

I don't want him to stop paying so I'm compelled to defend Smiley Girl. "That was Aija . She's a hard-worker and mother seems to like her."

"Mother told me that the carer she likes is someone called Melody. Do they come in pairs, like policemen?"

"No, Aija and Melody are the same person."

"What? Is mum going gaga?"

"No." I explain about the name issue and add, 'Aija's English isn't perfect, so she may not have understood about Abu Dubai."

"Her English was good enough to tell me that mum is 'Sad, sad' and 'The grandchilds must visit, soon, soon'. Mum always sounds cheerful enough when I ring. Is she depressed about something? You've never mentioned it." His tone is almost accusing.

"I think she just feels the world closing in on her and that every day is the same as the last, with nothing to look forward to." I surprise myself with this insight. "Is there any possibility of you all coming over...?"

After a pause, Rob says, "We've already booked to spend Christmas in Sidney but maybe we could come over in the new year."

"That would be good, but I won't mention it to mother until you're sure. I don't want her to be disappointed."

What I really don't want is to have to listen to mother making excuses for Rob not turning up.

"Fair enough. How are you doing, Meggy?"

"I'm...doing all right. I've got some pictures in an exhibition opening tomorrow and I'm just applying for a job in an art gallery."

"A job? That's great. We'd been wondering whether you might want to come and stay with us for a bit but it sounds like you're far too busy. Anyway, I know you wouldn't want to leave mother on her own..."

He waits for me to agree but I don't. Am I to be confined to this country now that I've become the kind of surplus single woman who traditionally gets the job of looking after the elderly parent?

"Perhaps we could both come on a long visit," I say, just to scare him, "if you can't make it over here."

"You know mother can't stand the heat..."

I let him jitter for a while, before conceding that the journey would be too much for her. The conversation ends amicably but I wish he hadn't spoken the word I've been trying not to think about – Christmas.

It doesn't seem worth the bother of getting dressed, so I go downstairs in David's dressing-gown. I make myself coffee and spread out the job application forms on the kitchen table. Vincent jumps up to sprawl on them so I open the back door and shove him out, even though it's raining. I fill in the 'Work Experience' sheet, mentioning every bit of teaching and demonstrating I can remember. I stress that I'm an artist who has always 'engaged directly with the public'. Does my voluntary work come under 'outreach'? That sounds like the sort of buzz word they'll be looking for. Perhaps I should get Nina to draw up a list of the currently favoured jargon.

I'm still not sure what to put in the 'Specific Information in Support of my Application'. How can I describe my painting in a way that doesn't make it sound hopelessly old-fashioned? Minutes pass, as Vincent howls outside the back door and my pen hovers over the page. To borrow a lumpen phrase from my guide to surviving divorce, I must incentivise myself. There is a pile of unopened bills and financial statements on the hall table. I should look at them to remind myself why I need a job.

I begin with the bank statement. The account is still in joint names but there seems to be considerably less coming in from David than I would expect. Is half of his income now going elsewhere? Or more? Can he do this? I must ask my solicitor. Perhaps she's already told me in one of her unopened letters. I scrutinize the bank statement again. There is a scarily long list of Direct Debits to pay the Council Tax and utility bills. Does it really cost *that much* to run this house? There must be cheaper ways of doing things. I shall make a list of possible cuts... After I've finished the Application form.

I decide to pitch my work as representing nature threatened by man-made pollution and climate change. That's one way of interpreting my shadows and splodges. Perhaps I should get one of the more fashionable members of Western Artists to act as a referee for me? I can think of several whose paintings don't change much but whose descriptive labels always reflect a current trend. I could button-hole them at the Private View tomorrow night. If I can bring myself to go on my own. It would be all right if Nina was going to be there but she has to attend some fund-raising event instead.

David always comes with me to exhibition openings but there could be any number of reasons for his absence. I mustn't assume that everyone will think that he's left me. If anyone asks me where he is, I shall say that he is busy with the Jenkins trial. What could be a better distraction than a juicy murder case? Or, if I'm feeling really brave, I shall shrug my shoulders and say, 'David? Oh we've been separated for some time now.'

November 20th

The word of the day must be something modern and meaningless, like proactive. I would rather be prolethargic but lethargic Meg must make way for proactive Peg. I shall take the initiative today and change my life. I start small by changing a light-bulb. I am sick of huddling up to the table lamp in the drawing room. I need more light, so I drag the heavy step-ladder out of the cupboard under the stairs and into position in the drawing-room. In a fit of eco-enthusiasm, David has stocked up with hideous energy-saving bulbs. I see that they are 'bayonet fitting', which sounds very aggressive. No wonder it's mainly men who change light-bulbs.

I mount the steps to remove the blackened bulb. David always made it look easy – just a flick of the wrist and the bulb was out. I balance on top of the step-ladder, hoping that if I fall it will be onto the sofa. I glance across the room to make sure the switch is off before reaching up. Is it twist and pull or squeeze and pull? Neither seems to work. I'm afraid of tugging too hard because the whole light-fitting seems rather insecurely attached to the ceiling. A puff of plaster dust drifts down as the chain swings. Suddenly the bulb comes away in my hand and I nearly overbalance. I gasp, steady myself and climb down with the old bulb. Then I fetch my reading glasses to read the instructions on the packet.

Not much wiser, I mount the ladder again, holding up the new bulb as if I'm hoping that it will leap out of my hand and into the socket. It doesn't. I struggle to get the bulb in straight. It doesn't want to go and if I try to force it, the bulb might break in my hand. I ease it upward and wriggle my fingers till something seems to click. I slowly take my hand away and stealthily climb down. I'm half way across the room to switch on the light when the bulb falls, hitting the edge of a table and smashing. It is ridiculous to sob over a broken bulb considering that I didn't cry when David told me our marriage was broken.

I tell myself I shall try again later, when I'm feeling calmer. After sweeping up the milky glass, I ring Nina to ask her to act as my referee for the gallery job but she's 'in a meeting'. So I go out and get the papers. I riffle the pages, looking for news of Martin Jenkins and find myself staring at a drawing of Rosa. She is shown questioning the Jenkins' next door neighbour. The court artist has made Rosa look slimmer than she really is and has given her a pugnacious tilt of the chin. I race through the text underneath the drawing. The neighbour claims to have heard screams on the day of the murder.

David wouldn't normally let a Junior handle such an important witness. Did he give the task to Rosa because he thought the elderly female neighbour would respond better to being questioned by a woman? Or is he just favouring Rosa because he's so besotted? Did she seduce him to further her career? Is the baby part of Rosa's game plan or a hindrance to it? When I picture Rosa in her low cut yellow dress I remember that she was wearing a small gold cross on a chain around her neck. Perhaps, unlike me, she had moral scruples that ruled out an abortion. Perhaps she is scared of being single and pregnant and sees marriage to David as her only option. I should find out her side of the story.

The newspaper reports that the trial was adjourned until Monday because one of the jurors is unwell again, so Rosa might be in Chambers today. I pick up the phone before I can change my mind and press out the number for David's Chambers. When the receptionist answers, I ask to speak to Rosa Winston. The receptionist crisply asks for my name and business.

"This is Mrs Claridge," I say, "and I want to talk to Miss Winston about my husband."

I hear a sharp intake of breath and expect the receptionist to call for Mrs Kingsley or the Chief Clerk or even to cut me off. Instead, with what sounds like glee, she answers, "Please hold, I'll see if Ms Winston is available."

I am switched to soothing Vivaldi for quite some time. Then the receptionist is back on the line. "I'm so sorry, Ms Winston is unavailable at present. Can I take a message?"

"Yes. Please ask her why she wants to marry my husband."

"I'll see that she gets the message, Mrs Claridge."

I'm sure she will. Obviously Rosa is not a favourite with the office staff.

I ring off and put the phone down on the kitchen table. I picture my message being conveyed to Rosa. Then I clutch my stomach. Why did I do that? My roiling gut is telling me that I just made a very bad decision. If a furious Rosa rings me back, I won't know what to say to her. Even the sound of her voice would make me physically sick, though she is the one who is pregnant, not me.

I feel safer after I switch off my mobile phone and unplug the land-line. Emails I can delete unread. She can't get to me now, unless she comes to the house. Surely David wouldn't let her do that? After all, she's bound to go whining to him about this. I check that the security chain is fastened across the front door and then take a sketch-pad upstairs.

I concentrate on drawing details of the bathroom – the clawed foot of my reconditioned Victorian bathtub, the head on David's power-shower that looks like the seed-case of a dead sunflower, delicate shells arranged on the windowsill, bold stripes from the bathmat and matching towels, the curve of a perfume flask. How long should I leave it before throwing out all the half-empty bottles of David's aftershave and cologne, not to mention the aniseed-flavoured toothpaste which only David likes? Rosa doesn't know his habits as I do. Perhaps David sees this as a good thing; a chance to rethink everything from core morality to toothpaste preferences. People get mired in dull habits just because their partners know everything about them. Not me though. We've only been separated for a few weeks but there are already things David doesn't know about me, proactive Peg.

I skip lunch and take my sketches to the glass-house to rough out a painting of the bathroom. I paint black water dripping from a decapitated shower-head, claw-feet rending a blue and yellow towel, and mildew-like patterns over everything. Then I tell myself that I am being ridiculously melodramatic, scrub it all out, and start again.

When the light fades, I go back into the house to change for the reception at the Western Artists Gallery. I wash and dry my hair in the perfectly ordinary bathroom. In our...my bedroom, I put on the black dress with the sparkly peacock-feather decoration. I ease my feet into black pumps and stay sitting on the edge of the bed. I ought to get going but I don't seem able to move. What if someone asks, 'Where's David tonight?' and I say, 'With his lover, his pregnant lover,' and burst into tears?

Once I've decided not to go, I start to feel better. Then

the doorbell rings. I fly down the stairs to answer it. My body believes that David has remembered the Private View and come to be with me, but my brain is catching up even as I fumble with the security-chain and open the door. It can't be David, or if it is, he's come to be furious at me, not to escort me to a reception.

For a moment, I only see flowers and my heart surges. Then I realize that it isn't David holding out a bunch of tinned-salmon pink carnations. This man is shorter and plumper, with gingery hair and a freckled face. It is David's colleague, Mark Arbuthnot. David usually refers to him as 'Tanker' because Mark specializes in the dull but lucrative area of marine law.

"Hello, Meg." Mark thrusts the cellophane cone of flowers into my hands, "I thought I'd come round and see how you were doing. We were all very sorry to hear about it. I mean, none of us had any idea..." I must be looking blank because he hastens to explain, "About David and Rosa Winston. I'd never have thought old David was the type, but once a girl like that gets her hooks in someone...Can I come in?"

"In? Yes, yes of course."

Without thinking, I lead him into the dark drawing room. As I switch on a table lamp, I remember that the stepladder is still standing in the middle of the room.

"Having a spot of bother?"

"I'm not very good at changing light-bulbs." I hear how pathetic this sounds and add, "The ceilings are so high in this house."

"Oh quite. Not easy, for a dainty little thing like you. Shall I pop in a new bulb for you? It won't take a moment."

I can almost see his chest swell when I mutter my thanks. I fetch him one of the hateful bulbs, half-hoping that he'll make a mess of putting it into the recalcitrant fitting. He doesn't and he's right, it only takes a moment. "Thank you so much," I repeat.

"Any time. Now, show me where this ladder goes."

I do and then say awkwardly, "Well, I better put these in water."

As I carry the bunch of carnations into the kitchen, he follows at my heels like a badly trained puppy.

I pick out a brown jug which won't clash with the sickly pink of the carnations. I fill it at the sink, snip through the cellophane, and drop in the carnations. There is no point in trying to arrange them artistically. Carnations always stand as stiffly as if they were the embalmed corpses of flowers. That's why I hate them.

"I know you love flowers," says Mark and again I'm reminded of a puppy. One who proudly presents its owner with a disgusting old bone.

"Yes, thank you."

Mark doesn't seem deterred by my cool response. He smiles in a satisfied way and sits down without being asked to.

"Thought they'd cheer you up a bit." He pauses, as if he's not sure whether what he wants to say next is a good idea, but he goes ahead anyway. "It was jolly brave what you did today, ringing up to hold La Winston to account. She should have had the decency to speak to you."

So the receptionist has made sure that everyone in Chambers knows about my message to Rosa. I wince but try to sound indifferent.

"Yes, after all, she should be used to handling hostile witnesses."

"Oh quite. She gets far too many opportunities in my view. You know what these ethnic types are like. They have such a chip on their shoulders but they don't think twice about taking advantage of quotas and so forth. I doubt she'd have got a place in our Chambers if she hadn't been female and black."

'Oh God,' I think, 'don't make me feel sorry for Rosa. I can't cope with that.' Aloud, I say, "She always struck me as being a very clever young woman."

Mark nods. "I know what you mean. Clever enough to get whatever she wants and no scruples about how she does it. I suppose David feels he has to marry her, now that she's up the duff, but I think he's a fool leaving someone like you for someone like her. The baby might not even be his."

My hackles are up. "David isn't a fool!"

But I am, for automatically defending him.

"You're so loyal," Mark says admiringly. "He doesn't deserve you. She may be young and... but it's not as if you're...I mean, you're looking good, Meg."

The unspoken words 'for your age' might as well have been shouted but I'm suddenly conscious of the clingy dress I'm wearing and the fact that the wrap isn't as securely fastened as it should be.

"I'm going out," I blurt.

"Oh, yes of course." Mark stumbles to his feet. "I just thought you might need bucking up, might like to go out for a drink. Perhaps another time?"

He looks so disappointed that I find myself saying, "I'm only going to a reception for the opening of an art show. You could come with me if you like."

"Right, yes," I can almost see his tail wagging. "Shall I get my car?"

"No, it's only a short walk to the Western Artists Gallery and there's never anywhere to park nearby. I'll just get my coat."

We are out of the house and walking side by side before I have much time to think about what I'm doing. I always assumed that Mark was gay because he never brought anyone to dinner-parties, but I do remember David insisting, 'Tanker has his lady-friends. He just likes to keep his professional and private lives separate.' If I'm right, I am stepping out with a safely gay 'walker' who is here out of pure friendliness – or pure dislike for Rosa. If David is right, the situation is more...ambiguous. It may mean that Mark considers I'm already banished from legal circles and so eligible to be part of his private life. As what? If he's fancied me for years, he never gave the least sign of it. Or not that I noticed. Perhaps when you are happily married, or think you are, the faculty that senses these things shuts down. I decide to focus on the fact that, either way, I won't be facing the reception alone.

"So," I begin brightly, "marine law must be much more exciting now that there are pirates again."

"Lord, yes. Contracts have to be drawn up really carefully. I had a case last sessions involving a cargo of jute where liability for losses hadn't been clearly apportioned..."

By the time we get to Victoria Square, I realize that David was right about one thing – marine law is very boring. I still try to show an interest and ask what he means by barratry. An explanation so convoluted you'd think I was paying Mark by the hour gets us all the way to the gallery.

As we approach the fluted columns of the giant portico, Mark suddenly falls silent, aware that once inside, he'll be out of his element. Predictably, he murmurs, "I don't know much about art."

I will him not to add, 'But I know what I like'.

"I like your flower paintings of course," he goes on. "There used to be such a pretty one in David's office. Apple blossom wasn't it?" Winter-flowering cherry, actually; just a few pale buds on a silvery branch against a blue-white sky. "I suppose we should have known something was wrong when David took it down."

He took down the picture I painted to celebrate our Silver Wedding Anniversary? I want to ask when, but I bite back the question as someone calls out, "Hello, Meg." I nod, smile and take Mark's arm to hurry him inside.

As usual, Crispin Shaw has volunteered to check invitations and hand out catalogues. He's standing at the foot of the stairs, like a Cerberus whose bark is worse than his bite. No-one can get past him without a knowing look, an intrusive question or an unwanted compliment.

"Meg darling, lovely to see you. Black could be your colour after all. Where's David?"

"Mark has come instead."

I'm quite pleased with this evasion but Crispin is giving Mark an unfriendly stare. "Are you one of Meg's pupils? You should be wearing L-Plates tonight."

"What?"

Mark is floundering and a queue is forming behind us.

"We mustn't hold everyone up," I start up the staircase and Mark follows. "I'm sorry, Crispin likes to emphasize his status as a professional artist by being rude to amateurs. He thinks that encouraging hobby painting is a peculiarly British vice ."

"I've never been mistaken for any kind of artist before."

He makes it sound as serious a category mistake as if someone had thought he was Chinese.

In the Grand Salon, waiters who look too young to drink themselves are offering red wine, white wine or orange juice. Normally, I'd plump for the orange juice but tonight I grab a glass of white wine. Mark chooses red and grimaces after the first sip. "Australian," he mutters; which is clearly meant as a term of abuse. David always complains about the wine at these events too.

"I'm afraid I don't know much about wine," I reply.

Mark beams at me as if I've said something clever and starts to tell me why only the French can produce great claret. As he goes on about vine root-stocks and alkaline soils, the Salon is getting crowded. I glance around nervously, expecting people I know to come up and ask why I'm with a strange man. Nobody does and I'm almost disappointed. When Mark pauses to drink the last of his despised wine, I say, "Well, we better look at some of the paintings."

The catalogues come complete with a price list so everyone can privately exclaim, 'Fancy so and so charging that much/that little for their paintings!' Mark has no difficulty with this part of the proceedings.

"Three thousand pounds for that? Good lord, it doesn't even have a frame."

He is gazing at a colourful abstract, a glorious lion's roar of a painting.

"Jacob's a highly regarded artist. I'm sure his work will appreciate in value."

I wait, hoping that Mark will stick to his guns and insist that he still doesn't like it. Instead he frowns thoughtfully, "A sound investment?" and scrutinizes the painting with new interest. I find myself missing David's barbed whispers, 'That one looks like she's sicked-up a year's worth of hair-balls onto the canvas' or 'Do all the people he paints need liver-transplants?'

"That's jolly," says Mark, jabbing a thumb towards a faux naïve seaside scene. "Where are your pictures?"

I consult the catalogue and see that my work has been hung in an insignificant side-room. On our way there, several members greet me. I smile back but I don't stop to talk as I usually would. Mark is one step behind me, so they probably don't even realize that we're together. Together...how odd that sounds.

You can tell which are the most successful artists by the clusters of people attracted to their paintings. I spot the lanky frame and spiky grey hair of Veronica, the distinguished painter I was hoping to cadge a reference from. She's wearing an orange trouser suit and big earrings that shriek confidence. I can't make myself go up to her and ask for help. Not in public. Not with Mark listening. I slink into the furthest side room.

"Oh, there they are!" exclaims Mark and goes up to one of my flower collages. If even Mark can recognize my style at ten paces, perhaps it is time for a change.

"Lovely stuff," he says, "so much detail. Tell me what all the flowers are."

I recite the Latin names like a litany but even as I speak, my collages seem to blur into incoherence. Why did I ever believe 'all that detail' amounted to a meaningful whole?

"Lovely stuff," repeats Mark, "They remind me of my mother's garden."

"She's a keen gardener?"

"Was. Used to spend most of her time in the garden. It was her refuge."

"Refuge from what?"

Mark shuffles uncomfortably, "Well, you know...life. And father I suppose."

"Evening, Meg."

I turn and find myself looking up at the sallow face and sparse goatee of Lukas Vazin. He's probably grumpy about his prints being relegated to this side-room but it's hard to tell because Lukas never looks happy.

"That one's a new departure for you, Meg,"

He's nodding at my 'Drawing Room' painting. For Mark's benefit I explain, "It isn't meant to be a naturalistic view, I was trying to capture the essence of our..my main living room."

"By reducing it to a pretty pattern," sneers Lukas.

"It is pretty," agrees Mark, assuming that this is a good thing.

Lukas is what David used to call 'one of the Uglies' and he never misses the opportunity to spout their manifesto. "Beauty is always superficial. The eye slides over it and there's nothing for the mind to engage with. Beauty doesn't ask any questions. Ugliness shocks the brain into action."

"Well I don't see the point of looking at a picture that isn't beautiful," says Mark stoutly, "I mean, it would be like going on holiday to a sewage farm."

I can't help giggling and Lukas stalks off to defend his bit of wall. His prints show emaciated black figures superimposed on Bristol landmarks. Even David admits that Lukas' work has atmosphere.

Mark is still studying my 'Drawing Room' painting, gallantly making an effort to understand it. "What's this bit that looks like a desert landscape?"

"That's twenty years of wear on an old leather arm-chair."

"Ah. And the grey triangle?"

"It's the space where David used to be."

"I'm sorry." He awkwardly pats my arm. "So is that horrible spiny thing, Rosa?"

"No! I'd never paint her inside my house." I picture Rosa's hands pressing against the windows; hear Rosa's fingers tapping on the glass, searching for a way in. "Never."

Mark now has that panicky look which men adopt when they think a woman is about to cry.

"Why don't we go somewhere more cheery for a decent glass of something?"

"All right," I say.

I don't want this to look like a retreat. I try to walk through the galleries like a person with somewhere better to go. I don't find myself missing the usual opening night conversations. There isn't much high-minded theorising going on. Even Lukas only wanted an audience, not a debate. Most of the artists I pass are whinging about gallery commissions, the art critic who writes for the local paper, or the price of paint. As a student, I used to copy a quote from Ruskin at the beginning of every sketch-pad – 'Without mingling of heart-passion with hand-power, no art is possible.' There is plenty of hand-power here tonight but where is the heart-passion? I talk about art with my 'amateurs' far more than I do with my professional colleagues. I should have asked one of my pupils to come with me tonight. Evangeline is all heart.

"My, she's a big girl!"

Mark has paused to admire a bronze of a pirouetting nude woman with the figure of a Neolithic fertility goddess. To me the figurine looks like a parody of all those impossibly slender Art Deco dancers, but for Mark it's seriously ogle-worthy. So, not gay then? In the entrance hall, Crispin is thankfully too busy interrogating a newcomer to ask me why I'm leaving so early but he throws me a sidelong look which almost makes me blush. As Mark helps me into my raincoat, I wonder if we look like a couple rushing off to bed.

After leaving the gallery, we walk down Park Street. Mark stops outside one of the bars and peers in. "This doesn't look too crowded. We should be able to hear ourselves think."

I always can, and what I think is that Mark is checking to see if there is anyone he knows in the bar before going in. He chooses a table as far as possible from the plate-glass window fronting on the busy street. Then he reads the wine list scrawled on a board and announces that he is going to order a bottle of something he's sure I'll enjoy. "Unless, you want one of those syrupy cocktails that women go in for nowadays." He nods towards a table where four skittish young women at the start of their Friday night out are drinking gaudy cocktails – giggles in a glass. I envy their sugar-rush conviviality but I know Mark will be disappointed in me if I opt for a 'Purple Hooter' or a 'Sex on the Beach'. "

"A glass of wine will be nice," I say.

When the wine comes, Mark pours me a very large glassful and asks me what my plans are. I consider saying that my plan is to become a bitter and lonely old woman but I remember that the word of the day is proactive. I tell him about applying for the job in Bath, making it sound more like a sure thing than a long-shot. Mark nods approvingly.

"Just the thing to keep you busy but Bristol to Bath can be a nasty journey in rush hour. Do you know, there isn't even a First Class carriage on most of the commuter trains?"

I truthfully say that this will not bother me.

"Oh, are you planning to move to Bath?" He sounds slightly dismayed and I wonder why.

"You enjoy living there, don't you?"

"Lord, yes. If you like rain and have sound knees, Bath's a wonderful place. All that architecture. Property is very expensive though. Almost London prices. Half the value of your Bristol house would only get you a small flat in a decent area of Bath."

I'm tempted to say that I'd prefer an indecent area but I just state that I am not planning to sell my home

"Waiting for the market to perk up again? That could be wise. You don't want to sell in a buyers' market."

Mark starts to talk about falling property prices, only pausing to ask how I like the Chablis. The wine is making me feel as if I'm in motion but will never get anywhere. I struggle for a more complimentary way of putting this.

"It reminds me of swinging in a hammock on a lazy summer's day."

Mark looks genuinely delighted. "That's it exactly – a real taste of summer. I knew you'd appreciate it. Some people are moving their money into vintage wine, but I still think that property is the best long-term investment..."

I'm happy to let him drone on about investments until I glimpse myself in a mirror on the far wall. I notice that I am leaning towards Mark till our knees almost touch and tilting my head to show that I am hanging on his every word. Is this the behaviour my body has learned over all those years of being married to David? Am I so ductile that any male can trigger these responses? I refuse another glass of wine. Mark asks if I would like to go on somewhere for 'a spot of dinner'. I say that I am tired. A little too consciously acting the gentleman, Mark insists on walking me home.

As we approach my street, I wonder whether I should invite him in for the traditional 'nightcap'. Since David left, I've been alone in the house through every evening and every night. As the daytime sounds die away, you notice the internal silence more. I'm tempted to ask Mark to stay just for the sound and touch and warmth of another body in the dark.

Then he starts talking about property prices again. I search my handbag for the door-key. In the orange glare of a street-lamp, Mark is looking faintly expectant and a nasty thought strikes me.

"Well, thank you. Thank you for going with me to the exhibition," I gabble, "though I'm sure it wasn't your sort of thing, and for the lovely wine, and the company."

After a slight pause, Mark seems to realize that he's being dismissed. "Not at all. My pleasure."

"I'd be grateful if you didn't tell anyone at work about our... evening."

"Oh, quite. Not a word. Perhaps we can do this again?"

"Perhaps," I say.

November 21st

I start the morning by reading over my diary entry for the previous day. If I'd been entirely sober when I wrote it, I probably wouldn't have mentioned David so often. I try to focus on Mark and picture the way that we said goodnight. If I hadn't turned my head at the last moment, would that peck on the cheek have been a real kiss? Did I want it to be?

When I remember to plug the phone back in, I see that my last caller was Nina. I call her back. She starts by apologizing. "I'm sorry I couldn't join you last night. I would far rather have been looking at paintings with you than spending an evening with a roomful of sozzled middle-management and bored spouses,"

Looking at paintings with Nina can be a rather unnerving experience. She has an encyclopaedic memory for everything that has already been done in art. She'll pause in front of a picture and say, "Oh that's very similar to one of Kurt Jackson's early landscapes but the stylised treatment of water is more like Piper." Thankfully, she refrains from doing this with my work. At least out loud.

"The after-dinner sucking-up speeches kept the corporate sponsors happy, so the Summer Sculpture Trail is now fully funded. This year the pieces are supposed to be inspired by Bristol's Industrial Heritage. One of the sculptors is planning a giant skull that belches black smoke to commemorate the tobacco industry. Health and Safety nightmare. How was your exhibition?"

"Fine. You know – usual people, usual paintings."

"Meg, you did go?"

"Yes of course. You didn't miss much – Veronica holding court; Lukus giving his 'Beauty is so superficial' speech."

"I know you didn't want to go on your own..." Nina still sounds suspicious.

"I didn't. I mean I didn't go on my own. One of David's colleagues – Mark Arbuthnot – called round to offer his sympathies, so I took him along. I think you met him at one of our dinner parties."

"Freckles and endless anecdotes about marine insurance, that Mark?"

"Yes. He's probably gay..."

"Definitely not. I remember him trying to play footsie under the table."

"Oh. Anyway, Mark doesn't like Rosa, which puts him on my side."

"Even though he's David's friend?"

"Well, that's the trouble. When he turned up on my doorstep, I was so surprised I just accepted his story, but later I started to wonder. What if David asked Mark to visit me and persuade me to go out for a drink? They could be setting me up to look as if I was having an affair too."

"Meg, you don't have to be pure as the driven snow to divorce someone any more."

"But it could make a difference to the settlement I'll get, couldn't it?"

"David doesn't need to resort to tricks like that. He already has better lawyers than you."

"It could be a way of punishing me for...for being awkward about selling the house."

"Meg!"

"I know it sounds paranoid but when you've trusted someone, trusted them completely, and then find out that they've been lying, how can you ever trust them about anything again? Once you've been given cause to be suspicious, it's hard to know when stop."

"Don't let one lie change your whole outlook. Tell me about Mark. Did you just go to the exhibition with him or..."

"We went for a drink in Park Street afterwards and then he walked me home."

"You didn't invite him in did you?"

"Now who's sounding paranoid?"

"It's just that he could be a mopper-up."

"A what?"

"The sort of no-hoper who specializes in catching women on the rebound. You know the type – presents himself as a gentlemanly shoulder to cry on, gets you into bed for a comfort fuck and then moves on to the next unhappy woman."

"I really don't think..."

"Just be careful, Meg."

I promise and firmly change the subject. When I ask Nina to be one of my referees for the Bath job, I can sense her reservations.

"I know I don't have much chance of getting this one but I feel that I have to try."

"As long as you won't get discouraged if they don't offer you an interview..."

"I'm not that easily discouraged," I say, though I suspect that I am.

Later, I visit my mother. I thought that I had timed my visit to miss her Carer but Aija answers the door, wearing a skimpy black and white outfit. Then, just like a 'French Maid' in a farce, she insists on announcing me – "It is Maar-gret. No David."

I wonder what my mother has been telling her about my marriage. Mother doesn't get up from her chair so I go over and kiss her.

"I asked Melody to make lunch for us," she explains, "it's going to be something Latvian."

"You don't usually like foreign food."

"She is liking my cooking," calls out Aija from the kitchenette. "The *piragi* are very good. Put fat on bones."

"I thought it would be a treat for you, dear," says mother. "I did ask Melody to make enough in case David came..."

"He's still busy with the big murder trial."

Aija's presence is almost a relief because I had been thinking of telling mother about David today. With Christmas creeping up on us, she'll have to know soon but it has to be a private conversation.

"Such a waste of time and money," mother is saying, "when the husband is so obviously guilty. Why doesn't he just admit it?"

Perhaps because Martin Jenkins doesn't think of himself as a murderer? I try to make a joke of it. "If they all admitted their crimes, David would be out of pocket."

"A waste of tax-payers' money," mother repeats, "but I'm sure your David will get him sent to prison for a good long time."

"David says that wife-murderers tend to get well treated in prison. Warders and prisoners all take the view that killing your wife is the sort of thing that might happen to anyone."

Mother frowns. "Not to nice people, though there was that polite young man who worked in the Fishmongers when we lived in Guildford. He just gave his wife a push because she kept complaining that his hands smelled of fish. She hit her head on the edge of a sink and died. You remember I told you about it, Melody?"

Aija has come out of the kitchenette, carrying two plates of food. "Yes, yes, the police say murder but people write the letters and so it is only slaughter."

"Manslaughter," corrects my mother. "With all those people giving him a good character, he only served five years in the end."

"And then emigrated to Australia," I finish, because I know this story too. It is one of mother's favourites. Being served with her Friday haddock by a killer is probably the most exciting thing ever to happen to mother. Aija puts a heaped plate in front of me.

"Your mother have very interesting stories."

She smiles as if daring me to disagree. Perhaps they are interesting, if you haven't heard them all a dozen times before.

"The *piragi*," says Aija pointing at the oozing pasties on our plates, "always we make them for family."

Beside the pasties are pale-green lumps.

"Eat, eat." urges Aija, and she stands over us to make sure that we do.

The pasties are stuffed with bacon that is nearly all fat and the lumps taste as if they have been moulded from mushy peas. Mother prods at her food with a fork and says, "As my son-in-law isn't here, why don't you have his share, Melody?"

I suppose I can hardly expect her to eat standing up in the

kitchen but it still seems like an intrusion when Aija draws up a chair and squeezes herself between us at mother's small dining table. Without being asked, she leans over and starts cutting mother's pasties into bite-sized pieces.

"This is better than the Meals on Wheels, yes? All fresh. No brown soup all over."

"Brown gravy. Mr Gladwin at Number Nine, says his Meals on Wheels are a few bits of stuff swimming in gravy. Or swimming in custard if it's meant to be pudding. Horrid."

I open my mouth to ask if Mr Gladwin has a date for his hip operation yet, but Aija gets in first.

"The poor man. Will his hip be fix soon?"

"When he rang the hospital to ask, they said they couldn't even find his name on the waiting list, so he's had to start all over again with a new letter from his doctor."

I am ready with an appropriately indignant response but it isn't needed.

"Bad, bad!" exclaims Aija. "How long have he wait before?"

Mother starts to tell her.

Are old people like cats? Are they equally happy with anyone who feeds them? Anyone who listens? After an undeniably delicious dessert of apple cake with sour cream, I arrange to visit my mother again a week on Sunday when Aija definitely won't be there. That will give me the perfect opportunity to tell mother all about David and Rosa.

November 22nd

Sundays are unbearable.

November 23rd

Word of the day is – economise. Perhaps I should give it a jaunty exclamation mark. Economise! Yesterday, when I was half dreading, half hoping, that David or Rosa would ring, I distracted myself by thinking of ways to save money. Now I go over the list.

Mortgage and Taxes – There is nothing I can do about the mortgage payments but I believe I get a reduction in my Council Tax for living alone. Will City Hall take my word for it that I'm now a singleton? Or do they send someone round to snoop? Perhaps they check your recycling bin for beer cans and other tell-tale signs of a masculine presence.

Energy Bills – It isn't the ideal time of year to economise on heating, especially as I've just given all my best sweaters away. I'll start with turning down the room thermostats by a few degrees and hope that the green glow of being eco-friendly will keep me warm. I will also turn on fewer lights. I'm almost sorry that Mark has fitted a new overhead bulb in the drawing room. When I inhabited my own small pool of light from the table lamp, I couldn't see the empty chair where David ought to be sitting.

Phone Bills – I must try to understand what tariff we're on and only ring people at cheap times. Thank God you don't have to pay for the calls other people make to you, or Deirdre would be a very expensive friend. I had a long weepy call from her on Saturday night. She's told Callum to leave but, as both he and I pointed out, it's his house. Living there for fifteen months without making any contributions to the mortgage, doesn't make for a persuasive claim to ownership. I tried to get her to see Callum's point of view without sounding harsh. I don't think I succeeded. She told me that she was just trying to keep a roof over her children's heads, adding that I wasn't a mother so I wouldn't understand.

Transport – I used to feel rather smug that we only ran one car when we could afford two. I let people assume that we were making some kind of sacrifice, when it was just that parking is such a nightmare around here. I might as well take my car keys out of my handbag as I've no idea where the car currently is. There won't be any question of running my own car. I don't mind using the buses. What I'll miss is the feeling that I can always take a taxi in bad weather or if I have something heavy to carry.

Cleaners – I have no faithful family retainers to sack but the monthly deep-clean can go. I cancelled the last one at short notice. At the best of times, I hate having strangers working in the house and last month I couldn't bear the thought of being scrubbed and polished and hoovered around by whatever random multi-lingual bunch of people the agency decided to send. David would have been happy to pay for the sort of daily help his mother has always had, but I actually enjoy most housekeeping tasks – or I did when there was someone to keep house for.

Societies and Charities – I've lost count of all the organisations David and I are supporters or patrons of. Museums, theatres, Art Centres, groups for preserving Georgian Bristol and wild flowers in the gorge. I'm sure most of them can survive without my patronage. When I know what my income is actually going to be, I'll pick a couple of charities that I really want to support.

There are, I must keep reminding myself, millions of people in the world who need help more than I do.

Clothing – All clothing catalogues must go straight in the bin. New purchases to be from Charity shops only. Not a great hardship. At the rate we're going there will only be Charity shops left in most High Streets soon. As a bonus, my reduced wardrobe has already cut down on washing-machine use and I haven't ironed anything since David left.

Beauty products – Do I really believe that the application of money to my 55 year old skin is going to make me beautiful enough to compete with youthful Rosa? No. I had already decided that there are to be no more monthly trips to the hairdresser. I may allow myself a small budget for make-up if I have to go to job interviews but all those blue glass bottles and jars of certified organic gunk won't get replaced when they're finished. A tin of Petroleum Jelly will probably do the job just as well, or a teaspoon of olive oil every day. No, expensive cooking oils will have to go too.

Food Bills – These should have halved, but somehow they haven't. I could stop going to the Farmers Market and the local delicatessen and do my big shop at a budget supermarket. Is the food at Waitrose really better quality or am I paying extra only to bump trolleys with middle-class people?

Today, I resolve to answer this last question. I have to look up where the nearest Bumpersave is. As I leave the house, I see my neighbour Susan peering suspiciously at me from her front window. She and Derek have probably worked out by now that David doesn't live here any more. When I get to the bus-stop, I nearly take the bus into the city centre instead.

From time to time over the weekend, I found myself

thinking about Martin Jenkins. His trial should continue today. I'm tempted to go again but I'm afraid that David may have spoken to the Court ushers about me. In theory, I have as much right as any other member of the public to attend the Jenkins trial. In practice, if David has warned the ushers that I might make trouble, I'll be humiliatingly turned away.

I catch a bus that soon takes me beyond my middle-class comfort zone. It is easy to recognize the stop for Bumpersave by the queue of pensioners struggling to retrieve their wheeled shopping bags from the luggage pen. I help two of the frailest of them off the bus. The supermarket is set into an aggressively hideous multi-story car park. Inside, I blink at all the banners which seem to be made of the same fluorescent material as workmen's' safety jackets. 'Cheap!' they scream in big black letters on yellow or orange grounds, "Buy Now!" I take a wire basket and wander up the nearest aisle but I can make no sense of what I'm seeing. Tins of baked beans and cardboard boxes full of oranges are stacked next to reduced-price barbecue sets and shiny packets of men's pants.

I look up for guidance but the dangling notices only tell me about current offers on multi-packs of unbranded Cola, chicken thighs and kitchen towels. The narrow aisles seem to be stocked at random with goods piled wherever there is room. Some customers are pushing their trolleys in a purposeful way, as if they know the trick of getting through the maze. Others are wandering disoriented like me, occasionally spotting something they might conceivably need and grabbing it. As I squeeze past a bin of plastic footballs dumped in front of shelves of biscuit assortments and Christmas puddings, I yearn for the calm and order of Waitrose. I tell myself to to stop searching for tinned tomatoes and just explore what they do have. Who knows what interesting bargains I may come across.

I find a section which is mainly pet food, though not with any brands I recognize, and put some disconcertingly cheap tins of 'Chunks in Gravy' in my basket. Chunks of what, it is probably best not to ask. From the chill cabinets I select semi-skimmed milk, plain yoghurt and feta cheese, all of which are reliably dull wherever you buy them. I can't bring myself to try any of the greyish mince or pallid sausages but I pick up a bag of mixed peppers grown in Holland just for the shot of colour. Round the next corner, I come across a display of pyramid-shaped shaped scarlet and white boxes. They seem to contain genuine Italian Panettone Gran Cioccolato for half the price I'd pay in the delicatessen. Serendipity. I take one for myself and another to give someone as a Christmas present.

As I scurry along an aisle mainly filled with soft drinks and giant bags of crisps, a familiar voice says, "Oh, hello, Meg." I almost don't recognise Joanne without Candy at her side. Her trolley is piled with two for the price of one frozen meals and multi-packs of toilet-rolls and washing powder. I hear myself stupidly saying, "I didn't expect to see you here."

A budget supermarket doesn't seem the right setting for any of my Wednesday-morning ladies. Joanne looks faintly embarrassed. "I started to come here when Patrick lost his job with the bank and it's really not bad for basics."

"I'm sorry, I didn't know about..."

"Oh, Patrick has another job now but it doesn't pay very well, so I'm working part-time again – fitting the shifts around the kids. Your Wednesday morning class is the only time I have left that's just for me." She leans forward and lightly touches my arm. "It means a lot to me, being able to forget about everything for two hours and just draw or paint. I do hope I won't have to give it up."

"I hope so too," I say feebly, but I mean it.

November 24th

I open a Bumpersave tin for the cats at breakfast time. Slimy beige chunks plop onto their plates. Theo takes a sniff, gives me a basilisk stare, and exits through the cat flap. Vincent gobbles down his own portion and then eats his brother's. I find the yoghurt I bought yesterday pleasant enough with a slug of maple-syrup – another item I won't be buying any more unless I discover a cheap stash at Bumpersave. If I take the bus-fare and my impulse panettone purchase into account, I don't think I saved much money on my scavenger hunt, but it was certainly a different shopping experience. Looking back, I realize that there was no 'us and them' feeling at the checkout. The cheerful Polish lady who dealt with my basket behaved as if I might just as easily be the one doing her job. Which will be true if I don't get that application off to the gallery in Bath.

I spread out all the pages on the kitchen table, checking that I've filled everything in. There is still a gap where the name and address of the second referee should be. It is rather early to ring Veronica, though she might already be in her studio working on one of her vast canvases with a brush the size of a broom. I should have made the call over the weekend but somehow I didn't. I even had a strategy planned. I was going to whine about being dumped for a younger woman first and then ask her to be my referee. Surely she wouldn't refuse after that sob story, even if she doesn't know me or my work very well? I decide to put down her name and ask later. I know her address and phone number from when we were on the 'Open Studios' committee together.

I am making sure that I've listed enough modish reasons for applying for the post, when the doorbell rings. By now, I'm pretty sure that David and Rosa have decided to ignore me, but the bell still gives me a jolt. I clutch at the papers in front of me, crumpling my list of competencies. Then I smooth the sheet out and resolve that if it is David at the door, I will apologize to him for embarrassing Rosa and try to explain why it is so important for me to understand their actions.

When I open the door it is only the postman asking me to sign for a Registered Letter, or rather to squiggle meaninglessly on the screen of the small computer he carries. As I go back into the kitchen, I see that the letter is from David's solicitors. I expect it to be just another form to fill in and sign, so at first I don't really take it in. Then the words 'harass' and 'Restraining Order' leap out at me. I feel as if I'm breathing in scorched air. I read the letter several times. It tells me that if I try to contact Rosa Mary Winston again, an application will be made to a court to issue a Restraining Order against me, forbidding me to contact her or come near her home or place of work.

All I've done is look at Rosa, like everybody else in the court-room, and then rung her at work to ask her one question. A question I'm surely entitled to have answered. How is Rosa suddenly the victim here? How can David let her brand me as a stalker? If they take out this order, does it give me a criminal record?

I realize that I need legal advice but David is now the one person I can't turn to. For a moment I consider asking Mark for help but criminal law isn't his field. Besides, when it came to the crunch, he probably wouldn't want to antagonize two members of his own Chambers. I scrabble for the number of my solicitors and ask to see Mrs Patel. "As soon as possible. I mean today." The receptionist tells me that Mrs Patel is fully booked all week. I insist that I need to speak to her. "I've just had a...a threatening letter from my husband's solicitors and I don't know what to do." The receptionist seems to understand that I'm in real distress. She asks me to hold while she sees if Mrs Patel can give me a 'phone consultation'.

I hold. This is probably going to be an expensive call but I don't have any choice. The phone plays Mozart at me and Vincent coughs, shudders and starts regurgitating his breakfast onto my favourite Turkish rug. I dare not put down the phone, so I prod Vincent with my foot until he's sitting on a bare flagstone. I have to listen to the same tinkly minuet three times before Mrs Patel comes on to the line.

"Good morning, Mrs Claridge. How may I help?"

"I've had this letter from David's...my husband's solicitors..."

"I have been informed by Hadley and Stokes that you haven't returned the forms they sent you..."

"It isn't about that. I know there are some letters I haven't got round to opening but I opened this one straight away because it came registered. The letter is about Rosa, David's ...lover. Just because I rang her at work and left a message, they're accusing me of harassing her. They say if I try to contact her again, they'll apply for a Restraining Order 'under Section 5 of the 'Protection from Harassment Act 1997.' Can they do that? How is one phone call harassment? I didn't even get to speak to her."

"Harassment is defined as causing distress or alarm by..."

"Then I'm the one who has been harassed! What about all the distress that Rosa has caused by stealing my husband, by making him lie to me?"

"Please calm down, Mrs Claridge...Peg. Read out the letter to me."

I do, though it makes me shake with rage. When I finish there is a long pause before Mrs Patel asks, "You are saying that you have not approached Ms Winston?"

"I did go to Number One Court last week, when she was appearing for the prosecution, but that was to see my husband, not her. I went to give David back his engagement ring. I didn't speak to Rosa."

"I see, and you haven't been to her place of residence or waited outside it?"

"How could I? I don't even know where she lives."

"But you rang her at work?"

"Yes."

"And this message you left, could it be construed as threatening in any way?"

"No! I just asked her why she wanted to marry David."

Spoken aloud this sounds a stupid thing to have done but Mrs Patel only asks, "And was the message left on Ms Winston's phone or with a third party?"

"With a...with the receptionist, after I didn't get put through to Rosa."

"I see." There is another long pause before Mrs Patel says, "I shall have to consult with a colleague who has more experience with Restraining Orders, but I think we should regard this letter as a bluff. If you have been frank with me, then I do not believe there would be enough evidence for any court to issue such an order against you. Please come and see me at," she pauses, presumably to check her calendar, "at three o'clock on Thursday and we will draft a formal reply."

I feel almost dizzy with relief. "Thank you, thank you."

"In the meantime, I strongly advise that you do not try to contact Ms Winston again, or go anywhere where you have reasonable cause to think that she might be."

"No, no I won't," I promise.

"Thursday at three," she repeats.

The relief doesn't last very long. Rosa and I live in the same city, how am I supposed to tell where she might be at any given moment? I know that Rosa will be dazzling a jury in court this morning while I'm in my kitchen clearing up cat-sick, but once the trial is over I might accidentally meet her anywhere. Well, probably not in Bumpersave. Do I now have to avoid all the nicer bits of Bristol? When David first left, I knew it was bad but I never imagined that my life was going to change for the worse in so many different ways.

When I've finished scrubbing the floor, I pick up the phone again. Mrs Patel didn't warn me against contacting David, who is, after all, still my husband. I can leave a message on his mobile phone. I will ask him to explain what the hell Rosa is doing. Why is she persecuting me, when I'm the injured party? I haven't taken a carving knife to her, like Martin Jenkins did to his wife, just made a phone-call. Isn't it enough for the bitch that she's... No. I stop pressing out David's number and jab the Off button. I mustn't do this until I'm calmer. Screaming abuse down the phone won't convince David that Rosa is the one who is acting unreasonably. I shall wait until later, or even tomorrow. Perhaps David will ring me first to apologize.

November 25th

I am nearly late for my morning class again. I wasted time searching my frosty garden for something worth painting but this is the drear low point in the year when all the summer plants are reduced to bare sticks or rotten leaves and none of the spring plants have yet emerged. Then there was a paper-jam in the printer just before I'd printed out the right number of registration forms for next term's classes. Punching the printer in frustration only bruised my knuckles. I always try to hand out the forms well before the end of the current term in the hope that people will fill them in and pay in advance. In the past, the fact that this rarely happens has only been something to grumble about to David or Nina. Now, it could actually be important to my finances. Of course, if I get the job in Bath there won't be any classes, but I've decided not to mention that possibility yet.

Pam and Janet help me to arrange the furniture as the rest of the class arrive. I notice that Candy is missing.

"I think she couldn't face any more chickens," says Joanne and she may not be joking.

"No chickens today," I promise. "People often say that they don't know what to paint, or imagine that only attractive landscapes or carefully arranged fruit or flowers are worth painting. I want to show you that everyone has access to interesting shapes and colours in the everyday stuff we carry around with us. So," I take a deep breath, hoping that the idea I thought up on the way over here will sound like an inspirational lesson-plan, "I want each of us to delve into our handbags and find something to draw or paint. I'll start."

I tip the contents of my handbag onto the table. As my wallet falls open, I notice that there is still a photo of a smiling relaxed-looking David in its see-through pocket. A photo I must have taken on one of our post-trial breaks. The grandiose building in the background could be in Paris – Turin – Barcelona? David's time off is so unpredictable that it is...was usually a case of booking at the last minute wherever a flight and a room was available. The randomness and rush were all part of the excitement.

I realize that the class is staring expectantly. I close the wallet and hastily pick up my house key.

"Everyone carries a key, and keys are beautiful intricate shapes. Like a snowflake, each one is different. Then there's the contrast between the metal, whether it has a silvery sheen or a matt bronze finish, and the material of the fob – in this case leather."

My current key-fob is imprinted with an image of the Cheshire Cat, grinning and orange, against a bright blue sky. Deirdre always sends me Christmas and birthday presents with cats on, as if the fact that I'm a cat person and she's a dog person is the defining difference between us. I do not retaliate with cute pooch presents.

"There is also a dimension visible only to me," I continue, "the thought of the friend who gave me this fob, the knowledge that this key unlocks my home, the one place where I feel secure... What I mean is, objects come with memories and associations, and those belong in the painting too."

"But how can you paint something you can't see?" objects Pam.

"You can hint at it in the style you choose," I answer. "If you were painting your car keys and they meant freedom to you, you might use bold dashing strokes. If you were painting a key that was mainly used for locking things away, you might put in a lot of shadow. Think about what the object means to you while you're painting or drawing and it will probably happen naturally. That's the advantage of painting something that belongs to you." Pam is still looking doubtful. "It doesn't have to be keys – lip-sticks, credit-card holders, lucky charms – have a rummage and see what you come up with."

Joanne and Alice copy me and upend their bags until they have a heap of small objects to choose from. The others peer into the depths of their handbags and dubiously fish out combs and handkerchiefs, packets of cough sweets and coffee-shop loyalty cards. Pam wonders aloud why she is carrying around a street-map of Glasgow and a ping-pong ball. Alice asks if she can do more than one object. "Of course," I say. Janet decides to paint her phone. I assume it's so that she has an excuse to read the texts people keep sending her. Joanne asks my advice before settling on a floral powder-compact.

"I know it's a bit gaudy," she says, "but it's the first present my son has chosen for me all by himself and paid for out of his pocket money. No help from Dad."

The compact is decorated with a bright yellow daisy that looks like a child's drawing of the sun.

It suggests that Joanne's son sees her as warm and open, or that he just bought the shiniest thing he could afford.

Pam has selected a bulbous orange object which turns out to be a combined torch and alarm.

"If I press this end," she explains, "it shrieks like a banshee.

Since I got mugged, I always have this with me. You never know, do you?"

I murmur sympathetically and suggest that she does the outline in paint rather than pencil. I've just noticed that Jean is already drawing what looks like some kind of military cap-badge. Oh God, it must be a relic of her soldier son that she keeps in her handbag. Almost as if she was carrying around his ashes. "Let me know if you need any help with that," I say, and hastily move on to Alice who has lined up her Royal Academy pocket diary and a black enamel pen blotched with pseudo-Mackintosh roses. "I'd be lost without my diary," she admits. I smile and suggest that she rearranges the pen to create a strong diagonal. Then I sit down and start drawing my house key with a soft silvery pencil.

At coffee time I get out the registration forms. I stare at the dates for next term's classes and they seem unreal. Until a few weeks ago, I thought I knew my future. Everything seemed fixed. Now I wonder what else might have changed by January. I start handing out the forms.

"I'm afraid I've had to increase the fee a bit." I try not to look at Joanne as I speak. "My expenses have all gone up."

There is a non-committal murmur of understanding from the class. This is a time when nearly everyone feels that their expenses are going up while their income is going down. Have I just priced myself into the 'luxury too far' category? Nobody gets out their cheque book straight away. I abandon my own intricate drawing and bustle about trying to be the perfect teacher.

Pam has smeared orange paint everywhere but there is a pleasingly defiant quality about her picture. I can almost hear the alarm shrieking, 'Stay away from me or else!' Joanne is quietly absorbed, so I don't disturb her. Alice's painting is neat and pretty but lacks feeling. Not unlike my own work. Jean wants to give up because her drawing looks so flat. I show her where to add shadows to give depth. Janet's picture is a surprise. She has painted her phone about four times its actual size in bold black and green. On the keys, instead of numbers there are stick figures or smiley faces and across the screen area she has written , 'How long do I cook kippers?'

Janet sees my puzzled look.

"Since Mum went doolally, Dad's been in charge of the house. He's always texting me to ask how to do things."

She goes on to identify the figures and faces on the keys. I don't need to know which face represents her best friend, Lawraine; or that the plumpest of the stick figures is her Aunty Barbara. I've already got the message that her phone makes Janet feel permanently connected to all these people. Almost as if she's part of a group entity.

My Wednesday morning class are becoming a group too. They linger after twelve, planning an end of term lunch. I almost have to push them out so that I can lock up and spend my lunch-break queuing up at the Post Office to send off my job-application. Normally, I would just guess how many stamps a weighty envelope might need, but today I dare not risk it. I wince at the cost of guaranteed next day delivery, but hand over the money. There isn't much left to buy flowers for my afternoon class, so in the Florists I ask the girl behind the counter what she considers to be the most beautiful flower in the shop. She gapes at me and starts to say that roses are always popular.

"No, which do <u>you</u> find the most beautiful?"

"Oh, I..." She glances around wildly as if she'd never noticed before that she worked amongst flowers. "Those lilies. They're so....queenly."

She is pointing at a bucket full of egg-yolk yellow lilies. They wouldn't have been my choice but I smile and say, "Then I'll take one stem of those."

I only just get back in time for my afternoon class. Rodney insists on moving a table for me. All the women present are probably stronger and fitter than Rodney but he prizes his status as the class's sole male, so I let him do it and pretend not to notice his huffing and puffing. Meanwhile I arrange the chairs in a circle so that everyone gets a good view of the lily, standing proud in my enamel flower-jug.

"We won't wait for Gina," I begin, "as she's probably off seeking the sun again." Or too offended with me to come back. "Today, I want us to make our paintings as beautiful as possible." So stuff you, Lukas. "I asked the young woman in the Florists to choose a beautiful flower for us."

"It's lovely!" exclaims Evangeline, "The colour is so bright."

"So, perhaps intensity of colour makes things beautiful. The florist called these lilies 'queenly'. I think she meant that to be beautiful, rather than just pretty, a flower must have a majestic quality."

Rodney nods. "Lilies have more structure than other flowers, they're almost a sculptural."

Other Sarah gives a little sniff. "I always think lilies are too perfect. It makes them look artificial."

I'm surprised because she is the one who always complains when I offer her imperfect specimens to paint.

"You think it's the tiny flaws that make a subject seem

natural and alive and therefore beautiful?"

Other Sarah just shrugs.

"Maybe it's because I associate lilies with Easter and funerals, but.." Sarah struggles to put a thought into words, "don't they make you feel that there is something better than the world we see, something perfect?"

"Consider the lilies of the field...." murmurs Evangeline.

"Those were actually anemones," puts in Other Sarah.

I intervene before an argument can develop. "Let us all try to bring out the best quality we can see in the lily. Don't think of this as a naturalistic still life. That jug is a neutral shade but you could change it to a colour that will make the yellow sing out..."

I get them all started and then sit staring at the blank sheet of paper in front of me. When I look up, the golden lily only seems to be flaunting its costliness. What's that line from Shakespeare? 'Lilies that fester smell far worse than weeds...' Today I'm finding it hard to believe in beauty but I still have an instinct that if artists don't go on trying to create beauty, the world will become uglier and uglier. I don't mean the world of art with all its fads and feuds, I mean the shared world of human thought and feeling. Is there an ominous reason why, in the 21st century, we no longer equate beauty with truth?

At the end of the afternoon everyone indicates, either in words or with defeated body language, that they have failed to convey their personal idea of beauty. Unusually, it is Evangeline who has come closest. Her painting may be full of slips and blurs but the yellow of her petals does glow against the rich blue background she has chosen and the green stem seems to surge up from her wonky red jug like Jack's magic beanstalk. I hold it up to show the others. "Now this has so much energy and warmth."

Evangeline chuckles. "I haven't got the shapes right but it does remind me of home."

I think she means Jamaica but Evangeline carries the sun around with her. Wherever she makes her home there will be brightness. I envy her that.

There are no phone messages when I get back. No-one has rung me since yesterday. After I've fed Vincent, I make some tea and find myself still automatically taking two mugs off their hooks. I drop David's favourite mug on the flagstones. The satisfying smash terrifies poor Vincent who flees upstairs. Of course the gesture would have been more effective if David had been here to see. I'm the one who has to get down on my knees with a dustpan and brush to clear up the mess. Perhaps I should post him the pieces. Or would that count as harassment?

When I've tipped the remains of the mug into the swing bin, I pick up the phone and dial David's mobile number. I don't expect him to answer straight away but he does.

"Meg?"

What if Rosa is right beside him? Suddenly I'm finding it difficult to breathe. I jab the off button.

I sit down, still gripping the phone. After a few moments it starts to ring. I look at the display and see that it's David calling me back. I gulp in air and make myself press the answer button.

"Meg? Are you there? What do you think you're doing?"

"I wanted to talk to you but then I was scared that I'd get another solicitor's letter if I did."

"Oh. I'm sorry about that. It wasn't my idea. Rosa just got nervous when she saw you watching her in court."

"I was watching the case, not Rosa. Not everyone finds her

as fascinating as you do. Besides, I was there to bring back your ring. Didn't you tell her that when you gave it to her?"

I hear David clear his throat before saying, "I haven't given her your ring."

"Why not?" My heart thumps with hope. "Are you having second thoughts about marrying her?"

There is time for me to think, 'You shouldn't assume that I'll take you back' and to know that I'm lying to myself, before David answers, "No. I...We had already a chosen a ring."

So now I have to imagine David and Rosa together in a jeweller's shop, viewing trays of diamond rings.

"Well, I suppose a second engagement ring is probably cheaper than an eternity ring, unless Rosa has more expensive tastes than I do."

"Meg! Look, you shouldn't have rung Rosa at Chambers and left her that message. You humiliated her in front of the people she works with."

"And you think I'm not humiliated, having to tell people that you've dumped me for a younger woman? Am I not even allowed to ask questions about what happened to my marriage?"

"I told you what happened. You seemed to take it so calmly, I thought you felt the same as I did about our marriage."

"And what is it exactly that I'm supposed to have felt about us?"

David snorts in exasperation as if it is outrageous to be asked to talk about feelings. "That we were good friends but not..."

"Not what?"

"Meg, none of this is your fault but you do have to accept that I'm with Rosa now."

"Do I also have to accept legal threats from your mistress?"

"For Christ's sake, Meg. Rosa just overreacted because she's pregnant. You should know how that..." He breaks off. "Meg....I'm sorry, I didn't mean to..."

Tears are sliding down my cheeks. "You will be hearing from my lawyers."

I end the call before he realizes that I'm crying. I go over and over the whole awful conversation in my head, wishing it hadn't happened. The worst word of all was only a small one – we – meaning David and Rosa not David and Meg.

November 26th

'You will be hearing from my lawyers' sounds very dramatic but I know that the reality of unenthusiastic Mrs Patel will be much more prosaic. On my way to her office, I stop off at the small café in the Western Artists Gallery for a double Espresso. Expensive coffees will have to go onto the occasional luxuries list but I need a strong shot of caffeine today. I hardly slept last night. Even after I'd finished writing my diary, I kept picking over David's words and silences, trying to get the last scraps of meaning out them. Apparently we were not a loving couple but 'just good friends'. Yet none of this was my fault. I think we can agree on that. We meaning David and Meg.

This morning I have been trying to paint. Trying and failing because if I've been so wrong about my marriage, I may be equally wrong about my work. Why should I believe that I know what I'm doing and that there is any passion in my painting? Today is what Crispin calls a 'popping in day' – about the stage in the exhibition when people 'just pop in to see how things are going'; meaning to see whether they've sold any pictures.

In the side gallery I discover that Lukas hasn't sold any of his prints but there is a red sticker on one of my flower collages. I knew that the June collage, with its easily recognizable flowers – rose and delphinium, peony and foxglove – would be popular. Foxgloves are another of the flowers that always sell, perhaps because they make people recall a childish sense of wonder. I painted this foxglove as if I was still a little girl looking up to count the freckles inside each cup. I remember my father telling me that the freckles were supposed to be fairy finger-prints. Is that a genuine tradition or did he make it up to please me? The only time I seemed to get his full attention was when we were both out in the garden, me playing, him gardening. Rob and I weren't allowed to pick the flowers, but I know father laughed when I pulled off some foxglove cups to see if they fitted my fingers. Now somebody is going to get a dose of summery nostalgia for Christmas. I hope they like it. Mark seemed to like my flower paintings but he hasn't rung since Friday. I didn't particularly enjoy his company but it would be pleasant to think that he had enjoyed mine.

To reach my solicitor, I have to get past the chuggers. It won't be hard today because two out of the three chuggers are letting prosperous-looking citizens scurry by unmolested while they chat-up attractive girls. A thought strikes me. Why are chuggers always young? Wouldn't people find it harder to say no to motherly middle-aged women? Or even unmotherly ones. I focus on the third chugger, a weedy young man with a sparse gingery beard. He is wearing an ill-fitting jacket emblazoned with the slogan 'Save the Children'. Whose children? The chugger looks apprehensive when I walk right up to him, deliberately making eye contact.

"Hi?" he says uncertainly. Perhaps he thinks I'm here to check his licence.

"You get paid to do this don't you?"

The chugger's face clears. He's obviously been briefed on how to handle this question.

"We do get paid but studies have shown that 30% more money is raised by employing...."

"I'm not interested in the money you're raising, just in what you're paid per hour."

The chugger tugs at the badge hanging round his neck as if it can somehow give him more authority. "The company who employs us is proven to give excellent value..."

"So it's a commercial company?"

"Yes but..."

"How did they come to recruit you?"

"I..um, I saw an advert on campus and..."

"So they target students?"

"Yeh, we're all students. They bus us to different places and..."

"Isn't that age discrimination? Why couldn't I do your job?"

"But you're..." he breaks off before he can say 'You're too old'. Then he tries again. "You wouldn't want to be standing up all day. In the cold and...everything."

"You are probably right, but just as a matter of interest, when someone signs up to a regular donation, are you rewarded with a warm glow of satisfaction or an actual bonus?"

"I...they…" He mutters something about incentives.

One of the other chuggers comes over. "Is there a problem?"

I open my mouth to say, "Only a moral one," but my first chugger bursts out with, "I do this job because I enjoy it! People are nice when you're raising money for a good cause. Most people."

Doing a job that I enjoy is something I've taken for granted until very recently, so I just say, "Thank you for clearing that up."

As I walk away, the chuggers mutter about me and I think I catch the word 'cow'. Although I've been known to use it myself, I've never understood why cow is a term of abuse in this country. Cows give us milk and butter and cream and have the loveliest eyes in the animal kingdom. I believe that there are African societies where being compared to a cow would be a very gracious compliment. Unfortunately I don't live in any of them.

When I get to my solicitors, the receptionist can't find my name on her screen, so I am a non-person. "Mrs Patel told me to come at three," I insist. The receptionist taps a few more keys and says loudly, "Oh I see, she fitted you into a time-slot where she had a cancellation but her three o'clock is still down as Mrs Lang."

I sense heads turning towards me in the waiting area. Are they all speculating about why I need an urgent appointment with my solicitor? Perhaps they think I've been caught shoplifting, or something equally discreditable. I catch the eye of a smartly-dressed woman and feel like running away. So I imagine myself entering the waiting area as a cow, squashing the smartly-dressed woman's ostrich-leather bag under one hoof, knocking over the flimsy coffee table, spilling glossy magazines all over the floor and leaving cow pats on the carpet. When I sit down I almost expect the chair to break under my weight. Cows may be stupid but they're hefty and strong.

I barely have time to start pretending to read a magazine before Mrs Patel calls me in. As I follow her into her poky office, I wonder about the absent Mrs Lang. Did she and her husband have a sudden reconciliation and take mutual pleasure in sacking her divorce lawyer? Could that still happen to me?

As soon as I sit down, Mrs Patel asks to see the letter from Rosa's solicitors. She takes her time over reading it. Today, her nail polish is coral.

"Have you had any further communications from Ms Winston's solicitors?"

"No."

"And you have not tried to contact her again?"

"No." It is irritating to be interrogated by my own solicitor. I'm paying her to be on my side. "I did speak to my husband."

Mrs Patel frowns.

"Why shouldn't I? We are still married. He admitted that she...Rosa panicked because her pregnancy is making her over-emotional."

"And was your husband a party to sending this letter? Did he know about it in advance?"

"I don't think so. I'm not sure."

Mrs Patel nods as if she is and hands me a piece of paper. "Here is a draft of the letter I suggest that we send in reply. Please read it carefully."

I do and note that I strongly deny the alleged harassment. Then I state that I have no intention of approaching Ms Winston again or attempting to communicate with her in any way. Without admitting to harassment, this letter is a promise not to do it again.

"This letter makes me sound guilty but I don't believe I've done anything wrong."

"There is no admission of wrongdoing, of course not, but at this stage in the divorce proceedings it is important for us to establish that you are behaving reasonably and co-operatively."

"Co-operatively?" So Rosa is allowed to be over-emotional but I have to be compliant. "I haven't even agreed to the divorce yet."

Mrs Patel looks pained. "Are you telling me that you wish

to contest the divorce?"

"Yes. No. I don't know."

"I must warn you that contesting the divorce would only put off the inevitable while costing you a great deal of money. Judges very rarely refuse to grant a decree nisi, even when one of the parties doesn't want the marriage dissolved."

"Dissolved. That's what it feels like. My whole life is dissolving. It's too much, I can't cope with this on my own. I just can't."

I see Mrs Patel lean back slightly as if she's afraid that a buffet from my emotions will disarrange her coiled hair or chip her perfect nail-varnish.

"Mrs Claridge, as your solicitor, I am not the right person to provide emotional support. I can give you a list of accredited counsellors. Or you could go to your GP."

Is that my choice? Parading my woes before someone who charges by the hour for compassion, or begging my doctor for pills to make the pain, and every other strong feeling, go away? I agree to sign the letter.

November 27th

A parcel arrived this morning. Inside are a hundred Christmas cards featuring a three-colour image of snowdrops and holly. I choose a different drawing of mine every year to feature on our card. People tell me that they look forward to getting a new 'Meg card' each Christmas. Deirdre claims to keep all hers in a special album, or she did till the album went missing during one of her flits. This year's image has come out well but printed inside every card are the words David and Meg Claridge, followed by our address. I should have remembered to cancel the order but I didn't. I can't bring myself just to throw the cards away. I put the box aside and go out for a walk.

Today Sion Hill looks like a water-colour landscape that someone has tried to rescue by holding it under a running tap. There aren't many people around to share my pleasure in the blurred shapes and pearly greys. Murk and drizzle have kept away all but the most seriously addicted joggers and one professional dog-walker who is struggling to control six dogs, all frantic to rush off in different directions. Their leads tangle around his legs as if he was a maypole and he swears in a language I don't recognize.

I stay near the road. I wouldn't want accidentally to stumble over a cliff-edge in the mist. David might think I'd done it deliberately because I couldn't bear to live without him. Would that fill him with remorse? Or would he just be relieved that he could marry Rosa straight away without all the hassle and expense of a divorce? If I die now, does my half of the house automatically go to David? There's a reason to survive. I've never got round to making a Will, since I was happy to think of everything going to David. Who else do I have to leave anything to? The nephew and niece I hardly know? At least they aren't going to drop me because of the divorce, unlike my mother in law. Thirty years as her daughter in law and she hasn't said or written one word to me since it happened....

I nearly shuck my skin when I hear someone shout, "Mar-gret! Mar-gret!" I turn, half-expecting to see some other Margaret being enthusiastically greeted, but it seems to be me that a group of people occupying the nearest benches are waving at.

"Mar-gret!"

Under assorted hoods, beanies and plastic rain-hats, I recognize Jake and five of his charges from my former Friday class.

Annie is bouncing up and down. She seems thrilled to see me, even though we've only met once. Jake pats her on the shoulder. "Yes, it's Margaret. Our Annie never forgets a face."

Annie and Etta now have matching hats with bobbles. They are holding hands but Etta looks more lost than ever. On the other bench, Carl is jabbing at the ground with a stick; Pete is sitting as motionless as a mouse when an owl flies overhead, and Morag is muttering swearwords which almost sound like a greeting.

I say hello to them all. "No Tom today?"

"Tom's been a bad boy," answers Annie.

I look questioningly at Jake who murmurs, "Set fire to his Care Unit."

"Oh dear. So what are you all doing out here?"

Jake takes a puff of his cigarette. "This is a nature ramble."

"We found snails!" exclaims Annie, "Look!"

She delves into Etta's pocket and brings out a large mottled snail-shell which I think is still occupied. Etta grabs it back.

"Do you like snails, Etta?" I ask.

Etta nods. "Snail has her own house."

I don't know what to say to that so I ask if some other activity has been found for the group on Friday afternoons.

"Nah, no funding," answers Jake. "We usually watch videos – kids stuff mainly. The same ones over and over. They don't mind it but I'm so sick of bloody 'Toy Story.'"

There is an expectant pause. I don't leap into the silence with any kind of offer, so Jake continues, "Pete keeps drawing though, don't you Pete?"

Pete ducks down so that even less of him is visible under his over-size anorak.

"That's good, Pete."

Jake gives me a shrewd look and actually takes the cigarette out of his mouth to ask, "What about you, Margaret? How are you doing?"

"Me?" He must be wondering what I'm doing out here on such a miserable morning. "I'm all right. Just going for a walk to get inspiration. For painters there's no such thing as bad weather."

"Is that right?"

"Even painters feel the cold though, so I must keep moving. Bye everyone. "

Annie waves at me with her own hand and Etta's. Pete gives a tiny shake of his hood, which might be some kind of acknowledgement. Carl throws his stick in my direction, as if I might want to play 'Fetch'. The stick is easy to dodge. What I find really disconcerting is that Morag smiles at me. She may just be pleased to see me go but it looks more like a knowing smile. The sort of smile that says 'now you're one of us'. I walk away fast.

On the way home I buy a Telegraph and a local paper to follow their coverage of the Jenkins trial. I have thought about Martin often this week but after the threatening letter came, even the idea of reading about what David and Rosa were doing together brought on a cold sweat. I needn't have worried. When I tear out the relevant pages from this week's papers and arrange them in order to follow the case, the story is all about the victim. The Defence team are trying to get the murder charge reduced to manslaughter by attacking Jenna Jenkins' character. As evidence of provocation they have uncovered two office affairs before the one that Jenna seems to have taken seriously enough to ask for a divorce. Her married lover, Raymond Noach, now claims that he had no intention of leaving his wife and children for Jenna, which makes him less faithful to her than Martin.

In Thursday's Telegraph there is a drawing of the leading Defence Counsel questioning the lover. Oh Jenna, how could you think of leaving reliable Martin for anyone called Ray, let alone one who is obviously going to have a paunch and a bald patch in a few years time? How did Martin feel as he listened to the sordid detail of assignations in coffee-shops and fumbling encounters in the photocopying room? How would I feel if I was forced to sit in open court listening to exactly what happened when David met Rosa? Did Jenna tell Martin everything when she announced that she was leaving? I flinch when the Telegraph mentions an intervention by David implying that Martin must have known about his wife's infidelities, just as he implied that I must have known that the passion had gone out of our marriage. Whatever Jenna said on that fatal day, I think it came as a total shock to Martin and that's why he picked up the knife.

From now on I suppose I will only see my husband in courtroom sketches. Some years ago I bought a drawing from the court artist of David cross-examining a defendant and had it framed as a surprise birthday present. It obviously isn't one of his prize possessions since it is still hanging in his study. He said at the time that it made his nose look too big but perhaps he didn't like it because the drawing was done during the Zubeyer case. David got Mukhtar Zubeyer convicted of causing death by dangerous driving but when the man had served a sentence that seemed insultingly short for the loss of two innocent lives, he couldn't be deported because he was entitled to a 'family life' here. Right here in fact, since the Probation Service got him rehoused only a few streets away. No wonder that case left a bitter taste in David's mouth.

I lug my easel up to the top floor to paint an impression of David's study before I strip the room to reclaim it as my space. I'm sketching in the frayed spines of a few of his oldest law books when the phone on the desk rings. Because I'm in David's study I somehow expect the call to be for David, but it is Mark Arbuthnot asking me to go out for a meal.

"Tonight?" I hesitate, not wanting him to know that I have nothing on tonight or any other night. "I'm afraid I can't do tonight. How about tomorrow?"

"No can do. Got a dinner party to go to."

Not with me evidently. We settle on Wednesday night. He will pick me up at 7.30. Just before he rings off, he tells me that he went back to the gallery and bought one of my paintings. What am I to make of that?

November 28th

I haven't been able to bring myself to go back to Bumpersave, so I'm using up all the odd packets and tins from the back of cupboards and shelves. I've decided not to read the 'Use By' dates and just go by whether things look or smell mouldy. For a cold weather breakfast I resort to my old student standby – porridge. I can remember times near the end of a term when my grant was all used up and I practically lived on porridge and tins of baked beans or spaghetti hoops. On porridge days there was rarely any fresh milk in the communal fridge, so I'd make it with a little water and eat the quivering grey slab sprinkled with dusty sugar. Today at least I have milk and I find a bit of treacle in the bottom of a tin. I'm just savouring my first mouthful when Deirdre rings.

"I've done it!" she announces.

"Done what?"

"What you told me to do. I've left Callum. We're in a hotel – well more of a B&B – but they won't let me have the dog in our room – I'm sharing with Emily – I tried leaving Jagger in the car but he barks all the time. People keep putting notes on the windscreen complaining, or telling me it's cruel. The kids are going to Grannie Logan at the weekend but she won't take Jagger because of all the bother about her neighbour's cat..." On she goes with no apology for ringing so early. "I can't afford to put him in kennels, or not for very long. Maybe I should have left him there, like I did the rabbits. Rory got quite attached to Jagger. They used to romp around the garden together."

"Rory?" I never forget the names of Deirdre's offspring but

it's hard to keep track of her step-sons and daughters and her boyfriends' children. Or is Rory a pet?

"Callum's son," says Deirdre impatiently, "he was only there every other weekend but still. Johnny claims to miss him. They hated each other's music, which is tough when you're sharing a room, but they did enjoy ganging up on Emily. I don't know what I'm going to do about her."

By this stage I would normally be trying to calm Deirdre down but I seem to have missed my cue.

"She says she wants to go and live with her Dad. Can you believe that? There's no way that's going to happen. He hardly ever takes up the access rights he does have."

I open my mouth to say. 'Well, he does live in Canada,' but decide not to bother.

"And he still sends her dolls. Imagine that, dolls for a fifteen year old! But she won't throw them out. She's unpacked some already. They're sitting on her pillow, creeping me out. I've tried with her, I really have..."

When I was happy and secure, I could cope with Deirdre off-loading her mainly self-inflicted misery onto me. Perhaps I even enjoyed her emotional turbulence as a contrast to my own placid life. Now I understand what it's like to feel so eviscerated by your own problems that you can't begin to care about anyone else's. It's not selfishness; it's self-defence. You simply can't spare the energy.

"Emily's blaming me for splitting up with Callum, even though he's been such a sod – and she never thinks about where the money's going to come from for all the whiny calls she makes to her friends on her mobile. Oh Meg, I can't believe I'm going through all this again. It's worse this time because I put most of my savings into that craft shop and even though it closed down months ago I still have to pay the rent. Unless I can find a subtenant..."

She'll expect me to start making practical suggestions about what to do next but I don't have any. I just want her to stop talking before she makes me believe that there are no right choices and that, sooner or later, everyone's life goes hideously wrong.

"Don't you sometimes wish ," Deirdre is saying, "that you could go back and start again? If I'd stayed with Adrian, and hadn't needed to worry about money so much, maybe my career as a textile artist would really have taken off, but he could be such a patronising shit. I remember once..."

"Deirdre, I'm sorry but I can't listen to this any more."

"What? Oh, were you about to go out? Is David waiting?"

"No, he isn't. I just can't do this."

I feel like the sort of animal that curls into a ball when danger threatens and pretends not to be there.

"But you..."

I cut Deirdre off in mid-sentence. What was she going to say? "But you always listen." Not any more. I go back to eating my now cold porridge.

For the rest of the day I try to keep busy. I divide my time between searching websites for arts-related jobs I could apply for and putting together my picture of David's study. Like a Chinese brush painting it is more about the space you leave than the lines you put in. Spaces that mark the absence of David's essential or prized possessions. All that remains are the bits of his life he was happy to discard – binders full of notes from his student days, a glass paperweight I bought him in

Venice, a non-Digital radio, a photograph in a silver frame of us on our wedding day.

I really look at the photograph for the first time in years. David and his best man, Christopher, are confident and timeless in their Morning Dress suits. It is always the bride and her bridesmaids who look absurdly dated in wedding photographs, as if their happiness was never destined to last beyond one era. Deirdre, in her hand-sewn bridesmaid's dress, has the radiant smile that is supposed to belong to the triumphant bride. I appear fragile and anxious in my pseudo-Victorian gown, overwhelmed by all the lace and ruffles. With hindsight, my bridal gown reminds me of abandoned Miss Havisham. Perhaps when couples just drift apart, their joint past remains stable. For me everything has dissolved and reformed into new shapes. The past poisoned by the present. How dare David do that to me?

I take the photo out of its frame and go out to buy a local paper. I informed Mark that I was doing something this evening so I feel I should make it true. I look at the Entertainment columns to see what's on offer. There's a classical concert on or a Japanese film showing at the local Arts cinema but these are both things I might have gone to with David. I look for something that I would never have dared suggest to my husband and spot a post-West End tour of an American musical. I phone the theatre to see if there are any seats left for tonight. Ominously, there are.

At seven o'clock I put on my black dress and set out for the Hippodrome. Half way there I have a panicky pause. If I do bump into David and Rosa on my evening out, will I be accused of following them around? David has an opera-lover's snobbish disdain for musicals but what do I know about Rosa's tastes? Perhaps she likes nothing better than dressing up as a nun and singing along to 'The Sound of Music'. I remind myself that I'm in the cheap seats, where well-paid barristers are unlikely to venture, and keep walking.

I'm relieved to get through the lobby and into my seat without seeing anyone I know. I don't think I've ever been to a theatre by myself before. I'm surprised by how out of place I feel amongst all the groups and couples. I read the director's pretentious notes and the potted biographies of the B-list cast several times but there's a limit to how long you can pretend to be deeply absorbed in the programme. I smile at the people who thank me for standing up as they squeeze past to their seats, but that is the sum of my human contact.

I try to absorb myself in the show but the gaudy figures strutting on the stage seem a very long way away and their over-miked voices sound jarringly artificial. Gradually though, I'm drawn into their tangled love stories. There is something cheering about listening to other people singing about misery, frustration and hopeless love.

As the interval starts, I get up purposefully along with the rest of my row but can't face the scrum in the bar. David's experience as a Rugby player made him the ideal person to fetch interval drinks. Since I'm on my own, I just queue up for a tub of ice-cream. When I sit down again in the middle of the now empty row, I'm glad that I've decided to carry my diary with me wherever I go. I take it out of my bag and fill in the details of my day. I think of making porridge my word of the day but remember that it is slang for doing time in prison. Definitely not positive enough to win Nina's approval.

Thinking of Nina somehow makes me feel guilty about Deirdre but I know that the ritual phone calls have sustained a friendship which should have faded years ago as we grew to have less and less in common. If Deirdre lived nearby, instead of in Scotland, we would probably have stopped being close when her first baby arrived. It is difficult for childless women to stay friends with women who suddenly become mothers before anything else. I can remember some of them saying, 'It's such a nice change to go out with you, Meg, and talk about something other than the kids...' but they never quite meant it. I could sense their thoughts drifting back to their little Alexanders or Charlottes.

Characters in musicals rarely seem to be encumbered by fractious babies to feed, overdue bills to pay, light-bulbs to change, or any of the other petty problems of daily life. They can just stand there and emote, or dance out their feelings without slipping on cat-sick or piles of unopened post. There was more in the local paper today about Jenna Jenkins' alleged lovers but I wonder if it was her dismissive attitude to her house-husband's daily routine that led to her death. Did Martin stab her because she let the dinner he'd so carefully prepared get cold while she insisted on telling him about her feelings for another man? When David told me about Rosa I clung to the routine that gave me purpose – cooking a hot meal, serving it on nice plates, watching David pour out the single glass of red wine which might be good for his heart. His heart...

November 29th

On the bus journey to my mother's side of town, I think about my walk home last night. It was foolish to go a West End musical. I should have predicted that 'love would conquer all'. If I wanted a tragic ending for the entire cast, I should have sat through that Japanese art film or one of the gloomy Italian operas that David adores. I can't explain why it suddenly seemed unbearable when the plot contrived to bring all the star-crossed lovers together. As the leading couple started to sing, in ridiculous rhyme, about how rapturously happy they were going to be. I wanted to jump to my feet and shout to the heroine, "Give up now. His love won't last. It never does."

Then, as if I was dreaming, I found that I had stood up. The people on either side were staring at me and someone behind hissed at me to sit down. I didn't shout. I just muttered, "Sorry, sorry," squeezed my way out of the row and blundered through the nearest exit. I felt guilty when an usherette hurried over to take my arm, assuming I was ill. Did I look as bad as I felt? I told her that I had a headache and needed fresh air.

Coming back up Park Street, I found myself pushing against a tide of brash young women just beginning their evening out. There seemed to be very few mixed couples about. The girls exchanged playful insults with passing men but stayed in their all-female gaggles. I tried to imagine how they felt about love and marriage and guessed that although they are tempted by the prospect of an extravagant wedding with all the trimmings, they don't have high expectations of men. In due course they'll mate and have a child or two but they will probably rely on family and female friends for support rather than husbands. Those confident young creatures wouldn't understand why the unexpected end of my marriage seems so terrible to me. They probably think traditional marriage an old-fashioned custom as bizarre and harmful as foot-binding. Today though, I have to face my mother, who still thinks that being a good wife is the happiest state a woman can aspire to.

I hesitate outside the door of mother's flat, afraid that when I ring the bell smiley-girl will be there after all. When I finally flex my finger to start the ding-dong chimes, there is a reassuringly long wait before the door opens.

"Hello, dear. You're looking peaky."

However much their eyesight may fail, mothers can always detect peakiness.

"I'm all right," I say and stoop to kiss her.

I never used to be this much taller than my mother. I have to steady her as she turns to go towards the kitchen.

"Melody stayed on yesterday to cook us something. All we have to do is warm up the stew in the microwave and take the plum tart out of the fridge. She made enough for three, in case David came."

"He won't be coming."

As I say this, I feel a tremor go through my mother's body. Has she, after all, sensed that something has gone wrong between David and me? She hasn't pressed me about David's absence but then 'If you don't talk about nasty things, they may go away' has always been mother's motto.

"Plenty for seconds then. Melody thinks you need feeding up."

I can't help letting my annoyance show. "You've been

discussing me with the help?"

"Why shouldn't I talk about my own family? Melody likes to hear about you all. Now where's that note about how long the stew needs?"

I find the idiot-proof instructions that Aija has left on top of the microwave.

"Such nice clear hand-writing," approves mother. "Most English girls can't write like that any more."

"Why don't you sit down, while I get everything ready?"

I busy myself putting the casserole-dish of rust-coloured stew into the microwave, setting the table, pouring cream into a jug and finding a pie-slice for the tart. My plan is to tell mother about David over coffee. There is no point in spoiling her appetite for Sunday lunch.

When the microwave pings, I remove the stew which now looks more like a soup. I put away the plates, get out extra spoons, and ladle the stew into soup bowls.

"It's steaming hot," I say, "better leave it for a minute."

I realize that I'm treating my mother as if she was child, but she just nods. "I do like hot food though. I never could stand things served lukewarm, like they do in some parts. Melody's the same. 'Very hot – good' she says, 'Very cold – good. Tepid – blah!'"

"I'm surprised that she knows a word like tepid."

I am beginning to suspect that Aija's charming broken English is something of an act.

"She reads a lot. Her mother is a teacher. Her grandmother was too. She taught in a school that used to be a palace, built by some Duke or other in the Russian style. Very grand, with hundreds of rooms. Melody's mother was brought up in a flat that used to be part of a ballroom, with naked ladies painted on the ceiling. I expect they were goddesses, or nymphs..." As the stew cools, mother gives me a detailed account of Aija's granny's childhood home, suddenly ending with, "The school's gone and the palace is open to the public now. You should go there with David on one of your breaks."

I open my mouth to say that there won't be any more breaks but I hesitate too long and miss the moment.

"Melody has a cousin who works in a hotel in Riga, the part they call the Old Town. That would be a nice place to visit. Melody showed me photographs. Only most of the English people who stay in the hotel are young men who just go there to get drunk. Stag-parties they call them. There was nothing like that when your father and I got married I'm pleased to say but nowadays.." My mother seems more animated than she has been for ages. Aija's conversation is obviously more stimulating than mine. "...and the women almost as bad. Whole groups of them going to pubs, and strip-clubs even."

"You can see that in Bristol too," I begin, "last night..."

Mother won't be deflected. "To act like that abroad is worse. What must they think of us? Latvian girls are brought up to behave nicely. Not like the Russian girls..."

I eat the mushy paprika-flavoured stew, while mother tells me what Aija says about Russian girls. Does any housework get done during her visits or is it all tea and chat?

"One of Melody's aunts was married to a Russian soldier but he didn't take her back with him when the Russians left in a hurry. He probably had another wife in Moscow, or wherever he came from..." Mother slurps up her stew between anecdotes but it takes her a very long time to finish the bowl.

"Melody's grandmother had a brother who was sent to one of those camps... Gulags is it? Anyway, he never came back and the family couldn't find out what happened. So when one of her daughters married a Russian, Melody's grandmother never spoke to her again. Not once and if the daughter came to the house, she wouldn't even open the door. Think of that!"

"I'm sure it's all more interesting than our dull English lives."

Mother refuses to take this as sarcasm. "A dull life is something to be grateful for. Melody says she'd rather..."

I can't stand to hear any more about what 'Melody' says.

"Well apparently I'm so dull that David has been having an affair with someone more interesting."

I hadn't meant to be so abrupt but I'm glad that it's out.

"An affair?" mother quavers.

"Yes, that's why you haven't seen David for weeks. It isn't the trial, it's because we're not living together any more."

"Oh, my poor Meggy!" Mother leans across the table to pat my hand and that nearly makes me cry. "Why didn't you tell me before?"

"I don't know. It didn't seem real at first and then you had your fall so I thought it wasn't a good time to tell you something upsetting."

"You should have told me. Is it someone he works with?"

I'm surprised at the shrewdness of this question. "Yes, it's one of his Juniors – Rosa Winston – I think you met at her at last year's garden party."

"Not the coloured girl?" Mother looks horrified. So much for equal opportunity adultery.

"Well, I'd never have thought it of him. Whatever you think

about Celia, she surely brought her son up to have better taste than that, but the girl probably led him on."

That's what I think too but it sounds cruder when you hear someone else say it.

Mother goes on, "Men of David's age, they can't help themselves when they're around an attractive girl, day in and day out. If their wife isn't well...as forthcoming as she used to be, even the best of them sometimes have a fling. It doesn't really mean anything. That's what you have to remember."

"This isn't just a fling."

Fling. As if David was throwing himself into an unknown future. Leaping before he looked. Not like him at all.

Mother squeezes my hand. "I know how angry you must be, but try to forgive and forget."

"I don't think that's an option. David..."

She doesn't let me finish. "Forgiveness is always an option. Darling, I'm going to tell you something I've never told anyone else. Your father was a good man but he did stray the once."

I really don't want to hear this about my father. Mother sees that in my face and starts making excuses for him.

"It was after Rob came along. I'd always wanted a baby and Rob meant the world to me. I think your father felt shut out. I should have taken notice when he started to stay later and later at the office, but I was just glad to have more time to get Rob bathed and into his cot. He wasn't an easy baby to get to sleep. I should have remembered that men always have to be first with someone. It's the way they're made."

"You shouldn't blame yourself for being a good mother!"

"I should have been a good wife too. It was Annie Perks who gave me the hint. Do you remember her?"

I nod. I remember 'Aunty Annie' as a deceptively jolly-looking fat woman who kept a sharp tongue hidden in her smiling face. I imagine she took great pleasure in disillusioning mother.

"It was his secretary of course. I'd never liked the look of Janice. She was what I'd call obvious. All bottle-blonde hair and shiny lipstick. Thought she was Marilyn Monroe. When I confronted your father he didn't admit what they'd been up to but he had the cheek to say what an understanding woman Janice was."

I can see that still rankles after all these years and I can almost hear the grinding noise as everything I thought I knew about my past changes again.

"Well, harsh words were spoken and your father packed a suitcase and went off to a hotel. After a week apart we were both miserable. After three weeks we met at the hotel, in the public lounge at tea-time almost as if we were courting again. Your father said he was sorry and told me he'd given Janice her marching orders. I asked him to come home and promised we'd say no more about it and we never did. I told Annie she'd been mistaken and that was that. Your father and I were happy together, especially after you came along. So you see, dear, however much it hurts now, it is worth giving them a second chance."

Mother takes my hand and weakly squeezes it. For her, this is a demonstrative gesture. I don't squeeze back. There may have been no words spoken about father's infidelity but there must have been thoughts. Surely mother must have wondered, as I am, about all the secretaries and office girls who came after Janice?

"That was just between us two," mother is saying. "Promise me that you'll never tell Rob. I wouldn't want him to think badly of his father."

"I don't think he would." I am remembering, though mother chooses not to, that Rob left his first wife for a woman he met at work.

"No, no, it must be our secret."

I promise and then mother tells me to make us a cup of tea. She seems to think that she's fixed something, rather than broken my childhood memories.

While the tea is brewing, I try to make her understand. "Mother, David and I won't be getting back together. He doesn't care whether I forgive him or not. He wants a divorce because Rosa is expecting a baby."

"A baby?"

"Yes, David's baby. Well, he assumes it is."

"Oh." There is a long pause before mother says, "I see, well at least he's trying to do the right thing by the baby, but you mustn't blame yourself for not being able to give him a son."

"I'm not!"

I retreat into the kitchenette and clatter cups, too furious to speak to her again for a minute.

When I bring out the tea, mother seems grimly determined to be cheerful. "I won't deny it's a shock about David but he'll make sure you're comfortably off and getting a divorce is so common nowadays..."

"I'm not getting a divorce. I'm being divorced."

Mother perseveres. "What I mean is no-one thinks the worse of a woman for being divorced. Mrs Lawton in the flat above – her daughter has been divorced twice but she's found a nice new man on the interweb – a tax accountant I believe. So, you see dear, divorce isn't the end of the world."

But how I wish it was – the end of the world in a swift searing flash and no waking up tomorrow to an empty bed, an empty house and a whole life to remake.

November 30th

I wake up because the world hasn't conveniently ended. There are cats to feed and rubbish to put out, so I wash and dress myself. I make porridge and eat several spoonfuls before Vincent sticks his head in the bowl while I am staring out of the kitchen window. I let him lick up the milk and mumble the remaining porridge. David would be horrified. He hated to see cats on the dining tables or the kitchen work-surfaces. Now I let Vincent and Theo tread wherever they like. Not that I've seen much of Theo recently.

There are two more days to go before I reach the black cross on the calendar. If I haven't heard from the gallery in Bath by Wednesday, it means that I won't be called for an interview. Rejected applicants aren't even worth the price of a stamp. So, word of the day must be Job-search. I take my lap-top up to David's study where the printer still hunkers in a dark corner. I google 'jobs for artists in Bristol' and optimistically print out the first six jobs that pop up. After thumping the printer a few times, I have a sheaf of paper to take downstairs to read over coffee in the glass-house.

The belief that I will feel more confident surrounded by examples of my work is rapidly eroded. Would I fit in at a 'brand-led, customer-focused design consultancy'? The job description for this one sounds faintly obscene – 'You will be responsible for giving high end graphic solutions'. Am I high or low end? I've no idea. A temporary job replacing someone on maternity leave requires 'experience of mentoring a creative team, no matter how big or small' – can I spin my art classes into 'creative teams'? The advert continues that it goes without saying that whether my 'skills have been honed agency or client side' I will have a 'stunning portfolio' and 'be an expert mac and adobe creative suite user'. I like to think that I have the stunning portfolio but as far as I'm concerned, a mac is a raincoat and an adobe is something you make out of sun-dried mud-brick. I pass on to the application headed – 'The art of hospitality needs artists like you'. This seems promising until I see that what hospitality needs are artists who can create a gif banner (probably not an embroidery) and understand the meanings of a whole string of non-words. I recognize PDF and jpg but what is or are tiff, eps and avi? Does nobody want artists who can just draw well any more?

I drop most of the application forms into the waste-paper basket. Does even having such an object mark me as hopelessly outdated? I love the feel of paper in all its variations. The glassy smoothness of a sheet of Hot Pressed, the slight dimpling of Not that only my fingertips can discern; the inviting textures of Rough.... but apparently I should have been paying more attention to art forms made with keyboards and screens. While I was living in my protective bubble, time and technology have whooshed past, so now I've emerged looking like a blinking idiot. If only I had a son or daughter to explain it all to me.... No. Don't fantasize about some perfect offspring who wouldn't follow the normal pattern of treating their parent as a primitive life form. This is something – another thing – I have to deal with on my own.

I start by going for a bracing walk. There is no fog this morning. A sharp wind harries grey clouds across the sky as if they were a flock of sheep which mustn't be allowed to scatter. Thinking this reminds me of Deirdre's dog, Jagger. He's notorious for chasing anything that moves – sheep, cats, cars, balloons, bicycles, postmen. I am feeling guilty about Deirdre. I ought to ring her and explain. Let her be the listener to a tale of woe for once, but I don't think I'm quite ready for that piece of role reversal. I also have a sinking feeling that if I told currently homeless Deirdre about my plan to keep the house, she'd suggest moving in with me. I decide to wait and see if she rings me again.

As I push Deirdre to the back of my thoughts, I notice that my feet have automatically taken me along David's favourite route to the gorge. I shall have to break habits like this but now that I'm here, I go and sit on 'our bench' in the shelter of one Brunel's pylons. Cast iron railings separate the platform on which the bench stands from a scrubby piece of land which ends abruptly in a frightening drop. The famous bridge is a magnet for the suicidal. Do they imagine angelic moments of flight before a plunge into welcoming darkness? And there is always the faint hope of miraculous survival; an infallible sign that life is meaningful after all.

I lean back against the slats on the bench and grip one of its metal arms. I am nowhere near the edge, but every nerve in my body seems to be screaming out a warning that I'm about to topple. I close my eyes. The last time I felt like this, I was seven years old and on a family day out to a ruined castle. We'd climbed to the top of a tower with battlements I could only just see over. I don't remember what set off my panic – just the absolute conviction that if I moved an inch, I would fall to my death. I crouched down, with my head jammed against my knees, and refused to budge. Mother was embarrassed and kept telling me to get up because people were looking at us; Rob was scornful and told me to stop acting like a baby, but Dad picked me up, held me close, and whispered, "I've got you, Meggy." He carried me all the way down the tower and back to the car.

I felt safe with my father. I believed he would always be there to protect me. Until the sunny Sunday afternoon when his heart failed as he tried to restart the lawnmower. One of the neighbours who had rushed to comfort my hysterical mother told me that my father had 'gone to heaven'. Apparently, I answered that my Dad wouldn't go anywhere without saying goodbye to me first. Now I've been made to see that my father was never the immovable fixture I believed him to be. At any time, he might have left mother and Rob and me for another understanding secretary.

Do men ever really leave because their wives don't understand them? Isn't it because their wives understand them all too well and they want a fresh start with someone who doesn't? Yet mother immediately assumed that with David it is all about doing right by the baby. What if he didn't leave me for Rosa but for the baby? Is being a good father more important to David than anything else? He had a very good father himself, so perhaps it's in his genes; an imperative he just can't ignore.....

The ground has stopped rocking, so I open my eyes. Perhaps there is a solution to this mess. All I need to do is show David that he doesn't have to choose between his marriage and his child. Rosa doesn't require saving from a shameful fate, as if she was a doomed heroine in a Hardy novel. In this day and age, her career probably won't suffer because she's an unmarried mother. I'd have no objection to David paying child maintenance and sharing custody with Rosa. We could even...

I get my phone out to ring David straight away. I wonder if I'll be able to get a signal but I do. I know I'll have to leave a message because he'll be in court today. My fingers hover above the buttons. It is so engrained not to disturb David for anything but dire emergencies during the last few days of a big trial. David will be psyching himself up to make his crucial closing speech for the Prosecution. The speech that will condemn Martin Jenkins to prison far more surely than anything said by the judge. Martin has so little chance of escape. Disturbing David is one small thing I can do for this Defendant who won't defend himself.

I reach David's message service. When the tone sounds, I gabble, "David, it's me. It's Meg." Did I need to add that? "David, I've been thinking about the baby. When you were uncomfortable with the idea of adoption, I thought that you weren't bothered about having children, but that was wrong, wasn't it? What you've always wanted is a child who is truly your own. Now she...Rosa is able to give you that, I'm sure you're determined to be a good father. Of course you are. That's the right thing to do and I should have said so earlier but it's all been such a shock...." I pause to gulp in air. "There is no need to break up our marriage over this. You must give Rosa all the financial support she needs and I'm willing...happy to share the responsibility of raising your child. It can visit us whenever you want. We can turn the study back into a nursery. Do you know yet if it's a boy or a girl? Anyway, please ring me so that we can work out how..."

The tone cuts me off. I should have recalled that David has set his phone so that messages can last no longer than sixty seconds. He says it encourages brevity in colleagues who are used to being paid for every word they utter. Still, I think I made myself clear. Not many wives would make an offer like that. I shall try to think of the child as a stepson or daughter from a previous relationship. Lots of women rear step-children without giving them poisoned apples.

December 1st

Word of the day – suspended. David didn't ring back last night. I wish there was some way of knowing whether he has listened to my message. He may be putting off opening it because he assumes that whatever I have to say will pile more guilt onto him. Or he may be ignoring all of his messages until the Prosecution has closed its case. I watched the local television news last night in case there was any coverage of the Jenkins trial. Another day of salacious evidence ensured that there was. A reporter standing outside the Crown Court described a claim by a female 'friend' of Jenna Jenkins that Jenna had slept with a teacher at her daughter's school during the same period that she was having an affair with Ray at the office. Child, full-time job, two lovers on the go – how did she fit it all in?

The picture switched to a court-room drawing of Counsel for the Defence gesturing as if he was in some Victorian melodrama about a fallen woman. Without quite saying so, the Defence implied that Martin Jenkins had learned about all Jenna's infidelities at once and understandably snapped. Will the jury believe this without hearing it from the distraught husband himself? Or will Martin opting not to give evidence, and his lack of visible emotion, condemn him as a murderer no matter how punctiliously the judge tells the jury to ignore these factors? So, I tell myself that David has obviously been too busy to listen to any of his messages. A more hopeful part of me thinks that he has already heard my proposal and is too overcome or too embarrassed to reply straight away.

I've been dreading November inexorably giving way to

December. Christmas is the great exposer of broken families. Now, as I turn over to the last page of my 'Great Female Artists' calendar, I wonder if David might have moved back into our home by Christmas. Which means I will have a mother-in-law to worry about again. Not having to think of a suitable Christmas present for Celia was one of the few benefits of being ejected from David's family circle. However hard I try to please, Celia always sneers at my taste, so for some years now I've deliberately selected things I know she won't like. Of course I have to do it in such a way that David won't notice, which adds to the challenge. Last Christmas we gave Celia an elaborately decorated folding walking-stick. Celia hates having attention drawn to her unsteadiness but David thanked me for choosing such a thoughtful present for his mother. Perhaps this year I should get her a book on how to be a good granny.

I banish Celia by studying December's picture on my calendar. It is a very unseasonal portrait by Laura Knight of a World War II factory worker. Clad in dungarees and a headscarf tied into a turban, a robust young woman is confidently bending over a fearsome-looking machine. Which reminds me to get back to my own search for work. Even if David does come home, it would be good to be able to show him that I don't need his financial support.

I make myself a coffee with the last spoonful of grounds in the bottom of a tin of Fortnum and Mason's Finest Java Blend. In future, I'll have to get my morning buzz from something cheaper. Anything hot and dark brown will probably jangle my braincells just as effectively. My new plan is to compile a list of local Graphic Arts firms and then go and target them in person with my portfolio.

I open the laptop which is sitting on the kitchen-table, turn it on and go for Google. I don't get there because a 'No internet connection' notice flashes up. It doesn't say 'Please try again' but I do, several times. Then I go through the rigmarole of closing down my computer, waiting just long enough to finish my coffee, and powering up again. Still 'No connection'. I try moving the laptop to another room but it doesn't help. That takes me to the limit of what I can do without asking someone who actually understands computers. Someone like David.

Somewhere, I have the number of our service provider's helpline. I spend ten minutes going through the bits of paper stuffed into an old letter-rack. On every one are scribbled numbers or addresses that must once have been important. I decide to throw away anything I don't recognize. It's quite satisfying to screw up the scraps and toss them into the waste-paper basket or to Vincent, who comes to join in what he thinks is a game. I nearly throw him the paper with the vital number on, but realize just in time.

I pick up the phone and press the button to make a call. What I still think of as the dialling tone doesn't hum reassuringly in my ear. I look at the miniature screen and see the words 'No Line'. A nasty suspicion forms, which I confirm by going into the drawing room and turning on the television. The cable channels are gone too. David must have stopped paying our subscription, or transferred it to...wherever he lives now. I have been cut off.

What else has gone? Water? Electricity? No, I've just filled and boiled a kettle, but those bills come in quarterly. Is David planning to deprive me of heat and light at the end of December? I picture myself shivering in a cold dark house as the new year begins. I find that I'm hugging myself, as if I was already desperate to keep warm. I sit down and try to be rational. This is clearly a ploy to push me into accepting a financial settlement. Can David just do this to me without warning? I suppose he can, since the utility bills are all in his name. What about my mobile phone? Has he cancelled that contract too?

I rush back into the kitchen and scrabble for my phone, which always sinks right to the bottom of my handbag. When I type in my pin number the phone responds as normal. I open one of the messages from the phone company which I normally ignore and find a reminder about last month's bill. I haven't been cut off yet, but presumably I will be if I don't discover how to pay this bill.

When the post arrives I get more shocks. I've made a new resolution not to put it all in a pile to open 'later' but to deal with anything that isn't obvious junk-mail straight away. The first letter is from an estate agent stating that they have been commissioned to value my house and could I ring them to arrange a convenient time for the valuer to visit. Do I have to let them into my home? My plan to consult my solicitor about this falters when I open an envelope containing her first bill. I shriek, 'How much!" so loudly that Vincent bolts down the hall. I thought I didn't have to pay until the settlement came through, or is this scary sum only the bill for responding to Rosa's threatening letter?

I shall have to go a cash machine to check how much money there is in the joint account, since I can't do it on-line. Or perhaps I should go straight to the bank and demand to talk to our 'account manager'. As I stare at my lap-top I realize that there is another thing I can't check. What if the gallery in Bath has sent me an email summoning me for an interview? Damn David. I go back to the filing cabinet and search for old bills from the company that provides our phone, cable and internet connections and find a letter with our account number and the answers to our security questions. Then I ring the number on the scrap of paper. The wait is long enough for me to work out what to say. I'm pretty sure that David won't have told whoever he spoke to that he was cancelling his subscription to spite his soon to be ex-wife.

When my call is answered I get over the first hurdle by giving the details of our account, David's date of birth and Celia's maiden name. Before the pleasant sounding women in customer services has had time to finish saying, "How may we help you today?" I'm in mid-gabble. "My husband cancelled our subscription for this address but now our plans have all changed and we need the services back again. My husband is too busy at the moment to deal with things like this." How true that is. "I do hope you can help us because it is so awkward to be without the phone and the internet. It's such a problem when people let you down and you don't know what's going to happen."

This seems to strike a chord and we chat for a minute about the horrors of moving house when everything can fall through at the last minute.

"For a resumption of services we really ought to have notification in writing..."

"We'll send you a letter to confirm the instruction, but it would be really helpful if we could have the services back right away."

"I'll see what I can do. I've got all the details on my screen now."

I hear faint tapping noises. After a minute, she says, "There, I've marked the new subscription at Porto as postpone and cancelled the collection of your box from your current address. Your services should be back within an hour."

I thank her effusively and ring off. Let David see what it's like to be unexpectedly cut off.

Porto? I think it's the name of one of the new blocks of flats down by the harbour in a once seedy area near the old Mud Dock which the developers have cannily re-branded as Lower Clifton. I remember walking along the tow-path with David to look at all the buildings going up in the property gold-rush. He was the one who sneered at the Lego-like architecture and now he lives there. At least, temporarily. Harbourside isn't the sort of place that anyone stays for very long. It's aimed at 'young professionals' – more like 'young irresponsibles' who want somewhere close to bars and clubs until the time comes for them to sober up and move to the kind of home you can raise a family in. The kind Rosa has her eye on.

I put on my raincoat and go out to the bank. Half-way there, words leap at me from the board outside the newsagents – JENKINS CHANGES PLEA. I can't walk past that. I fumble for the right change and buy the late edition of the Bristol paper. I try to read it in the street but the rain is now pelting down. I almost run back home, my heart pounding, the headline repeating over and over in my mind – 'Jenkins admits murder charge'. Why would he do that at this late stage? If I'd been in court, would I have seen his facade of calm begin to crack? Or was this some crisis of conscience that happened overnight? I imagine Martin Jenkins looking into a mirror and suddenly seeing himself as a murderer.

When I get home and spread out the rain-spattered newspaper on the kitchen table, I find that there isn't much new information beneath the sensational headline. In court this morning, Counsel for the Defence announced that his client was changing his plea to guilty. The judge thanked and dismissed the jury and remanded Martin Jenkins in custody to await sentencing at a later date. The rest of the columns are taken up with a rehash of the juicer bits of the case and the usual photograph of Jenna on the beach. A photograph that it is now impossible to see as a picture of innocence. The barristers on both sides will be furious about the late change of plea but they won't say so in public. At least they'll only lose a few days' fees. I feel sorrier for the jury which has sat through all that harrowing evidence without even getting to have their say.

The judge won't give Martin any credit for pleading guilty when his expensive trial was nearly over. So why did he do it?

After thinking about it for quite a while, I believe I know. I distract myself by checking to see if the services have come back. I reach my email account, but there is no message from the Bath gallery asking me to come for an interview. I use the phone to call my mother. She has apparently been trying to reach me. "But I couldn't get it to ring. I just got this voice telling me that your number 'wasn't available'. Melody tried for me and said the number had been cut off. I knew that couldn't be right. Was there something wrong with your phone earlier?"

"Yes, but it's fixed now. Has something happened?"

Damn David for not thinking about the effect of his actions on my elderly mother.

"No, no. I was just a little bit worried because you didn't

ring yesterday at your usual time.'

Double damn. I forgot to make the brief five o'clock 'are you still alive?' call yesterday. I apologize and remind mother that she can always call me on my mobile number if she can't get through on the main line.

"Well, I would if it was urgent."

I can't persuade my mother that mobiles aren't just for emergencies. She keeps the expensively simple mobile phone Rob gave her in a drawer and has never yet used it. Mother asks me how I am. 'Having a foul day,' I think.

"I'm fine," I say, "just busy preparing classes."

"You won't sit in the house moping all the time will you, dear? Perhaps you could go out somewhere with your friend, Nina."

"Actually, I am going out to dinner tonight with...another friend. Someone from David's Chambers."

I shouldn't have added that. Mother immediately says, "I know you must want to find out what's going on with David, but wouldn't it be better not to think about him any more?"

I don't see how it is possible to stop thinking about someone you've been bound to in every possible way for nearly thirty years. It's like telling me to stop breathing.

"That's not why I'm going out with Mark. He's just good company."

"Oh, a gentleman friend..."

Before mother can offer me any more advice I tell her that I have to go.

I had been thinking of ringing Mark to cancel our dinner but I have spent so much of the day struggling to communicate via machines that the thought of a face to face conversation with another human being seems very attractive. I suppose it is possible now to live almost entirely through phone and internet and never the leave the house. It wouldn't matter then if I shrank into the hunched and spiny creature of my drawings because no-one would ever see me and be shocked or repelled.

Tonight though, Mark is going to see me and I don't know what to wear. I contemplate rushing out to a charity shop to get something new but decide to put on the black dress with the peacock feather motif again. It's unlikely Mark will remember that I was wearing it last time. Whenever I asked David what I should wear for an evening out, he'd say, "Your pretty blue dress." The particular blue dress he was thinking of had long since gone to the rag-bank but whatever I actually put on, he always nodded approvingly. I used to find that endearing but perhaps he had just stopped looking at me. Really looking.

If David rings me back before 7.00 there will still be time to put Mark off. I check my email every half hour, but the only new one is from Janet telling me that she can't come to my morning class tomorrow. This reminds me to think about lesson plans but I'm not in the mood. I decide that I'll just have to wing it. At 6.30 I watch the local news programme. There is an interview with the stolid policeman in charge of investigating Jenna's murder and a brief statement from the family expressing relief that Martin Jenkins has finally admitted his guilt.

At 7.00, I go upstairs and change into the peacock dress and my black pumps. I look in the mirror and feel almost too weary to walk. There has been no slow fading of hope. One moment I really believed that David might want to come back to me; the next my offer seemed like a futile attempt to turn back time.

When the doorbell finally rings, I know it won't be David.

I make myself smile as I open the door to Mark. He is standing there under the canopy of a luridly striped umbrella.

"Hello, Meg. Awful weather, so I got us a taxi."

I grab my raincoat and let him hurry me out of the house and into the taxi. He takes care to keep the umbrella over me so that I don't get wet. I feel protected and cherished again. Mark gives the driver the name of a restaurant in Whiteladies Road.

"I hope you like Chinese food."

I'm tempted to say that I've never had any, only Chinese restaurant food, but I just smile and nod and talk about the weather. When we arrive, Mark leaps out to come round and open the door for me, but the taxi driver beats him to it. I notice that he gets a very small tip for his pains.

The restaurant has a soothingly pastel interior. There are panels reproducing paintings of Chinese tree peonies on the walls and silk flowers on the tables. It strikes me as the sort of place that you could safely bring your mother or your aunt, but I assume that Mark chose it because he imagined the floral decoration would please me. It was a kind thought, so after he has ordered drinks, I dutifully admire the panel closest to our table. It's the kind of elegantly understated painting that makes my work look fussy and garish.

"The artist has used different parts of his brush to make thick or thin strokes..."

Mark interrupts my explanation. "Yes it's all strokes and space isn't it? I prefer your style of painting. It's so much more real. With your pictures, you can practically smell the flowers."

If he was one of my pupils, Mark would get the 'virtues of negative space' lecture at this point. Since he's just a...friend, I say, "I don't think I thanked you properly for buying my June picture from the exhibition."

"My pleasure. Mother's birthday is in June. I'm going to save it to give to her then."

"Your mother? Does she live near you?"

"I've had the basement flat in my house done up for her. Mother's wonderful for her age but she needs keeping an eye on. You know how it is."

"I do indeed."

Oh God, another man who thinks his mother is wonderful. At least Celia never moved in with us.

"Mother was a great gardener before her arthritis got too bad," Mark is saying, "so I'm sure she'll love your picture."

Unless it reminds her of all the things she can no longer have and do. I smile and dip my head to study the suspiciously long menu.

"The beef in black bean sauce is always good," suggests Mark, "or the sizzling pork."

I don't care what I eat, so I let Mark order one of the set meals for two.

We chat about the difficulties of finding suitable carers at reasonable rates. For my age-group, this seems to be the conversation that has replaced the moan about house-prices and school-fees. I keep wondering if Mark knows that Rosa has branded me as a stalker. If he does, there is no indication that it has changed his opinion of me. When the crispy duck starter arrives, I tentatively mention the Jenkins trial.

"Lord, what a mess!" exclaims Mark as he shovels shredded duck into one of the circular pancakes and piles on slices of cucumber and chunks of spring onion. "I gather both sides repaired to 'The Wig and Gown' to drown their sorrows, except for La Winston who went home with a headache. Not a smart move if she wants to be considered one of the boys. David was still seething about the case when he got back to Chambers."

"He must have been frustrated that he didn't get to make his big closing speech to the Jury."

"You are so right. He likes a firecracker ending, does David. Matt Bolton – who was leading for the Defence – is a good sort. Apparently he tried to talk his client out of changing his plea but Jenkins kept insisting he'd done it and that he knew exactly what he was doing – which I rather doubt. A wimp, like that. Anyhow, Jenkins was warned that pissing off the judge by pleading guilty at this late stage wouldn't get him a shorter sentence but he would do it. God knows why."

"Perhaps," I say carefully, "he always knew that he was guilty but he wanted the truth about Jenna to come out in court. If he'd pleaded guilty to begin with, no-one would have heard about her lovers. Now the whole country knows how she cheated on her marriage."

"You're saying he planned the whole trial as an act of revenge?" Mark looks genuinely horrified and then shakes his head. "Nobody would be that calculating. She was the mother of his little girl after all. However angry he may have been with his wife, surely he'd be thinking about what was best for his poor daughter? I mean, the children always have to come first, don't they?"

Mark bites into his rolled-up pancake, crunching on the raw onion. He doesn't seem to expect an answer, especially the one I might have given him. I arrange a few slivers of duck on a pallid moon of dough as carefully as if I was composing an abstract collage.

"A bad business all round," continues Mark, "makes me glad that I went into Commercial Law, though I could tell you some pretty grim stories about the big shipping companies. Now most of the tanker crews are Filipinos and what not, no-one seems to think it matters if corners are cut and they lose a few sailors."

"Surely not?"

I assume that this bland query will be the only encouragement Mark needs to tell me about his work, and I'm right. His 'grim stories' last all through the starter and the main course. Mark seems to have a remarkable talent for eating and talking at the same time. As I pick at my lemon chicken with egg-fried rice, he tells me that some companies won't pay ransoms for the sailors kidnapped by Somali pirates because it is cheaper to hire a new crew. I realize that somewhere inside this wealthy middle-aged barrister there are traces of an idealistic young man who went into law to fight injustice. Just as David did. David still looks the part. It is harder to imagine Mark as the bewigged avenger of wronged Filipino seamen but I try. A glass of wine helps.

"...so at least the company got a huge fine and agreed to pay compensation to the widows." Mark suddenly reaches across the table and touches my hand. "You're such a good listener, Meg. It's rare to find someone who takes an interest in what I do and sees how important it is. Barristers like David behave as if we Commercial chaps were all second-raters and only criminal law matters. It can really get you down."

Mark obviously noticed and resented David's mockery far more than we ever realized.

"Criminal law certainly grabs the lion's share of the

publicity," I say.

"Oh yes, the papers make far more fuss about the killing of one randy blonde than they do about the deaths of twenty hard-working seamen. Convicting someone like Jenkins won't stop jealous men killing their wives. That's just human nature. Enforcing safety laws at sea actually makes a difference."

I suppose he's right. There will always be another Martin and another Jenna. Everyone likes to think that their own tragedy is unique but to outsiders it must look like the same dreary pattern repeating generation after generation, marriage after marriage.

As stony-faced waiters clear away the detritus of our meal, Mark finally asks, "And what about your work? Are you going to take that gallery job in Bath?"

"No. It...it wasn't right for me."

"No point in taking a job you won't enjoy."

The point was to earn enough money to pay the bills. Do I detect a whiff of relief that I won't be coming to work in his home town? I wonder how many of Mark's lady-friends get introduced to his wonderful mother.

"Plenty of things to do in Bristol," Mark is saying. "What are you painting at the moment?"

Is it pathetic to feel a flush of gratitude at being asked? I tell him that I've just completed another of my semi-abstract house interiors. This sounds a bit thin, so I explain that I'm waiting until the end of term to start a new project and make my teaching commitments sound greater than they are.

"The Floral Art class is a tricky one to teach. Most of the students are quite advanced and I have to keep finding new challenges for them. Last week we...."

Mark interrupts. “Is that your phone?”

It is. I seem to be the only person who doesn’t have a tune for my ring-tone but it is such a horrible thing to do to music. A bit like torturing trees into bonsai.

“I’m sorry,” I hoick the phone out of my bag. “I forgot to turn it off.”

Even as I press down hard on the off button, I register that it is David’s mobile number on the screen. Mark is beaming at me.

“I knew you wouldn’t be the sort of woman who constantly answers calls and texts, instead of paying attention to the person they’re actually with.”

I slip the phone back into my bag and agree that such people are abominably rude. As our dessert arrives, Mark begins an anecdote about a shop assistant who wouldn’t come off her phone to serve him. I nod sympathetically and wonder if I can slip to the Ladies to check if David has left me a message.

“It’s the same on the train,” Mark is saying, “people have the most bizarrely personal conversations on their mobiles, as if there was no-one sitting next to them. They behave as if the rest of the world just doesn’t exist. I’m sometimes tempted to tap them on the shoulder and say ‘I’m not deaf, you know!’ or tell them to speak up because someone at the far end of the carriage didn’t quite hear the details of their sex life.”

I laugh for the first time in quite a while. It feels good, so I tell myself to forget about David and pay attention to the person I’m actually with.

“You have a lovely laugh, Meg. Do you want that other banana fritter?”

“No, please take it.”

"You should eat more," says Mark as he helps himself to the greasy fritter. "Can't have you fading away. Shall we have coffee here, or back at your place?"

I don't like his assumption that he has a standing invitation to come into my house, like a vampire after they've once been allowed to cross the threshold, so I say, "Oh, let's have it here. My budget doesn't run to good coffee at the moment."

"Right you are." Mark summons a waiter and orders the coffee and two liqueurs. Then he launches into a rather good story about a judge being incensed about a mobile phone interrupting his summing up, until he realized that it was his own. Mark is pleasingly indignant on my behalf when I tell him how much I hate my art pupils answering their phones or checking for texts during my classes. The coffee is stewed and bitter and the liqueur much too sweet but I drink both.

When a waiter brings the bill, I offer to pay half, just as I would with Nina or any other friend. Mark is already getting out his credit card.

"No, no. This is my treat. I know money must be tight for you until everything is settled."

I shouldn't have mentioned my budget. If this is a date, have I just given Mark the wrong signal by letting him pay? After being married for so long, I have very little idea what the conventions of modern dating are. Mark is going to ring for a taxi but I can see that it has stopped raining. I suggest that we walk back to my house. The alcohol is making my head muzzy, so I could do with some fresh air.

In Whiteladies Road I let Mark take my arm. With his other hand he twirls his umbrella, as if he's ready to fend off anyone who tries to take me from him. I giggle a little at this absurd idea. As a group of people hurry past, I wonder if they assume that Mark and I are a couple. Then I realize that they are far too young to take any interest in us at all. 'We can't have you fading away' Mark said, but that seems to be what's happening. I clutch his arm tighter, just to be sure that he can still feel me.

"Are you all right?"

"The pavement's a bit slippery."

"A chap I read Law with now specializes in getting compensation for people who've tripped on cracked or slippery pavements. It's made him so nervous of falling that he drives everywhere. Won't walk even a few yards in the street."

"What about you? Do you know too much about Marine Law to ever go to sea?"

"You certainly won't find me hitching a lift on a cargo ship, but when it comes to liners and ferries, some companies have a much better safety record than others."

Mark launches into a full comparison of the major cruise lines. Apparently he takes his mother on a cruise every year.

It's because I'm not really listening that I notice the cat in the window. The first house in my street hasn't closed its wooden shutters yet. Across the deep and narrow yard that divides the house from the pavement, I can see into the brightly lit living room. Theo is perched on the high back of an armchair, looking out through the sash window. I stare up into his copper eyes. After a moment, Theo turns his head away. He starts grooming his ruff with great concentration.

The tug on his arm makes Mark notice that I've stopped walking. He asks me what's wrong. I point at the window and say, "That's my cat!"

"Are you sure? There are lots of ginger cats about."

"I'm sure. The nick on his left ear is unmistakable."

"Ungrateful buggers, cats," says Mark, "when they find somewhere they like better, they just slope off."

At least he didn't say *someone* better, but I still let go of his arm.

"Theo's *my* cat. They have no right to him. It should be obvious that he belongs to someone, that he's been well cared for..."

I want to march up the steps, bang on Number One's door and demand my cat back but Mark puts himself between me and the house.

"He'll probably slink back to you before morning. Best to leave it for now, Meg."

He obviously doesn't want me to make a scene.

"Yes, I suppose so."

Mark offers me his arm again but I pretend not to notice as I delve in my bag for the front-door key. As we approach my house, Mark suggests that I get a dog instead. "Might be a good idea, now that you're living on your own."

That makes me wince, so I say, "I'm thinking of taking a lodger. Or two."

"Oh. Yes, I see. A couple of nice girls would be company for you and help with the bills. Very practical. I do so admire how you're coping with all this, Meg."

I'm standing on the top step now, pushing the key in the lock. This is the moment to thank Mark for the lovely dinner and firmly bid him good night. Instead I hear myself say, "I don't think I'm coping with any of it."

"There, there, don't cry, Meg."

"I'm not," I say, but I probably am, so I let Mark put his arm around me and we go into the house together.

December 2nd

Over breakfast I make a list of the reasons why I didn't have sex with Mark.

I wasn't quite tipsy enough

I don't like men with piggy eyes

His breath smelled of spring onions

I remembered what Nina said about 'moppers-up'

Our bodies didn't fit together.

Mark isn't David

It so nearly happened though. Almost as soon as we were inside the house, Vincent came trotting hopefully into the hall.

"Ah, there's your ginger cat!" exclaimed Mark. "I told you there was nothing to worry about."

I told him that this cat was Theo's brother, Vincent. Mark obviously couldn't see why anyone would need more than one cat. I launched into the usual explanation about getting two cats so that they could keep each other company. Only they don't. Theo alternately bullies and ignores his sibling, while Vincent always seems desperate for human attention. "They're not much like the real Van Gogh brothers," I finished weakly.

"Well they are cats, not crazy Dutchmen. Was that a smile? Why don't we crack open one of David's bottles of claret and see if I can cheer you up some more...unless he took his whole cellar with him?"

"I don't know. I haven't looked."

David's 'wine cellar' is actually a damp coal-hole opening off the front yard. I never go in there. I took Mark down to the kitchen, unbolted the door to the yard and gave him the cellar-key and a torch. As soon as he was gone, I took out my mobile phone and checked for messages. There were three unopened messages from Nina, one from Deirdre and one from a local number I don't recognize but nothing from David.

By the time Mark came back with a dusty bottle, I had put the phone away, dabbed my eyes with a tissue, and was calmly feeding Vincent.

"There are quite a few spaces on the racks, but I managed to find a bottle of the good stuff. Why don't you grab a corkscrew and a couple of glasses? Then we can settle down somewhere comfy."

I resented being ordered about in my own house, but at least this man still wanted to talk to me. I kicked the door shut behind us, trapping Vincent in the kitchen, and led Mark up to the drawing room. He made a great fuss about opening the claret and letting it breathe. Then he joined me on the sofa instead of taking the chair opposite.

"Now then, Meg, what's getting you down? Is David not playing fair in the divorce settlement?"

"David and Rosa want this house. They want to turn me out of my home."

"Ah...well, I suppose David is fond of the place too, but try to see this as a positive. If you have something the other side wants, you've got more leverage. You can negotiate a better deal. Who's your solicitor?"

When I told him, Mark frowned. "Patel? Never heard of her. Still, courts tend to favour the wife's claim when it comes to the marital home, especially if..." He stopped before actually saying, 'especially if there are children'. "Wouldn't you rather screw more money out of David and move to somewhere new?

Somewhere with fewer memories?"

"But my memories of living in this house are nearly all happy ones, right up to the moment when he..."

Mark put his arm around me.

"Of course they are. You were always a good loyal wife to David. I used to envy him his happy marriage. He's made a right fool of himself over La Winston. She'll probably use him to get a leg-up in the profession and then move on to a younger man after a few years. It happens all the time with second marriages."

I found myself protesting, "There is a baby involved,"

"It's so decent of you to worry about the baby, Meg. David's a double fool for abandoning a sweet woman like you and shacking-up with a super-bitch."

He leaned in and kissed me on the cheek and then got up to pour the wine.

"Only a little for me," I said, but he still handed me a glass so full it was almost slopping over the rim. That reminded me of the incident of Belinda spilling her wine. "I can't help wondering now whether David has had other affairs in the past, with women he's met at work." Mark didn't respond but I kept fishing. "Perhaps with other pupils, like Belinda?"

"The flashy redhead? I don't know anything for certain, but there was a bit of talk... The fact is, David wasn't worthy of you, Meg. So here's to new beginnings!" He raised his glass. "Drink up, Meg."

"New beginnings," I repeated but I only took a sip. I associate the taste of claret with kissing David at the end of a dinner party when we are...were finally on our own.

Mark shuffled closer and put his arm around me again. I think I shrank away slightly. He put down his glass and began to stroke my hair.

"Meg, there's no need to be lonely."

"I'm not, and I'm all right now, really I am."

"But you're trembling. You poor little thing..."

When David pulls me against him for a kiss, I know exactly how our bodies fit together and the precise angle to tilt my head so that David's lips press down on mine. As Mark enveloped me, our noses clashed as if we were teenagers fumbling towards a first kiss. It felt like being embraced by a feather-filled cushion. David's body has thickened over the years but he isn't soft and flabby. Yet, when Mark's lips touched mine and his hand slid down my neck towards my breasts, my body arched in response.

"Oh, good girl." His fat fingers slithered under the insecure wrap-front of my dress and I let them. His tongue pushed into my mouth. Then he drew back for a moment and whispered, "I've always fancied you, Meg." One hand was exploring under my dress; with the other he gripped my right hand and pulled it down to rub at his groin. "Forget about that black bitch and show me what David's missing..."

Looking back to last night, can I really have thought so many different things in the few seconds before I pushed Mark away in a great heave of revulsion? 'It's so long since I had sex with anyone but David, what will it be like?' 'Mark thinks I'm desperate for revenge sex. An easy lay, even for someone plain and paunchy like him.' 'Does he even fancy me, or is this a way of getting at David?' 'What would David think of me now?' Even, 'Poor Rosa, what she must have to put up with'. Aloud, I think I stuttered something about it being too soon.

I don't know why I kept saying "I'm sorry" to Mark. He didn't persist after I pushed him away but he was slow to school his face. I could see that he was furious at not getting the sex he thought he'd already paid for with spurious sympathy, a round of drinks, and dinner at a moderately expensive restaurant. Not to mention the picture.

"I quite understand," he said.

We were very polite to each other as he finished his glass of wine but I couldn't bear the thought of him touching me again. Mark seemed as anxious to get out of the house as I was to have him gone. I thanked him for the dinner as I hurried him to the front door.

"We must do it again some time, Meg."

"Yes. Good night."

I kept the door between us, so that he couldn't kiss me goodbye.

"Meg...I...Good night. Take care."

I bolted and chained the door while he was still going down the steps.

Would any man have jumped on a recent widow like that? Surely not, but divorcing women are thought of as fair game or assumed to be sexual predators. I knew then that there was no possibility of keeping Mark as a friend. Another relationship over and done with. I went to bed, promising myself to be more wary in future. Every night the darkness seems to shape itself into a figure lying beside me. A figure who is no longer a comforting and protective presence. A stranger in the bed.

Mark was right about one thing. While I was washing up my breakfast bowl and mug, Theo slipped in through the cat-flap. I turned to see two ginger heads feeding from the same dish.

"Do you think I don't know where you've been? How dare

you go off to someone else when it suits you and then come back bold as brass..."

Vincent thinks I'm yelling at him and squeezes himself under the dresser. Theo calmly goes on eating. I might have gone on pointlessly shouting at a cat with no conscience if the phone hadn't started to ring.

When I pick up the handset, David's voice says, "Ah, so you are answering this phone."

I can hear street noises in the background. David is obviously making this call where Rosa can't overhear him.

"I am when it isn't cut off without warning. When you cancelled our phone contract, did you give any thought to the effect on my poor mother? She was so worried when she couldn't reach me. She's been in hospital after a fall recently."

"I'm sorry, I didn't know that..but don't you think it's about time you took some financial responsibility for yourself? The changeover shouldn't have been unexpected. I told my solicitor to inform your solicitor that I wasn't going to continue paying all of the utility bills after the first of December unless you agree to leave the house within a reasonable period. I am still putting enough money in the joint account to pay a half-share. Most people would consider that an equitable arrangement."

There may have been something about it in those documents from Mrs Patel which I haven't got round to reading yet, but that's hardly the point.

"I'm still your wife, you could have had the courtesy to tell me in person."

"We're separated, Meg, and you could have had the courtesy to respond to the legal forms you've been sent instead of dragging your heels over everything."

I find myself answering as if we were compelled to keep to the script of a ritual exchange of grievances, "I'm sorry I'm so slow at getting over thirty years of marriage. And you haven't answered the message I sent you on Monday. Do you think it was easy for me to think about the baby and say all that to you?"

"I've been caught up in the wretched Jenkins case. I only heard your message last night. I rang straight away but you were too busy to answer your mobile phone."

I think of all the wasted hours I've spent waiting for David to come home or hoping that he'd call, but when he wants to speak to me, he expects an immediate response. I can't resist saying, "I was having dinner with Mark."

"Mark? Mark Arbuthnot?" David's tone suddenly changes to what sounds like genuine concern. "God, Meg, don't let Tanker get his paws on you. He's notorious for smarming up to vulnerable women and then boasting about his conquests."

"I'd worked that out for myself. Apparently deserted women are regarded as fair game."

"You make it sound as if I'd marooned you on some desert island. You do have friends and family in Bristol, unlike..."

He stops. Was he going to say 'unlike Rosa'. Did she win David over by being lonely and needy?

I may not have Rosa's youth or Rosa's curves but I can probably do lonely and needy better than her.

"You've no idea how isolated I feel. Have you told Rosa about my offer?"

"God no! She'd think..."

His stops again. The distant rumble of traffic and the shrieks of seagulls replace his voice.

"What would she think? What?"

"That you were trying to take the baby away from her."

"That's absurd. All I'm offering is a civilized arrangement that should suit all three of us. You said when you first told me about Rosa that you hoped we could be 'civilized.'"

"So what are you saying? That you'll turn a blind eye to my relationship with Rosa, if we carry on pretending to be a devoted couple, with Rosa's baby as the child we never had? Rosa isn't some surrogate mother you can forget about as soon as you've grabbed the baby. She certainly wouldn't be happy just being my mistress. She deserves better than that."

"Why is she so much more deserving than me? You break every promise you made to me and still expect to have everything – job, home, new wife and baby – while I'm left with nothing!"

"Hardly nothing. Don't be so melodramatic. I never thought you'd be like this. You've always been so...reserved."

"So you thought I'd placidly accept your sudden change of heart?"

"I thought you had, but after these crazy phone-calls..."

"Crazy? I'm not imagining things. I really have been betrayed by you and Rosa..."

"This is a pointless conversation. We had some good years together and I'm grateful for that, but you have to accept that our marriage is over. I love Rosa now. I'm committed to her..."

I put the phone down to stop this 'pointless conversation'. Word of the day 'pretending'. It sticks in my throat like a fish-bone. Does David really believe that I was only pretending to be devoted to him?

I sit there shaking until the numbers on the dial of the kitchen clock begin to register. I need to leave the house right now to be on time for my art class. I think that I can't do it, I can't face them, but it's too late to get in touch with everyone to cancel. They'll already be on their way to the hall and I still don't know what I'm going to ask them to paint. Then the bright packets of Panettone catch my eye. I grab one, and a cake knife, shove them into my bag of art stuff and set out.

Three of the class are already waiting when I arrive at the hall. I've been walking so fast that I hardly have the breath to apologize. Joanne tells me not to worry. They've been too busy chatting to notice the time. She and Candy cheerfully help me to set out the tables and chairs. Alice looks on because her back is 'having one of its cranky days'. The others arrive in a group. Janet's absence is noted but somebody knows that she's taking 'the old codger' to a hospital appointment. This provokes a spate of anecdotes about how long you have to wait in various hospital clinics until Alice cuts short Pam's moan about the Fracture Clinic by quietly asking what we are going to paint today.

Suddenly, everyone is looking at me. I have an impulse to strip off my clothes and tell them to paint me as a naked hag in the style of one of Goya's nightmare witches. Instead, I take the Panettone out of its box, hack out two slices and place one on either side of the cake.

"I thought we could use the first hour to paint this Panettone. Then we'll eat it at coffee-time and spend the last hour painting the box."

"Ooh lovely!"

They all seem delighted with this idea. I take up a little time suggesting techniques for portraying the different textures of the inside and outside of the Panettone but everyone is raring to start. I make sure that each person can see one of the slices as well as the cake, retune my radio to find some cheery music and leave them to it.

I hold my pencil over a sheet of paper for a long time without making a mark, as the disastrous conversation with David replays in my head. Am I crazy for squatting in the ruins of my life rather than rebuilding straight away? Rebuilding isn't as easy as David seems to think. I put down my pencil and pick out a brush to do a quick painting of one of the Panettone slices. The pale golden cake looks as if it is studded with gems; emerald angelica, citrine lemon-peel, ruby cherries, topaz apricots, amethyst raisins. I thin some Aureolin and try to immerse myself in the world of colour and texture, the world where I have the skills to stay in control.

During a pause while I am waiting for a yellow wash to dry, I glance round at the absorbed faces and busy hands and realize that I am in a room full of contented people. Even Jean appears serene as she dabs at her painting with a small piece of sponge.

I try to focus on my own work again. The cake still looks jewelled but now they seem the sort of glittery fakes you might find in a cheap Christmas cracker. That's what David is doing to my memories of our life together. Saying 'We had *some* good years' implies that we had many years which weren't so good. Did he really think that at the time, or is he creating false memories to justify his recent behaviour? Or, and this is worse, is he reassessing our relationship in the light of what he now has with Rosa? A relationship which lasted longer than Rosa has been alive.

I don't want to think about that so I ask, in what seems an unnaturally loud voice, if anyone needs my help. Nobody does. I go to the cloakroom and splash cold water on my puffy eyes. Then I return and pace around the room until the news headlines sputter out of the radio and I can finally make the coffee. People stretch and smile and push back their chairs. Someone says, "Is it time to cut the cake?" as if we were at a wedding.

I wield the sharp knife as though I was cutting into their complacent happiness. Chopping it into bits. Chop, chop, chop. They probably mistake my scowl for a puckering of concentration. Janet, who seems to be on a perpetual diet, shakes her head but everyone else accepts a slice. As I bite into mine, I remember that Panettone is never as good as it looks. The crumb is too dry and bits of candied fruit stick between my teeth.

The 'what are you doing for Christmas' conversations are starting already. Pam asks me about my plans. I say that I'll be having a quiet Christmas at home.

"Oh, I do envy you," burbles Pam, "it's our turn to go over to Henry's brother in Lincoln. The house will be packed – thirteen adults and eight children, if you count the babies. It will be bedlam."

With no David to fetch mother on Christmas morning, I'll have to go to her, but how will I carry everything? Do the buses run on Christmas Day? Is it too late to book Christmas Lunch somewhere and a taxi there and back? If I can afford that. It all seems desperately difficult. I'm sure David hasn't given a thought to organizing Christmas. He'll expect Rosa to do everything. Will they be visiting Celia? Or Rosa's family? Either scenario is hard to imagine. Perhaps they'll book into a luxurious hotel somewhere snowy. I always longed to do that over Christmas but we never did because of 'the mothers'. Once a man has severed one inconvenient tie, he may start cutting the rest. Has Celia thought of that?

I have to pay attention again when people start talking about the arrangements for the last class of term. Then I get them started on painting the Panettone box. Nearly everyone needs help to draw the basic shape in perspective, which makes the hour pass more quickly. Even so, I'm grateful when they start to pack up their paints, their chatter and their smiles. Just before she goes, Jean asks me if I'm all right. "Of course," I say.

I ought to go out and buy or gather specimens during my lunch hour, but I just sit there, soaking up the silence. So, when my flower-painting class arrives, there is nothing for them to paint. I pretend that this is carefully planned.

"This week, I want to test how much you've learned from observing the flowers and foliage we've painted this term."

"That sounds ominous," says Sarah.

"Ooh, I wouldn't have come if I'd known there was a test," chimes in Gina, whom I'm surprised to see back again. "You will take into account all the sessions I've missed?"

Evangeline pats her arm. "I'm sure you'll still do better than me, dear."

Other Sarah gives a very slight snort. She is the sort who always does well in tests. Rodney slides his spectacles up and down his nose in an anxious manner.

"So," I continue, "I want you to think back to something you enjoyed painting this term, or something that you were particularly pleased with when you finished it, and then draw or paint it again from memory."

There is a chorus of exclamations from the ladies. Rodney

asks if he can look over his paintings first.

"No peeking," I say firmly, "I want the image to come out your head."

"But I can't paint nothing!" Other Sarah sounds angry but looks frightened. "How can I be accurate when I've got nothing to copy?"

"Art isn't about accuracy," declares Gina, "it's the interpretation of what you see that counts. Isn't that right, Margaret?"

I think it is, but Gina isn't helping.

"You're such an accurate observer, Sarah, I'm sure that everything you've painted is stored in your memory. You just have to access it. Why don't you try recreating the yellow lily you did last week? Start with remembering the colours you used."

Other Sarah opens her meticulously arranged box of paints. Her fingers hover uncertainly over the yellows.

Rodney seems to have even more difficulty getting started. He keeps adjusting his glasses even though there is nothing in the centre of the table for him to focus on. I go to the cloakroom and take my time so that he can cheat by looking at his term's work if he wants to. When I come back, Rodney has covered a whole sheet with leaf outlines, Sarah is drawing the carnations from the garage bouquet, making them much prettier than they actually were, and Gina is laying down swirls of violent purple which are probably her boisterous interpretation of the delicate colchicum. Evangeline, no longer trammelled by the need to copy something real, is painting poppies that glow with all the warmth and colour of her sunny mind. They make me smile just to look at them.

Other Sarah has ignored my advice about starting with the right hue and is trying to draw a lily from memory. She keeps rubbing out bits of the outline and starting again until she suddenly drops her pencil. "I can't do this. I really can't!"

In her eyes I see the panic of someone forced into a situation that she can't control. Welcome to the club.

"Just relax," I suggest, "and let the line flow. Do the whole flower in one movement, without worrying about any bits you think are coming out wrong."

Other Sarah crumples up her sheet of expensive paper. "I know that won't work."

"Perhaps you could try something else," I say soothingly.

"No, I'm going home." She stands up and snaps her paint-box shut. "This is the wrong class for me. It always has been."

"For mercy's sake, this is just a bit of fun," puts in Gina, not helping again. "What does it matter if you're the worst at this exercise?"

Evangeline hastily tells Other Sarah that she is a wonderful artist. The others nod and look at me, willing me to defuse this tense situation but I don't want to. I want to let the fuse burn and watch somebody else's life blow up in their face.

"It's a pity you feel that way, Sarah, but perhaps you're right. I believe that they run some good botanical art classes at the Bristol School of Drawing. They'd probably be more in your comfort zone."

Other Sarah stares at me in shocked silence. She must have been expecting me to grovel a bit and then persuade her into staying. She would look very foolish if she just sat back down again now, so she has no choice but to carry on packing up. Evangeline is still trying to mend bridges.

"Do come back for our last week, even if it's just to keep us company."

Everyone but me makes encouraging noises. Other Sarah nods stiffly, murmurs that perhaps she will, and leaves.

"Well, what a kerfuffle!" exclaims Gina. "Some people just can't cope when things don't go their way."

No, some people can't.

December 3rd

I get up late. I didn't manage to sleep until about two in the morning, after a long walk to try to tire myself out so that I wouldn't just lie there going over and over the conversation with David. Word of the day is to be – self-promotion. My plan is to go out and promote myself and my work to local Graphic Design agencies. For sale – a reliable, fully-trained and experienced artist. Only one previous owner.

At least this is what I told Nina that I was going to do. After Other Sarah walked out, the spirits of my afternoon painters wilted like flowers left too long without water. When I got home, I tried to shake off my sour mood by checking my phones for any messages, just in case David had thought better of some of the things he said to me. There was nothing from David. Only yet another message from Nina. I listened to it and discovered that she was planning to come round that evening to check up on me since I hadn't responded to any of her other messages. I rang her, fended off an invitation to lunch the next day, on the grounds that I would be busy job-hunting, but had to agree to coffee at the Arnolfini Gallery on Friday.

Before she rang off, I asked, "Do you think I'm reserved?"

"Well, you're not a gushy person. Neither am I, which is probably why we get along."

I thought it was one of the reasons David and I got along too.

I don't bother with breakfast, even though skipping breakfast is high on my mother's 'things never to do' list, along with swimming immediately after a meal and wearing too much make-up. Instead, I go to the glass-house in order to make a final choice of works for my portfolio. I put in copies of half a dozen greetings cards based on my water-colours and several recent drawings. Is it all too flowery and feminine? I dig out some poster designs I did for local societies and events. I'm particularly proud of one I produced for a cat show, with black and white felines playing with punctuation marks between the rows of lettering. I put in several copies of this poster. How about the Halloween Party invitation with cupcakes decorated with spiders and miniature skulls? Does that count as edgy? Probably not. I include it anyway, along with a couple of drawings that look like abstracts but are based on lichen shapes, and one of the insect studies I made on the roundabout. I tie up the portfolio and get ready to leave the house.

I am at the door with my coat on before I remember that I haven't got the list of addresses I scribbled down from the websites of half a dozen Graphic Design firms. I go into the drawing room to find it and notice a man in the street who seems to be taking a photo of my house with his mobile phone. I wait a minute before opening the front door, hoping that he will have gone away, but he is standing at the bottom of our steps looking delighted to see me.

"Mrs Claridge? So glad I've caught you."

The young man is wearing an ill-fitting pinstripe suit with a ghastly purple shirt but I find myself responding to the warmth of his smile.

"Did you know that your chimneys need repointing?" He beckons me down the steps. "And some of the front sashes are in a bad way."

"If you're selling double-glazing..."

"No, no, I'm Barty Hutch." I must be looking blank because he adds, "Your ex asked us to pop over and do a quick valuation. I did leave a message."

"I've been very busy, and I'm just going out..."

"It'll only take a minute or two. Ten tops. It's great to see a period property with potential. We've got lots of clients wanting to do up houses in this location."

I thought my house was already done up. We had been meaning to get all the sash-windows repainted this summer but I never got around to organizing it. Now it will have to wait until spring, or until I can afford to pay for the work. I suddenly picture my home getting shabbier and shabbier until it turns into a 'little old lady house'. The kind with yellowed lace curtains at the windows, damp patches in the stucco, flaking paintwork and missing roof-tiles. The kind that has developers circling like sharks, waiting for the executor sale.

I brandish my portfolio at him. "I'm sorry. I have business appointments today. You'll have to come back another time."

"If you lent me the keys, I could put them back through the letter-box when I'm done."

"Certainly not, I don't know you from Adam."

"Adam who?"

He seems genuinely baffled. Am I talking like a little old lady already?

"Another time," I say firmly.

We agree on 12.45 the following day, when I may or may not be back from having coffee with Nina. This will give me time to ring Mrs Patel. As Barty doesn't move, I step around him and set off for the bus-stop. When I glance back, it makes me shudder to see him running his hands along my iron railings. I feel as if I'm being groped.

The right bus comes along straight away, which seems a good omen. I push my way to the roomy back seat because my portfolio is wider than I am. This is like being a student again. Deirdre and I used to visit publishers and print-shops and likely local businesses together, trying to get commissions for artwork. As soon as we were in the door, she would come out with a spiel about how this was their big opportunity to buy our work before we were famous. Combined with a suggestive smile and a low cut blouse, it was a winning approach. I wonder if Deirdre is still stuck in the awful B&B or if she has already inserted herself into the life of some new man. It is mean of me to think of Deirdre as an opportunist. For all her moaning, she's much better at coping with change than I am. Off with the old love and on with the new.

My destination is a Victorian factory complex, now converted into workshops, studios, and office space for architects and media companies. Two of the firms on my list hang out here. When the place first opened I toyed with hiring a studio in this complex. I imagined myself going to work each morning, as if I had a real job, having stimulating conversations with new creative friends in the organic coffee shop, and getting my work seen by the gallery owners who would be attracted to this artistic hub.

When I tentatively mentioned the idea to David, who would probably end up paying the rent, he said, "But I thought you loved working in the glass-house." "I do, except when it's very cold. I just feel a bit isolated there sometimes..." I found it hard to explain why the privacy and quiet that I used to value so much no longer seemed quite as desirable. Was I already sensing that our home was no longer a protected place where both of us would always be happy and secure? David bought me a new paraffin heater for the glass-house and I dropped the idea of renting a studio.

I study the board at the entrance to 'The Cannery' and see that 'Logic-Tree Design' are just across the main courtyard. Their door is painted an assertive viridian with their leafless tree logo in the centre. There seems to be no handle. I have to press a button on an intercom and beg to be let in. There is a crackle and a tinny voice answers before I'm ready with what to say.

"Er...hello, my name's Meg...Peg Claridge. I'm a freelance artist. I wanted to show you some of my designs..."

"Do you have an appointment?"

"No, I hoped someone might take a quick look at my portfolio. A lot of my work has featured on..."

"All our designs are done in-house and the Art Director doesn't see anyone without an appointment."

"Then perhaps you could arrange a time for me to..."

I realize that the crackling has stopped. I've been cut off.

I feel like pounding on the door but I just slip one of my business cards under it and retreat to the café. It turns out to be vegan as well as organic, so I order a very expensive soya latte which tastes subtly off. I spread my business cards out on the old cable-drum that serves as a table, as though I was doing a Tarot reading. I designed the cards, which describe me as Margaret Claridge, Painter and Illustrator, but David gave me the antique silver case I keep them in. Should I give away all his presents, as I gave away all my clothes? Or sell them.

I suppose I should shake off his name as well and become

Margaret Rice again, but I've disliked my surname ever since it earned me the nickname of 'Pudding' at school. At a school reunion, I was greeted with cries of 'Hello, Pudding, you haven't changed a bit!" I wanted to believe that I'd changed a great deal from the shy schoolgirl they remembered; that I was too confident and successful ever to be that girl again. I never went to another reunion.

My business card is decorated with a drawing of a half-open winter iris which I was rather proud of at the time. I thought it captured the exact moment when an unpromising bud unfurls into unexpected beauty. A beauty that lasts about two days in the average English winter. Why did I choose something so transient as my symbol? Did I always know that my artistic moment in the sun was going to be brief? I glance around at the other people perching on metal stools in the café. They are all at least twenty years younger than me and hunched over electronic devices of one sort or another. Dressing in black does help me to blend in but I can't imagine striking up friendships in here.

I gather up my cards, abandon my sour coffee, and make my way to the far end of the complex to find a company called Flow! I think the name makes them sound like something in sanitation, but according to their website they offer 'new-wave graphic design'. I find myself facing another locked door with a baffling key-pad entry system. Why is every office now as hard to get into as a high-security prison? What are they afraid of? This door has a glass panel through which I can see two men coming down the corridor. As they open the door from the inside, I pretend to be having difficulty holding on to my handbag and portfolio and pressing the keypad at the same time. The first man ignores me, "Charlie, we have to get this sorted a.s.p. or the client may bolt..." but the second man pauses and says, "Need a hand?"

I give him my best daffy smile, "If you could just...Oh, thank you."

He is holding the door open for me. I slip through and set off along the corridor, trying to look as if I know where I'm going.

I find 'Flow!' on the top floor. They occupy the entire roof-space of one side of the Cannery. A series of huge sky-lights bathe the desks and drawing tables in cool north light. There is a computer at every 'work-station' but this still looks like a place where actual artwork is produced. I itch to have a good look around but my way is barred by a thin black desk that curves like a snake. Behind it sits a girl with striped hair admiring the patterns on her own nails.

"Hello?" I say tentatively.

She stops wiggling her fingers, looks up from the sparkly swirls, and scowls. "I didn't buzz you in."

"Charlie let me in." I hope she'll assume that this means I know Charlie. "I've brought my portfolio..."

"All work should be submitted on line."

She chants it like a mantra. I'm obviously about as welcome as a gypsy selling white heather.

"I'm sorry. I didn't realize, but as I'm here, perhaps someone could just..."

"Everyone's busy," the receptionist says, without looking behind her.

As far as I can see most of the people in the office are gathered around a fancy-looking coffee machine. I take out one of my cards. "Perhaps you could give this to whoever is in charge of commissioning artwork?"

She looks at my business card as if I had dropped a slug on her desk.

"He's out. You can email him. The submissions address is on our website."

I stubbornly unzip my portfolio and take out a copy of my cat-show poster. "Perhaps you could give him this with my card when he gets back?"

She glances at the poster and says, "Sweet."

It sounds like a compliment but I know in my heart that she means it dismissively. Flow! doesn't do sweet.

"Thank you so much," I say and retreat.

I make my way to the Harbourside path. One of the new developments I can see in the distance is Porto but I don't go in that direction. I walk towards the city centre, fighting against the icy winds coming in off the estuary. My next stop is Welsh Back. I find the office block I'm looking for and speak into their entry-phone. I hear myself pleading to be let in and the polite but negative response....No I can't do this any more. I can't write down the full list of my humiliations.

I return home, lugging my unwanted portfolio. I can almost see Barty's sticky finger-marks on my front door. I ring Mrs Patel and am told that she is with a client. I leave a message asking if I have to let David's estate agent into my house. She returns my call after half an hour. I remember her bill and don't argue when she says that the court will expect me to be co-operative about the valuation of marital assets.

"If you are unhappy with this agent's valuation you can ask another estate agent to act on your behalf."

"Just to be clear, do I have the right to refuse to let this man in?"

"You do, but if you take that course of action, the court might regard you as guilty of defective disclosure and order a valuation."

"I understand," I say and ring off.

I understand that somehow once again I am the defective one.

I get through the evening. I make myself some soup. I dip into some of my favourite poetry anthologies. I go for a walk. I take a bath and wash my hair. Then I lie in bed listening out for signs of life in the houses on either side. Derek and Susan in Number 6 have always been quiet, though I can sometimes hear their yappy little dog. Susan seems to be deliberately avoiding me, as if being abandoned by your husband was a contagious disease which she might catch if she gets too near me. Number 10 is rented out to a shifting number of young professionals. "At least they're not students" David used to say. I can faintly hear rock music coming from one of the bedrooms. I used to regard any noise from the neighbours as an intrusion into my private space. Now I welcome it as proof that the entire population of Bristol hasn't left me too.

December 4th

Word of the day – scathed. If there is such a word. I'm certainly not unscathed by David's behaviour, so I must be scathed. I imagine a scathe as some kind of sharpened comb which has left permanent marks on every layer of my skin. When we were first married, David liked to let down my hair and comb it before... No, don't think about that.

I get up and get dressed, although this seems increasingly pointless. I take a bus to the bottom of Park Street and then walk along Canon's Road towards the restaurant that was going to be my first choice for celebrating our wedding anniversary. The whole damn city is imprinted with memories of my married life.

I cross the Floating Harbour at the Horned Bridge, which leads to a spit of land where once-useful warehouses have been converted into architects' offices and art galleries. As I reach the twist in the centre of the bridge I pause to admire the dramatic curves of the horn-shaped counterweights. Then I spot David about to step onto the far end of the bridge and my heart gives a joyous leap, as it always does when I see him unexpectedly. David sees me, I'm sure he does. He stops in mid-stride and turns on his heel as though he'd suddenly realized that he was going the wrong way. As David walks rapidly back towards Queen Square, I cling to the side of the bridge as if it was rocking.

"Are you all right, my lover?"

A wrinkle-faced man is staring at me with concern. Older Bristolians still use this traditional form of address, even though it is officially forbidden to Council staff. Too much like sexual harassment apparently. I don't feel harassed by this kindly pensioner.

"Someone just walked over my grave."

Why did I say that? The old man just nods understandingly. "Gives you the shudders that can."

I let him take my arm until we are across the bridge. He only lets me go when I assure him that I am meeting a friend inside The Arnolfini. The sullen brown building looms over us.

"Ar, the weirdie place," he says. "I hear they charge something awful for a cup o' tea."

"I'm afraid they do."

The Arnolfini claims to be 'one of Europe's leading centres for the contemporary arts' but 'the weirdie place' is a more accurate description. I thank the old man and he walks away briskly, as if helping me had given his day a new sense of purpose.

I pause in the lobby to see what's going on in the building because if I don't stop thinking about David being repelled by the mere sight of me, my heart may burst in my chest. I concentrate on my surroundings. I am a contemporary artist because I am still alive but of course that isn't what The Arnolfini means by contemporary. The main exhibition seems to consist of photographs of naked women holding joints of meat, accompanied by a noisy video of cattle being butchered in a slaughter-house. There is an excellent art bookshop off the lobby. I want to numb my thoughts by reading the title on every spine or flicking through the pages of the fattest book on each shelf. Instead, I go straight to the café-bar to find Nina.

She is sitting at a table that is littered with empty glasses and half-drunk cups of coffee. Has she been meeting people here all morning? Nina stands up when she sees me coming. "Hello, sorry about the mess. We were having a breakfast meeting about the Art-Science Link project and it rather over-ran. Are you all right, Meg? You're looking very pale."

"I'm...a bit tired."

"Hmm, perhaps it's just that I'm not used to seeing you wearing black. What can I get you? The Fairtrade double espresso they make here would perk up the dead."

I nod and she strides off to the counter.

This is another pseudo-industrial café, perhaps so that the artists who exhibit here can think of themselves as 'makers', though making things with their own hands is the last thing most of them seem to do. The coffered concrete ceiling seems to be pressing down on me and the black metal lamps are swinging too low. Above the chatter of people at nearby tables I can faintly hear the lowing of distressed cattle. At least it isn't Christmassy.

When Nina returns with a languid young waiter, who collects up the soiled cups and glasses with obvious distaste, I say, "I don't know how the people who work here cope with listening to a soundtrack like that all day."

"Not all of them do. Apparently one of the gallery stewards is off with 'stress' and is talking of suing for psychological trauma. There's art with impact for you."

Another waiter soon arrives with my espresso and a ring doughnut big enough to use as a bracelet.

"Go on Meg, you need feeding up."

I take a sip of the bitter coffee and ask, "So, what is this Art-Science thing?"

She tells me. Apparently it involves artists designing robots and a team of research students in the university's Robotics Department building them.

"Well, hopefully. Some of the designs may have to stay on paper if they're impossible to construct."

"So, is that what I should be painting? Machines not flowers?"

"Only if machines genuinely inspire you. Trying to be modish never works, or at least, not in the long run. You know that."

"I thought I did, but painting what I love doesn't seem to be the way to get design work."

I finish my espresso in one defiant gulp and tell Nina about my abortive visits to the local graphic design firms. I aim for a tone of resigned amusement but what seems to come out are squawks of indignation.

"...and when I tried the one just down the quay from here, they glanced at my work and suggested I try wallpaper design."

"That may not be a bad idea, floral and figurative wallpapers seem to be in fashion again."

I am not to be reasoned out of being aggrieved. "And at Dot-Dash-Dot they treated me as if I was still painting on cave walls because I didn't know what Joomla was. They didn't like it when I told them that the only 'Content Management System' I use is my brain."

"You really should try drawing on a Tablet, Meg. You might even enjoy it. I believe they do evening courses at the Art College..."

Can I bear to regress from teacher to pupil? I tear my doughnut into manageable chunks while Nina gives me her full

'Don't be such a technophobe' lecture. I try to catch a waiter's eye to get more coffee but they always seem to be looking the other way. When she notices me yawning, Nina effortlessly summons a waiter and orders two more espressos.

"Was it a very bad night? Perhaps you should ask your doctor about sleeping pills..."

"No, I've tried those in the past and they just made me feel as if my head was full of wet sand. I'd rather walk myself tired."

"I don't like to think of you walking about late at night all by yourself – though I suppose Clifton should be safe enough."

"Oh, it is." I don't tell her where I actually went last night. "There are plenty of people about."

"It's the people I'm worried about. You're not likely to be attacked by the architecture."

"Actually I did nearly walk into a lamp-post the other night when I was distracted by a wall-full of new graffiti."

"There isn't a Banksy in your area is there?"

"No, we're far too bourgeois to be honoured by Banksy. It was just the usual slogans and standard urban images produced with spray paint and bought stencils."

Nina sighs. "The street-art equivalent of junk-food."

"You should commission me to do some slow street-art. Clifton could do with a better class of vandal."

Nina takes this as a joke but her laughter seems a little forced. I know that she has always felt relaxed with me because, unlike most of the artists she meets, I never badgered her for a grant or introductions to gallery owners. Now I've started asking her for favours, the relationship is bound to change. It strikes me that Nina hasn't bothered to ask me if I got onto the short-list for the gallery job.

I try to sound casual as I say, "I haven't heard back from the New Bath Gallery."

"It was a bit of a long-shot Meg. Don't take it as a reflection on you as an artist. They're probably looking for someone with more management experience. "

"After the big rejection, it's hard not to take everything personally."

"The big...Oh, you mean David. Meg, don't think of it as a rejection, you probably just grew apart..."

"I didn't! I was growing closer and closer to him."

I suddenly see myself as a creeper clinging to David's trunk; the sort of creeper that someone eventually uses a chainsaw on to save the tree. Rosa as a chainsaw, all teeth and roar.

"You don't understand," I hear myself bleating, "You're so competent at everything. Stop shaking your head. You are, even the waiters can tell. You don't know what it's like to be made to feel unwanted and useless."

I've spoken louder than I intended to and heads turn at nearby tables to look at the unwanted woman.

"Meg, you mustn't feel that way," whispers Nina. "You have friends and family who love you. How could you be unwanted or useless when you have a mother who needs you so much?"

How? Because Aija seems to be doing a better job of caring for mother than I can. When I don't answer, Nina goes on, "You're an intelligent, creative person with so much to offer. I know life seems bleak at the moment but I'm willing to bet that in a few years time you will have done things, achieved things, that would never have happened if you were still safely married to David."

So, we are back to divorce as a wonderful opportunity for

self-improvement. Would people say this kind of thing to me if I had lost David in a car-crash instead of to the human chainsaw?

I look at my watch. "I expect you're right. I have to go now because David's estate agent is coming to value my house this morning. If I don't let him in I shall be deemed uncooperative, rather like those cattle making such an unseemly fuss in the slaughter-house."

"Meg!"

"Just joking. Thanks for the coffee."

"You haven't even eaten your doughnut."

I tip the bits into my handbag. "I'll share it with the seagulls on my walk back."

I hate seagulls. They are greed and aggression covered in feathers; feathers that smell of rotting fish. I try to hit one with each stodgy piece of doughnut but my aim isn't good enough. I am late for my appointment with Barty but he is still sitting on my front-steps when I get home, chattering into his mobile. His shirt today is candy-floss pink. He gives me a cheery wave of acknowledgement but keeps on talking. Normally I would try not to listen to somebody else's phone-call but I don't have much choice as he is blocking my way to my own front door. Barty seems to be trying to get a vendor to accept a 'lowish' offer on their house.

"I wouldn't call it an insulting offer. He's a genuine cash-in-hand guy, keen to buy places he can carve up into student Lets. What? But you wouldn't be there to see it, would you?"

I wonder if I can step over him to unlock the door.

"OK, you might get more if you hung on but hey – you might not. Viewer feedback hasn't been good. There is the dog problem..."

"Excuse me." I go up another step so that I'm towering over him.

"Oh, right...gotta go. Just give it a think through and we'll talk later."

As he gets up, I squeeze past and use my key. I'm not quick enough to stop Barty following me inside. He hands me a copy of Malling and Hutch's terms and conditions as soon as he's in the hall.

"You do realize that I haven't agreed to sell the house?"

"Sure, your ex just..."

"He's not my ex. We're still married."

Even as I say it, I believe for the first time that he is my ex; that the man who turned his back on me at the Horned Bridge is never coming home.

"Right, got you. Are you OK, Mrs Claridge?"

"Let's get this over with." I take off the hideous poncho and hang it up. "This is the cloakroom."

"Hang on a tick," Barty gets out some kind of miniature recorder and presses a button. "No 8 Amelia Street, continued. Entrance hall with recessed cupboard."

Vincent trots into the hall to greet me and then flees in panic when he realizes there is a strange man beside me. Barty says, "Hello kitty," and sniffs the air. Oh God, does the house smell of cat pee? Vincent does spray on the furniture when he's feeling nervous and I've probably stopped noticing. I guess that Barty is already knocking a few thousand off his valuation because of the 'cat problem'.

"The drawing room is this way."

I mentally kick myself for using this term. Barty won't understand the joke and will think I'm just being pretentious.

I've always loved this room. To me this, and not the kitchen, is the heart of the house because it is...was the place that David and I spent the best of our time together. The time when we really talked and later the time when we stopped talking, which I mistook for the silence of mutual contentment.

I have made no effort to tidy up the house because that would be an admission that I was planning to sell. Now, as I notice Barty noticing the grimy window-panes, the sooty cobwebs in the corners of the room, all the cat hair clinging to the sofa, the half-drunk mug of coffee left on a table and the screwed up balls of paper – failed sketches turned into cat-toys – on the floor, I wish that I had. What I think of as charmingly Bohemian, he probably sees as squalor.

"Nice high ceiling," says Barty, "and plenty of light. That'll tick boxes." He presses a button and starts recording again. "Living room with original fireplace and stripped floor-boards..."

"Will you please stop that! You're meant to be doing a quick valuation, not drawing up For Sale particulars."

Barty's face crumples as if I'd snatched a sweet away from him. "I'm only trying to save time in case you do decide to put the house on the market. Once the basics are in here," he pats the recorder. "I can get your details onto Rightmove in a flash."

"I am not moving!"

Barty flinches. Perhaps I am almost shouting. I try to speak more calmly. "I'll show you the dining room." "Don't see many of those nowadays," says Barty as if sitting down at a table to eat was a quaint old custom he'd only encountered in the kind of Period Dramas they show on Sunday night television. As he stares at the oxblood-red walls and the dusty mahogany table, the dining room seems redundant to me too. I realize that apart from the day I did sketches for my painting of this room, I haven't been in here since David left.

"You could could call it a study," I suggest.

I take Barty down to the kitchen, where I know that Vincent will have taken refuge. He is sitting in the sink, licking one of last night's unwashed pans. As I open the back door and bundle Vincent out, Theo strolls in.

"More cats," sighs Barty.

"He's just a visitor."

Barty prods at the uneven flagstones with the tip of one of his shiny shoes and asks if there is an Aga. When I say no, I realize that my home has failed yet another desirability test. Barty seems unimpressed by the walk-in larder and the laundry room but perks up a bit at David's coal-hole cum wine cellar. When I offer to show him around my garden, Barty just sticks his head out of the back door. "Courtyard garden and...is that a home-office?"

"It's my studio," I say. "I'm a painter."

"Oh, right, but we could call it a home-office if there's a broadband connection..."

He looks sad again when I tell him there isn't.

We go back up to the hall. I know that estate agents must have to deal with divorcing couples all the time but I still don't want to watch him noting the tell-tale signs of David's absence from what Barty will no doubt call the 'master bedroom'. I send him to look at the upper floors by himself and distract myself by picking up the post which arrived while I was out. This turns out to include my first Christmas card of the year. It's from Beth, an old art school friend. Inside she has scrawled in big letters 'Merry Xmas to Meg and David'. Should I tear the card in two and send David his half?

I can hear faint muttering from upstairs. Either Barty has gone back to using his recorder or he's talking to another client on his phone. The second envelope is obviously from a charity appealing for donations, so I put it straight in the bin. The third letter is last month's bill from the company who supply mother's carer and it is for a lot more than I was expecting. A lot more than I can now afford. How many hours has Aija been working? I shall have to have words with mother about this when I go over to see her tomorrow. The fourth and fifth envelopes are subscription renewal reminders. Why does everything seem to be about money?

Just for a split-second, the sound of footsteps coming down the stairs makes me think that David is in the house, but of course it's only Barty.

"I've had a good look-see. Pity there's no en-suite but you could convert that little bedroom into a wet-room." He gives me what he calls a 'ball-park figure' which is rather less than I was expecting and promises to email an official valuation.

"You do have an email address?"

He probably doesn't mean to make me feel so past my use-by date.

When Barty has gone, I fasten the chain across the door as if that will give me back my privacy. I feel as if my home has been opened up like a doll's house for the curious to peer in at my life. Do I really want to go on living here? Is it possible to make this into my house rather than our house? Perhaps Nina was right all along and I should be planning to make a new start somewhere. I think I could cope with moving if I'm not forced to sell up to David and Rosa – that would be like the house itself betraying me for a younger and more attractive owner. I probably need another expensive chat with Mrs Patel.

I go out to my despised studio because at least that is undoubtedly my space. David never came in here unless he was looking for me. I grab some sketch paper and charcoal. Drawing is what I do. If I focus on that, everything else will be blotted out.

For a while, everything is. I let my hand choose what to draw, one line at a time. The light starts to fade but I don't pause to turn on a lamp. I'm soon shivering with cold and grubby with charcoal but I keep making strong downward strokes, bold upward curves and smaller patterns executed with dashes and jabs. I finally step back to look at my work. They are not just patterns, they are leaves.

I realize what it is that I have been drawing over and over again. A mound of leaves – arched over ferns and branches – a scattering of wild flowers. Wasn't this how I imagined Martin Jenkins burying his wife in the woods? He still hasn't been sentenced. Presumably the judge is waiting for some psychiatrist's official report. I picture Martin sitting as silently as he did in court, refusing to co-operate with the picking and prying into his thoughts and feelings. Will he be blamed for 'defective disclosure' too? I consider sending him a letter of sympathy but I don't want to become one of those pathetic women who inject some melodrama into their dreary lives by writing love letters to famous murderers. Do murderesses attract admirers too? Probably only the young and attractive ones. After what happened this morning I almost believe that I

Page torn out here.

December 5th

On the way to my mother's, I look down from the top-deck of the bus and think about how Park Street changes its character after dark. By day, it seems dominated by high-end shops and by cafés plastered with layers of posters for student activities. People of all ages are moving purposefully up and down the pavements, shopping for clothes or books, visiting the museum or heading for the grandiose building that houses the University administration. Last night it was the garishly lit bars and basement night-clubs that I noticed and the youngsters swanking in or spilling out of them.

I hadn't meant go on another late-night walk. After coming in from the glass-house, I tried to read myself tired with a stack of poetry books. I thought I could rely on Edward Thomas to soothe me with delicate evocations of ash groves, bright clouds and green roads. Then I happened on his chilling poem to his wife Helen -

'If I could choose
Freely in that great treasure-house
Anything from any shelf,
I would give you back yourself,
And power to discriminate what you want
And want it not too late.'

I have been given back myself by David. Though I still have the power to discriminate, it seems to be too late for almost everything I want.

So, I shoved my largest size brushes and palette knives and the sort of poster paints that will cover anything into my art bag and went out. The night was dry but not yet frosty. My plan was to replace ugly graffiti on the walls of Clifton with my signature flowers. It wasn't as easy as I expected to find a quiet spot to work in.

At one in the morning there were still couples returning in various degrees of drunkenness from evenings out and individuals trying to tire out over-active dogs or, in one case, a colicky baby. The harassed father, whom I vaguely remembered meeting with his much younger wife at a neighbour's party, was so desperate for adult company that he stopped to say hello. Talking above the wails, he told me all about his son's bedtime routine and then added, "You're out late."

"I'm...looking for one of my cats who hasn't come home."

"Ah, cats. I wish we'd had cats instead of children."

I noted the protective way he was holding his son. "No you don't. Well, I better keep looking for Theo..."

"Right, but you and..."

"David."

"Yes, you and David must come round some time."

I told him that would be nice.

Around the next corner, I stopped calling for Theo and eyed an end-wall disfigured by a few black scrawls. I paused under a street lamp and fumbled inside my art bag. Even as my fingers closed on a tube of yellow paint, I knew I couldn't do it. Not so close to home, not in the familiar places where I was respectable Margaret Claridge who lives in that nice house in Amelia Street. I needed to be in the city centre, where nobody knew me and I could be anybody I chose. So, I let myself be caught up in the tide of people flowing towards Park Street.

When I got half-way down the hill, I nearly turned back.

The Friday-night crowd on the pavement reminded me of a Brueghel painting, their alcohol-fuelled jollity tinged with cruelty and incipient violence. Brueghel the Elder who made peasant revels and the Massacre of the Innocents look much the same. Forced to push my way through groups of revellers, I was afraid of being mugged or groped until I remembered that one of my sharpest kitchen knives was still at the bottom of my art bag. When a drunken lout nearly jostled me into the road, I thought about how surprised he'd be if I whipped out my serrated knife and stuck it into the gap where his t-shirt failed to meet his low-slung jeans. I wondered how far the knife would go in before it struck bone. I've always been a better carver than David but of course you have to let the man do it at dinner parties.

Aloud I think I said, "I'm more dangerous than you because I don't care what happens to me."

The drunk gave me a bleary look, muttered, "Sorry, love," and got out of my way.

The pavement was still like an assault-course. I had to keep pushing through the surprisingly patient queues of youngsters trying to get into the more popular nightclubs and stepping over soggy boxes of half-eaten pizzas and burgers. Blasts of music bludgeoned my ears every time a nightclub door was opened by a bouncer and the bars all favoured the kind of electric blue light used to repel flies in butchers' shops.

The steps down to dark, dank Frog Lane seemed like an escape route. I paused to glance across the road bridge to the building whose side-wall was adorned by the city's most famous Banksy mural. It shows a man and woman framed by a window while a naked man – presumably the woman's lover – hangs by his fingertips from the windowsill. Like the rest of Bristol I used to be amused by the suspicious husband's failure to notice the lover under his nose. Now I imagined myself standing with David by the open window, oblivious to a naked Rosa hanging there. I made myself go down the steps.

Some of the nightclubs had basement back entrances on Frog Lane where a few smokers lurked among the rubbish bins. None of them took any notice of me and beneath the road bridge I found the perfect pocket of urban ugliness for me to work in. Dimly lit, graffiti spattered, smelling of urine and ankle-deep in litter; just the kind of place I would normally avoid. I set down my bag on the pavement. The irregular sandstone blocks of the underside of the bridge don't provide a smooth enough surface to appeal to most street-artists so the graffiti was nothing but names, slogans and swearwords. I got out some turps and wiped over a particularly offensive section of wall.

Fumbling amongst my tubes of quick-drying acrylic paint, I realised that I should have brought a torch, preferably the sort you wear on a headband to keep your hands free. Eventually I managed to squeeze thick pools of red, yellow and blue onto the palette I was holding in my left hand. I knew that I would have to work fast and confidently with the palette-knife I was clutching in my right hand. I stood there imagining a perfect striped tulip growing in that squalid place. The street-noise above me seemed to get further and further away.

When I knew that the paint would start hardening if I didn't act, I jabbed the blade of the knife into the yellow and flung it at the wall as if I was flinging it at Rosa. I smiled as I imagined her immaculate black and white courtroom outfit spattered with yellow paint. Would the Jenkins jury have listened to her then?

The paint didn't cling evenly but I kept on adding layers of yellow until I had almost covered one block with an open flower-shape. The occasional car rumbled past, blinding me for a moment with their headlights, but they seemed to exist in a different world. I was adding streaks of scarlet to yellow petals when I became aware of a faint scuffing sound just behind me. I turned my head. A young black man was watching me. He was wearing a hoody and there was a feral quality about him that made my skin prickle. I had a few seconds to think that I was about to be mugged before I saw the white flash of his smile and a hand moving in what seemed to be a gesture of approval. Then he melted back into the shadows.

I carried on working, adding the outline of a leaf. Then I moved on to another block, painting an orange lilyform tulip with red-tipped petals. I was mixing a brighter green for the stem when I heard footsteps entering the tunnel. It was two policemen and unfortunately neither of them was art-loving Jack. This duo weren't looking in the mood for art appreciation but I could see their bodies relax as they got close enough to notice that I wasn't some teenage hooligan. One muttered, "Everyone thinks they're Banksy now." The other demanded to know what I was doing.

"I am trying to make this place less ugly."

"You do realize that what you're doing is a criminal offence?"

"Surely not."

If they confiscated my bag of paints, they would find the carving knife. I wondered if that meant that I would automatically go to prison. I ought to have been worried, but somehow I wasn't.

"What's your name."

"Peg," I said.

"Peg what?"

He got out his notebook to take down my details but then the radio he was wearing in a kind of holster crackled into life. I overheard the message about a disturbance in one of the bars. The sour-faced policeman closed his notebook.

"Go home. If you're still here when we get back, I'll book you for criminal damage."

I opened my mouth to ask how painting flowers over swearwords could possibly be criminal or damage, but thought better of it. I watched them race up the steps towards Park Street and then painted in a soldier-straight leaf for my tulip while the shuddering wail of police sirens came nearer and nearer. Then I scrawled 'Beauty is Truth' in large red letters.

I considered throwing the carving knife away before I left the underpass but you never knew who might pick it up. So I just packed up my paints, went back up the steps, and crossed to the opposite side of the street to avoid the police vans clustered outside one of the nightclubs. As I walked back up the hill, it was obvious that the party-atmosphere had soured. Huddles of smokers were coughing and shivering, rejected night-clubbers were arguing with bored-looking bouncers and several couples were having screaming rows in the street.

This time I had to step over the legs of prostrate drinkers, some of them giggling, some semi-conscious. In the distance, I glimpsed a girl who, from the back at least, looked very like Aija. She was arm in arm with two men. I thought of trying to catch up with her but two other figures in uniform were coming towards me. I was afraid they were more police, who might question the streaks of paint on my hands and clothes if I drew attention to myself by running. As they came closer, their yellow tabards identified them as Street Pastors. Instead of handing out tracts about the dangers of demon-drink this pair were offering bottled water to exhausted dancers and giving flip-flops to girls too drunk to walk home in their high-heels.

"Is it like this every Friday night?" I asked one of the pastors, an apple-cheeked woman of about my own age.

She looked me up and down, obviously checking for signs of drunkenness, before saying cheerily, "Unless it's raining heavily or snowing. Then we get a night off. "

"You want to be getting home," put in her stocky male companion, "before things turn nasty."

I thought they already had.

A little further up the road an orange street-light was shining directly onto a single red stiletto shoe abandoned in the middle of a pool of vomit. If you could ignore the stench, the colours were extraordinarily beautiful. I did a quick sketch before making my way home. It was on the drawing room mantelpiece this morning, so I know I didn't dream the whole episode.

The bus carries me away from my night-walk territory and I get to my mother's around 11o'clock. I have brought a flimsy cardboard box containing two chocolate éclairs from the best bakery in Clifton. I have had to keep it carefully upright throughout the bus journey and the walk to mother's housing complex. Mother usually leaves her front door open when she knows I'm coming. Today, when I push on the door I find that it is locked. Has she fallen again? Aija should have been here earlier but something might have happened since then. My heart does a flip, as I picture mother helpless on her bedroom floor or even...

I try to tuck the cake-box under my arm without squashing it, while I find mother's door-key on my ring. I could use my spare key every time I come, but we have an unspoken agreement that it is only for emergencies. That way, mother can keep her privacy. I turn the key and push open the door, calling out, 'Mother, it's me."

I find Aija standing in my way. Her skimpy clothes and slightly smeared make-up suggest that she has come straight from the nightclubs of Park Street.

"It is the daughter," she announces.

I stupidly state the obvious. "You're still here."

"I stay to keep the mother company until you are coming."

"Hello, dear," says my mother from her chair, "I was expecting you a little earlier."

"I stopped on the way to get you some of those éclairs you particularly like."

"How nice. Melody brought me some cake too."

Aija snatches the box from me. "I make the coffee."

"There is no need for you to stay, now that I've arrived."

"Is no trouble," says Aija and disappears into the kitchenette.

"She's such a dear," murmurs mother.

I know exactly how dear Aija is. I have the bill in my handbag.

I kiss my mother, take off my raincoat and agree that I should have worn something warmer. Then I say that I'm going to help Aija in the kitchen. I find her dumping my expensive éclairs on to a plate. I keep my voice low.

"Aija, you've been doing more hours here than I arranged

with the agency."

"This is OK. Your mother is very nice lady, so I do extra."

"No, it isn't OK," I whisper. "My brother and I agreed to pay a certain sum each month for mother's care but the bill is nearly double that."

Aija slams a saucer on to the tray she has got out. "So, so, you do not want to look after the mother and you do not want to pay. British daughters are cold like..." Her English seems to fail her, but only for a moment. "Cold like fish."

"If Latvian daughters are so wonderful," I hiss, "why are you living in a different country from your own mother?"

"Because I am not rich lady like you! I have to work, work, to send money to my family."

"Meg? Is everything all right?"

The quaver in my mother's voice instantly makes me feel guilty. She may not have been able to hear exactly what Aija and I were saying but she knows that we are quarrelling.

"Everything is fine," I say as I come out of the kitchen and sit down close to mother. I jump slightly when she asks what I've been doing with myself.

"Painting tulips."

"At this time of year."

"I don't need the real thing to paint them any more. I can see them in my mind's eye."

"You were like that as a child too, living in your head and not noticing what was going on around you."

Was I?

Aija emerges with the tray.

"Coffee," she declares, "with special honey cake from my mother's recipe...and the bought cakes."

"Thank you, Melody. It all looks lovely," says my mother diplomatically.

"I go now," Aija says.

I bitchily tot up how much of the money that was supposed to be sent home, Aija has spent on her red leather skirt and sparkly mohair sweater and the little white raincoat she's now putting on. I'm sure that it was her I saw last night in Park Street.

"Goodbye," I say loudly.

Once Aija has gone and mother is occupied trying to eat her half-squashed éclair without getting cream all over herself, I tell her about Barty's visit. I attempt to make it sound as if I found the whole experience amusing. I list all my house's apparent faults and finish by saying, "So, it's a wonder David still wants to live there."

"You did choose that house together. Perhaps David can't see himself living anywhere else. Men can get very attached to places they're used to."

"You make him sound like a cat. Should I have buttered his paws to stop him running away?"

Even as I joke about it, I'm wondering if mother could be right. I'd always thought that what David felt for our home was pride, not love; pride that his career had been successful enough to pay for an aspirational property. Perhaps pride and love are the same thing for David. As it gradually became clear that I was never going to be a famous artist, did I cease to be something to be proud of? If I move out, will David and Rosa be able to live happily in a haunted house? Won't the ghost of my presence linger in every room, as David's presence does for me?

Mother is telling a rambling anecdote about the time that

one of my childhood cats went missing. "Three days he stayed in that cupboard," she finishes, "and not a mew out of him!"

I say that I remember and then raise the delicate topic of money.

"I see from the agency bill that Aija has been spending more time here than she's supposed to."

"Well, she isn't always looking at her watch, like Mrs Green's girl. Melody stays until she's finished the job and she never makes me feel that she's keen to get away."

"That's nice, but it all goes on Aija's charge sheet – the bill, I mean."

"I didn't think she...the agency would charge for the extra minute here and there."

"It's more than minutes. Mother, I want you to have the care you need, of course I do, but you know that money is a bit of a problem for me at the moment because of...the separation, and Rob has all those school and college fees to pay..."

Puckerings of worry appear on my mother's face. The importance of paying for the grand-children's education is something that she would never contest.

"Poor Rob, he works so hard and he has so many things to worry about. From now on I'll make sure that Melody doesn't stay any longer than she's supposed to, or run any more errands for me."

What errands? I try to be magnanimous. "See how it goes for a while. Then if you do need more carer-hours, Rob and I will manage it. Don't worry about that."

Mother takes a sip of coffee and then says hesitantly, "If money is tight...well I'd already been thinking...now that David is gone, wouldn't it make more sense if we lived together?"

I almost choke at this surprise attack and then say feebly, "But you know you couldn't manage the stairs..."

"It's true those awful stairs would be too much for me but if you sell your house and I sell this flat, we could buy somewhere together. A really nice bungalow perhaps, with a garden for you. Then Rob wouldn't have to pay for a carer."

She has it all worked out and everyone but me will think it's a very good idea. I sit there chewing Aija's disgustingly sweet honey-cake, trying not to let out the scream that is welling up inside of me.

December 6th

I wish I could sleep right through Sundays. Instead I go for a walk, letting the cold rain soak me. So when the wind comes in off the river, my hair is too wet and heavy to blow into my eyes. I told my mother that I couldn't be her carer because I was going to have to find a full time job, but I promised to think about moving in with her. I do think about it. Aija is right to say that my mother is a nice lady, so why does the prospect of living with her fill me with such dread? Is it because I feel that my life is being sucked backwards, like a tide flowing the wrong way?

I had two phone-calls last night. I couldn't cope with answering them. I waited for a while and then listened to the messages. I must, as Aija says, be a cold fish because when I heard Deirdre's sobs I didn't immediately ring her back. She was calling me from the house of her former mother-in-law, with whom she'd been warming up old quarrels. She didn't feel she could stay there a moment longer but she had nowhere else to go. There was a lot about having to give away the dog before she remembered to ask, "Are you all right, Meg? I'm sorry if I've upset you but I really don't know what I've done to make you go silent." Actually, I've always been the silent partner in this relationship. Deirdre hasn't done anything but become a more desperate version of her usual crisis-prone self. There doesn't seem any point in ringing back to tell her that.

The other phone-call was from Nina to say that she is worried about me. She urged me to focus on my new freedoms and repeated that I was going to come out of this a stronger person.

If she really believes that I'm strong, why is she so worried about me? To show willing, I picked up the book on surviving divorce again and opened it at random. The exercise for the day was identifying with an 'empowering character' from fiction or myth. My first thought was to pick some doomed Hardy heroine but Tess of the d'Urbevilles is no-one's idea of a positive role model. The first Mrs Rochester? At least she got to burn the house down. The Snow Queen? La Belle Dame Sans Merci? I mentally flicked through a list of goddesses. Jealous Juno who turned her husband's lover into a cow? Something angry and Indian with extra hands for painting with? Hel, ruler of the Norse underworld? She probably had to keep explaining to other deities, 'No, that's Hel with one L.' Eventually, I made my choice, left the house and walked through the semi-dark streets much more confidently.

It was during this night-walk that Nina's words suddenly began to make sense. Concentrate on the new freedoms. The new freedom of being unloved and unneeded. David no longer loves me. Mother thinks she needs me but Aija seems to make her happier than I do. If I am the obsolete woman, with no husband, no lover, no child, I can take risks that ordinary people can't. Do extraordinary things without caring about the consequences. I had it right when I faced down that drunk. "I'm stronger than you are because I don't care."

Even so, it may take a while to nerve myself up to carry out my plan. I turn away from the river and enter the Harbourside development area. The block names in this section are meant to commemorate the port and sherry trade (so much more respectable than slaves or tobacco) but everything here seems disconnected from the city's architectural past. The flat roofs, sun balconies and glaring white walls with panels of electric blue create a spurious Mediterranean atmosphere that the British weather is doing its best to destroy. In spite of the concrete and tarmac, the railings and security gates, there is a flimsy and transient quality to it all. Grey stains are already appearing on the white walls. Strips are peeling off the sodden advertising hoardings that have been claiming for a very long time that only three flats are still available. There are weeds growing through the standard shrubs you find in every new development: laurels with sickly variegation, wind-burned conifers, and berberis with crisp packets and discarded till-receipts impaled on their thorns.

In the daytime, Porto looks more like an office-block than a collection of homes. It's not the sort of place where people bother to close their blinds, so at night you can see them in their glowing boxes. I was wrong to think that the inhabitants were all young. There are older 'irresponsibles' here too. The separated, and the down-sizers who want somewhere they can lock up and leave whenever the fancy takes them. I try to imagine Rosa pushing a baby-buggy through the bleak car-parks and fail. No wonder she wants my house.

Of course I don't know that they are here together. David may just be renting this flat as a temporary measure, so that he has his own space somewhere. I always tried to give David space. I never went into his study when he wasn't there. I wanted him to feel that he had his own territory, as the glass-house was mine. For the same reason, I never pressed him to let me into his thoughts if he didn't choose to share them. Did he mistake my restraint for indifference?

I walk around the perimeter wall until I reach the place

where I painted my tulip last night. In pallid daylight, the flower doesn't look as bold and colourful as I'd hoped. The outlines are blurred in places where I worked too quickly. I will have to practise creating something beautiful in just a few strokes. Something defiant. Even if my painting is cleaned off, come the Spring there will be some surprises among the dreary shrubs. I forgot to plant my tulip bulbs in November and there seemed no point now in putting them into a garden I can no longer keep.

December 7th

Today I choose to go down the street that I usually avoid. One side of Fitzherbert Street looks similar to Amelia Street but it's easy to see that the terrace on the other side belongs to a Housing Association – there are far too many doorbells and wheelie-bins. I pinch my nose at the stink of the over-filled bins as I walk past, stepping around two veiled women talking to each other in a language I can't even name. I glance up at the terrace. Many of the draughty windows are lined with cling-film or permanently darkened by drawn curtains. Some of the delicate iron-work balconies are draped with washing failing to air on this dank winter day; others are crammed with miscellaneous objects – a punctured football, rolls of carpet, a folded baby-buggy, parts from dismembered bicycles and what looks like a discarded video-player. The Bromdon Trust provides accommodation in Fitzherbert Street for deserving cases such as single mothers, recent refugees, and foreign killers whose Human Rights must be respected. Number 14 is the house that David pointed out to me. It looks no better or worse than any of the others. I don't see the man I'm looking for so I head back towards Clifton village.

In the window of one of my favourite quirky shops a jacket catches my eye. It is woven in damson and inky blue shades set off by bright turquoise buttons. The fabric is as luscious as a slice of summer pudding. For a moment I long to put colour back into my life, but that would mean pretending I was still the old Meg. The foolishly complacent one who thought that David found my faux-Bohemian style adorable. Besides, the jacket is ridiculously expensive. It strikes me now that these boutiques aren't genuinely quirky. Their stock is cynically targeted at the sort of women who live in Clifton Village, or aspire to. I go into a charity shop instead and spend £2.99 on a thick black sweater that comes pre-kneaded by someone else's cat.

On the way home, I walk past the newsagents before I register the headline on the billboard – 'Jenkins Sentenced'. I turn on my heel, buy a paper without trying to scan the front page, tuck it under my arm and walk home. Somehow it would seem disrespectful to read about Martin Jenkins' fate in the street.

Once I'm back, I take the paper into the drawing room and sit down opposite David's chair. I look first at the court-room sketch on the front page. Martin Jenkins is shown standing in the dock between two prison officers. The artist has given Martin a face so devoid of expression it might be a death-mask. Unlike the obsessively neat man I saw in court, this Martin is dishevelled, with untidy hair and buttons left undone. His shoulders are hunched, his upper body sagging. Did Martin really look like this as he listened to the judge shred his character? Or were these signs of disintegration added by the court-artist to turn his picture into a satisfying moral tale?

I read the story below the picture. The judge apparently told Martin that he was a jealous and possessive husband. Or, to put it another way, he was someone who took marriage vows seriously in an age when most people think nothing of breaking them. The judge emphasized that Martin had shown no remorse for brutally cutting short the life of a young woman and depriving a child of her mother. How can anyone know Martin's true feelings about what he did? They probably change from minute to minute. Perhaps he is just too honest to make the facile apologies expected in court. A formal statement of regret read out by a lawyer isn't remorse. Remorse is regretting something that was done every waking moment. Remorse is longing to turn back time and set things right. Remorse is something I hope that David may one day feel for what he has done to me.

For murder, a life sentence is still mandatory but I know from following David's cases how little that means nowadays. By some strange equation which seems the opposite of justice, the longer people live, the shorter Life sentences become – and marriages. Jenna Jenkins probably had a life expectancy of at least fifty years but for taking this away, the judge has ordered Martin Jenkins to serve a minimum of seventeen years. His daughter will be a grown woman, possibly with children of her own, before he gets out of prison. There are quotes from Jenna's family expressing disgust that the sentence wasn't longer. Is Martin satisfied with the Devil's bargain he made? Were those few intense minutes, in which he made his wife sorry for what she'd done, worth seventeen dreary years in prison?

I go out to the glass-house and fasten large sheets of sugar-paper to the back wall. I load my palette knife with paint and stand at arms length. I close my eyes to think through the strokes I must make to create a striped tulip as beautiful and startling as a sudden appearance of the Northern Lights. I try to move instinctively, so that the image is transferred directly from my mind to the paper but I find myself sneaking a look at how it's going. That destroys the spontaneity. I'm left with sparse, unfeeling lines. If they evoke anything, it's the rigidity of a plastic flower.

I drop the knife, close my eyes again, and squeeze the tubes of red and yellow onto the palm of my right hand. I clench my fist and revel in the silky squelch of paint. I picture sensuous red and dazzling yellow blending into furious orange. As soon as my fingers are coated I use them to smear colour across the paper. Curve and slash, curve and slash. When I open my eyes I see that what I've painted is more like a rose than a tulip. It takes me a long time to scrub the remaining paint off my hand.

In the evening I sit down with our Christmas card list. Even if I ignore the people who are work colleagues of David, it is a long list. I am at the stage of life where I seem to have a very large number of acquaintances but few real friends. After signing each card with just my name I carefully cross out the 'David and' above our printed address. I will post them off tomorrow in the hope of pre-empting any more cards offering cheery greetings to David and Meg, a joint entity that no longer exists.

December 8th

I am woken by a call from Rob. We have our usual exchange about the weather. Rob tells me that his day is going to be a scorcher. I tell him that my day is going to be grey and wet. Then he gets to the point. "What's this about you and mum moving in together?"

"It's her idea, not mine."

"I guessed that but she said you were considering it."

I make an exasperated noise which might mean that I am.

"Mum seemed in quite a state about money and about you having to find a job at your age. Are things really that bad, Meggy? Is David not paying up like a gent?"

"Nothing is settled yet and if I keep the house I won't have much to live on."

"You need a better lawyer. When I divorced Sylvia I was lucky to walk away with my own skin."

"I can't afford a better lawyer than David."

"I suppose not but why was Mum going on about costing us too much? I know she's capable of blaming herself for just about anything but surely..."

"I had to point out that she was running up a massive bill by letting her carer work lots of extra hours."

"You mean the care we arranged isn't enough?"

The care I arranged.

"It should be. The extra time wasn't for anything she really needed. She just likes Aija's company and forgets that she's paying for it by the minute."

"Well that's understandable. Nobody likes to live alone." He pauses and I know what he's about to say. "So, you and Mum moving in together would kill two birds with one stone. It would be company for you both and save you money. Of course, Mum could still have someone come in for bit each day if you have to go out to work."

I notice that he doesn't suggest help would be needed so that I could stay in to work on my paintings. Meg the artist would be the bird killed by that stone.

"Of course I can see that it makes sense for mother to live with me. I'll look into it when I've got through the divorce and sorted out my finances."

Can't Rob hear in my voice that I no longer believe any kind of normal future is possible for me? Apparently not. We were never that close. I tell him that I have things to do and end the call.

I get dressed, pulling on the new old sweater, stuff the pile of envelopes into an old Waitrose bag and set off for the postbox. I should have put my raincoat on, even though the box is only as far as the end of my road. I loathe sleet. It has most of the coldness of snow but none of the beauty. I walk briskly to the postbox and delve into the bag for a handful of envelopes. It should be so easy to push them through the slot but once I post these cards nearly everyone I know will learn that my marriage is over. So I stupidly stand there, sheltering the cards with my body while sleet soaks into my bowed back like liquid misery.

Only when I sense someone hovering behind me, do I shove all the cards through the slot, not caring if they are bent out of shape. As I turn away, I see that the man behind me is Derek from next door, clutching a single brown envelope.

"Posting early for Christmas?" he enquires brightly.

"That's right."

Even this banal exchange seems to exhaust me.

"We're just sending e-greetings this year, except to a few old-timers."

I want to tell him that this is bad news for charities, and for artists like me, but I don't have the energy. I move my lips into something that might look like a smile and walk away.

When I get back, I have to take off the sodden sweater and drape it over a radiator. I put on a thinner black sweater and sit down to make a list of new reasons to hate David.

He has exposed my home to the contempt of an estate agent.

He has made moving back in with my mother seem the only logical option.

He has caused me to discover that I am unemployable and far more helpless about money than I ever realized.

He has made me dread opening Christmas cards this year in case they contain messages of sympathy. Or don't.

Because crossing the Horned Bridge will always be painful from now on.

Because I hesitated over posting the cards in case there was still a chance of David coming back.

Standing in front of that postbox, I knew that if David suddenly appeared on the doorstep I would let him back into my life as cravenly as my mother took my father back. Is capitulation in my genes? I can't forgive myself for still being willing to forgive him. No forgiveness for Rosa though. I'm not that pathetically nice.

December 9th

Word of the day is – conviviality. My morning class will be in a holiday mood so I mustn't spoil it for them. I thought about all of my students last night when I was standing in Fitzherbert Street. It was too wet to be painting outside, so I went back to Number 14. Through a lighted basement window I spotted a man who might be the one I was looking for. I pictured myself opening the gate, walking down the slippery metal steps, squeezing past the bins to the door and ringing the bell. My plan was to say that I was from Social Services. I didn't need him to let me into his flat, only to open the door. I got as far as putting my hand on the gate before I decided it wasn't the right moment. I owed it to my artists to turn up for their last classes.

We always do Christmas cards during the final class of the winter term. I dig out my sample cards and some Christmas tree baubles and then go into the garden to pick a few sprays of variegated holly. I usually try to take a so-called Christmas Rose for people to paint but this hellebore is as elusive as the perfect Christmas. It never seems to flower on time or be as beautiful as you anticipated when it does. True to form, my stunted specimen has leaves disfigured by black spot and something is eating the meagre flower buds. I consider digging the whole thing up and bringing it in as a realistic symbol of many people's Christmas. Then I remember, word of the day – conviviality.

On my way to the hall I stop off at the local florist to buy a poinsettia. These scarlet monsters may have nothing to do with Christian symbolism but they flaunt all the gaudiness of the season. I pause when I notice how the price of these short-lived plants has been raised to the maximum that desperate present-givers will pay. While the florist is occupied with a weepy customer ordering funeral flowers, I use my finger and thumb nails to nip off a couple of bracts and drop them into my art-bag. I don't feel too guilty as I walk out. They've had plenty of my money over the years.

I get to the hall just before the first of the ladies arrives. It's Joanne. After she helps me to set out the tables she offers me an envelope.

"Here's my form and the money for next term."

When I don't immediately take it, she misunderstands my hesitation.

"Don't worry, our finances have improved a bit. Patrick's just got a better paying job but it's in Northampton so he'll only be home at the weekends."

"You aren't going to move to Northampton?"

"Not till we're sure this job is going to last, and maybe not even then. The kids are so settled in their schools and my mum and dad look after them when I'm working. I couldn't uproot my parents. They've lived in Bristol all their lives. So, it's complicated, but..." Joanne pushes the envelope into my hand, "...we'll work something out."

I ought to tell her that I almost certainly won't be giving any more art classes but the others all arrive in a bunch, laughing and chattering. They keep on talking even after they are all sitting down.

To get their attention, I say loudly, "As this is the last class before Christmas, I thought we'd draw turkeys instead of chickens..."

Candy is the only one who doesn't immediately realize that I'm joking. There is a chorus of groans and Pam calls out, "I've got so many young Vegans to cater for, I'll have to draw a Nut Roast."

Everyone but me laughs. As I pass out blank cards, I wonder if any of them have practised their chicken-drawings enough to master the subject. I imagine not.

I give them the usual speech about choosing a strong and simple image for their Christmas card and warn them to think carefully about where to place it before they start drawing or painting. The response to this good advice ranges from Janet immediately sloshing on the scarlet for a dead-centre poinsettia bract, to Alice making a dozen tiny sketches of a holly leaf and a Christmas star from a variety of angles.

The end of term spirit means that there is very little chance of silent concentration this morning. I endure the conviviality by moving from person to person concentrating on the small rectangle of paper in front of each one of them. I help Jean to make the glass bauble she's chosen convincingly rounded and persuade Pam to add more berries to her holly than are actually there. "Isn't that cheating?" she asks. I tell her that artists improve on reality all the time.

As I'm reshaping the head of a camel-shaped ornament for Joanne, someone mentions Martin Jenkins. I must have jumped because there is now an ugly break in the line I was drawing. The others are discussing the verdict and the length of his sentence.

"Seventeen years is nothing for what he did," declares Pam. "Burning her body in the woods like that. Horrible."

"He should never be let out again," Jean agrees.

"No wonder that poor woman wanted to end the marriage," says Janet. "She must have known what he was like. He obviously couldn't cope with her having a successful life outside the home."

Alice nods. "So jealous and controlling."

They all seem very certain that Martin should be defined by his one desperate act rather than by everything which led up to it.

"And that poor little girl," Alice goes on, "left without a mother."

Or a father. For all any of us know, she was closer to Martin than to Jenna. His daughter might have been Martin's best character witness, if only she'd been allowed to speak.

Joanne looks up at me. "Meg, wasn't your husband leading the prosecution?"

"Yes, but David doesn't discuss his cases with me."

"Still, you must be proud that he puts people like Martin Jenkins behind bars."

"It's the jury and judge who do that."

I quickly move on to Candy, who is still staring at her blank card.

"Is there nothing on the table that you fancy trying?"

"I suppose I could do the star, if I'm allowed to use a ruler."

She obviously can't summon up an ounce of enthusiasm for any of my Christmas card clichés, which is strange because I'd have cast exuberant Candy as the person who adores everything about Christmas.

"Not in a festive mood?" I ask quietly.

"This isn't my favourite time of year. Not since we lost my mum on Christmas Day three years ago." She answers my unspoken question. "Breast cancer. She so wanted one last family Christmas together but...". Her voice tails off .

My father died on midsummer's day and since then I associate high summer with bewilderment and misery rather than strawberries and tennis, but I don't say that I know how she feels because I probably don't. Instead, I briskly offer to find her something non-seasonal to draw. Candy shakes herself like a wet dog and says that she'll just make something up.

I retreat to make everyone a cup of coffee. I should have known about Candy's mother – and about Jean's son. I thought I was the one people always confided in. Have they stopped doing it because they sensed that I was no longer really listening? When did that happen?

The class work through coffee so that we can finish half an hour early to go off to lunch in one of the local cafés. Most of them seem pleased enough with their cards to inflict them on a relative. Joanne has done one for each of her boys. "Perhaps *my* work will get stuck on the fridge for a change."

Before they pack up, I walk around the table searching for something to praise in every painting. I do find it. Janet has painted the stolen poinsettia with carefree panache. Alice's card is beautifully composed and delicately drawn. Jean has remembered to leave enough areas of white paper to make her bauble look as if it is catching the light. Pam's generous cluster of red berries sings out against the green and gold of the holly leaves. Joanne's camels have naïve charm. Candy has drawn a childishly simple Christmas tree hung with glass baubles that look like tear-drops. You can't create talent, only nurture it. After my last Wednesday morning class, I can feel that I've helped all of them to improve. If only a little.

"Well done, everyone!" I say heartily.

Jean sighs. "I feel like I'm running as hard as I can just to stand still."

The others tell her not to underrate herself and point out how far she's come since her first lesson. This should be my job but I'm preoccupied with wondering if I can get out of the lunch by pleading a headache. Then Joanne hands me my coat and I allow myself to be swept off to Salvatore's, where she's reserved a table in one of the side rooms.

As he hands out the Christmas lunch menus, the Sicilian owner of the café flirts with us all in the likeable way that British men don't have the knack of. During the prolonged ordering process it transpires that Janet isn't perpetually on the latest faddy diet as I'd assumed. She has Crohn's Disease; something else I should have known. I don't have the energy for trivial decisions, so I copy Joanne's choice of chestnut soup followed by Aubergine Parmagiano.

While we wait for the starters, Alice and Pam try to pump me for more information about the Jenkins case. They obviously didn't believe my claim that David doesn't discuss his work with me. I used to joke that the Defendant in David's current case was the third person in our marriage. I knew how intensely David would be thinking about that person while the trial lasted, rather as I would be thinking about my current painting. So perhaps it isn't so extraordinary that on sleepless nights I've been imagining Martin Jenkins lying in bed beside me instead of David.

To stop the interrogation, I say, untruthfully, that I don't want to think about murder during our celebration lunch. Jean supports me.

"You're right. We come to Art classes to get away from all the depressing things in the news."

Art as escape. Are Lukas and the Uglies correct to assume that people who paint pretty flowers are turning their backs on real life?

While I'm brooding about this, Salvatore brings our first courses. The chestnut soup looks like greasy dishwater but smells enticing. As I drink it, I notice that Joanne is skilfully covering for Candy's unusual silence and deflecting the conversation away from Christmas and towards recent films. All I have to do is interject an occasional, "Is that worth seeing?" and sit back and listen to Pam and Janet argue, since they seem to have diametrically opposed tastes. Janet is passionate in her dislikes but she has to keep pausing the conversation as her father texts her more items for the shopping she is doing for him later.

"I'm beginning to wish I hadn't taught the old codger to text. It will be easier when the annexe is finished. At least I'll only have to drive to the supermarket and back, instead of half across town to Dad's."

I can't help exclaiming, "He's moving in with you!"

Janet shrugs. "It's not ideal but Dad's not good at managing on his own and when his flat is all set up we may be able to have Mum home for visits. There's been another delay though. One of the builders managed to drill through a vital bit of the underfloor heating and now the whole system may have to be installed again..."

Everyone groans sympathetically and we move on to a 'bad builders' conversation. My class can come up with plenty of examples. While Pam describes the increasingly bizarre excuses offered by her roofer for not turning up, I think about

Janet and her parents. No-one tells stories about women like her. There is no drama in quietly and cheerfully doing the right thing. I watch Janet's fingers nimbly texting while the others talk and try to work out what makes her so different from me. I tend to match people with media. I've always thought of Janet as resembling a pastel drawing, made up of feathery lines and pale powdery colours, but there must be more strength there than I'd imagined.

Our main courses arrive. Aubergines, like Christmas Roses, always disappoint. Their taste is so much blander than their sumptuous skin-colour suggests. While I'm waiting for the cheese crust on my aubergines to cool, the conversation suddenly shifts from builders to babies. Pam has explained that she's having her attic turned into a 'rumpus room' for her grand-children. Pictures are demanded and passed around the table so that everyone can declare how adorable the children are. I can see that the man at the next table, who has ordered a succession of black Americanos as he hunches over his lap-top, is getting irritated by the rising noise level, but I do my bit and ask who the little girl takes after. When her strawberry blonde hair, snub nose and stubborn chin have all been attributed to various members of Pam's extensive family, Jean chooses this moment to announce that her daughter Kate is expecting her first baby. There are shrieks of delight and the man at the next table signals for his bill.

"If it's a boy, they're going to call him Michael."

I silently hope that the baby will be a girl, who won't then grow up with the burden of expectation that the name of a dead hero would carry. There is much discussion of due dates, the propensity of first babies to be late, and whether fathers are a help or a hindrance in the delivery room. I'm expecting a baby too but it isn't mine. Will David's child even be told about me? At some point he or she is bound to ask about the missing thirty years in David's life. Then I remember that I'm not the only one cut off from a child I feel a strong connection with.

I turn to Alice and ask, "Have you managed to get access to your grandson yet?"

The question comes out sounding more blunt than I intended but Alice merely sighs. "It seems that in English law being a grand-parent counts for nothing. All we can do now is support Peter's case to stop Leanne – his ex – leaving the country for good but anything that involves lawyers is so expensive... Sorry Meg, I didn't mean to imply that lawyers like David aren't worth every penny."

"No, you're right. Unless you're very rich or very poor, the law is terrifyingly expensive." As I now have reason to know.

"Are you trying to get the court to award joint custody in this country?" asks Jean.

Alice nods. "But the awful thing is, deep down, I agree with Leanne that a child is better off living with its mother rather than shuttling from one home to another. So we'll just have to accept what the court decides and make the best of it."

Making the best of it is what these women do. I look at them with an artist's eye and see Alice in precise silver-point, Jean in dark ink with a wash of tears, Candy in bright acrylics, Pam in bold crayon, Joanne in multi-textured collage and Janet in pastels. They are all 'middlers' – middle class, middle-aged, middle income, middle generation, middle ability and middle intelligence. There is nothing remarkable about any of them and yet they seem to be coping with everything that life throws at them. Death, divorce, disease, dementia... They are the 'walking wounded' who keep on walking. Why can't I join their steady march into the future? Why am I the one who has fallen and can't get on her feet again?

Salvatore starts clearing our table, reciting the choice of desserts as he piles up plates. The others declare that they couldn't eat another thing and then let themselves be persuaded. I say that I'll be late for my afternoon class if I stay for dessert. I put a couple of ten pound notes on the table to cover my unwanted food and hand round my Christmas cards. This causes a general flurry of bringing out and swapping of cards. I hope that no-one will have a chance to open mine and interpret the crossing out of David's name before I'm gone, but as I'm leaving to a chorus of "Have a good Christmas!", Jean gets up and squeezes my hand. Then she kisses me on the cheek and whispers, "You'll come through this."

If I do, it will probably not be in a way that stalwart Jean will approve of.

I make my way back to the church hall. When I get there, I realize how inadequately prepared I am for my flower-painters. They always do Christmas cards too but a few scraps of holly and one wilted poinsettia bract are hardly worthy of them. I leave the hall unlocked, which is very much against the rules, and rush to the Florists. This time there are no other customers in the shop so theft seems out of the question. The girl behind the counter is the one who picked out the golden lily as her most beautiful flower. I ask her if she could quickly make up a posy in red, white and green. "With everything fully out, please. It doesn't have to last long."

It's almost like watching some exotic dance as she

confidently plucks individual flowers out of the tall jugs, using her right hand to weave them together in the palm of her left hand. Then she binds the posy with a length of scarlet and gold ribbon As she names its price, I realize that I should have set a limit. Now I have no choice but to get out my credit card.

I insert it in the machine and type in my pin number. I use the birth-years of famous painters for pin-numbers, so then I only have to remember which card goes with Cézanne and which with Matisse. When my pin-number isn't accepted I think I must have got them the wrong way round and try again. Still rejected. I feel slightly sick. Has David cancelled our joint credit card? I withdraw the card and say, "I think I've got the out of date card by mistake. I'll have to pay by cheque."

The florist tells me that they don't accept cheques any more. I scrabble in my bag and get out all the notes I have with me. They aren't going to be enough. When she sees me counting coins, the Florist scoops up the notes and says, "This will do. You are one of our best customers."

I thank her and leave the shop feeling far more guilty than I did earlier.

I rush back to the hall. As I enter, I hear someone talking. My flower-painters, including Other Sarah, are sitting in their usual places while Gina tells them all about the Christmas cruise she has booked.

"And at Christmas lunch, there'll be crackers and paper hats and as much champagne as you can drink and the Stewards make sure that no-one feels lonely. You should try it Evangeline."

Evangeline just smiles and then says to me, "You have run out of puff. Sit down and catch your breath, dear."

"Sorry," I gasp, "there was a delay at the Florists."

Sarah gestures at the posy. "Are those for us to paint? How lovely. Let me put them in a vase."

I gratefully hand over the posy and lean back in my chair. I consider giving Other Sarah a special welcome but decide we'd both prefer to pretend that last week's quarrel never happened.

I take a deep breath, pass round the blank cards and say, "I'd like you to regard this as an exercise in reduced scale. Obviously you can't do the posy full-size on a small card, so you have to think hard about the basic shape and edit down the detail."

Other Sarah is looking interested but doesn't say so. I wonder who persuaded her to come back. It certainly wasn't me.

"Remember to leave enough space for lettering if you want any on the front."

Sarah places the vase containing the posy in the middle of the table and everyone stares at it intently. Gina complains that she can't see the red carnation from where she's sitting and carnations are her favourite flower. Rodney good-naturedly changes place with her. I suggest that everyone starts by making a quick sketch or two on rough paper. Then I have to scrounge some rough paper for Gina who hasn't brought any. I do a couple of sketches of the posy, one from above and one from the side, to show how the subject might be fitted into the space. I'm determined to get my money's worth out of these damn flowers.

I allow the class ten minutes' grace before I start pacing around the table to peer over people's shoulders. Rodney has made a good start but asks for advice on which red to use. His finger is already hovering over the right tube. Sarah keeps standing up to view the posy from above. She has cleverly reduced it to a brilliant pattern-filled circle, like something seen through a kaleidoscope. Gina has gone for fancy lettering but is trying to squash 'Merry Christmas' into too small a space. We agree that she'll have to change it to Xmas. Evangeline has managed to draw an outline which fits onto her card but when she puts in her first flower – a star-burst gerbera – it is way too big. She nods when I point this out.

"Oh dear, you did warn us about that but I'm not good at making things tiny. I think it must be my stubby fingers."

I think it must be her generous spirit which instinctively enlarges rather than reduces everything. Other Sarah has relaxed into the task of down-scaling. She is a natural miniaturist, like poor timid Pete. How insulted Other Sarah would be if she knew I was comparing her to that lost soul.

I still think about my Friday people and wonder if they were lost from the start. Were they always condemned by their genes to struggle on the margins of society? Or was there a specific moment for each of them when their life ran off the tracks?

After an hour, I make tea and bring out the second of my bargain panettones as an end of term treat. I still have the carving knife in my art bag and this time I make a neater job of cutting thick slices for everyone. Purist Other Sarah remarks that 'authentic' panettones don't contain chocolate chips. She still eats every crumb. Gina and Rodney have two slices each.

After Evangeline sucks the last of the chocolate from her sticky fingers she asks what we'll be doing next term. I ought to tell them that there will be no next term but I can't face the questions that this announcement might raise. Before I have to answer, Gina bursts out with, "We should work towards an exhibition! Everything looks so much better in a nice frame.

Isn't that right, Meg?" She doesn't give me a chance to reply. "We could join in that 'Art at the Harbour' thing, or do an Open Studio."

Evangeline chuckles. "No-one would pay for my fumbles but the rest of you paint as well as fancy artists you see in galleries."

Rodney looks interested. Other Sarah says she couldn't think of selling any of her work.

"We could do one of those days when artists leave their work around the city for people to take," suggests Sarah. "We could call it 'Flowers for Everyone' or 'Flowers for Free.'"

"Free!" exclaims Gina, "Definitely not."

I don't join in the argument but it does amuse me to think of my flower-painters as part of the same movement as anti-capitalist, guerilla street artists. As a painter still trying to make a living from my art, I am the one out of tune with the times. I offer more tea but everyone is keen to get back to work on their cards. I watch them with a rising sense of panic. I've been putting off the big change until I'd fulfilled my obligations to all of my students. By four-thirty that excuse will be over and done with. There will be nothing to hold me back.

I circle the table, trying not to keep glancing at the church hall clock. Only Evangeline needs my help. We decide to start a fresh card and I do most of the drawing for her, leaving Evangeline to fill in the colours. I sit down again and do the same with one of my own sketches.

I try to absorb myself in capturing the tiniest nuances of tone and hue but something is different. I realize that Gina has been uncharacteristically silent for quite some time. She is staring at the posy, concentration deepening her wrinkles. I ask if there is a problem.

"Oh no, dear. I'm all done. I was just enjoying the flowers. Don't they make your heart bounce just to look at them?"

Even Other Sarah nods in agreement.

"But don't tell my cardiologist," says Rodney, "or he'll put me on even more tablets."

"Ooh, death by flowers," cries Gina. "What a lovely way to go."

Death by flowers. If modern art is supposed to be confrontational, why shouldn't people be confronted by the fact that the beauty of flowers is as much a part of the real world as all the ugliness, squalor and pain? Death, decay and renewal. People used to see the whole cycle of life in a flower. Now we seem to be mired in decay. I want to ask Rodney and Evangeline, Gina and the Sarahs why they love painting something that will be dead by tomorrow but it is time for them to pack up and go.

Other Sarah hasn't quite finished her exquisite drawing, so I pluck the posy out of its vase and offer it to her.

"Here, take this home with you."

Other Sarah hesitates, allowing Gina to make a grab for the flowers. "Well, if you don't want them..."

I'm reminded of how I tried to toss my bridal bouquet to Deirdre only to have it intercepted by David's sporty cousin Josephine, last heard of living in Dorset with a pug-breeder named Cora. Superstitious Deirdre liked to claim that this piece of bad luck caused the failure of her first marriage. I put it down to her affair with a gallery-owner.

The scrape of chairs being pushed back returns me to the present. My afternoon group is more reserved than my morning class. They have never exchanged Christmas cards but

Evangeline suddenly brings out jars of home-made marmalade for everyone. I hold my jar up to the light to admire the amber glint.

"Don't let any little ones have a lick of it," warns Evangeline, "there's a dollop of rum in every jar."

Other Sarah manages to refrain from saying that authentic marmalade does not contain rum and Rodney seems particularly delighted.

"Just the thing to liven up breakfast. This'll give me a reason to get up in the mornings."

His choice of words makes me wonder exactly how dreary his home life is. I'm never likely to find out because if everything goes to plan tomorrow, this is the last time I shall see any of my flower-painters.

December 10th

I wake up feeling more positive because my word of the day is – **hate**. It is such a relief to stop pretending to be reasonable and admit how much I hate David and Rosa. With David, the hate comes in quick stabs, with Rosa it is more like a steady ache. I must use that hate to fill up all the hollow places inside me and give me the strength to act.

Before I get dressed I look over the long diary entry I wrote last night. I'm amazed by the trivialities I bothered to record. Yesterday's Meg seems like a different person, pointlessly going through the motions of her old life. Today's Peg moves with new purpose. I put on the anonymous black clothing and for the first time it looks right on me.

In the kitchen, Vincent whines for his breakfast but I've run out of cat food. If...when I'm not here, who will look after the cats? Will David feel obliged to take them in? I remember Rosa giving a foolish little shriek when Vincent brushed against her leg during the garden party. I'm guessing that she's no animal lover. Theo seems to have made his own arrangements, I haven't seen him for a while now. Vincent will probably end up in a Cats Protection shelter. Why isn't there a charity that re-homes abandoned wives?

I search the dustier recesses of the larder and find a tin of French paté which I think someone gave us the Christmas before last. I peel back the lid and scoop half the creamy fat and pallid meat onto Vincent's plate. He drags a mouthful off the plate and retreats into a corner to eat it, as if he's afraid I'll want a share. I'm itching to leave the house and get it over with before I can change my mind but I ought to wait until there are fewer people around. That will give me a greater chance of achieving my goal before I can be stopped. After filling in all those application forms, I know the difference between goals and objectives. My goal is a death and my objective is justice, or at least vengeance.

Mother always told me to eat a good breakfast on days when I was doing something important. I look around the kitchen. Evangeline's marmalade is sitting on the kitchen table, shining 'like a good deed in a naughty world'. I search for some bread to go with it but can't find even the dry heel of a loaf. I unscrew the jar lid and plunge in a spoon. Then I close my lips over the spoon and savour the sweet jelly, the bitter peel and the kick of rum. I eat half the jar before beginning to feel queasy. I make some coffee and drink it black because there isn't any milk.

I wonder if I should leave a note to explain my actions. David will probably understand as soon as he hears the man's name. He used to stress that a prosecutor who allows distressing cases get to him is no use to anybody. David did stay cool during the trial of Mukhtar Zubeyer and ensured that he was found guilty of causing death by dangerous driving. It emerged that since Zubeyer came to England from Somalia as an asylum-seeker, he'd been involved in drug-dealing and petty crime. One Autumn day in Swindon the police were called when Zubeyer drove off from a garage in an uninsured stolen car without paying for his petrol. When he saw the patrol-car behind him, Zubeyer started to drive very fast. He didn't slow down when April Lyons and her two children stepped onto the pedestrian crossing. The little girl was killed instantly. The little boy was dragged under the car but Zubeyer still didn't stop. He abandoned his car and the boy's mangled body a few streets away and ran for it. The police soon tracked him down. April was horribly injured. The doctors did their best but no drug can kill the sort of pain she must have been feeling. She died a few weeks later by jumping out of a hospital window.

At the trial the judge ordered that Zubeyer be deported at the end of his prison sentence. After he'd served a mere five years, Zubeyer's lawyers argued that Somalia was too dangerous a place to send anyone back to and that Zubeyer had a right to a family life in England with a woman he'd abandoned as soon as he knew she was pregnant. No matter that Clive Lyons had lost his entire family and that innocent people living here were left exposed to a dangerous man. David exploded when he heard on the legal grapevine that Zubeyer and his 'family' had been given new identities and rehoused only a few streets away from us. For a day or two he even talked about quitting the law. Then he settled back into doing his job with grim determination. Was that when a fault line opened up in his life? Should I have tried harder to talk to him about it?

No. I must stop playing David's game in which his feelings are important, and must be acted on no matter what the consequences, and mine are tiresome and just about 'making a scene'. I'm guessing that the affair started with Rosa encouraging David to talk to her about work-related problems, implying that she was the only person who could possibly understand him. I hate the way that Rosa hasn't just taken David's body away from me. She has got inside his head and changed the way he thinks about me. I wish I could take my carving knife and cut Rosa out of our lives, cut her into such tiny pieces that it would be as if she had never existed.

I hate what her existence has done to me. Clever Rosa, sensuous Rosa, young Rosa has made me into scorned Meg, the obsolete woman. Now I am going to do something that should shock David and Rosa into seeing the new person they have made. Meg may not capable of harming pregnant Rosa, but Peg has the will to punish a monster like Zubeyer and give Clive Lyons the vengeance he can't take for himself. I don't care what happens to me afterwards. I shall leave my diary open on the table so that people can read it and understand.

Half-way to Fitzherbert Street it occurs to me that I may not be caught. I'd pictured myself being arrested at once, as if there was still a policeman on every street corner, but I might be able to walk away after the stabbing. I am wearing gloves because it is cold and my features are hidden by the hood of my raincoat. There will be nothing to connect me with the person the police will label as 'the victim'. What would I do then? As I step out of the way of a woman pushing a double buggy, I decide that I will choose more people to punish and keep going until I am caught.

I walk fast, nearly bumping into an old man as I turn into Fitzherbert Street. I murmur an apology and slow to a more normal pace. As I approach Number 14, I realize that it is silly to assume that Zubeyer will be there just because I have screwed up my courage to the sticking place. I resign myself to coming back in the evening but when I look over the railings into the narrow forecourt of Number 14, there he is. That is the face, with its half-moon shaped scar on one cheekbone, that I know so well from the courtroom sketch hanging in David's study. It seems that my plan is destined to succeed. I let myself imagine David's shock when he finds out what I have done and feel a surge of pleasure that is almost sexual.

Dressed in a garish fleece top over tattered jeans, Zubeyer is just lighting a roll-up cigarette. He looks up and scowls as I open the gate and come slowly down the slippery metal steps, holding my art bag.

"You from the Bromdon?"

It takes me a moment to understand that Zubeyer is asking if I am from the Housing Association.

"No."

"Benefits?"

I shake my head. He is looking shifty now.

"What do you want?"

His voice seems full of barely suppressed anger that a woman might have any control over his life.

I stay on the bottom step, so that he won't tower over me. With my right hand I reach across to my bag and feel for the handle of the carving knife. If meek Martin Jenkins transformed himself into a righteous killer, surely I can too.

"What do you want?" he repeats.

I knew I would have to be quick. If I tried for the heart, the knife might stick on a rib. I had to thrust the knife as far into his stomach as it would go and then twist the handle. I want him to know what this is for.

As I begin to whisper, "Do you remember the Lyons family?", his voice overrides mine.

"You from the school? I tell you on the phone, Leila's sick. Coughing all the time. This flat is too cold. Why don't you people do something?"

He gestures at the damp-stained wall of the basement flat and I notice a child's pink bicycle beside the door. From inside the flat I can hear jagged coughs and the anxious murmur of a woman's voice. I let go of the knife-handle and back up the stairs, muttering something. I may even have told him that I was sorry. Zubeyer shouts after me, "Why don't you do something?" but I don't stop.

I run as far as the street corner, drop my bag and lean against a brick wall. Stupid, stupid, stupid. How could I ever have believed that I was capable of killing someone? Even if Zubeyer hadn't made me see him as a father, I couldn't have touched him. Peg the avenger was a ludicrous fantasy, invented to distract me from my pathetic failure of a life. I can't stop myself crying right there in the street even though I hate public displays of emotion almost as much as David does. Not the dainty tears of Romantic fiction but great ugly snorting sobs.

I don't notice the old woman until she gently touches my arm. She is wearing two thick cardigans over a long shapeless black dress and carrying a plastic bag bulging with fruit and vegetables. Her wrinkled sepia face is framed by a headscarf that hides all of her hair and she looks ancient in a way that Western women no longer do until they are well into their nineties. She peers up at me, obviously searching for the English words to ask me what the matter is and not finding them. She clucks with frustration, and reaches up to stroke me on the cheek – a gesture of sympathy from one sad woman to another. I read into her expression the assumption that some man is the cause of my tears.

I find a tissue, scrub at my eyes and blow my nose. She nods approvingly and then delves into her shopping bag and presents me with a scarlet pomegranate. I can't help smiling and she smiles back, showing more gaps than teeth. It is only later

I remember that a pomegranate was the fruit which trapped Persephone in the Underworld.

As soon as I get home, I slam my diary shut. I know I would cringe if I read the morning entry, know that fearless Peg is gone for good, know that the only thing I have left which is separate from David is my work. So, I take the pomegranate out to the glass-house. I try to forget everything but the need to record this unexpected and ambiguous gift.

The shape of a pomegranate is simple to draw but they aren't easy to paint. When you look at one closely there are no areas of solid colour. The scarlet is made up of tiny speckles and the surface of the fruit has the shine and solidity of glass. I do my best and then finally take the carving knife out of my art-bag. It takes me several goes to to hack the fruit in half and I nearly cut off one of my finger-tips when the knife slips. Seeds spill out of the pink flesh. The pomegranate is a traditional symbol of fertility; far more suitable for pregnant Rosa than for me.

I change my mind about painting a cross section of the pomegranate. I dip my brush in water and drew the sharp outline of a lemon beside the pomegranate. Next I mix an acidic yellow with a green undertone. Lemons may be sour but they are much more versatile than pomegranates. I flood in the colour and create the pitted skin with tiny dabs from a sponge. Then I sit back and watch the paint dry – a process which I find fascinating though to almost everyone else it is a byword for boredom. Paper and paint should metabolise into something more than just a copy of what the everyday eye sees. I tell myself that I am trembling because, even with the heater turned up to maximum, it is still cold in the glass-house.

I was cross when Lukas once peered at some of my flower-paintings during a Private View and accused me of being a Stuckist. I had to explain to David that, depending on your point of view, Stuckists are either boring unoriginal traditionalists or brave Remodernists working 'towards a new spirituality in art'. Now I'm reminded of a discomforting phrase from one of the Stuckist manifestos: *'Truth is what it is, regardless of what we want it to be'*. Am I painting what touches my soul and telling the truth about it? Or am I stuck, stuck, stuck in a life built on pretty lies?

I search my painting for hints of revelation and don't find any. There is nothing about these two competently rendered pieces of fruit which would transport anyone into a different world. In the past, when I got colour and form exactly right, there was something more. I begin going through my folders in search of a painting or drawing which will prove that my work once had that intangible quality that even non-believers like me might call soul. It is not just beauty. It is more like a signpost to a rightness beyond beauty.

There isn't room to spread everything out in the glass-house, so I lug my folders into the house. I decide to colonise the dining-room and use the long table and its set of formal chairs to display my work. The phone rings several times but I ignore it. Vincent gets under my feet yowling for more food but I ignore him too. When he jumps onto the table and sits on a fragile half-finished collage, I don't try to push him off. The collage now looks gaudy and trivial. I cover the rest of the table with small pictures of fruit and foliage, flowers and cats and then arrange taller paintings on the chairs, as if they were guests at a dinner party. I imagine my inky trees and teetering rust-speckled hollyhocks making polite conversation with rain-swept views of the gorge and semi-abstract studies of Clifton terraces. They would have to talk about the weather since none of them has anything profound to say.

I fetch more folders and shake the carefully packed contents out onto the floor. Fluffed-up birds on bare twigs, berries with the eerie brightness of poisonous frogs, the false gold of autumn leaves – I don't even feel conventional melancholy when I look at them. The bluebells whose elusive colour I was once so proud of capturing, the Red Admiral butterfly perfectly poised on white buddleia, the luscious pinks of the Comte de Chambord rose and the peacock displaying its multi-eyed tail no longer give me a jolt of joy like a minor electric shock. Only the best of my tulip paintings provoke a faint tremor; a promise of a more intense mode of existence. It isn't enough. It isn't enough. I need to forget everything that I've ever done and start again.

Can I, while my old work is all around me? Even if I lock up the glass-house and shut the door on the dining room and never go in there, my paintings will still jeer at me from almost every wall in the house. What am I going to do? Bundle them all into sacks and give them to Oxfam, as I did with my Mrs Claridge clothes? Charity shops don't find art easy to sell. They might, humiliatingly, refuse my offer. Or only accept it on the grounds that someone might buy my pictures at give-away prices to reuse the frames.

Give-away. Of course. I think back to my last art class – how could I imagine I had anything to teach them? – and hear Sarah enthusing about taking part in an 'Art for Free Day'. Big steps not little ones. I shall leave my paintings all over the city and whoever finds them will decide their fate. Perhaps I better make it an 'Art for Free Night' so that no-one sees what I'm doing and tries to stop me. Then I laugh at my timidity. This morning I thought I was capable of committing murder and now I'm afraid of being accused of dropping litter. Even so, I will wait until it is dark.

I go from room to room taking down framed pictures and pile them on the kitchen table. Then I use a Stanley-knife to gut them like fish, not caring if anything tears as I pull out the mounted paintings and drawings. I wonder whether I should cut off anything that might identify me as the artist, but I only ever sign my work with the initials MC and the outline of a tulip-flower. The truth is that my work isn't well known enough for anyone but a few fellow-artists to recognize it.

The phone rings again. I ought to answer it. I ought to open the letters piling up in the hall. I ought to pick up the threads of my life again as my Wednesday morning ladies would, but gathering as much artwork as I'm able to carry seems more important. I can always build a bonfire with the rest.

December 11th

I am woken by the doorbell. I do not expect it to be David. Of course I don't. The caller is a Parcelforce driver with a parcel to be signed for. In the past I might have made some excuse for still being in my night-things at ten in the morning but now it doesn't seem to matter. I have no particular reason to be up or dressed or alive.

After I close the door, I stare at the square package in disbelief. I know the neat handwriting on the front but I turn the parcel over to confirm my suspicion. There it is – a return address in Chipping Camden headed with the name Celia Claridge. My soon to be ex mother-in-law has sent me her usual Christmas present – a bottle of Chanel No 5. I can hear the liquid slosh as I tilt the package. I have never liked perfumes that blend the fugitive scents of real flowers into something cloying and artificial. Chanel No 5 is what Celia's ideal cool and sophisticated daughter-in-law would wear, not her real one. Will she start giving it to Rosa too?

I can't bring myself to unwrap the parcel, so I leave it on the hall table. My usual response to this gift is to splash some on for our Christmas visit to Celia and then shove the bottle to the back of the bathroom cupboard with the others. At least I don't have to do that this year, which gives me an idea. I fetch all the old bottles from the bathroom and go out through the kitchen into the front yard. There is a drain beside the steps that go up to the street. I take the fancy glass stoppers out of the dusty bottles and start pouring the perfume down the drain.

"What are you doing?"

I look up towards the voice. It is my neighbour, Susan, standing on her front steps.

"Getting rid of old perfume."

I start on another bottle.

"But why?"

"It's gone off," I say, which applies to just about everything in my life at the moment. "I've got a new bottle if you'd like some."

Susan waves her hand in front of her nose. "I don't think you should be doing that. There are rules about what you can put down the drains. The fumes might be dangerous."

"Don't drop any lighted matches or cigarettes then."

Susan turns, unlocks her front door and retreats into her house with a slam. I've always wondered if she was the person I could smell smoking over the wall in their back garden. My eyes are watering as I pour the last of the Chanel No 5 down the drain. Then I pack the empty bottles into the glass-recycling box. I should have the classiest rubbish in the street this week.

I can still smell perfume when I go back into the kitchen and so can Vincent. He tilts his head, opens his mouth and then backs away from me. I realize that my Marks and Spencer velour slippers (a present from mother) are spattered with Chanel No 5 which must be bludgeoning his superior sense of smell. I stuff the slippers in the washing machine along with a bundle of underwear to see if they survive the delicates cycle. My feet are instantly chilled by the flagstone floor, so I put the kettle on to make myself a hot drink and retreat to the rickety chair that stands on a rag-rug.

I got extremely cold last night. In the end I didn't set out until around eleven o'clock. I'd spent hours scrawling 'Free Art

– Please Take' on bits of card and attaching them to my pictures with paper-clips. Now, I don't know why it seemed so urgent to get rid of my work. Perhaps I hoped that if I could only get it out there, something that I'd drawn or painted would turn out to be meaningful to someone. After a while I lost patience and started tearing the more disappointing paintings into strips. I do recall how oddly satisfying that felt. I gathered up a big bag of scraps to lay trails of random images, put on my hooded coat, went out into the clear, frosty night and headed away from Clifton.

Vincent approaches warily and sniffs at my feet. I lift him onto my lap and run my fingers through his coat, finding several tangles. He needs regular grooming but I've been neglecting him. He begins to purr because he thinks I'm showing him affection rather than guilt. Poor Vincent. It just shows how easy it is to be deceived by rituals of touch, by familiar fingers and lips...

I wish I could remember more about last night. I only stopped in one bar for a drink, leaving a still life of a bunch of grapes and a slice of Stilton as a tip. I know that I placed some pictures against walls and shop-fronts and bus-stops and dropped others over railings into basement courtyards. A few people asked me what I was doing. I said it was 'Art Night' and they seemed to accept that explanation because it sounded official.

One man swore at me as he flung back a sketch of willow trees on Spike Island. "I don't want your fucking rubbish!" I ran then, down towards the Floating Harbour. It was starting to get windy, so some of my paintings probably ended up in the water. As I wandered through the development zone, I tucked drawings under the windscreen wipers of parked cars or between the bars of gates. I looked up at the windows that still had lights, at the people who put themselves on display to the world and his wife. Couples living in bright boxes like specimens in a collection.

Coming back up Park Street I offered scraps of painted paper to young drinkers. People who thought I was handing out leaflets went out of their way to avoid me. Others dropped the scraps after a baffled moment but some seemed surprised in a pleased way. I remember one girl shrieking to her friends. "Look, it's a flower – so pretty!" I think that verdict made me cry.

Just as the kettle finally boils, somebody rings the front-door bell. I decide not to answer but the unwanted visitor keeps on ringing and starts using the knocker as well. I stump upstairs and wrench open the door. Aija is standing on my doorstep, bundled up in a faux-fur coat that still leaves a remarkable amount of leg exposed. The surprise is like a punch in the gut. Has she come to tell me that she has found mother ill or injured?

"Ah," she says, "you are in bed."

"What?"

"You are sick. This is for why you have not called the mother."

I open my mouth to say that I'm not sick, but as I'm standing here in my nightie and tatty dressing-gown with bare feet and rat's tail hair, I can see why Aija might think so.

"Is mother all right?"

"No. She is not all right. She is so so worried. You do not call her. She calls and calls but you do not answer your phone. She thinks something bad has happened to the daughter, so I say that I will come and see. I will come to your big house where you live all alone though," she pauses to sniff as suspiciously as Vincent, "it smells like...like a House of the Night."

Does she mean a brothel? I'm tempted to ask how she knows.

It is true that I didn't ring yesterday. What could I have said – "Hello mother, I meant to kill someone today but it turns out that I don't have the nerve." I do feel guilty that she's been so worried but I'm determined not to show this in front of Aija.

"I haven't been myself," I say, "one of those sudden winter things."

Aija leans forward and grips my arm. "You are thin, too thin. You are sick because you do not eat. I will come in now and make you hot soup."

For a moment that sounds comforting but there is no way that I am going to let Aija see the current state of my kitchen – unwashed plates and cups in the sink, next to nothing in the larder and picture frames and glass everywhere.

"No thank you. I was just getting myself something. Please go back to mother and tell her I'm fine now and that I'll ring her later."

Aija lets go of my arm but doesn't budge from my doorstep. "You do not look fine. I will make you better, even for free because your mother is such nice lady."

"If I need any care, I shall pay for it, but while you're here I have something for you. Regard this as your Christmas bonus."

I duck back inside and rip the paper off Celia's parcel. Ignoring the card that drops out, I hand Aija the cellophane-wrapped black and white package. She looks at it blankly for a moment and then asks, "Is for real?"

"Of course it's for real. You can wear it when you go clubbing on Park Street. Goodbye, Aija."

I firmly shut the door on her.

When I'm sure she's gone, I pick up Celia's card. It has a tasteful snow scene on the front and a printed message inside – 'Wishing you Christmas Joy'. I can't imagine Celia feeling an unruly emotion like joy. Under her signature Celia has written, *I hope we can keep in touch.* Keep in touch? Is that all she can say to me after I've been a dutiful daughter-in-law for thirty years? Not even a hint of an apology for David's behaviour. She always did think that David was in the right about everything, except perhaps about marrying me. I'll give her 'in touch'.

I want to ring her right away but I know that this would be unwise, so I go back down to the kitchen and make myself a lumpy mug-full of packet soup. Then I settle down with the phone and listen to my messages. There are three anxious ones from mother, each more quavery than the last, a brisk one from Aija telling me to call 'the mother', a curt one from my solicitor's secretary informing me that I will be charged for the appointment I missed with Mrs Patel – did I? – a patronising one from Nina about some possible paid part-time work on a local arts project, a vague one from Joanne promising to 'be there if I want to talk about things' and a probably fraudulent offer of free loft-insulation. I delete all the messages and call Celia.

She answers, as she always does, by reciting her phone number. I've never been quite sure how to respond to this but now I say, "I know what your number is."

"Who is this?"

Can she really not recognize my voice or is she just giving

herself time to think?

"It's Meg. I'm ringing because I got your parcel. Why did you send it?"

That throws her. "Why? Well, I didn't want you to think that I'd forgotten you."

"Which I might indeed have thought, as I haven't heard a word from you since David walked out on me."

"To be honest, Margaret, I just didn't know what to say to you. It is very..."

I fill in the words for her. "Awkward? Embarrassing?"

"Very unfortunate...but David is my son. I have to support him, whatever I might think about... I'm sorry, Margaret, but these things happen and Rosa does seem to make him happy, so we both have to accept it and move on."

Even old-fashioned Celia is using the 'moving on' platitude to absolve her from dealing with the mess that David's selfishness has created.

"And we all have to think about the baby," Celia continues.

As if I could stop thinking about it. "Are you looking forward to being a grandmother at last?"

"Oh yes...although of course I wish that the circumstances were different."

Circumstances is a very Celia word, covering things that she doesn't want to call by their proper names. She hastens on. "Are you spending Christmas with your mother? Do give her my regards."

"I haven't decided what to do about Christmas yet."

"I appreciate that it won't be a happy one for you this year, but in the long run we'll probably all look back and think that this happened for the best."

"How convenient for you all."

"Do try not to be bitter, Margaret. I'm sure you'll agree that David has always treated you generously. He wants the divorce to be as amicable as possible."

"Amicable?"

"I believe it is quite common for divorced couples to remain friends nowadays. I hope that will happen with you and David, so..." Celia is obviously searching for a way to end this conversation before it gets too emotional. "So, try to have a happy Christmas with your family and do enjoy the perfume."

"Actually, I've always hated Chanel No 5. It's the sort of scent that call-girls think is classy. I gave your bottle to my mother's carer."

"A carer?" Celia splutters down the phone. "Well! There's no need to be so rude..."

"If I can't be rude in these 'circumstances' when can I?"

"I warned David that you'd be spiteful..."

"Did you? I know you've always bitched about me to David behind my back. 'Margaret doesn't look after you properly', 'Margaret shouldn't spend so much time on her paintings', 'Margaret should dress like a barrister's wife not an art student'. We used to talk about it, David and I, and laugh at your attempts to cause trouble. I wonder if Rosa knows what she's letting herself in for."

"There is no point in continuing this ridiculous conversation. Please do not ring me again."

She cuts me off. So there is my new Word of the Day – ridiculous.

The act of writing all this down is the only thing which gives me a purpose; a reason to keep going. I make myself get dressed, though all of the available choices in my wardrobe, like all of the available choices in my life, are not what I want. I wonder if Martin Jenkins feels the same. Or is it a relief that in prison nearly all his choices are now made for him?

As I come back down the stairs, the letter post is pushed through the door. A splatter of cards falls onto the mat. I'm tempted to put them straight in the bin. I'm not in the mood for filling up my mantelpieces and windowsills with cheery pictures of robins and choirboys. I try opening one of the envelopes and find a card from Mark – the first I've heard from him since the night of what he probably saw as his ignominious rejection. The card has an illustration of 'I Saw Three Ships' on the front and Mark's business address inside. He – or his secretary – has signed it with his full name. I clearly don't merit a more personal card.

I feel a twinge of regret that I didn't allow myself to find comfort in his clumsy embrace, however much it would have made David despise me. If we'd gone on, if I'd let my body's needs drive me, would I have discovered what every modern young woman seems to know – that sex can be just as satisfying with someone you don't love? Which would have given me one more reason to fear that I've wasted the last thirty years. My life is a story that has lost the meanings I thought it had. I put the rest of the cards aside to deal with later and go down to the kitchen. I wash up my soup mug and clean the draining board and the sink, scrubbing at old tea-stains with pieces of kitchen-roll that come apart in my fingers.

When I do sit down with the phone I even consider ringing Deirdre and letting her troubles wash over me. Anything to delay the moment when I have to speak to my mother. I'm afraid that if she asks me what's wrong, I'll howl like the four year-old who used to bury her face in mother's skirts to hide from the world. One of my earliest memories is of mother telling me to, "Stop that awful noise, Margaret. You won't get things to turn out the way you want by wailing." Dad used to give me sweets when I cried. He always seemed to have a bag of Liquorice Allsorts in one of his pockets. The taste of aniseed still makes me think of him.

I force myself to press out mother's number. She answers so quickly she must have had the phone right beside her.

"Margaret...I've been so worried about you."

"I'm sorry I didn't ring yesterday. I wasn't feeling myself."

I was trying, and failing, to be someone completely different from myself yesterday. It would be a relief to tell her about it but before I can find the words to begin, mother says, "Melody rang me straight away to tell me that you weren't well."

Ah, more points for Aija. She rings as soon as she has news. I don't. Can't mother read my silences by now? Perhaps she can and that's why she's filling this particular silence with chatter about flu jabs and keeping warm and eating properly. My mother doesn't want to hear me wail, doesn't want to know that I seem to be disintegrating like the cheap kitchen-paper I've just used on the sink.

"Melody thought you were looking very pale. She thinks you should eat more red meat. Liver and bacon is always nice in cold weather. Do you remember how I used to make it with stuffing on top?"

I gag at the memory – dried up liver, fatty bacon and dusty packet-stuffing with an overpowering smell of sage. I used to drown it all in gravy to make it edible.

"I'm not feeling like eating anything solid at the moment."

"Some good thick soup then. I could get a taxi and come round..."

I appreciate the magnitude of this offer and say hurriedly, "No, really it's just a 24 hour thing really. I'll be fine tomorrow."

"Well, if you're sure. Melody said something about you giving her some expensive perfume as a Christmas present. That was very nice of you, dear."

She has interpreted my impulsive regifting as a gesture of reconciliation towards her precious Aija. Perversely I say, "It was just the usual bottle of Chanel No 5 that Celia gives me. I didn't want it."

"Celia's been in touch? I'm glad to hear that she's treating you properly. I shall send her my usual card after all."

So Celia is behaving 'properly' and I am in the wrong again.

"You do that," I say.

"And you needn't worry about booking somewhere for Christmas. Melody is going to do all the shopping and make a special Latvian dessert for us. She'll get us a turkey-roll and some ready prepared vegetables. All you'll need to do is pop a few things in the oven."

"How lovely."

I say that I have to lie down again and promise to ring her tomorrow morning to tell her how I am. Perhaps tomorrow I really will tell her.

December 12th

It is 4.00 in the morning but I can't sleep. I need to talk to someone but who can I ring at this hour? Only Rob, though I'm hazy about the time difference between us. I try his office and just get an answer-phone which tells me to leave a message after the tone.

"Rob, it's me – Meg..." I realize that he'll think I'm ringing with bad news about mother. "Mother's fine. She's looking forward to Christmas." But when I look forward all I can see is emptiness, as if the entire fabric of my life had been destroyed by some natural disaster. "I just wanted...I just need..." My throat closes up. I don't know what I need from Rob. Or from anyone, except David. I end the call.

Yesterday, as I was putting pieces of broken frames and scraps of paper into a rubbish sack, the phone rang. I'd just decided to keep one of the scraps which had a painting of a single orange petal – an almost successful attempt to capture the pleated silk texture of a California poppy. I'd finally trained myself not to expect David's voice, so it took me a moment to register who was speaking.

"Meg. What the hell are you playing at? I've just had mother on the phone telling me about some crazy call you made to her and I know you were outside our flat last night."

'Our flat'. I'd read somewhere that looking at something beautiful can lower high blood-pressure, so I kept staring at the orange of the petal.

"I found your paintings in the car-park this morning. Did you think I wouldn't recognize your style?"

Actually yes.

"You never seemed much interested in what I was painting."

"That is such an unfair thing to say. I did come to all your exhibitions, even when I was in the middle of a case."

"I never realized how much you resented wasting your valuable time on art."

"I didn't resent....that isn't the issue here. The issue is your bizarre behaviour. Thank God I left first this morning. I dread to think what would have happened if Rosa had seen those ripped up flowers. Are you trying to make her lose the baby?"

"No, of course not!"

"Then stay away from us. The only reason that Restraining Order isn't being implemented is that I don't want to tell Rosa about your visit. She's spooked enough by you already."

"But I'm still not allowed to be upset by what she's done to me?"

"Rosa's done nothing to you. She barely knows you. If you want to blame anyone, blame me."

"I do." A grim echo of my wedding vow. "But you're wrong to assume that the paintings were just a message to you and Rosa. I've cleared out most of my old artwork and left it all over the city for people to find."

"What? Why on earth would you do a thing like that?"

"To see if it meant something to anyone. You've ripped the meaning out of everything I've done for the last thirty years."

"I don't see how I can be responsible for..."

"Imagine if you discovered that everyone you'd successfully prosecuted in the last thirty years was innocent; then you might begin to understand how I'm feeling. I can't even go on living in my own home because it's just a shell now. Four walls and a roof that I can't afford. I have to sell up and go away." Until I said the words I didn't know that I had made the decision. "So you've won, you and Rosa. You can have the damn house. Are you happy now?"

"Meg, it isn't a matter of winning or losing..."

"With you, winning is always the point."

He wouldn't have been such a successful barrister if it wasn't. I cut David off before he could tell me that it would all turn out to be for the best. He rang back almost immediately but the achingly familiar number on the screen wasn't enough to make me answer.

I held on to the edge of the table for a while because I felt so light, as if everything had dropped away and if I let go I might just float. To tether myself, I returned to tidying the house, fetching a dustpan and brush to gather up scraps and splinters from under tables and chairs. Then it occurred to me that if I was about to sign my home away, any housework I did would only benefit Rosa and David. I left the dustpan on the dining table. No more cleaning and tidying from now on. Let Rosa deal with the dust and the cat-sick. If she was assuming that David would do his fair share of the housework, she'd soon be disillusioned. That thought was the first thing to make me smile in quite some time.

I had to do something with my hands so I went out to the glass-house for a sketch-book. The mess in there made it look as if I'd been burgled. I suppose I have by the woman I attempted to be yesterday. I wondered what Rosa would decide to do with my studio and imagined it full of candy-floss pink pelargoniums and garish begonias, or as dumping ground for things discarded from the house and David's previous life. It seemed important to finish my drawings of the rooms in the house while they were still mine.

The kitchen had always been my domain but none of my drawings seemed able to capture the sense of security I used to feel there. I tried to make a satisfying pattern out of the lovely curves of favourite pans and jars and plates but when I stood back all I could see were the empty spaces inside the circles. I fetched some chalk pastels and filled in the spaces with blue gas-flames, stylised flowers from the Provencal table-cloth, and the multi-coloured zig-zags of the rag-rug. Then everything seemed to flicker with a feverish energy and that was wrong too. Where was the energy on the night that David told me he was leaving but I just sat at the kitchen table meekly eating lamb with apricots? Why didn't I throw something then? I took two dinner plates off the dresser and hurled them onto the flagstones to hear them smash. Nothing changed.

I had been leaving what I still think of as our bedroom until last. I made a charcoal sketch of the rumpled duvet lying in the corner where I'd tossed it in frustration after failing to get a clean cover all the way onto it. That was always a two-person job. I'd dug out an old top-sheet and a slightly moth-eaten blanket to replace the downy warmth of the duvet. I drew the bed with David's side in complete shadow and mine in a bright cold light. The stripes of the blanket still join the two halves.

Now I lie here wondering why David rang back. I have read over the account of our conversation which I wrote last night. Was that really all I said to him? Or did more of the pain and anger gush out of me than I remember? I make myself wait until I hear the long-case clock in the dining room strike five before listening to the message David left when I wouldn't answer his second call.

"Meg, I think you need help. You should go to your doctor." Does he hope that a doctor will prescribe pills to banish raging Peg and bring back calm and reasonable Meg? "I'm worried about you. I never meant to hurt you like this." Oh God. David the heartless bastard I can just about deal with now but a kind David, a David I would still want back, is much harder to bear. "I'm so sorry but we all have to live with what's happened." Do we? Do we really? "About the house...Rosa...we have changed our minds about wanting to live there. You were right. It was never a good idea. So take all the time you need to sell the house. It doesn't have to happen at once."

But it does. I'd finally made the decision to sign a bit of paper and walk away and found a kind of peace in that. Now you're saying that I must let crass Barty and any number of strangers crawl all over my home. I can already picture them sneering at my taste and planning to make brutal improvements that will strip away all traces of my time here. I can't stand the thought of this violation. I have to get out of the house.

I dress in my warmest clothes, with David's old sweater as a top layer. I carry the diary under my arm because I never go anywhere without it now. Vincent is excited at the prospect of an early breakfast and follows me around the house as I try to remember where I left my raincoat. Is the mixture of exasperation and affection which I feel for my cat, all that David now feels for me? I remember David's face when he saw me on the bridge and know the truth is worse than that. What David truly wants is for the problem of my existence to go away.

In the kitchen I search the fridge for something to put in Vincent's bowl. He's unlikely to eat a withered lemon or half a jar of stuffed olives. I look in the larder and between some tubs of stale herbs and a tin of solidified custard powder I find a packet of suet. Vincent always steals some when I put suet out for the birds in winter, so I needn't feel guilty about shaking the unappetising white pellets into his dish. Sure enough, Vincent gratefully gobbles them up with his usual lack of discrimination. For some stupid reason this makes me cry.

I find my raincoat on the living-room floor and put it on. I nearly open the front door and go straight out with nothing but my key and my diary. Then, because I'm not sure whether I'm coming back, I think about Vincent and his pathetic inability to use the cat-flap. I return to the kitchen, unbolt the door to the garden and shoo him out. I stand looking at my garden as Vincent goes from shrub to stone, marking what he fondly believes to be his territory. I suppose he's no more deluded about that than I am. By April, all the dark earth, bare branches and dead stems should be transformed into a miniature paradise of colour and scent but I have lost my faith that it will happen. I planted no tulip bulbs this autumn and the promise of primroses isn't enough for me.

I turn my back on the open door. I know I ought to leave a note for mother. I tear a blank page out of my diary but I can't think what to write. I just scrawl, 'I'm sorry'. I pick up my handbag and go.

Outside in the street I don't consciously choose a direction but my feet take me towards the gorge, the gash of wildness that has always been there at the edge of my comfortable life. My footsteps are the loudest sound in the eerie pre-dawn hush. No cars or cyclists pass me. There are no lights in any of the windows I walk by. Everyone is asleep in their own intact worlds. I say to myself that if I encounter just one person in the street, see even one light come on, I won't do it. I will turn around and go meekly back to the remnants of my life.

Silence and darkness. Nothing and nobody stirs as I pace towards the gorge. Not even a chugger. I'm not just an obsolete woman, I seem to be invisible and inaudible too. I feel like a ghost unable to make any meaningful contact with the living.

When I reach the grassy slope of Sion Hill there is just enough glow from the lamps on the suspension bridge for me to find my way to our special bench. Its splintery wooden slats are damp with dew but I sit down anyway and wait for the sunrise. While my body chills, I listen to the dawn chorus. Another world of communication that I am not part of. The sunrise isn't beautiful or dramatic. The new day seems to creep reluctantly across a grey sky. As soon as it's light enough, I scribble in my diary.

I have my back to the massive sandstone wall supporting the Clifton end of the suspension bridge. The bench sits on a paved platform jutting out from the edge of the hill – a small rectangle of order and safety on the edge of the abyss. The bench is chained to the wall as if there was some danger of it trying to leap to freedom. Iron railings separate us from the wooded slope of the gorge but they are not high or sharp. An Old Man's Beard, still covered with fluffy seed heads, is coiled around the railings and long bramble stems are poking through the gaps. One of them has snaked across the paving stones and is nearly touching my foot, as if to show me how impossible it is to keep the thorns out for ever. I knew all along that I would have to take one big step, not lots of little ones, so I throw my diary over the railings and clamber after it.

There is still no-one about to stop me. My feet find a narrow strip of level ground to stand on but my handbag sliding down off my shoulder nearly overbalances me. If I slip I might be saved by crashing into one of the trees that almost miraculously grow out from the cliff-face or I might fall through the gaps, down and down and down... I grip onto an iron spike protruding from the sandstone wall to steady myself. My heartbeat is skittering and I picture my heart as a trapped bird trying to escape from a sealed room. I take deep calming breaths. Then I use one foot to beat down the grass and ivy and brambles growing along the top of the cliff to make a kind of nest for myself.

I let go of the spike for a moment and grab for the railings again. I slide cautiously into a sitting position, with my left arm folded around one of the railing posts and my feet braced against the branch of a whitebeam that is reaching up for light. When I feel secure I reach into my handbag and scrabble one-handed for my phone. I place it on my thigh and manage to press out David's mobile number. When I hear the ring-tone I carefully move the phone up to my face.

David has always been an early riser, so he may be awake already. Phone-calls at this hour rarely bring good news. He'll check who is ringing in case something has happened to his mother but when he sees the caller identity, he'll probably choose not to answer. I'm trying to collect my thoughts into a message to leave for him when David's voice snaps, "It's six o'clock in the morning. What the fuck are you thinking?"

David never used to swear at me, however annoyed he got. Is he trying to fit in with Rosa's foul-mouthed generation?

"I'm sorry but I have to talk to you. Nothing makes sense any more so I need to understand why you left me."

In the background I hear a woman's voice asking, "Who is it? Is it her?"

"Go back to bed," David says. "I'll handle this."

I raise my own voice. "I have to know. Was it something I did or something I stopped doing? Did you gradually get tired of me or did you just wake up one morning and think, 'Why am I married to that?'"

"Where is this coming from?" I hear a door close as David shuts himself away from Rosa. Precious Rosa who must not be upset by the rawness of my feelings, "You were so calm when I first told you about this. You hardly seemed to mind what I did. You even helped me to pack."

"I couldn't believe that you were leaving for good. That evening was like a bad dream I was sure I'd wake up from soon and you'd laugh when I told you about it. I felt like that for weeks. I cooked meals for two every night in case you were home for dinner. One day I sat in the chair by the front window for hours on end, watching for you to come along the street and up the steps. I was so sure you were coming back to me...."

"Oh Meg...God, I don't know what to say."

"So now I've come to our favourite bench on Sion Hill because I can't stop remembering all the happy times we spent here but if I was wrong about that, if the happiness was just a sham, I've lost everything I thought we shared. I can't survive with that kind of gaping hole in my past. I can't see any point in going on. I just want it all to stop."

Handle that, David.

"Meg, you're not seriously thinking of...."

"Why not? Isn't that what you and Rosa want, to have me out of the way for good? Could *you* survive if you thought that the person you loved best in all the world wanted you dead? I might as well jump."

"No! Meg, please calm down. Of course I don't want you dead. How could you think that even for a moment?"

"Because when you met me on the Horned Bridge a few days ago it was obvious that I was the last person in the world you wanted to see. Once, I'd have been the first."

"On the bridge? Pero's Bridge? I'm sorry, I must have been preoccupied and just didn't notice you." I think he is lying but if this were the truth it would hurt even worse. I press on. "Now I can't even speak to you face to face. If I could just do that one more time, if we could have a proper talk about everything that's happened between us, maybe I could start to understand, maybe I could find a way forward."

"All right, look I have a meeting at ten, but that should be over by twelve so we could..."

I scream down the phone, "I'm your wife, not some client! I'm still your wife. The person you promised to cherish. How can you treat me like this? I can't bear it. I can't..."

"Meg..."

"You've taken everything away and you're too busy even to say goodbye. I can't deal with this any more..."

"Meg, please don't cry..."

"I can't face another day of feeling so unwanted..."

"Meg, listen – I'll come to you right now and we'll talk. I'll get over there as quickly as I can. Do you promise to wait for me? Do you promise not to do anything stupid?"

"I do. Please hurry."

I drop the phone because my hands are shaking. I manage to grab it before it slides down the slope but I scratch my hand on bramble thorns and that really does make me cry. Will David race over here as he promised, or will he just ring the emergency services and tell them that a mad woman is threatening to jump into the gorge? Even though he earns a living from dissecting people's unfortunate private lives in public, David has always hated the idea of his own life being exposed to scrutiny. He takes traditional English reticence to extreme levels, so I'm guessing he'll opt to deal with this crisis discreetly and alone. I wonder what he'll tell Rosa to explain his hurried departure. Will she try to stop him? Does triumphant Rosa ever feel any pity for the woman she must think of as the loser in this game?

As I rub spit into the scratches on my hand, I am startled by the rumble of a car crossing the bridge. Then I hear a dog barking in the near distance. There will be more traffic and people about soon – delivery vans and long-distance commuters, dog-walkers and joggers. There is only one point on the path that skirts Sion Hill which gives a good view of our special bench and now that I am beyond the safety railings it is unlikely that anyone will notice me unless I stand up. I feel oddly secure sitting in this perilous secret place, writing in my diary.

How many minutes will it take David to drive here from Harbourside? While I'm waiting I start doodling in the margin of my diary – curves and spirals. Suddenly I'm drawing the curl of a fern and the many-faceted shape of a withered blackberry. There is so much life clinging to the almost bare rock, even in midwinter. It makes me remember a summer day I spent beside the gorge, lying flat on my stomach so I could peer over the edge and sketch tiny cliff-face plants like mouse-ear and rock-cress. Now I can see the ghosts of summer in the desiccated flower-spikes of tall speedwells and the bleached seed-heads of the crimson allium affectionately known as the Bristol Onion. Part of me yearns to forget about David and start trying to capture their skeletal elegance but my eye is drawn to the void beyond them.

I put my pen back in my pocket and wedge my diary between the railings to keep it safe. Then I open my legs and edge my body forward until I am gripping a thick whitebeam branch between my knees. I'm uncertain whether it will bear my weight but I want a clear view of the drop. I look down. How far below me is the Portway road? Perhaps as much as a 100 metres. My stomach roils at the thought of striking that unforgiving surface. Beyond it I glimpse the silvery river at the bottom of its gorge; a river which must be so much more powerful than it looks to have sliced through these hills. I fancy that the faint roar I can hear must be the sound of the fierce waters assaulting rock but it is probably just traffic on the Portway. A quotation floats into my mind – 'Many waters cannot quench love.' Beautiful words but just words. Given time, water can erode anything.

I wonder if it is possible to reach the river by falling from this part of the cliff. The centre of the bridge is the obvious place to jump from but there is a high barrier to get over and more chance of being stopped by some officious passer-by. I pull my handbag off my shoulder and hurl it as far out as I can to see where it lands. I should have zipped it shut first. A shower of small objects falls out – pen, powder-compact, reading glasses, wallet, key-ring. The bag deflates as it empties and a small gust of wind is enough to blow it back against the cliff where it snags on a branch. One impulsive moment and my money and credit cards and house-keys are all gone. It feels good to be free of the detritus of my old life and I laugh. Am I finally moving on?

There is quite a crowd on Sion Hill now but I think I have time for one last diary entry. The people watching me aren't certain what they saw so I shall write down my account of what happened.

At first I thought I was imagining that someone was calling my name. Then I recognized David's voice. I used my feet to push myself back from the tree and twisted my head to peer through the railings. David was slithering across the damp grass. He looked around and then stopped beside the wrong bench – the one on the crown of the hill which gives him his favourite view of the suspension bridge. He couldn't even remember where our special place is. Word of the day – quenched.

I shuffled sideways before reaching behind me to find the railings. Once I was gripping them tightly, I twisted my torso and slowly hauled myself to my feet.

"David! I'm here."

"Meg."

He rushed down the slope, across the path and onto the platform, only stopping his momentum by crashing into the side of the bench.

"God, Meg, look at the state of you."

I obediently looked at myself – at my damp dirty clothes and the brambles clinging to my legs. There seemed to be seeds and dead leaves caught in my hair.

"Mad Margaret," I said and expected him to laugh with me

but he didn't.

"Meg, we need to get you home."

"We don't have a home any more."

"Back to the house," he explained as if he was talking to a small child. "Back to Amelia Street."

"I threw the keys into the gorge. I wanted to see what the fall from here would be like."

"Christ...give me your hand, Meg."

He lunged for me and I stumbled backwards, losing my balance.

"Meg!"

I managed to catch hold of the protruding spike. I was shaking and gasping for breath but I didn't think he could reach me unless he climbed over the railings.

"Meg...I better get help."

"No! I can't bear anyone else to see me like this. Just talk to me. You don't know what it's like to wake up and remember that there's no-one in the bed, no-one in the house, no-one to talk to when you most need it."

"You're not alone, Meg. You have family – friends. You were always going out with Nina or talking to Deirdre on the phone."

"Deirdre is only interested in her own troubles and Nina – Nina is so perfect she never sets a foot wrong. She can't possibly understand why I'm failing to cope with all this and I am failing. Everyone keeps telling me that I'll come out of this a stronger person but I'm not. I'm breaking up..."

"Hang on, Meg. Stay exactly where you are. I'm coming over to you."

He made quite a business of climbing over the railings, swearing when he tore his new-looking trousers, which were tighter than I would ever have let him wear. But when he took me into one of his bear-hugs, it was so good to bury my face in his Arran sweater and smell the familiar scents of his body.

"You're shaking – are you cold?" he asked me. "Do you want my sweater?"

I remembered giving him that sweater two Christmases ago, so Rosa hadn't yet succeeded in expunging all traces of me from David's wardrobe.

"No," I pulled away from him a little, though there was barely room for both of us to stand on level ground. "Make me understand why this happened to us."

David grimaced as he always did when asked to talk about his own feelings.

"I can't. I thought we had a pretty good life but everything changed when I really saw Rosa for the first time. If you must know...it was the night of our last garden party. Rosa told me later how of out of place and unhappy she felt at that party. She was intimidated by you and most of the guests ignored her, so she retreated into the glass-house. Underneath all that prickly intelligence she was so vulnerable..."

"It didn't have to be you who brought her out of her shell. You could have resisted her charms."

"No!" David sounded genuinely frustrated by my obtuseness. "That's what I'm trying to explain. There wasn't some long process of falling in love. There wasn't a time when it was possible to turn back. When Rosa smiled at me as I joined her in the glass-house, my old life was...over. If you want the truth, I knew loving Rosa meant that I was going to behave very badly towards someone who didn't deserve it but that no longer seemed important. Don't look at me like that Meg. If you'd ever really..."

"If I'd ever what?"

"Meg, I'm sorry. I never intended to be unfaithful to you and I hated the deception. We both did, Rosa and I. The baby wasn't planned either. We...I was careless but it did seem like a sign. So please don't blame yourself for our marriage ending. You were always a good wife to me – a real support, but there was nothing you could have done to stop this happening."

I tried to get this straight in my head.

"You are telling me that nothing I do or say or feel makes any difference to you?"

"You always twist what I say... Meg, I'm still your friend and you have to let me help you now. I want you to let go of that spike and take my arm. Then we'll move very carefully to the railings. I'll climb over first and then help you. Meg, are you listening? Come on." He tugged at my arm. "Be a good girl and just let go."

So for a moment I did let go of the spike; let go of everything that I used to be.

David staggered backwards and lost his balance. His arms flailed and his feet slipped from under him. His body slid down the cliff face, gathering speed.

"Meg..."

On the way down he clutched at the speedwells and alliums but their fragile stems snapped in his fingers and he kept on falling. The noise of his descent, the crashing and the screaming, seemed to go on for a long time but I suppose it was only seconds before I heard the final thud. Death by flowers.

Someone on Sion Hill called out, "God, did you see that?" and another voice answered, "I think she pushed him! He was trying to help her and she made him fall."

But that can't be right, because nothing I do makes any difference.

It was my name that David shouted as he fell, not Rosa's. I found myself wondering if this mixture of horror and exhilaration was what Martin Jenkins felt when he finished stabbing his wife, when he realized that he still had power over her, even if he regretted the way that he had chosen to use it.

Very carefully, I let go of the spike, lowered myself to the ground and leaned my back against the railings. It would have been very easy to slip forwards, to launch myself down the cliff as if it were a playground slide. Everything would have been over in seconds, but I remembered how long those seconds had seemed for David. Besides, I wanted to make a list of the reasons why I loved – still love – David. My diary was stuck between the railings. I reached out with my left hand and just managed to reach it without destabilizing myself. I ignored voices on the hill saying, "What's she doing now?" "Have you rung the police?" and started my list.

I love David -

Because he made me feel desirable when, after Leo, I thought that no-one could want me.

Because of all the Sunday mornings making love and lazing in bed until lunchtime.

Because he tried so hard not to show how much he minded about not having children.

Because he never gave less than his best in court, no matter how dull or distasteful the case.

Because on every holiday he let me drag him around art galleries.

Because I was the only one who knew how frightened he was of dogs.

Because the shape of his rugby-battered nose made me smile.

Because he stood between me and so many of the difficulties of life.

Because when I really needed him, he came back.

Because he'll always be mine now.

'The proof of love is in the letting go.' What poem is that from? I can't remember. It was David who told me to let go.

"Miss, can you hear me? What's your name? Tell me your name."

The shouting was irritating, so I looked up from my diary. A policeman was standing on the platform with one hand on our bench. That seemed wrong.

"What's your name, luv?"

I had to think for a moment before I called back, "Peg."

"Peg, I'm Craig. Can you tell me what happened?"

"My husband went over the cliff. You should be looking for him."

"We will. Now Peg, I want you to stay calm..."

"I am calm. Go away."

"OK, Peg, OK. You just stay where you are and we'll get you help."

When I looked at him more closely, I saw that his badges identified him as a mere Community Police Officer. I knew that I could ignore him. The chances of this plump, pasty-faced servant of Health and Safety doing anything as heroic as climbing over the railings to rescue me were extremely low.

"Go away," I repeated.

He backed off but I could hear him talking into his radio, summoning reinforcements.

I wrote as fast as I could. It was...is...so important to get everything on paper because it seems less and less real. When I look back at the bench I almost expect to see a contented couple sitting there – David and Margaret, married for thirty years. David will be admiring details of Brunel's bridge, basking in the afterglow of British genius, and I will be gazing across at the wild woods which the bridge failed to tame.

Craig hasn't gone very far. He calls to me from time to time but I don't answer. Perhaps I should tell him about Vincent, who won't have the sense to go and find himself a new home when the person who looks after him doesn't return. If I didn't, what hope is there for poor silly Vincent? I suppose I should be thinking about Rosa and her baby but I'm sure that vulnerable Rosa will have men queuing up to console her. I wonder if Mark will take her flowers.

I can hear sirens down on the Portway. Are they coming for David or for me? Can he really be dead? Pictures start to form in my head of a broken body but I can't bear that. I shall focus on the image of a hand clutching flowers. If I draw that image, I'm sure I can give it meaning. I see now that I have to keep drawing flowers because they are my native language and it doesn't matter if I am the only speaker left.

I hope I shall be allowed to choose the flowers for David's funeral. After all, David's obituary will say, 'He is survived by his wife, Margaret.' I am a survivor, like the plants that cling to these cliffs. Was everyone right when they said that this whole experience would make me stronger?

I will need that strength to face my day in court. A day I am determined to have. Whoever they choose as prosecutor, it will be David's questions that I shall have to answer. It will be David's voice I'll hear asking me, 'Why did you do it, Meg?' All I shall be able to say is, 'There wasn't a time when it was possible to turn back.'

Was I ever the nice person that everyone, including me, thought I was? Could it be that I was born a killer but would never have found this out if life had gone on giving me most of what I wanted? I shall sit here drawing until the police finally make their move. Perhaps in prison I shall have time to paint the perfect tulip.

Printed in Great Britain
by Amazon

61466355R00210